ALSO BY DAVE BARRY

FICTION
Tricky Business
Big Trouble

NONFICTION
Dave Barry's Money Secrets: *Like: Why Is There a Giant Eyeball on the Dollar?*
Boogers Are My Beat
Dave Barry Hits Below the Beltway: *A Vicious and Unprovoked Attack on Our Most Cherished Political Institutions*
Dave Barry Is Not Taking This Sitting Down
Dave Barry Turns 50
Dave Barry Is from Mars and Venus
Dave Barry's Book of Bad Songs
Dave Barry in Cyberspace
Dave Barry's Complete Guide to Guys
Dave Barry's Gift Guide to End All Gift Guides
Dave Barry Is NOT Making This Up
Dave Barry Does Japan
Dave Barry's Only Travel Guide You'll Ever Need
Dave Barry Talks Back
Dave Barry Turns 40
Dave Barry Slept Here: *A Sort of History of the United States*
Dave Barry's Greatest Hits
Homes and Other Black Holes
Dave Barry's Guide to Marriage And/or Sex
Dave Barry's Bad Habits: *A 100% Fact-Free Book*
Claw Your Way to the Top: *How to Become the Head of a Major Corporation in Roughly a Week*
Stay Fit and Healthy Until You're Dead
Babies and Other Hazards of Sex: *How to Make a Tiny Person in Only 9 Months with Tools You Probably Have Around the Home*
The Taming of the Screw

# PETER AND THE SHADOW THIEVES

### By DAVE BARRY
### and RIDLEY PEARSON

*Illustrations by* GREG CALL

### DISNEY
#### EDITIONS

Hyperion Books for Children/*New York*

*We dedicate this book to our children—Paige, Storey, Rob and Sophie—and to all the other children who read* Peter and the Starcatchers, *and asked us what happened next.*

## ACKNOWLEDGMENTS

We thank Wendy Lefkon, our unflagging champion, and her colleagues at Disney, for all their encouragement and support. (Not to mention the passes to Disney World.)

We thank Greg Call for his inspired illustrations, and his patience while we endlessly debated the question of what certain imaginary creatures look like.

We thank the many people who helped with research (Yes! There was some actual research!) and copyediting, especially Norman Anderson, Judi Smith, and David and Laurel Walters.

We thank the people who manage our lives despite all our efforts to thwart them: Louise Marsh, Nancy Litzinger, Joeylyn Lambert, and (again) Judi Smith.

We thank Jim Dale, who recorded the audio versions of both of our books, and who has a thousand voices, with a funny story for every one.

Most of all, we thank our wonderful wives, Michelle and Marcelle, who smile benignly when their husbands dress like pirates and talk like porpoises.

—*Dave Barry and Ridley Pearson*

# TABLE OF CONTENTS

CHAPTER 1: *A Speck on the Horizon*   1

CHAPTER 2: *The Choice*   8

CHAPTER 3: *The Wrong Side of the Mountain*   16

CHAPTER 4: *The Voice*   23

CHAPTER 5: *The Agreement*   30

CHAPTER 6: *The Darkest Way*   38

CHAPTER 7: *An Ally*   41

CHAPTER 8: *The Mission*   46

CHAPTER 9: *A Tasty Meal Lost*   51

CHAPTER 10: *Dead Eyes*   60

CHAPTER 11: *Strangers*   70

CHAPTER 12: *Something Familiar*   74

CHAPTER 13: *The Coming Danger*   78

CHAPTER 14: *The Farewell*   85

CHAPTER 15: *Into the Night*   91

CHAPTER 16: *One Look Back*   99

CHAPTER 17: *Ombra's Feeling*   104

CHAPTER 18: *"No Bees at Sea"*   107

CHAPTER 19: *Anything Unusual*   113

CHAPTER 20: *The Signal*   116

CHAPTER 21: *The Scuttlebutt*   124

CHAPTER 22: *Tubby Ted's Discovery*   130

CHAPTER 23: *A Second Visit*   134

CHAPTER 24: *The Stowaway*   137

CHAPTER 25: *Genius*   148

CHAPTER 26: *St. Katherine's Dock*   154

CHAPTER 27: *Into the Storm*   163

CHAPTER 28: *Not Safe at All*   166

CHAPTER 29: *A Bone to Pick*   173

CHAPTER 30: *Somehow*   177

CHAPTER 31: *A Tiny Heart Beating*   180

CHAPTER 32: *A Feeling*   182

CHAPTER 33: *A Way Out*   183

CHAPTER 34: *A Visitor*   193

CHAPTER 35: *A Walk in the Dark*   196

CHAPTER 36: *A Few Seconds*   200

CHAPTER 37: *"I'll Find You"*   202

CHAPTER 38: *The Shadow Thief*   206

CHAPTER 39: *The Market*   212

CHAPTER 40: *The Fear in Her Eyes*   221

CHAPTER 41: *Play It Safe*   227

CHAPTER 42: *The Standoff*   231

CHAPTER 43: *Thunder Down the Trail*   235

CHAPTER 44: *The Collector*   241

CHAPTER 45: *The Cold Iron Ring*   254

CHAPTER 46: *Hopeless*   259

CHAPTER 47: *The Drunken Centipede*   261

CHAPTER 48: *Something Strong*   271

CHAPTER 49: *Either Way*   272

CHAPTER 50: *Grasping Hands*   273

CHAPTER 51: *The Message from Egypt*   277

CHAPTER 52: *The Letter*   281

CHAPTER 53: *Potato Soup*   291

CHAPTER 54: *A Fine Name Indeed* 293
CHAPTER 55: *"Take All His Air"* 300
CHAPTER 56: *A Very Strange Business* 303
CHAPTER 57: *At Last* 307
CHAPTER 58: *Visitors* 310
CHAPTER 59: *Something Odd* 315
CHAPTER 60: *Overheard Words* 321
CHAPTER 61: *Footsteps* 323
CHAPTER 62: *Rough Hands* 325
CHAPTER 63: *The Thing on the Stairs* 327
CHAPTER 64: *The Black Pool* 331
CHAPTER 65: *An Urgent Search* 333
CHAPTER 66: *The Envelope* 335
CHAPTER 67: *The Phantom Light* 341
CHAPTER 68: *Conversation in a Tree* 347
CHAPTER 69: *A Cry on the Wind* 356
CHAPTER 70: *Reluctant Allies* 364
CHAPTER 71: *The Secret Place* 373
CHAPTER 72: *The Warder and the Watcher* 378
CHAPTER 73: *The Messenger* 385
CHAPTER 74: *The Ravens' Cries* 390
CHAPTER 75: *Traitor's Gate* 394
CHAPTER 76: *McGuinn* 398
CHAPTER 77: *Wolves on the Steps* 404
CHAPTER 78: *A Deadly Fall* 406
CHAPTER 79: *The Silent Struggle* 413
CHAPTER 80: *The Metal Man* 415
CHAPTER 81: *The Secret* 419

CHAPTER 82: *The Keep*   421

CHAPTER 83: *Ombra's Plan*   426

CHAPTER 84: *A Voice in the Dark*   428

CHAPTER 85: *Dark Kites*   437

CHAPTER 86: *An Offer of Help*   441

CHAPTER 87: *The Golden Weather Vane*   447

CHAPTER 88: *A Good Friend of His*   457

CHAPTER 89: *No Choice*   461

CHAPTER 90: *George's Thought*   473

CHAPTER 91: *The Destination*   485

CHAPTER 92: *Not Much Time*   487

CHAPTER 93: *A Raven's Eye*   495

CHAPTER 94: *The Return*   499

CHAPTER 95: *A Swift, Sure Shadow*   536

CHAPTER 96: *Over Their Heads*   545

## CHAPTER 1

# A Speck on the Horizon

*A* MANGO, THOUGHT PETER. *The perfect weapon.*

The scrawny, sunburned boy, dressed in a tattered shirt and pants torn off below scabby knees, brushed the unkempt reddish hair out of his face. It fell right back into his eyes as he bent to the sandy soil and scooped up the plump red-and-yellow fruit sphere, a bit bigger than an orange. The mango was squishy to the touch, too ripe for eating. But it was just the thing to drop on somebody's head from a great height. And Peter knew precisely whose head he wanted to drop it on.

Holding the sweet-smelling mango in his left hand, Peter raised his right hand over his head and, pointing his index finger skyward, sprang up and rose swiftly from the earth. It was a dramatic takeoff, and totally unnecessary: Peter—an expert flyer now, after three months' practice—could float easily upward in any position. But he enjoyed impressing the other boys.

"Peter!" shouted young James as he trotted toward the mango tree. He was followed by the rest of the Lost Boys, as they had come to call themselves—Prentiss, Thomas, and, lagging far behind, Tubby Ted.

"Where are you going?" asked James, his thin voice cracking.

"To pay the pirates a visit," Peter announced. "I've a delivery to make." He held out the oozing, overripe mango.

"Please, can't I come?" begged James.

Peter was silent for a long moment. The only noise was the distant sound of surf pounding on the reef outside the lagoon. Then, reluctantly, Peter said, "'Fraid not, James. You can't . . . I mean . . . You know."

"Right," said James. "I can't fly."

James said it matter-of-factly, but Peter saw the now-familiar look of disappointment in his eyes. He saw it also on the faces of Prentiss and Thomas, though all he saw on Tubby Ted's face was mango pulp, as Tubby Ted had decided it was time for a snack. (For Tubby Ted, it was *always* time for a snack.)

Peter hovered for a moment, feeling a flicker of guilt. It seemed that more and more lately, he'd been having his best adventures alone. He almost decided to return to the earth and to carry out his attack by land, so his mates could join in the fun. Almost . . .

But walking took so *long*, and if they were on foot, the

perfectly well that Lord Aster left you to look
and I appreciate it. But that was when I was new
this." He gestured at his airborne body, then the
w. "It's different now. I've learned a lot. I can take
elf. I don't need a fairy watching—"

interrupted by an angry outburst of shrill bells.
disliked the name "fairy," which she saw as a
r heritage.
said Peter. "I mean, I don't need a *birdgirl* watching

lls. Instructive.
dangers?" said Peter. "There's nothing on this
e to worry about except old Captain Hook down
e's too scared to come near our side of the island
ollusks about. Even if he does come, how's he
ch me if he can't fly? Face it, Tink, nothing here
. Nothing."

lls.
at's your opinion," said Peter. "But I don't agree,
lan to stay up here all day arguing with a . . . a

d his back on her and angled his body to start
d swoop. Tinker Bell flew in front of him, still

ter said, impatient now. "I can't stop you from
don't get in the way, okay?"

pirates might catch them. No, flying was the only way to do
this.

"You'll be safer here," he said. "I'll be back soon! We'll
have a game, or a snake hunt."

"But," said James, "I—"

"Sorry!" interrupted Peter, shooting skyward, not looking
back. He soared above the treetops, his pangs of guilt changing to irritation tinged with self-pity.

*It's not my fault I can fly and they can't*, he thought.
*Besides, they're safer back there. Can't they see I'm looking out
for them?*

These thoughts were quickly driven from Peter's mind by
the sweeping view that greeted him as he shot into the radiant blue sky between two small, puffy, bright white clouds.
He ascended at a steep angle, keeping his body parallel to the
dark green mountain ridge that rose sharply to form the
backbone of the island.

As he cleared the summit, he could see the whole of
Mollusk Island. Far below, on the side he'd come from, was
the shimmering blue-green expanse of calm, protected water
that the boys called Mermaid Lagoon. Peter could see the
tiny figures of a half dozen mermaids sunning themselves on
the broad, flat rock they favored. One of the figures waved—
probably their leader, the one known as Teacher. She was
quite fond of Peter, a fact that both embarrassed and pleased
him.

Peter returned the wave, then continued his aerial survey of the island. Curved around the blue-green waters of the lagoon was the island's widest beach, a semicircle of soft, sugar-white sand, fringed with coconut trees. Behind the beach, in a small clearing nestled at the base of the mountain slope, was the boys' home—a dome-shaped driftwood hut, covered with palm thatch, that they'd erected with the help of the Mollusk tribe. A quarter mile from their hut, in a bigger clearing surrounding a massive tree, was the Mollusk village itself, where gray smoke was drifting skyward from several cooking fires.

The Mollusks—whose chief, Fighting Prawn, owed Peter his life—had proved to be generous hosts. They'd shown the boys how to spear fish, which fish to spear, how to clean and cook them, where to get fresh water, how to keep a fire going, what to do when a hairy jumping spider the size of a squirrel leaped on your head—all the basic skills of island survival.

Peter suspected that Fighting Prawn also had men posted in the jungle to keep an eye on the boys' hut, lest the pirates decided to pay a visit. This had been reassuring at first, but as the weeks and months passed, Peter had become more and more certain that the pirates didn't dare venture to this side of the island, where they would be greatly outnumbered by the Mollusks. His fear had turned to confidence, then to cockiness. In recent days he'd taken to amusing him-

self by flying across the islar
taunting the pirate who
entire seafaring world—Bl
But Peter had given hi
Peter looked down th
toward what the boys call
looking the cove was the
of logs that had been lab
and bound with thick jun
Reaching the apex of
hovered for a moment. I
when he heard a sound
would have sounded li
melodious bells. Peter co
words inside his head, a
sighed and turned slow
Bell, her silvery wings b
pinched with anger.
"I did not run off,"
not my fault if you don'
More bells. Peter cr
"Listen, Tink," Pe
father. I have no moth
you. I don't have to an
The sound of more
"Yes, I do know

understan
out for me
to . . . to
island belc
care of my
He wa
Tinker Be
slight to h
"Sorry,'
over me."
More b
"What
island for n
there, and
with the M
going to ca
can hurt me
More be
"Well, t
and I don't
birdgirl."
He turn
his downwa
tinkling.
"Fine,"
coming. Just

With that, he gripped the mango, let out a whoop, and began his dive toward the pirate fort, his mind focusing now on his plan of attack. He was so intent on landing the mango on his target that he failed to notice two things: one was a small human form below, making its way laboriously up to the summit of the mountain. Had Peter looked closely, he would have seen that the form was James, who was determined that, this time, he would not miss out on the adventure.

The other thing Peter missed was a speck on the horizon—a tiny dark shape, far out to sea.

A speck that was, ever so slowly, growing larger.

## CHAPTER 2

# THE CHOICE

THE AIR SUDDENLY TASTED OF LAND.

Captain Nerezza turned his pox-eaten face windward, where two small, puffy clouds hugged the horizon, reminding him of the mashed potatoes in a shepherd's pie.

Everything reminded Nerezza of food these days: he and his crew had dined on hardtack and skinned rats for the past two weeks, having run low on food and, far worse, water, as they wandered the sea aimlessly, increasingly desperate. Nerezza had begun to wonder if there really *was* an island, or just a madman's confused memories.

But now these midmorning clouds hovered, stationary, all alone, not another spot of white in the rich, cobalt-blue sky. And that tantalizing taste lay ever so gently on his salty, parched tongue.

*Land.*

Nerezza started to bark out an order, then caught himself.

But the crewmen around him had heard his intake of breath and—knowing the painful punishment that awaited any man who failed to instantly obey Nerezza's orders—were watching him intently.

The sight they saw would have shocked anyone unaccustomed to it. Nerezza's cheeks and brow were deeply cratered and scarred from a disease he'd picked up in some godforsaken port. His eyes were small, close-set, ratlike; his teeth, a disaster. But these weren't the most distinctive features of his ravaged face.

Nerezza had no nose.

The one he'd been born with had been lost in a knife fight. In its place was a smooth-finished piece of African blackwood, shaped remarkably like the original, though without any nostrils. It was held to his face by a leather strap. When Nerezza wanted to smell something, he lifted the nosepiece to reveal a black hole in the center of his face. Through that hole he could pick up a scent as well as a bloodhound—although when he sneezed, you didn't want to be standing in front of him.

Nerezza lifted his nosepiece and sucked sea air into the hole. No question. Land.

Nerezza replaced the nosepiece and, ignoring the crewmen awaiting his orders, strode toward the mainmast. He grabbed the ratline and began to climb toward the first yardarm. The entire crew had stopped to watch this unusual sight; the only shipboard sounds were the whistle of lines and the random snap of dry canvas.

Hand over hand, Nerezza climbed. He was careful with his feet: where most of his crew went barefoot, he wore a fine pair of black leather boots, polished with whale oil for waterproofing, but ill-suited to climbing rope.

*Steady now*, he thought, glancing at the deck far below and the curious faces of the crew. Normally he'd have ordered them back to work, but he wanted them to see this. Wanted to make a point about who ran this ship, and what would not be tolerated.

He switched to another rope, avoiding the bulge of a sail. He pulled himself up onto the second of three yardarms and climbed the mast the rest of the way, passing the topgallant and coming up through a hole in the bottom of the crow's nest. He pushed the trapdoor out of his way and pulled himself up. The lookout, a sallow, thin-faced man, was slumped against the side of the crow's nest, snoring.

"Palmer!" bellowed Nerezza.

"Aye, sir! Captain, *sir!*" said the startled lookout as he clambered to his feet. He kept his face turned away from Nerezza, fearing the captain would smell the grog that had put him to sleep on his watch. "Captain," he stammered, "sir, I—"

Nerezza cut him off, his voice calm, cold. "South-southeast, Mister Palmer. See anything?"

Palmer spun in the wrong direction, corrected himself, and finally raised his spyglass. "A pair of cumulus, sir! Captain Nerezza, sir." He was sweating now.

Slowly, deliberately, Nerezza pulled his knife from his belt. He held it in his right hand, the blade sparkling in the sun. Palmer pretended to keep looking though the spyglass, but his free eye was locked on the knife.

Nerezza's voice remained calm. "Wind speed, Mister Palmer?"

Palmer took a look at the long pieces of cloth tied to the rigging at the ends of several yardarms. "Fourteen, fifteen knots, Captain, sir."

"And those clouds, Mister Palmer . . . are they moving with the wind?"

The end of Palmer's spyglass shook. Nerezza reached out and steadied it for him. Nerezza said, "Well?"

"No, sir. They ain't."

"Ain't moving, you say?" Nerezza asked. "And why would that be?"

Palmer lowered the spyglass. Terror turned his face from deep tan to the color of dirty soap.

"Can't you smell it, lad?" Nerezza asked, lifting his nose-piece and sniffing loudly in the direction of the two clouds. "Or has the grog *clouded* your ability to smell, eh?"

Nerezza smiled at his wordplay. Not a pretty smile.

Palmer, shaking, tried to answer; words formed on his

lips, but they were too soft, and the wind carried them away.

"What's that you say?" Nerezza bellowed.

"They ain't moving because . . . because they're over an island, sir."

"And what exactly has we been out here searching for these past eight weeks, you pitiful excuse for a sailor?"

"An island, sir."

"Yes, Mister Palmer. An island. *That* island, I'm willing to wager. The island that you missed because you was sleeping on your watch. Now wasn't you, Mister Palmer?"

"I was, yes, sir," Palmer said, shaking harder now.

"Cold, are you, Mister Palmer?" Nerezza said. It was hot enough to melt the pitch between the planks on the deck. Nerezza leaned close, to where his breath played against Palmer's ear. "You want to experience cold, Mister Palmer, perhaps I could arrange a visit with our esteemed guest, the one who travels in the cabin next to mine. The one who don't come out except at night. Would you like to meet *him*, Mister Palmer? Want to spend a few minutes *alone* with him?"

"NO!" said Palmer, a new level of terror in his eyes. "I mean, no, sir, Captain. No. Thank you, no." His teeth were clattering now. He put a hand over his mouth to shut himself up.

"You sure, Mister Palmer?" Nerezza said. "I could arrange it."

Palmer shook his head violently.

"I didn't think so," said Nerezza softly. "Not that I blame you."

Nerezza stepped away from Palmer and looked down. The crow's nest towered a hundred feet above the waterline. The ship, on its current tack, was heeled over, so the sea was directly beneath Nerezza. The deck, to the side, looked impossibly small in the vast expanse of blue ocean. Nerezza saw the upturned faces of the crew, all intently watching the drama taking place aloft. That pleased Nerezza. He wanted their full attention.

He turned back toward Palmer and held his knife up for all to see. Raising his voice—the powerful voice of a captain used to making himself heard throughout his ship—he addressed Palmer's cowering form.

"I offers you a choice, Mister Palmer," he bellowed. "*Three* choices, in fact, as I am a fair and evenhanded captain. One, you can pay a visit tonight to our esteemed guest in the cabin next to mine."

This brought gasps from the men below. Palmer whimpered, and again shook his head violently.

"Two," continued Nerezza, "I can carve a set of gills into you and toss you into the sea for the sharks to play with." He turned his knife so it glinted in the sunlight. Palmer was sobbing now.

"Three," bellowed Nerezza, "you can jump. Right now.

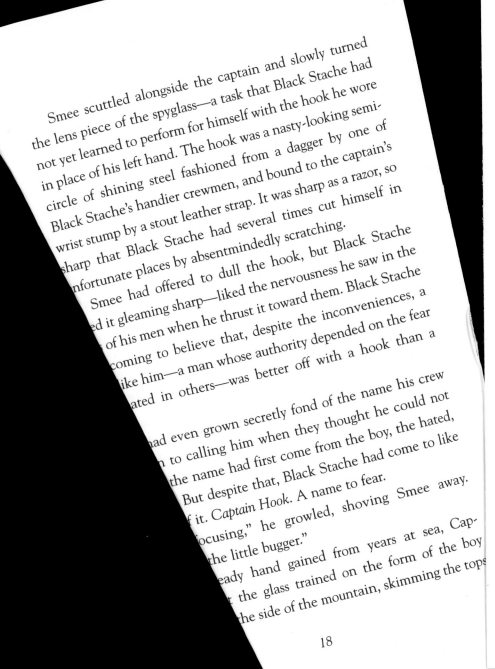

Smee scuttled alongside the captain and slowly turned the lens piece of the spyglass—a task that Black Stache had not yet learned to perform for himself with the hook he wore in place of his left hand. The hook was a nasty-looking semicircle of shining steel fashioned from a dagger by one of Black Stache's handier crewmen, and bound to the captain's wrist stump by a stout leather strap. It was sharp as a razor, so sharp that Black Stache had several times cut himself in unfortunate places by absentmindedly scratching.

Smee had offered to dull the hook, but Black Stache liked it gleaming sharp—liked the nervousness he saw in the eyes of his men when he thrust it toward them. Black Stache was coming to believe that, despite the inconveniences, a man like him—a man whose authority depended on the fear he created in others—was better off with a hook than a hand.

He had even grown secretly fond of the name his crew had taken to calling him when they thought he could not hear. The name had first come from the boy, the hated, despised boy. But despite that, Black Stache had come to like the sound of it. *Captain Hook.* A name to fear.

"Keep focusing," he growled, shoving Smee away. "Focus, you little bugger."

With a steady hand gained from years at sea, Captain Hook moved the glass trained on the form of the boy scrambling up the side of the mountain, skimming the tops

18

---

Without another word from your worthless trap. If you can reach that island—the island *you* should have spotted—I'll welcome you back aboard, Mister Palmer, as I am a forgiving man."

Nerezza drew in a deep breath, the air whistling past his wooden nosepiece.

"Now, which is it to be? The swim? The sharks? Or a visit with—"

Palmer was gone. Nerezza leaned over the side and calmly watched as the receding body grew smaller, then disappeared in a splash of white foam that quickly dropped behind the fast-moving ship.

Whether Palmer surfaced or not, Nerezza neither knew nor cared. He never looked back as he gave the orders— orders that the crew executed even more quickly than usual—to start the ship tacking toward the two small clouds in the distance.

15

# CHAPTER 3

# THE WRONG SIDE OF THE MOUNTAIN

"CAP'N," BAWLED THE LOOKOUT perched atop a tall palm. "It's the boy!"

"Where away?" bellowed a rasping voice from inside the fort. A moment later the owner of the voice appeared in the doorway: a tall, rangy man with long, greasy black hair, a hatchet face, close-set dark eyes, and a hooked nose protruding over the extravagant foot-wide flourish of facial hair that had given him his legendary and feared pirate nickname: Black Stache.

"East-nor'east, Cap'n!" shouted the lookout. "Coming down the mountain!"

The fort was made of felled palm trees, vines, and nameless barbed and spiked plants, lashed together into an ugly but surprisingly sturdy wall, which enclosed a half dozen huts

16

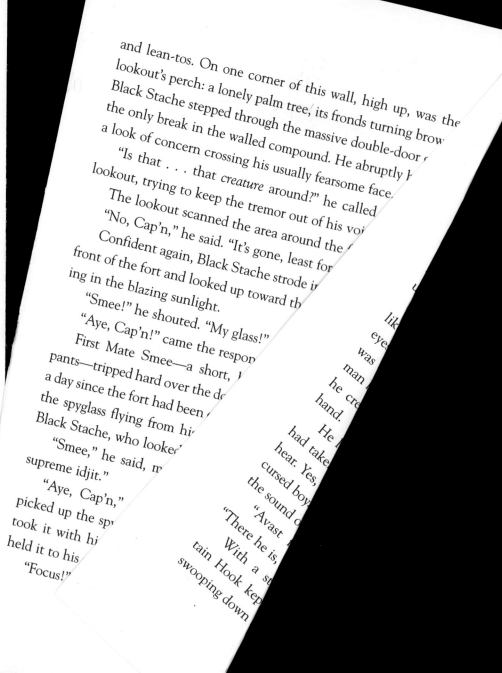

and lean-tos. On one corner of this wall, high up, was the lookout's perch: a lonely palm tree, its fronds turning brow

Black Stache stepped through the massive double-door the only break in the walled compound. He abruptly a look of concern crossing his usually fearsome face.

"Is that . . . that *creature* around?" he called lookout, trying to keep the tremor out of his voi

The lookout scanned the area around the

"No, Cap'n," he said. "It's gone, least for

Confident again, Black Stache strode i front of the fort and looked up toward th ing in the blazing sunlight.

"Smee!" he shouted. "My glass!"

"Aye, Cap'n!" came the respon

First Mate Smee—a short, pants—tripped hard over the d a day since the fort had been the spyglass flying from hi Black Stache, who looke

"Smee," he said, m supreme idjit."

"Aye, Cap'n," picked up the sp took it with hi held it to his

"Focus!"

of the jungle trees. As the boy drew nearer, Hook could see that he carried something dark and round in his hand—a coconut, perhaps, or a piece of rock. He knew what was coming—of late, the boy had taken to raiding the pirate encampment almost daily.

"Smee!" Hook snarled. "Fetch my pistol!"

"Aye, Cap'n," said Smee, running to the doorway. "OW!" he added, tripping into the fort.

"Hurry, you idjit!" shouted Hook.

"Got it, Cap'n," said Smee, re-emerging from the fort. "OW!"

As he tripped, the pistol flew forward, past Hook; it hit the ground and went off, emitting a puff of smoke and a sad little sound: *phut*. The pistol ball dribbled out the end.

Hook picked up the pistol. "Smee," he said, in the calm, reasonable tone he used only when he was very close to killing somebody. "Do we have any more gunpowder? Any *dry* gunpowder?"

"No, Cap'n," said Smee, getting warily to his feet. "You used it all up yesterday, when you was—"

"I *know* what I was doing yesterday," snapped Hook. He had been shooting at the boy, who had spent a half hour dropping coconuts on the fort. The boy avoided the pistol shots with infuriating ease while laughing—*laughing*—at the man who had once been the most feared pirate in the world.

Hook cursed and hurled the pistol to the ground, almost

weeping with frustration. He could not believe that he had come to this: marooned on this strange island; taunted by this horrid boy who had cut off his hand; unable to retaliate against the horrid boy's horrid little friends because of the horrid savages protecting them.

Worst of all, Hook, who had once roamed the seven seas at will, no longer dared venture more than a few yards from the cramped confines of the fort for fear of encountering the beast that had gulped down his hand after the cursed boy cut it off—the giant crocodile, longer than a longboat, known as "Mister Grin." It had taken to lurking near the fort, watching, waiting, its vast, jagged jaws smiling a hungry, toothful, expectant smile.

Hook had tried sending men out to lure Mister Grin away, but the beast showed no interest in others. Having tasted Hook, it seemed to want only him, lumbering forward when Hook showed himself, sometimes brushing its massive tail against the outside of the log walls while Hook cowered inside, drenched in fear-sweat, his wrist-stump throbbing.

Oh, yes, Hook hated his situation with a white-hot fury that burned in his brain. And the cause of it all was this boy flying down the mountain toward him now, ready to jeer at him yet again. And he was helpless to do anything about it.

"Cap'n," said Smee, picking up the useless pistol, "you best get in the fort, before he starts dropping things on you again."

Hook stood a moment longer, staring in frustrated fury at the oncoming form of the boy, less than a mile away now. But Smee was, for once, right: better to go into the fort. Without his favorite target, the boy would become bored in time, and leave.

Hook turned toward the door. He was stopped by another hail from the top of the tall palm tree.

"Cap'n," called the lookout. "There's another one."

Hook whirled and looked up. "Another what?" he shouted.

"Another boy, coming down the mountain."

"Flying?" asked Hook.

"No, Cap'n. He's on foot. Maybe a third of the way down."

*A boy, on foot. On the wrong side of the mountain.* The plan formed instantly in Hook's mind.

"Crenshaw! Bates!" he barked.

Two crewmen stumbled from the fort, blinking.

"There's a boy coming down the mountain," said Hook. He turned toward the lookout and said, "Davis, show them which way."

The lookout pointed toward the mountain; Crenshaw and Bates nodded.

"I want you to go up there and get him," said Hook. "I want you to stay under the trees, away from the clearings, so the flying boy don't see you, understand?"

The two men nodded.

"When we get him," said Bates, "do we kill him?"

"No," said Hook softly. "You bring him to me." He glanced toward the mountain again; the flying boy was only a few hundred yards off. Hook turned back to the two men. "Go," he hissed. "Hurry!"

Crenshaw and Bates trotted into the jungle.

"Cap'n," said Smee. "You best get inside now."

"No, Mister Smee," said Hook. "I think I'll stay outside for a bit."

"But, Cap'n," said Smee. "If the flying boy sees you, he'll stay around bothering you all day."

Hook smiled for the first time in months, showing a mouthful of yellow-brown, sharklike teeth.

"Exactly," he said.

CHAPTER 4

# THE VOICE

CAPTAIN NEREZZA ADDRESSED the man peering through the spyglass.

"Well, Mister Slank?" he said. "Is that your island?"

Slank put the glass down. He was a tall, sturdy man with big, rough hands and shaggy hair that, like Nerezza's, was held back in a ponytail. His face, in its own way, was as shocking as Nerezza's: though he still had his original nose, Slank's skin had been badly damaged by more than a month drifting at sea in an open boat. The relentless sun had burned his skin into a hideous mask of angry blisters and scabs through which could barely be discerned the features of a man.

"Aye," he said, his voice harsh, as if his throat was still parched. "As sure as I'm standing here, that's the island, Captain. The single cone of a mountain is what tells it, and the shape. That's the one, all right."

It was then they felt the chill. Every man on the ship had felt it; every man dreaded the sound of the voice that was sure to accompany the chill. The tropical sun still hung bright in the sky, but it was as though the air around the ship had gone cold and dank, like in a dark London alley near the docks in December. There was a smell, too—a faint but distinct odor of decay.

The sailors—trying to look casual about it, but clearly terrified—moved forward, away from the quarterdeck; one of them crossed himself. The man at the wheel, who could not leave his post without being flogged, went rigid and pale, his eyes fixed on the horizon. Nerezza and Slank also stiffened, neither daring to turn toward the companionway behind them, the companionway that led down to the officers' cabins.

The crew had been ordered to keep away from that companionway, but no orders were necessary. No sailor on the ship would go down there, not for a year's pay. Not with the rumors that had been scurrying around the ship since the . . . *visitor* had boarded the ship, at sea, in the dead of night, under very strange circumstances.

For openers, there was the matter of how he had arrived. It happened a few minutes into the middle watch, just past midnight. Only Nerezza and Slank were on deck. Nerezza, taking the wheel himself, had ordered the entire crew, every last man, to go below and close all hatches behind them—something that *never* happened aboard a ship at sea.

The crew, needless to say, had been intensely curious about what was happening on deck, and as it happened there was a witness: the youngest cabin boy, a slight, mischievous towheaded lad named Michael Doakes, nimble as a squirrel in the rigging. Rather than going below, Doakes had concealed himself aloft, lying on a furled sail, from which he had an excellent view of the moonlit deck.

The story that Doakes—a subdued and shaken Doakes—told belowdecks later was so strange that some of the crewmen were convinced he must have gone mad, or gotten into the grog. For the boy claimed that a man—or *something*—had come on board, and yet . . . *no ship had brought him.*

"I swear it!" he said, responding to the doubting looks of the men gathered around him. "There was no ship in the water."

"Then how'd he get here?" asked a skeptical voice. "We're five hundred miles from land."

"I . . . I don't know what it was," said the boy, his normally ruddy face gone pale and sickly. "I thought I saw a . . . a . . ."

"A *what*, boy?"

"A shape in the water. Big as our ship, but it weren't no ship. It came alongside, and then I thought I saw an . . . an arm come aboard. . . ."

"An arm?"

"Yes, a great huge arm, like a snake. . . ."

"You're mad, boy!"

"Hush! Let him talk! Then what, boy?"

"Then the arm was gone," said Doakes. "And the shape was gone. And there was this *thing*, or man, or whatever it is, standing there on deck."

"What'd he look like?"

"I couldn't say. It . . . he was all dark, like he was wearing a cloak, head to toe. When I looked at him, all I seen was black, just black. He walked across the deck. It was strange, the way he moved—like he was *gliding*, on wheels. Anyways, he went up on the quarterdeck, and he said something to Cap'n Nerezza and Mister Slank."

"What'd he say?"

"I couldn't get the words, but the *sound* of it was strange, like wind moaning in the rigging. It gave me the strangest feeling, like I was cold all of a sudden. I could tell Cap'n Nerezza and Mister Slank didn't care for it, neither. They was backing up away from the man, and turning away, like they was afraid to look at him."

"*Nerezza?*" said an incredulous voice. "*Afraid?*"

"That's what it looked like," said the boy.

"Then what?"

"Then the man went down the companionway, quick as anything—it was like he *flowed* down, like water down a drain. And then he was gone."

26

Doakes's account of the strange visitor was instantly the talk of the ship. Most of the crew believed the boy, but there were a few doubters—for a while. Their doubts vanished the first time the chill descended over the ship. It had done so several times since, and each time, it was followed by the dreaded voice.

Nerezza and Slank, standing on the quarterdeck, heard that same voice now, a cross between a hiss and a moan, emanating like a winter wind from the companionway behind them.

"You found the island," the voice said.

Nerezza and Slank looked at each other, then Nerezza answered.

"Yes," he said.

"You are certain, *Slank?*" the voice said.

Slank flinched, then said quietly, "I'm certain."

A pause; neither Nerezza nor Slank moved. Then the voice spoke again.

"You had better be right, Slank," it said. "*You had better not fail us again.*"

Slank said nothing, still staring at the island. He had, indeed, failed; had somehow, incredibly, let the most valuable trunk on earth—the most valuable *thing* on earth—slip through his fingers, because of some mindless mermaids and a . . . a *boy*. Defeated, humiliated, he'd barely escaped the island with his life; he'd spent weeks at sea, drifting on a tiny boat with Little Richard, his huge and loyal servant, whom he had ultimately, with some regret, been forced to kill and eat so he could stay alive. Because he *had* to stay alive, if only for revenge.

And stay alive he had, long enough to be picked up by a trading ship, and finally make it back to Rundoon, where he'd had to report his failure to King Zarboff. Zarboff, enraged by the loss of the trunk and its priceless cargo of starstuff, had wanted to feed Slank to the giant snake he kept as a pet. But Zarboff was only a king; he was subordinate to higher-ranking members of the Others, the secret group that for centuries had controlled much of the world through the powers they gained from starstuff. They knew they needed Slank alive, to lead them back to the island, and the trunk. For the time being, Zarboff's snake went hungry.

And so Slank had found himself hastily put aboard this ship—called *Le Fantome*—commanded by the brutal Captain Nerezza, a man often employed by the Others, a man known for getting things done by whatever means nec-essary. *Le Fantome* had spent weeks—too many weeks—wan-dering the sea, searching for an island that didn't seem to be on any of the charts; an island that, Slank suspected, Nerezza sometimes did not believe existed.

The recent midnight arrival of the mysterious visitor had increased the urgency of the search. Clearly, the Others were growing impatient in their desire to get the trunk back.

So Slank was relieved and pleased to see the island. Relieved, because it meant that he might yet escape from this debacle with his life. And pleased because the boy would be on the island.

He meant to kill the boy. The thought brought a rare and painful smile to his face, his badly worn teeth showing briefly amid the mass of sunburn scars.

Slank turned to Nerezza. "There's a decent anchorage off the eastern side," he said.

Nerezza nodded.

Then the voice again, behind them: "How long?"

Nerezza considered, squinting at the island. "About two hours," he said. "We can be ashore before sunset."

"*No*," groaned the voice, a sound that caused skin to crawl throughout *Le Fantome*. "Not before nightfall. It must be at night, do you understand?"

Nerezza, too shaken to speak, nodded.

"At *night*," the voice repeated.

And despite the heat of the day, Slank's teeth began to chatter.

## CHAPTER 5

# THE AGREEMENT

PETER, WITH TINKER BELL CLOSE BEHIND, swooped low, his belly just brushing the jungle treetops as he zoomed toward the pirate camp. He cradled the mango in his left hand and changed direction quickly, in case Hook shot at him again.

At first the shooting had scared him, but he'd quickly learned that he could evade it easily enough if he changed direction when he saw Hook's trigger finger twitch. Peter's eyesight was very, very sharp—far sharper than that of the other boys, or for that matter, anybody else on the island. It was one of the changes—like the ability to fly—that had come over him since he'd been exposed to the mysterious material called "starstuff." As he discovered his new abilities, he'd become increasingly convinced of his superiority to others, and his invulnerability. He no longer feared Hook's pistol. In fact, he almost *enjoyed* being shot at.

With the clearing just ahead, Peter shifted the mango into his right hand, his throwing hand.

Now over the clearing, he looked down and found himself staring straight into the eyes of Captain Hook, who stood out in the open.

*He was expecting me.*

Peter raised the mango, anticipating Hook might flinch, or even run toward the fort. But Hook didn't move, didn't so much as blink. He just stood there staring right back at Peter. In place of the pirate's usual hate-filled look, Peter saw an expression of disconcerting calm—almost *amusement*. Surprised by this change in the man, Peter forgot to throw the mango.

Instead, he flew across the clearing, banked into a rising turn, and settled into a high, slow-spinning hover, like a hummingbird, from which to assess the situation. He searched for signs of an ambush—pirates in the trees, perhaps, armed with pistols or spears—but saw nothing. A few pirates lounged against the wall of the fort; a few others rested by the spring at the side of the clearing, where the pirates got their drinking water. But there was no apparent threat; only Hook and his bumbling first mate, Smee, with Hook still watching Peter calmly, as though Peter were a mildly interesting bird, instead of his blood enemy.

*Odd.*

Peter decided to try to goad the pirate into reacting.

"Greetings, Dark Whiskers!" he shouted. "No, sorry, that's not your name, is it? Mister Stache? No, no, my apologies. It's Captain *Hook*, isn't it?"

This outburst brought muffled giggles from some of the pirates. Peter was certain this nickname must be infuriating to Hook, but the pirate's expression remained irritatingly calm.

"Greetings, boy," the pirate responded. "How are you and your little . . . *insect*?"

Enraged, discordant bells arose from Tink. The pirates laughed out loud this time.

Frustrated, Peter descended toward the clearing, displaying the mango.

"I brought you some lunch, Captain Hook," he said. "You didn't seem to enjoy the coconut yesterday. So how about a nice juicy mango?"

He raised the mango. Smee stepped away from Hook. Hook stood statue-still.

*Not like him at all.*

Bells chimed in his ear.

"Trap?" said Peter. "He can't trap us, Tink, not as long as we stay up here and he's stuck down there."

More bells.

"You worry too much," said Peter. "Watch this." He raised the mango over his head. "Enjoy!" he shouted, letting it fly.

His aim was perfect; right at Hook's head. Smee raised his hands defensively, but Hook held motionless, watching the fruit sphere hurtling toward him until . . .

*WHOOSH!*

A lightning movement. A flash of steel. And there stood Hook, his left arm held high, the mango impaled on his hook. A bit of its juice dribbled down the blade. Hook brought it down to his mouth, licked it daintily, then looked back at Peter and smiled.

"Thank you, boy," he said. "Delicious."

This was *not* what Peter had expected. Now he was becoming quite irritated.

"Then perhaps you'd like some more, *Captain Hook*," he said.

"That would be lovely, *boy*," sneered Hook, peeling back the skin and nibbling at the fruit.

"All right, then," said Peter, through gritted teeth. Ignoring Tinker Bell's warnings, he darted toward a clump of palms beyond the clearing and picked two large coconuts.

*Let's see him catch these*, he thought, swooping back.

"Ahoy, Hook!" he shouted. "Here's your second course!"

Peter noted with satisfaction that when Hook saw the coconuts, a trace of alarm crept across his face.

*That's better*, he thought. He angled his body upward, then arced into a steep dive directly at the pirate. Closer . . . closer . . . he raised his arm . . .

A scream from the direction of the mountain.

A boy's scream.

Peter whirled and swooped upward, listening, looking.

Another scream, then: "PETER! HELP!"

Peter looked at Tinker Bell's horrified face, saw that she, too, recognized the voice.

*James.*

Dropping the coconuts, Peter, with Tink at his side, shot toward the mountain, his eyes frantically scanning the jungle growth below him, his ears straining to hear. But the dense vegetation prevented him from seeing beneath the tree canopy, and he heard no more shouts or screams.

Time slowed to a crawl as Peter and Tink zigzagged frantically back and forth across the mountainside, calling for James, getting no response. Finally one of his passes took him near the pirate clearing. Hook stood exactly where he had been. He was smiling and still eating. Mango juice dribbled from his moustache.

"What's the matter, *boy?*" Hook called. "Missing something? Or should I say, some *body?*"

Hook laughed a very unpleasant laugh, a laugh that told Peter exactly why Hook had stood in the clearing, taunting him, daring him to attack.

*He was distracting me.*

Peter's stomach felt hollow.

"Where is he?" he shouted, flying closer.

34

"Your little friend?" asked Hook. "The one who *can't* fly? Oh, don't worry. We'll take care of him." The pirate raised the mango—still impaled on his hook—and took another delicate bite.

"Let him go!" said Peter. "He's done nothing to you!"

"That's true," said Hook. "He has done nothing. It's a shame that *he* should be the one to suffer." Another bite.

Peter, hovering almost directly over Hook now, stared down at the pirate.

"What do you want?" the boy asked softly.

Hook glanced up at him, and Peter saw it now, the hatred the pirate had been holding inside.

"Why," said Hook, "I want *you*, of course."

"Me for James," said Peter, very softly.

"That's right, boy," said Hook. "A trade: you for James."

A minute passed, Peter hovering, Hook watching. Peter finally broke the silence.

"Where is he?" said Peter.

"Your little friend?" said Hook. "He's unharmed, I assure you. For now."

Peter thought some more.

"You can't have me until I see you let him go, see that he's safe," he said. "I need to see him in the hands of Mollusks. Then you get me."

Now it was Hook's turn to ponder.

"Very well," he said. "Come back to the clearing tonight,

one hour past moonrise. You may bring two savages."

"Ten," said Peter. "Otherwise your men can—"

"*SILENCE, BOY*," thundered Hook. "If you want your young friend to live, you will bring no more than *two savages* with you. My men will be inside the fort, watching. I shall meet you there"—he pointed—"by the spring. I will be holding your friend. You will place yourself within my reach. I will grab you, and at the same time release your friend."

In response to Peter's doubting look, Hook said: "Think about it, boy! I'll *have* to let go of him, won't I? I have just the one hand, thanks to *you*."

Peter nodded. Hook went on: "Once your friend is free, the savages can take him and melt into the jungle, as they do so well. If I fail to release your friend, your savages can spear me, yes? And if you fail to return here at the proper time, or you arrive with *more* than two savages, or you try any other tricks, then your friend . . ."

Hook quickly raised his hook, flipping the half-eaten mango into the air. As it came down . . . *WHOOSH* . . . the hook flashed and the mango fell to the ground, sliced cleanly through the middle into two equal-sized pieces. Even the big seed in the middle was perfectly halved.

Hook tilted his head and addressed Peter. "Understand, boy?" he said. "This is no *game*."

Peter nodded.

"Good," said Hook. "Be back here an hour past moon-rise. *Don't forget*, boy."

"I won't forget," said Peter.

"Good boy," said the captain. He held up his hook, turning it so that it flashed sunlight into Peter's eyes. "I'll be waiting."

Peter shielded his eyes, turned in midair, and was gone, swooping straight up the curve of the mountain, all the while getting a nonstop I-told-you-so earful from Tinker Bell.

In the clearing there was silence, finally broken by Smee.

"Cap'n, d'you think he'll come back?"

"Of course he'll come back," said Hook. "The fool boy thinks he's a hero. He'll do what he must to save his little friend."

"Ah, so you'll let the other one go?" said Smee, relieved.

Hook barked out an ugly laugh.

"Smee," he said, "you are a *supreme* idjit."

## CHAPTER 6

# 𝒯HE 𝒟ARKEST 𝒲AY

𝒜s THE LAST VESTIGES OF DAY gave way to night, the sea and sky thickened into a paste of grayish black. *Le Fantome* glided into a small bay, and its crew lowered the anchor, easing it into the water as quietly as possible. Some flying fish leaped and glided, silhouetted against the disappearing horizon as the eerie cries of monkeys rose from the vast, formless jungle.

Nerezza, standing with Slank on the quarterdeck, said, "It'll be as dark as the inside of a whale in a few minutes. I'd best alert our guest."

The plan they'd settled on was a simple one. Coming into the bay, they'd spotted a tendril of smoke rising from the island; that was their target. They'd row ashore, two boatloads of armed men—brutal men; handpicked fighters—and search out this camp. If the boy wasn't there, whoever was in the camp would likely know where he was on an island this small. And the boy would know where to find the starstuff. And the starstuff was why they'd come.

Slank assumed the camp belonged to the pirates he'd left on the island—the pirates he'd defeated, before he in turn was defeated by the boy, and those hideous demon she-fish.

But it didn't matter whose camp it was. Anybody—or any *thing*—who got in their way would be no match for Nerezza's raiders and their . . . *guest*. If the starstuff was on the island, they would have it.

Slank tried not to think about what could happen to him if the starstuff wasn't on the island.

*It has to be here,* he told himself. *It has to be.*

The men were lowering the boats now. Slank eyed the dark water; his face betrayed the apprehension he felt.

"What is it?" sneered Nerezza. "Afraid of the *fishes,* are you?"

"I ain't afraid," snapped Slank. "But I ain't eager to meet up with them she-fish again." He shuddered, remembering when he had last been there, remembering the feel of the mermaids' teeth sinking into him, recalling his blood clouding the water.

Nerezza, who wasn't sure he believed in these she-fish, coughed out a laugh. It wasn't natural, coming from him; it sounded a bit painful. He pointed to the darkened companionway. "There's no fish—no creature alive—can possibly match our dark friend down there," he said. "Nothing on that island, neither."

Slank looked back to the island. He figured it to be about two miles to the smoke if they went along the shore; far shorter if they cut directly across the island. Slank wanted to take the coast—he didn't care to be in the jungle at night, not on this island—but Nerezza overruled him.

"We'll set off through the jungle," Nerezza said. "Not only for the sake of speed, but for the sake of darkness. Our guest don't want no light whatsoever. We go the darkest way."

"No light? How do we find the way?"

"That ain't up to us," said Nerezza. "Our guest leads, and we follow. Mark my words, Mister Slank, there's only one man in command once we reach that shore. And it ain't you. And it ain't me."

*And it ain't a man*, thought Slank.

# CHAPTER 7

# AN ALLY

"So," said Fighting Prawn. "You got your friend into trouble."

The Mollusk chief looked at Peter with piercing dark eyes, made all the blacker by their contrast with Fighting Prawn's flowing, snow-white hair.

"But it's not my fault!" said Peter, panting, still out of breath from his frantic flight back across the mountain to the Mollusk compound. "James followed me to the pirates! I told him not to, but . . ."

Peter's tongue was stilled by Fighting Prawn's stern stare, a look so disconcerting that Peter had to turn away.

"He followed you," the chief said, "because he wanted to join in your *game*. Because you boasted about how much *fun* you were having taunting the pirates. Isn't that right?"

Peter, still looking away, nodded. He was grateful that Tinker Bell, for once, was silent, though she listened with approval to the lecture as she perched on Peter's shoulder.

"What have I told you about taunting the pirates?" said Fighting Prawn. "What have I told you a dozen times and more?"

"It's foolish," Peter answered softly. "And dangerous."

"That's right," said Fighting Prawn. "It's a misuse of the gifts you've been given. I can protect you on this side of the island; the captain won't come for you here. But on the other side, you've got the captain and his men, any of whom would be happy to slit your throat. And you've got Mister Grin running loose, with a taste for human flesh. There's no reason to go over there except to look for trouble. But you chose to look for it. And now you've found it."

Peter's lip quivered. A tear slid down his cheek; Tink reached out and gently wiped it away.

"Listen, boy," said Fighting Prawn, his voice softer now. "You have a good heart. You have great courage. You fought the pirate. You saved my life. For that you will always have my friendship and protection. But you're still a boy, and you must learn to become a man."

Peter looked up, about to say something; then he closed his mouth, thinking better of it.

"I know," said Fighting Prawn. "Because of the change in you"—he pointed to the golden locket that hung at Peter's throat—"you will never grow old. You will always have the *body* of a boy. But in here"—now Fighting Prawn touched

Peter's forehead—"in your *mind*, you must become a man, because the other boys need you. You are their leader. They trust you. You must become worthy of their trust."

"But it's too late," said Peter, a flood of tears welling from his eyes now, streaming down his cheeks. "I've let them down. Hook has James. He'll kill him if I don't surrender myself."

"You do," said Fighting Prawn, "and he'll kill *you*."

"But it's my fault. You said so yourself. It's *my fault*." He looked down, sobbing, his tears spattering the dusty ground. Tink fluttered down and caught one in midair. In her hand, it turned into a tiny diamond. She showed it to Peter; ordinarily, a trick like this would have delighted him. But now he only shook his head.

Fighting Prawn put a comforting hand on Peter's shoulder.

"All right, boy," he said. "We will see what we can do to get your friend back." He glanced toward a small group of Mollusk warriors who stood a respectful distance away, watching. With a tiny movement of his head, he summoned them over.

Peter looked up. "Are you going to attack the pirates?" he asked. "Because Hook says he'll kill James if you do."

"I'm sure he would," said Fighting Prawn. "I'm sure he means to kill him anyway."

"But," said Peter, "he said you could send two savag—I mean, warriors—and they could bring James back."

Fighting Prawn smiled a thin, mirthless smile. "He means to kill the *savages*, too," he said. "He'll have men hidden nearby. The instant he has you in hand, you're all dead."

"So what can we do?" said Peter.

"I've been thinking about that," said Fighting Prawn. "Can you possibly fly your friend out?"

"No," said Peter. "Hook says he won't let go of James until he can grab me. And even if James and I were both free, I'm not sure I can lift him. I've tried flying him before, and I usually go all wobbly and come right back down."

Fighting Prawn pondered for a moment, then said: "You say Hook told you to surrender yourself next to the spring?"

"Yes," said Peter. "The spring at the edge of the clearing."

"I see," said Fighting Prawn thoughtfully. He turned and said something to one of the warriors in the Mollusk language—a mixture of grunts and clicks, sounding very odd to the English ear. It always sounded especially odd to Peter when Fighting Prawn spoke it; he was accustomed to the Mollusk chief's impeccable English, learned from his years as a forced laborer aboard British navy ships.

The Mollusk warrior answered Fighting Prawn at some length, Fighting Prawn listening intently. After another brief exchange, he turned to Peter.

"Just as I thought," he said. "That spring rises from a cavern. There's a tunnel leading to the cavern underground—a tunnel just wide enough for a person to fit through. But it's a long way from the spring to the tunnel mouth. A very long way. And it's all under water."

"I don't understand," said Peter. "Are you suggesting that James and I could *swim* out of there? Because I'm not much of a swimmer, and James can barely swim at all."

"No, it's too far for you," said Fighting Prawn. "But we may be able to use the tunnel to disappoint Captain Hook. We must make some preparations, and quickly." He grunt-clicked something to the warriors, a long and complicated set of instructions. They listened closely, occasionally smiling (*Why are they smiling?* Peter wondered). When the chief finished, they trotted off.

"Now," said Fighting Prawn. "We need to enlist an ally."

"An ally?" said Peter.

"Yes," said Fighting Prawn. "We need somebody who's reliable. Trustworthy. And brave."

Tink flew between the two men, chiming loudly and pointing to herself.

"Somebody who's a *very* good swimmer," added Fighting Prawn.

Tink, deflated, went back to Peter's shoulder.

"But," said Peter, "I can't . . . I mean, none of the boys can . . ." Then he stopped, finally understanding who Fighting Prawn meant.

"Oh," he said.

"Yes," said Fighting Prawn. "You have a big favor to ask."

## CHAPTER 8

# THE MISSION

TWELVE HARD MEN, KILLERS ALL, slipped over the side of *Le Fantome* and clambered down rope ladders to the two longboats, where Nerezza awaited them. Sheets of fog rose from the water, hovering at eye height between the ship and the shore, broken into patches and wisps by an intermittent breeze.

Ahead of the raiding party, a dory slid through the water, manned only by a lone oarsman, and *Le Fantome's* mysterious black-cloaked passenger sitting in the bow.

The unhappy oarsman was Slank, ordered by Nerezza to take the passenger—*Lord Ombra*, Nerezza had called him—ashore. Slank had protested: Lord or no lord, he didn't want to be alone in the boat with him. But Nerezza had given him no choice.

Slank pulled on the oars, his back to the shore and his unwelcome passenger. The night air was warm, but Slank felt a chill through his back, a chill to his bones. He'd felt it from the moment Ombra descended to the dory. Ombra hadn't exactly climbed down the rope set out for him, nor had he slid. It was more like he'd *oozed* down the rope, Slank thought, like harbor mud dripping down an anchor line.

Slank didn't want to think about that. He wanted only to get to the island and get out of this boat.

Lazy waves lapped the shore, on this, the leeward side of the island. Slank pulled toward that sound, wondering why Nerezza had assigned him this task.

"Steady on," came Ombra's voice, a deep groan that sent a shudder slithering down Slank's spine.

Moonlight broke through the swirling mist. Slank leaned sideways to study the surface of the water, looking for signs of the hated mermaids. He would never admit it, but he was terrified of the demon she-fish. As he moved, his moon-cast shadow moved with him, playing across the small boat.

Slank glanced toward the ship, saw the longboats pushing off. What Slank didn't see was the strange behavior of his shadow behind him. As if taking on a life of its own, it began to stretch and shift, slithering toward the bow, toward Ombra.

Slank felt suddenly light-headed. Behind him, he heard Ombra's wheezing groan, but in a low murmur, not addressed to him, as if Ombra were talking to himself. But then Slank heard a *second* voice . . . a voice eerily familiar to him, a voice so familiar that it was as if . . .

Ombra spoke again, this time to Slank. "So," he groaned, "you're afraid of the she-fish. . . ."

*But how . . .*

"I ain't afraid of any kind of fish, nor anything else on this island," Slank said aloud. His thoughts were quite different: *You'd be afraid, too, Lord whoever you are, if you'd tangled with them fish in this water like I did. And you might not find that flying boy so easy to deal with, neither.*

"I see," groaned Ombra. "You think the flying boy might give *me* trouble, as he did you?"

Slank froze, halting the oars in midstroke. *It's like he hears me thinking.*

"Exactly," groaned Ombra. "Row."

Slank resumed rowing. The moon passed behind a cloud; the sea went dark again. Slank lost sight of the longboats following.

"They're fierce, them she-fish," Slank said defensively. "Teeth like razors. And cunning . . ."

"How many she-fish?" All business.

"Were a sea full of 'em. Circling my dory. Five . . . six . . . ten. Taking bites out of the transom. You ain't never seen anything like it."

"Indeed, I've seen a great many things you've not dreamed of, Mister Slank. We needn't concern ourselves over a few she-fish. Nor pirates. Nor a flying boy. Nor the little girl, the daughter of the Starcatcher." Ombra hissed the beginning of "Starcatcher," a hiss of disdain.

"We concern ourselves with one thing, one thing only," continued Ombra. "To retrieve the starstuff *you* left behind."

Slank started to say something but thought better of it.

"Wise decision, Mister Slank. Now, with your knowledge of the island, and those men in the longboats, and my special . . . *capabilities*, we should have no trouble carrying out our mission. But you, Mister Slank, must be a help to us, not a hindrance. Do you understand?"

"Yes," said Slank, through gritted teeth.

"That means you must remember that our purpose here, our *only* purpose, is to get the starstuff, do you understand?"

"Yes."

"It is *not* to gain revenge."

Slank stiffened.

"That's right," said Ombra. "I know of your plans for the boy."

Slank said nothing.

"You will *not* waste time pursuing your personal agenda, Slank. You will *not* jeopardize our mission. You will obey my orders. Failure to do so would be very, very unpleasant for you, do you understand?"

"Yes."

"Good. Here we are."

The dory was lifted by a small wave and came down to rest on the beach. Slank never felt his passenger move, heard no splash of boots in the water; but when he turned, Ombra was gliding up the beach.

The moonlight broke through again, though only briefly. Ombra glided swiftly away from the advancing light—*Like he's scared of it*, thought Slank—into the darkness of the jungle.

Slank clambered out of the boat and hauled the dory out of the water. He looked up the beach, now pale white in the moonlight. His eyes traced the path Ombra had taken across the wet sand, and he felt the chill again.

There were no footprints.

## CHAPTER 9

# A Tasty Meal Lost

Peter stumbled down the dark jungle path, tripping over what seemed like every rock, root, and vine. Behind him followed a young Mollusk warrior named Running Snail; ahead of him went Fierce Clam, second in seniority only to Fighting Prawn himself. The two Mollusk warriors, unlike Peter, moved effortlessly no matter how steep, twisting, or muddy the terrain.

At one point Fierce Clam disappeared altogether in the gloom ahead. A warning chime sounded in Peter's right ear.

"I know, Tink," he snapped. "I'm going as fast as I can."

Peter would have preferred to fly, but Fighting Prawn had insisted that he remain on the ground with the two warriors, ensuring that the three arrive at the pirate encampment together. And so Peter stumbled forward.

*I hope this works*, he thought. The plan had sounded

foolproof when Fighting Prawn had explained it back in the village. But now, out here in the thick of the jungle, enveloped in darkness, approaching Hook's camp on foot, Peter felt less confident. In his mind he pictured the pirate's sharp hook slicing through the mango. He also knew only too well that the giant, hungry crocodile roamed this side of the island, looking for an easy meal. For an instant, fear seized his belly, and he considered turning back. But then, remembering James, he forged ahead.

Lost in thought, he almost collided with Fierce Clam, who had stopped on the path. They were nearly at the pirate encampment. Now the three of them—Peter and the two Mollusk warriors—exchanged looks: *Ready?*

*Ready.*

Fierce Clam gave a signal, pointing upward. Peter nodded, and flying now, raised himself a few feet off the ground. The two Mollusks moved beneath him and helped Peter adjust his sailcloth trousers and eel-skin shoes. When they were all three satisfied with the results, Peter, with Tinker Bell hovering close by, soared up through the tree canopy into the moonlit sky.

He drifted a few feet forward, saw the clearing with the hulking rough shape of the pirate fort at the far end. His eyes scanned the clearing, and then he saw the two shapes, one large, one small.

Hook holding James.

"Peter!" James squealed in a fear-squeezed voice that tore at Peter's heart.

"It's all right, James," answered Peter. "I'm here."

"Yes, James," said Hook, in a rasping, ugly mimic of Peter's high-pitched voice. "Your heroic friend is here to rescue you."

Peter swooped closer. The pirate had his good hand firmly gripped around James's left arm, leaving his hook free. As Hook had promised, they were alone—or so it appeared. Peter had little doubt that Hook's men were hiding in the thick vegetation surrounding the clearing.

For now, that did not concern Peter. What did concern him was that Hook and James were standing too far from the spring. The spring lay to Hook's left, at the edge of a clearing. In the moonlight, its clear water welled up from underground, forming a round pool perhaps six feet across; from the pool a small stream trickled off into the jungle.

*I have to lure them closer to the spring,* thought Peter. He drifted forward until he was almost directly over Hook's head. He heard James whimper as Hook's grip tightened on the boy's arm.

"No tricks, boy," growled Hook. "If you try anything— like making your little friend here fly—he'll have me hook in him before you can think about it, understand?"

"I understand," said Peter. He hitched up his trousers and drifted a bit closer to the spring. *Come on, Hook. Follow me.*

53

"But did you come alone, boy?" asked Hook. "Where are the sav—ah, *there* they are."

Fierce Clam and Running Snail had slipped silently into the clearing. They stood calmly at the jungle's edge, watching the pirate, who moved his hook near James's throat. He addressed Peter.

"Do they understand the agreement, boy? If they approach me, if they take so much as a step toward me, your friend is in pieces."

"They understand," said Peter.

"Excellent," said Hook. "Now, here's how we do this, boy. You lower yourself to me, nice and easy. When you're within reach, I let go of your friend."

"All right," said Peter. Slowly, he drifted lower, but he also moved closer to the spring. *Come on. . . .*

Peter's legs hung close to Hook now, his shoes just out of the pirate's reach. Hook, still gripping James firmly, eagerly edged closer, looking at Peter with hatred in his eyes. Peter glanced over at the spring—*Am I close enough?*—and drifted just a bit nearer to it. His legs dipped a bit lower, the right one now within Hook's grasp.

With a ferocious roar fueled by months of pent-up fury, Hook released James and, with a snake-quick motion, latched hard onto Peter's leg. "GOT YOU NOW, BOY!" he bellowed in triumph. Then: "GET THEM, MEN!"

In an instant, a dozen pirates sprang from their concealment and into the clearing, racing toward the Mollusk warriors. Hook, gripping the leg of the boy, felt a surge of elation. His plan had worked. At last, at long last, he had the boy. *The hated boy was his!*

And then, in the next instant, Hook saw it all go wrong. His first inkling of trouble came when he yanked on Peter's leg to pull him down, still undecided as to whether he would kill him then and there, or take his time, make it last for the pleasure of it.

He yanked, and the leg came down—both legs came down, in fact—but not the boy.

*The boy was still hovering up there.*

Hook looked down at the leg in his hand, still inside the trousers, eel-skin shoes still sticking out the bottom. . . .

*Long trousers. Shoes.*

*The boy didn't wear long trousers or shoes.*

His triumph turning to horror, Hook looked up to see Peter wearing his customary cutoff shorts. Peter was grinning as he demonstrated to Hook how he'd tucked his legs up in front of him inside the trousers that Hook was now holding. Bellowing in rage, the captain slashed his hook through those trousers, which was an unfortunate decision, as the Mollusks had fashioned the false legs using rancid fish guts wrapped in animal skin. These foul innards exploded all over Hook, filling the air with putrid fumes, which mingled with . . .

Laughter. The boy was *laughing.*

Hook lunged upward at Peter, stumbling forward as he slashed the air with his hook. This was exactly what Peter wanted him to do, as it took Hook away from James. Peter drew him forward a few more steps, then darted over the pirate's head—the arcing hook missing him by perhaps an inch—and swooped down to James, who still stood exactly where Hook had released him, frozen in fright.

Not daring even to land—for Hook had whirled and was charging back toward them—Peter took James by his shoulders and, to James's utter shock, shoved him into the spring.

"HOLD YOUR BREATH, JAMES," he shouted, and spun to see Hook and two of his pirate crew coming for him. Peter, leaping up, felt Hook's hand on his leg—his real leg, this time—but just as the grip was closing, Hook yelled "YOW!" and clapped the hand to his eye, which had just received a hard poke from a tiny but amazingly potent fist.

"Thanks, Tink!" shouted Peter, shooting upward and out of Hook's reach. He stopped and looked down just in time to see James's moonlit face—the expression of shock still intact—disappearing beneath the dark surface of the spring.

"GET THAT ONE!" screamed Hook to one of the crewmen, shoving him into the spring after James. The crewman ducked beneath the surface, reappearing a few moments later, soaking wet, water streaming from his shoulders.

"He's gone, Cap'n," he reported. "He musta sunk to the bottom."

Hook looked up, the fury on his face now mingled with mystification.

"You drowned your own friend, boy!" he shouted. "Some hero you are!"

Peter only smiled, enraging Hook still more.

"I thought we had a bargain, boy!" shrieked Hook. "You coulda saved the lad!"

"You never planned to hold up your end," said Peter. "Your men were going to capture James *and* the Mollusks."

Remembering the Mollusks—at least he would have *them* as prisoners—Hook whirled, looking around the clearing. He saw only his men, sheepish looks and downcast faces. The two Mollusk warriors were gone.

"Where are the savages?" bellowed Hook.

"They . . . they got away, Cap'n," a crewman said. "We followed 'em into the jungle, and they was right in front of us, and . . . they just *vanished.*"

Giggles from overhead. Giggles, and the sound of tiny, mocking bells.

For a moment, Hook stood absolutely still, reeking of fish guts. And then it erupted from him, a string of oaths so vile that Peter reached out to cover Tink's tiny ears. The sound of the oaths filled the clearing for thirty seconds, a minute, with both Peter and the pirate crew watching in fascination.

And then there was another sound, this time from the

jungle. A deep growl. Then a tremor in the ground. Then the sound of thick vegetation being thrust aside by a massive, lumbering shape.

"Cap'n!" shouted Smee, bursting from the fort. "It's . . . coming!"

At first, Hook, still loudly spewing bile, didn't hear. It was only when he felt Smee's urgent tug on his tattered coat sleeve, and saw the terror on the faces of his men sprinting past him toward the fort, that Hook looked to the clearing's edge and saw, emerging from the jungle, the giant crocodile known as Mister Grin, his two cannonball-size eyes glowing red above the gaping, tooth-studded jaws, big as a grand piano.

Shoving Smee aside, Hook turned and sprinted for the fort. Mister Grin, with astonishing agility for his vast bulk, launched himself across the clearing, his quarry, as always, Hook. It was a close race: Hook sprinted through the fort gates only a few yards ahead of the beast, screaming "CLOSE THE GATES! CLOSE THE GATES!" The men behind him managed to slam the two gates shut and bar them a half second before Mister Grin reached the fort. The giant croc, finding his path blocked, emitted an earsplitting roar, sending Hook racing to his hut, where he lay on the floor and curled into a ball, whimpering like a child.

Watching from above, Peter smiled in radiant triumph; he'd beaten Hook *again*. His smile disappeared at the discordant sound of angry bells in his ears, reminding him that all was not yet resolved.

"James!" he said, clapping his hand to his forehead. Then he whirled and shot forward, zooming across the jungle tree-tops, leaving the great beast roaring in frustration at a tasty meal lost.

CHAPTER 10

# $\mathcal{D}$EAD $\mathcal{E}$YES

$\mathcal{S}$LANK LED THE WAY DOWN the overgrown jungle path, followed by Lord Ombra, Captain Nerezza, and the dozen large scurvies.

Head of the line was not a place of honor. Slank knew that if the natives were unfriendly, he would be the first to take an arrow or spear. His eyes nervously roamed the darkness ahead. A lifelong sailor, he'd never taken to land, especially when he could barely see it. He didn't care for the squishy things underfoot, the crying things in the darkness overhead.

Another step, and he shuddered as his face was suddenly caught in an invisible, clinging, and sickeningly sticky spiderweb. He clawed at it, trying to untangle himself, spitting to keep the acrid taste out of his mouth. Just then, its creator—a hairy spider the size of his hand—landed on his head, apparently planning to eat him.

Slank grabbed at the spider, felt its thick fur and scrabbling legs. He was about to emit a most un-seamanlike scream when he felt something touch his hand from behind . . . something very cold. In an instant, the spider stopped twitching and slid from Slank's head. A dead thing now, it landed on the jungle floor with a muffled thud.

Slank stood still, panting, sweating, not wanting to turn around. Then came the groaning voice.

"I will lead," Ombra announced.

Slank gladly stepped aside to allow the dark form, near-invisible in the jungle gloom, to glide past. With Ombra in front, the raiding party moved quickly, soon reaching the base of a steep mountain slope. They turned right, following a narrow trail that led through a berry patch—the prickly branches grasping at the men but seeming to have no effect on Ombra—then across the crunch of volcanic rock and down to a small creek and a larger path that curved to the left, into deeper gloom.

Ombra raised an arm and groaned, "Halt"; the sound of his voice causing the unseen screeching creatures overhead to suddenly go silent. Ombra waved Nerezza forward, and Slank watched as the captain loosened the leather strap securing his wooden nose to his face. Holding his nosepiece at his side, he sucked in the jungle air, making a harsh, wet sound that reminded Slank of a wild boar. Nerezza pointed to the right, and the raiding party moved that way.

Another fifty yards; another halt. Nerezza again sniffed the air, then said something to Ombra. Ombra nodded—at least there was a movement of his hood—then said, "You will wait here."

"Yes, lord," said Nerezza.

This reply turned heads among the men. Nerezza, brutal ship commander, *never* showed this kind of deference.

Ombra moved off, but to Slank's surprise, did not take the path. Instead, he melted into the jungle, making no noise whatsoever. Slank knew this was impossible—the vegetation was far too thick for a man to move through it soundlessly. But there was no noise, no rustling of vines, nothing.

Five minutes passed. Ten. Then Ombra reappeared *in front* of Slank, coming not from the jungle, but from down the path ahead. He halted, a dark wraith in a flowing cape, and beckoned.

"Move," Nerezza ordered his men.

The group started forward. Ombra in the lead, followed by Nerezza, then Slank, then the rest. Another twenty yards and the trail widened, the tree branches overhead parting enough to allow some pale moonlight to reach the ground.

Slank peered ahead, and froze.

Not ten yards up the trail stood two men—natives, one on each side of the trail, each with a spear in his right hand. Sentries, apparently.

Slank drew his knife and held his breath, waiting for Ombra and Nerezza to react. But there was no reaction from them, and—incredibly—none from the natives. Ombra, with Nerezza right behind, glided toward the men, closer . . . closer . . . and still the sentries stood motionless. Ombra, taking no notice, glided right between them and continued up the path, followed, after a moment's hesitation, by Nerezza.

When he reached the sentries, Slank paused for a moment to study them. Their dark eyes were open, but their faces were blank. Slank waved his knife in front of the eyes of the sentry to his right: nothing.

Resheathing his knife, Slank passed between the sentries and moved up the path, followed by the men. Behind him, a voice from somewhere in the line whispered, "*witchcraft.*" Nerezza, hearing this, spun and glared back. There were no more comments from the men.

Twenty-five yards down the path, they passed through another pair of sentries, also standing like statues. Shortly after that, they came to still another motionless pair, these two stationed at the entrance to what appeared to be a large compound. The compound was surrounded by a high wall made of thick logs sharpened to points and lashed together with stout vines.

Keeping in line, the raiding party passed by the sentries—neither of whom moved a twitch—and into the village, a group of several dozen huts made of jungle thatch. The ground was packed sand. Fire circles, some still smoking, dotted the areas between the huts. The only light in the clearing, aside from the moon, came from a torch burning in the center of the village. Other than its flickering flame, there was no movement. The villagers, believing themselves protected by the sentries, were asleep.

The invaders, following Ombra, moved quietly into the village. As he glided past the torch, Ombra waved a cloaked arm at it, and Nerezza pulled it from the ground.

Ombra led the group directly to a hut that was larger than the others. Without pausing, he glided inside, followed by Nerezza and Slank, who ducked through the opening, Nerezza holding the torch low.

Inside they found a woman and girl sleeping in rope hammocks. By the smoky torchlight, Slank could see that the girl was perhaps nine or ten years old. Next to the woman was a third, larger hammock, empty. Ombra, standing over the empty hammock, groaned, "The chief is not here." He did not sound pleased.

At the sound of his voice, the woman stirred, rubbing her eyes and uttering strange soft sounds. She opened her eyes and, seeing the dark form of Ombra looming over her, screamed. This awakened the girl who, seeing the intruders, emitted a loud, piercing shriek.

Instantly there were shouts from the nearby huts, then the sound of running feet.

"Cap'n!" shouted a voice. "Men coming!"

Nerezza ducked his head outside, then turned back to Ombra. "Too many for us to fight," he said.

"There is no need to fight," said Ombra. He turned to Slank, who noticed that, even looking directly at Ombra in the flickering torchlight, he could see no face—only darkness under the black hood.

"Take the girl," groaned Ombra.

Slank reached down and yanked the fear-frozen girl up by her arm. The girl shrieked again. The woman, wailing, moved to stop Slank, but Ombra glided between them. Slank, busy trying to hold the struggling girl, didn't see what happened next, but suddenly the woman's wailing stopped. When Slank glanced down, she was absolutely still, with the same vacant expression as the motionless sentries on the jungle path. The little girl saw it, too, and lapsed into shocked silence.

"Bring her outside," Ombra said, moving to the hut opening. "Hold your knife to her neck."

Slank unsheathed his knife and, pressing it against the terrified girl's smooth, brown neck, dragged her through the opening behind Ombra and Nerezza.

Outside, they found a tense standoff. The raiding party, knives and pistols drawn, faced a semicircle of at least two dozen Mollusk warriors holding spears with blades fashioned from razor-sharp shells and turtle-shell shields. The natives, aware of their advantage in numbers, were spreading apart, clearly preparing to attack. They were directed by a compact, muscular man who spoke in strange sounds. When he caught sight of Slank holding the girl, his eyes widened, and he shouted something that stopped the others cold.

For a moment the two sides stared at each other, with the Mollusks focusing most of their attention on Slank, and the knife he held pressed to the throat of the girl.

*She's the only thing keeping us alive*, thought Slank.

Another tense, silent moment, then Ombra oozed forward into the space between the two groups—looking, Slank thought, more like a moving cape than a person. The Mollusks eyed the dark, advancing shape nervously, but did not back up.

Ombra stopped in front of the compact man, the leader, and spoke—his voice filling the silence like a chill wind.

"Your chief," he groaned. "Where is he?"

The leader frowned, then said something in clicks and grunts.

"He doesn't speak English," said Nerezza.

"No," said Ombra. "Bring the torch forward."

Nerezza, puzzled by the order but not daring to question it, stepped forward.

"Over there," said Ombra, waving a dark arm to the right of the Mollusk leader. Nerezza moved slowly to the right, watching the Mollusks as warily as they watched him.

"There," said Ombra, and Nerezza stopped, perhaps five feet from the Mollusk leader. Nerezza's face glistened with sweat in the flickering torchlight.

"Now the girl," said Ombra. "Bring her next to Nerezza."

Reluctantly, Slank dragged the whimpering girl forward, still holding the knife to her throat. He placed the girl next to Nerezza, to the right of the Mollusk leader. The eyes of the warriors were on Slank: he could see their helpless rage—their desire to kill him, and their fear of causing harm to the girl. Slank could also see that, as the warriors' attention was focused on him, Ombra drifted slowly, silently forward.

*What is he doing?*

And then Slank saw it. As the bottom of Ombra's cloak drew close to the torch-cast shadow of the Mollusk leader, the shadow elongated and curled toward Ombra like a dark snake. As it touched Ombra's cloak, expression drained from the warrior's face. His head turned slightly in Ombra's direction, then toward the Mollusks. As his gaze swept past, Slank saw a lifeless, flat blackness in his eyes.

Then the warrior spoke. He made the same clicking and grunting sounds he'd used before, but his voice had a strangely different tone—deeper, breathier. The other Mollusks noticed this and were clearly disturbed. But whatever the warrior said disturbed them still more. When he finished, two of the younger Mollusks sprinted out of the village, into the jungle night.

"Where are they going?" asked Slank. "What's happening?"

He addressed the questions to Ombra, but it was not Ombra who answered. Instead, it was the Mollusk leader who turned his face toward Nerezza and Slank.

As the Mollusk leader turned, Slank again noticed the strange deadness in his eyes.

Then the Mollusk spoke. But not in grunts and clicks. A chorus of gasps arose from the men watching, sailors and Mollusks alike; a chill slithered up Slank's spine.

The warrior spoke English. And *he spoke in Ombra's voice.*

"They are going to find the chief," groaned the warrior. "They will tell him that if he does not return immediately, his daughter will die."

Then Ombra glided back. Slank saw his cloak separate from the Mollusk's shadow, which slithered back to its appropriate position relative to the torch. The warrior's head slumped forward, then snapped up, eyes blinking, expression confused, as if he were awakening from a nap. He stumbled backward; two Mollusks grabbed him and held him up.

Regaining his bearings, the leader looked hard at Ombra,

then grunted something at length to the others. When he was done, the warriors, keeping their eyes fixed on the dark, hovering shape before them, backed up several steps and stopped. They would wait from a safer distance.

Slank, still holding his knife to the throat of the whimpering girl, hoped the wait wouldn't be long.

# CHAPTER 11

# $S$TRANGERS

$W$HEN JAMES HIT THE COLD WATER, his first reaction was shock. *Why did Peter push me in?*

He struggled to get back to the surface, and his confusion turned to terror as he felt something grip his left ankle and pull him down. He screamed underwater—losing more air— and kicked as hard as he could, but the grip only tightened, pulling him deeper into water that grew colder and darker.

James thrashed to free himself but could not. Seconds passed, and still the grip pulled him down. His lungs burned and he was weakening.

And then, as he started to drift into unconsciousness, he felt it.

A kiss. His first, actually. Soft lips, right on his. Suddenly his lungs stopped burning. In the underwater blackness, he felt the kisser—whoever or whatever it was—move around behind him, then felt arms lock around his chest. Water surged past James's face as he shot forward, twisting and turning, apparently avoiding obstacles that James could not see. Then he burst into an underwater cavern, and he saw a silver disc overhead—the moon!—and veered sharply upward, breaking the surface.

James gulped the sweet air as strong hands pulled him up and set him on the ground at the edge of the pool. Wiping water from his eyes, he saw the face of Fighting Prawn; behind him were two other Mollusk warriors.

Then he saw a shadow flash across the sky. *Peter.*

"James!" shouted Peter, landing. "Are you all right?"

"Oh, Peter!" said James, his pale face brightening at the sight of his friend. "I . . ." He coughed up some water. "I'm sorry! I just wanted to watch you have some fun with the pirates, and they . . . they got me! I'm so sorry, Peter."

Peter exchanged glances with Fighting Prawn.

"It's not your fault, James," he said. "It's mine."

"Peter, I was so frightened," said James, the words tumbling out. "The hook pirate told me the most awful things. . . . Said he was going to kill me *and* you, and feed us to Mister Grin. . . . And then, when you pushed me into the water, I tried to come up, and next thing I knew something was pulling me *down*, and then . . . "

James stopped, looking puzzled. "Peter," he said. "How *did* I get here?"

Peter smiled and pointed to the pool of water. Floating in

a shadow at the edge of the pool was the mermaid known as Teacher. Her long, wet, blond hair flowed down each side of her delicate face, a face dominated by impossibly large brilliant green eyes. She gave Peter a lingering look that he felt as well as saw. Among the strange changes that had come over Peter when he'd been exposed to the starstuff—besides the ability to fly—was that he could understand the thoughts of the mermaids, who were also starstuff creatures. Teacher was quite fond of Peter, and what she was thinking now made him blush.

*Thanks*, he thought back to her, and she nodded.

To James, Peter said: "It was Fighting Prawn's idea."

"Thank you, Mister Prawn," said James. "And thank you, too, Teacher. You saved my life."

Teacher smiled modestly, then resumed flirting with Peter. Tinker Bell, who felt that Peter had paid quite enough attention to Teacher already, flitted between them; Peter brushed her aside, an act that resulted in an angry burst of chimes, which Peter hoped Teacher did not understand.

"But, wait!" said James, frowning. "Teacher lives in the lagoon. So how . . . ?"

"The Mollusks," answered Peter. "They made a sort of chair from sticks and vines and carried her here, like the Queen. She looked quite regal, actually."

Teacher beamed. Tinker Bell sulked.

James turned once again to the Mollusks.

"You're welcome," said Fighting Prawn, before James could thank him a second time. "But from now on, you and your friends"—he gave Peter a hard look—"must stay away from the pirates, do you understand?"

"Yes, sir," said James.

Fighting Prawn glowered at Peter. "There are certain rules on this island," he said. "Laws, you might call them. And now that you and your friends are living here—"

He was interrupted by two young Mollusk warriors bursting into the clearing. The warriors ran to Fighting Prawn, the one in front emitting a rapid-fire series of grunts and clicks. Fighting Prawn listened, his expression increasingly grave.

"We must go," he said, when the warrior finished. He spoke in Mollusk to the others, and then to Peter and James: "Fierce Clam and Running Snail will take the mermaid back to the lagoon. You boys must return to your hideaway now, and *stay there*."

"What is it?" said Peter. "What happened?"

Fighting Prawn was already running for the jungle. "Strangers!" he called back over his shoulder. "They have Shining Pearl!"

CHAPTER 12

# Something Familiar

With Tinker Bell flitting far ahead, Peter and James labored up the mountainside in the dark. James, weary from his ordeal in pirate captivity, stopped to rest every twenty steps or so. It was slow going—agonizingly slow for Peter, who felt he had to stay with James, but desperately wanted to launch himself upward and fly over the mountain to the Mollusk village.

*They have Shining Pearl*, Fighting Prawn had said. Peter wondered who *they* were. Some of Hook's men? That seemed unlikely: the pirates knew better than to anger the Mollusks, who outnumbered them and barely tolerated their presence on the island.

But if not the pirates, Peter wondered, then who? Strangers on the island? Shipwrecked sailors? But why would they take Fighting Prawn's oldest daughter? And—this question nagged at Peter—would they have been able to take her if Fighting Prawn had not been on the other side of the island rescuing James from the mess Peter had gotten him into?

*If only I could fly to the village,* Peter thought. *Maybe I could help Fighting Prawn.*

But he couldn't leave James alone in the jungle at night. Not after what James had been through. What if James got lost on his way back? What if Hook's men were out here looking to even the score?

*Unless . . .*

"Tink!" Peter called. "Come back here! I need your help!"

Tinker Bell, still angry about Teacher's flirting with Peter, made some unhappy, dull sounds, which could be loosely translated as: "If you need help, why don't you ask your girlfriend, the big fat grouper?"

"Tink!" said Peter sternly. "I'm serious!"

Tinker Bell, her arms folded in a dramatic show of annoyance, drifted back toward the boys, glowing with pouty-ness.

"Listen," Peter said, "I think I should fly to the Mollusk village and try to help Fighting Prawn."

James gave Peter a wan smile. "Go ahead, Peter," he said. "I'll be fine."

Peter gripped his friend's arm. *Good old James.*

"Tink," Peter said. "You'll stay with James, and make sure he gets back to the hut. All right?"

With a burst of much brighter-sounding bells, Tink

replied that she would be happy to remain with James, since she did not intend to spend another moment with Peter ever again, and hoped he and his fat grouper girlfriend would be very happy together until an octopus ate them.

"What did she say?" asked James.

"She said . . . she's happy to take you back," answered Peter. "Tell the others to stay near the hut and not to go near the Mollusk village, all right?"

"All right," said James. "But be careful, Peter."

"You too," said Peter. Then, after giving James's arm another reassuring squeeze, he jumped upward and soared into the night sky. Angling his body so he was parallel to the steep mountain slope, he shot straight to the summit, reaching it in only seconds. From this vantage point he had a sweeping view of the island, its lush, jungle greenery turned a dark and ghostly gray by the moonlight. Peter spun a full circle, looking in every direction. As he looked east, he gasped at the sight of four thin fingers rising through the mist blanketing the bay. Masts.

A ship. A big ship.

Peter shifted his weight forward, putting his body at a steep angle to the ground. He swooped down the mountainside, his ears filled with the sound of rushing wind. He flew recklessly, far faster than he'd ever flown at night before. At one point he had to swerve sharply to avoid something large—a bird, perhaps, or a fruit bat—that shot up suddenly out of the jungle. He quickly reached the base of the mountain, slowed and leveled off, gliding just above the treetops, scanning the jungle ahead for the wide clearing where the Mollusk village lay.

There! Just ahead. . . . Slowing still more, Peter arrived at the edge of the clearing. He let himself down into the treetops and onto a stout branch, where the foliage hid him.

Through the enormous leaves, he spotted a gathering next to a large hut that he recognized as Fighting Prawn's. Drifting silently from treetop to treetop, Peter flew until he saw more clearly that the gathering was actually two groups. On one side stood Mollusk warriors holding spears and shields. They looked grim-faced at the smaller, second group of men, all strangers to Peter. These strangers carried swords and pistols. One of the men had an arm around Shining Pearl, a knife held to her neck. Peter studied the man with the knife for a moment. He couldn't see his face clearly, yet there was something familiar about him. . . .

Before Peter could consider this further, a noise rose from the jungle, below and to Peter's right. Fighting Prawn—his body glistening with sweat from what must have been a grueling run over the mountain—sprinted into the clearing. The strangers turned to face them.

Peter moved a giant leaf out of his way so he could see clearly what happened next.

## CHAPTER 13

# THE COMING DANGER

With the long, powerful strides of a chief who could still outrun a young warrior, Fighting Prawn arrived at the standoff between the Mollusks and the men from the ship. As he neared, he raised his spear over his head and drew it back, its sharpened tip pointed directly at Slank. But then, seeing the knife at his daughter's neck, Fighting Prawn stopped. Slowly, he brought the spear back down, his black eyes brimming with fury.

The clearing was silent; nobody moved. Fighting Prawn studied Slank for a moment, then scanned the other strangers. His gaze lingered on Nerezza's fearsome face, then longer on the dark, hooded form of Lord Ombra. Seconds turned into a half minute, and still nobody moved.

When Fighting Prawn spoke, he addressed Slank.

"Let go of my daughter," he said, "and I will let you live."

Slank swallowed but did not answer. He tightened his grip on the girl; he could feel her shallow breathing.

Fighting Prawn glanced at his own men. "You see how many of us there are. How few of you. This is your last chance to live. And I promise you that your death—yours in particular—will not be pleasant."

Slank swallowed again. But it was Ombra who spoke, his voice coming from the darkness of his cloak's hood like a cold wind from a cavern.

"We don't want your daughter," Ombra said.

Fighting Prawn now directed himself to Ombra, his rage still distorting his normally kind face.

"Then what *do* you want?" he asked.

"Not long ago," said Ombra, "a box washed ashore on this island. It was the cause of a great deal of trouble. You know the box of which I speak."

Fighting Prawn nodded. "Yes."

"We have come for that box," said Ombra, "and its contents. We want no trouble, only the box. It belongs to us—was stolen from us. Once we have that box back, we will leave. We will release your daughter unharmed."

A pause, then Fighting Prawn spoke. "We do not have the box."

"He's lying!" said Slank. "It was—"

"*Silence*," hissed Ombra, in a voice that chilled the spine of every man there.

Ombra's hooded form faced Fighting Prawn once again. "Then tell us where it is," he said.

"It is gone," said Fighting Prawn. "It was taken off the island."

"By whom?"

Fighting Prawn hesitated. Then, looking at his daughter, he sighed.

"An Englishman," he said. "His name is Aster."

Nerezza and Slank reacted to the name, looking at each other.

"I see," said Ombra. "And where did Aster take the box?"

"I do not know," said Fighting Prawn.

"How do we know he's telling the truth?" asked Nerezza.

"That's right," said Slank. "The savage could be lying."

"Savage?" said Fighting Prawn, turning to Slank. "I am not the one holding a knife to the throat of a child."

As Fighting Prawn spoke, Ombra glided forward almost imperceptibly. Only two pairs of eyes saw what happened next. One pair belonged to Slank, who, having noticed it earlier, knew what to watch for; the other pair belonged to the flying boy concealed in the nearby treetops, whose vantage point gave him a good view.

Ombra advanced to within inches of Fighting Prawn's wavering shadow, cast by a flickering torchlight. Ombra made contact with the shadow, and as he did, it stretched and slithered forward, flowing under and into Ombra's dark cloak. Fighting Prawn emitted a low moan. His eyes went dead; his posture slumped; his head drooped to the side. The warriors looked apprehensively at their chief, but they were looking at his face, and thus did not see what Slank and Peter saw: Fighting Prawn was no longer casting a shadow.

A few seconds passed, and the dark shape flowed back out from under Ombra's cloak and reconnected with Fighting Prawn. Ombra glided back a few feet. Fighting Prawn, once again casting a shadow, jerked his head upright and staggered sideways a step, a puzzled expression on his face.

"He is telling the truth," Ombra announced. "The box is not on the island."

"Then where is it?" asked Nerezza.

"Aster will take it back to England," said Ombra. "He will take it to the Return."

"Then we've lost it," said Nerezza. "If he's taken it to the Return, we've lost it."

"What do you mean?" said Slank. "What are you talking about?"

Ombra, ignoring Slank, spoke to Nerezza. "No," he said. "We have not lost it, not yet."

"But he's had three months' head start," said Nerezza. "He's well back to England by now."

"Yes," said Ombra. "But as we understand it, the Return can happen only at certain times—and those times seem to be rare. Aster will likely have to wait for the next opportunity. We must get the starstuff before that happens. We must sail for England at once."

"But how will we find the starstuff?" said Nerezza. "Aster will have it hidden, and he won't tell us where it is. He would die first."

"Perhaps," groaned Ombra. He looked between Shining Pearl and Fighting Prawn. "But fathers have a special place in their hearts for their daughters."

In the tree, Peter flinched at those words, thinking about Aster's daughter, Molly, the brave girl who had once saved his life.

Nerezza smiled and said, "Ah, yes . . . the daughter."

Slank grinned as well, though his face was grimmer. He had reasons of his own for wanting to see Aster's daughter again. She had caused him great torment and embarrassment the last time they'd met, here on this island—she and that cursed boy.

Fighting Prawn, now fully recovered, followed the conversation carefully, his eyes moving back and forth from Nerezza's face to the dark hole surrounded by Ombra's hood.

"Then you will leave the island," Fighting Prawn said. It was a statement, not a question.

"Yes," answered Ombra. "We will leave. But you will understand that we must keep your daughter with us until we reach the beach. Once we are safely in the boats, we will release her. You have my word."

"And you have my word that if any harm comes to my daughter, none of you will ever reach your ship," said Fighting Prawn. "Not a single man." He stared at Ombra, then added softly, "or whatever you are."

"Then we have an understanding," said Ombra. To Nerezza, he said, "I will lead the way back to the ship. Your men will form an escort around Slank. Slank, do not harm the girl, but do not release her, either."

And so they formed a procession—Ombra in front, gliding out of the compound, followed by Nerezza and his men in a loose formation around Slank and Shining Pearl, followed by Fighting Prawn and his warriors.

They came to the first pair of Mollusk sentries, still standing statuelike. As Ombra passed by, they suddenly went limp and fell. Then they sat up slowly, clearly disoriented but no longer in a trance. A few minutes later the same thing happened to the second pair of sentries, and then the third.

The uncomfortable procession continued down the path to the beach, where the dory and longboat waited.

Under the watchful eyes of the Mollusks, Nerezza and his men slid the boats into the shallow surf as Ombra and Slank stood by, Slank still restraining Shining Pearl.

"Have your pistols ready," Nerezza ordered. His eyes met Fighting Prawn's. "If you come after us," he said, "we'll shoot your daughter where she stands."

Fighting Prawn said nothing, his rage barely contained.

As Nerezza and his men climbed into the longboat, Ombra spoke to Shining Pearl. "We will let you go now," he said. "But you will not move until we row away, do you understand?"

Shining Pearl, not looking at Ombra, nodded.

"Let her go," said Ombra.

Slank released the girl and quickly climbed into the dory. In an instant, without apparent exertion, Ombra flowed aboard.

"Row," he said, but Slank was already pulling on the oars, as were the men in the longboat with Nerezza. As the boats slid away, Shining Pearl stood absolutely motionless. Then, as the longboats rowed out of pistol range, Fighting Prawn opened his arms, and his daughter ran up the beach and into his waiting embrace. Fighting Prawn hugged her hard, but his eyes remained on the two receding boats, his thoughts far away, in England.

It was not Fighting Prawn's business anymore, now that these outsiders were gone from his island. But he knew Aster was a good man and a loving father. And as a father, Fighting Prawn wished that he could warn Aster of the danger now heading toward him.

Peter, watching from the night sky, was thinking the same thing.

## CHAPTER 14

# THE FAREWELL

*I*N THE DRIFTWOOD HUT where the Lost Boys lived beneath a roof of withered palm fronds, only Thomas had managed to remain awake. So he was the first to hear the faint but distinct sound of bells in the distance. As it grew louder, he realized it was coming toward him from somewhere in the jungle.

"They're here!" he announced, shaking Prentiss awake.

"What?" said Prentiss, sitting up, yawning.

"Peter's here!" said Thomas. "I hear Tinker Bell."

"Peter?" said Prentiss, wide awake now. "Where?" He and Thomas had grown very worried when neither James nor Peter had returned by nightfall.

"Will you be *quiet*?" said Tubby Ted, sticking his head out from under the piece of canvas—an old sail—that the boys used as their collective blanket. Tubby Ted had been dreaming of chocolate cake and wanted to get back to it.

"But Peter's back!" said Thomas.

"Good for Peter," said Tubby Ted, ducking back under the canvas. "Wake me up if he's brought anything to eat."

Thomas and Prentiss rose and untied the hut door, a ship's cargo hatch that had drifted to the island. On the outside was a sign with these words scrawled in charcoal:

LOST BOYS ONLY
NO PIRRATES
NO GIRLS

The two boys stepped outside into the moonlit clearing around the hut and the relative cool of the deep jungle night. They peered at the trees, and Prentiss shouted, "There she is!" He pointed to a glowing ball of light dancing toward them through the treetops. In a moment, Tinker Bell was flitting in front of them, an unhappy expression on her tiny, delicate, birdlike face.

"Hello, Tink," said Prentiss tentatively. "Is everything all right?"

Tinker Bell answered with a discordant din. Thomas and Prentiss didn't understand her bell language—none of the boys did, except, of course, Peter—but it became immediately obvious that, in Tinker Bell's opinion, everything was most certainly *not* all right.

Prentiss was about to seek clarification, when he and

Thomas heard a noise at the edge of the clearing. They turned and saw a figure coming toward them in the moonlight.

"James!" shouted Thomas. He and Prentiss ran toward their friend, who looked very tired and had scratches on his bare arms and legs from the trek over the mountain in the dark.

"Are you all right?" said Prentiss.

James managed a weak smile. "I'm . . . Yes, I'm all right. Is Peter here?"

"No," said Thomas. "Isn't he with you? I mean, Tinker Bell is here."

"Yes," said James. "Peter sent her with me, to guide me back."

"Where's Peter, then?" said Prentiss.

James told them briefly about his rescue, and the little that Peter had told him about Shining Pearl. Eagerly, Prentiss and Thomas prodded him for more details, and he recounted his watery mermaid-aided escape from the pirate lair. He was just finishing when an angry and accusing burst of bells from Tink caught the boys' attention, and they looked up to see Peter swoop down into the clearing, his bare feet skidding ruts in the dirt as he landed.

"Peter!" shouted all three boys at once. They peppered him with questions, but he silenced them with an upraised hand. Silencing Tink took a little longer.

"There isn't much time," Peter said, once they were all quiet. "You must listen carefully. There are bad men on the island. They came by ship and they captured Shining Pearl. But it's not her they want; it's the starstuff."

"But the starstuff is gone!" said Prentiss. "Molly's father took it!"

"That's right," said Peter. "It's all gone, except for this." His hand touched the gold locket that hung on a gold chain around his neck—the locket given to him by Lord Aster. "Fighting Prawn told them that Lord Aster took it, and now they're going to England to get it."

"So they're leaving the island?" said James.

"Yes," said Peter.

"So we're safe," said Thomas.

"Yes," said Peter. "*We're* safe. But Lord Aster isn't. And neither is Molly. These are *very* bad men." Peter did not tell them about the troubling figure in the dark cloak, and the strange thing Fighting Prawn's shadow had done. He didn't want to scare his friends. Besides, he wasn't exactly sure *what* he had seen.

James studied Peter, frowning. "Peter," he said, "what did you mean when you said there isn't much time?"

Peter looked at his friends. He felt a tightness in his throat. "I have to go to England," he said.

"*What?*" said all three. Peter looked down, not wanting to see the fear on their faces.

"But how?" asked James. "Even if you could fly all that way, how could you *find* it? The sea is enormous."

"I know," said Peter. "I'll have to follow the ship."

"The *ship?*" said Thomas. "The *very bad men's* ship?"

Peter nodded.

"But what if they see you?" said James. "What happens when you get tired? Where will you sleep?"

"I dunno," said Peter. "But I have to try. I have no choice. I can't just stay here and do nothing while they go after Lord Aster and . . . and Molly."

Tink made an unpleasant sound. She did not care for Molly.

"But if you leave, what will *we* do?" said Prentiss. "Who will be our leader?"

"James will," said Peter. He stepped forward and put his hands on James's shoulders. As he did so, he realized that James, who had always been smaller than Peter, was now precisely the same height.

*He's growing older,* thought Peter. *By the time I get back, he'll be taller than I am. If I get back.*

"You'll take care of them, won't you, James?" he said.

James, his eyes wet, sniffed and nodded bravely.

"There's a good fellow," said Peter, squeezing his shoulders, then turning away and coughing to cover up a sniff of his own. Turning back, he said, "The Mollusks are here, if you need help. Just stay away from those pirates, all right?"

James, Thomas, and Prentiss nodded, and Peter saw tears on all six cheeks.

"It's all right," he said. "I'll be back. I promise you."

The three nodded again, not looking the least bit convinced.

"All right, then," said Peter. "I've got to get going before the ship leaves."

He rose a few feet into the air and hovered, looking at Tinker Bell. She turned her back on him and folded her arms.

"Well . . . I guess I'm going alone, then," he said. Then, with a wave to his friends—displaying a jauntiness he did not feel—Peter swooped up over the trees and turned toward the water.

For a moment the clearing was silent. The silence was broken by an explosion of bells—and it was a very good thing that the boys did not understand these bells—as Tink shot into the sky, turned in the direction Peter had taken, and was gone.

And then once again the clearing was silent, except for the sniffling of three very worried boys, and the sound of angry bells fading in the distance.

## CHAPTER 15

# $I$NTO THE $N$IGHT

$N$IGHT FELL EARLY ON LONDON. The pale, sinking, northern sun was no match for the city's blanket of clouds and dark gray fog, thickened by coal smoke and soot drifting out of ten thousand chimneys. The air, chilly enough in daytime, had turned a biting cold, made all the worse by the penetrating damp of the North Sea.

With darkness came danger. London's vast twisting tangle of streets, lanes, and alleys, confusing enough in daylight, by night became a baffling, impenetrable maze to anybody who did not know it well. And those who knew it also knew enough to get inside before darkness came. Because the London streets at night were a grim, grimy jungle prowled by thugs and lowlifes of every kind; a hunting ground where the weak and vulnerable were prey. For London's poor, night was a time to huddle together in a tiny room (if you were lucky enough to have one), wrapped in rags to try to stay warm, waiting for the long, black night to turn into another cold, gray dawn.

In the city's wealthier areas, the streets were illuminated—somewhat—by gas lamps, each creating a small, round island of light (or at least diminished gloom). But the upper classes rarely ventured out on foot at night, for well-dressed people were prime targets of criminals who would kill for a lady's necklace or a gentleman's watch.

So London's wealthy also spent the dark hours indoors, although, of course, they passed the time in far greater comfort than the poor. The wealthiest lived in grand homes, eating servant-cooked meals in rooms kept warm by servant-tended fires.

On this particular night, in a particularly fine home, on a particularly broad street, not a hundred yards from the grandeur of Kensington Palace, the family of Leonard Aster was eating dinner. The dining room was large enough to serve as a croquet court; the table could easily seat two dozen, and had often accommodated that many. But tonight it was just the three Asters—Lord Aster; his wife, Louise; and their daughter, Molly.

Molly looked much like her mother—the same thick, cascading, brown hair, the same delicate face. But her most distinctive feature was the one she shared with her father: her eyes, unusually large and radiantly green. Molly was a beautiful child; all of London society agreed on that. But she was also, it was widely whispered, *unusual*—especially since she had returned with her father from their sea voyage a few months earlier.

The story was sketchy: what little was known in London had come from Mrs. Bumbrake, Molly's governess, who had, unfortunately, spent most of the adventure locked in the hold of a pirate ship. She came back to England telling tales of a mysterious treasure chest and a strange island where Molly apparently had had some kind of ordeal. But Mrs. Bumbrake did not really know what had happened out there, and neither Molly nor Lord Aster would talk about it.

The lack of information did not, of course, prevent London society from endlessly discussing the matter. It was generally agreed that there was something odd about the Asters—some said there always had been—and especially about young Molly, who did not seem to be at all interested in the kinds of things that girls of her class were supposed to be interested in. Molly often seemed distracted, people said, as though her mind were elsewhere.

Which it often was.

But on this night, Molly's attention was fully focused on her father. Leonard Aster had been uncharacteristically silent throughout the meal, leaving Molly and her mother to make polite, meandering conversation. It was not until the serving maid had cleared the dinner plates and left them alone with dessert that Leonard, looking around to make sure he would not be overheard, began to speak, his voice low, his tone somber.

"I'm afraid I must leave you two for a while," he began.

Louise Aster nodded once slowly but said nothing.

"A while?" said Molly.

"A few weeks," said Leonard.

"Why?" said Molly.

Leonard Aster studied his daughter for a moment. He remembered her bravery at sea, and on the island—how she had fought, at times alone, to protect the trunk and its treasure from dangerous, desperate men. He decided that, despite her youth, she had earned the right to know more than he had told her so far.

"I must move the starstuff," he said.

"Move it?" said Molly, surprised. "But you said it was safe."

"I thought it was," said Aster. "But this afternoon I received some disturbing news from Ammm."

Molly's face brightened. "Ammm!" she said. "How is he?"

"He's fine," said Aster, smiling. "He sends his regards and asked me to tell you something."

Suddenly, Leonard began emitting strange squeaking, whistling, and popping sounds. Neither his wife nor his daughter was surprised; Leonard was simply quoting Ammm, who happened to be a porpoise. The sounds translated roughly to, "My teeth are green."

Molly laughed, for this was exactly what she, with her

minimal grasp of the Porpoise language, had told Ammm a few months earlier—it seemed so long ago—when she stood barefoot on the deck of a sea-tossed ship at night, trying to get an urgent message to her father.

"Please tell Ammm that my Porpoise is improving," she told her father. "But what was the disturbing news?"

"Well," said Leonard, "it's a bit muddled because Ammm got the message from the local Mollusk Island dolphins and, as you know, Dolphin and Porpoise are not quite the same. But the essence of it is that a strange ship arrived at Mollusk Island, and some men went ashore."

"Is Peter all right?" Molly blurted it out, then blushed.

"I don't know," said Leonard. "There was no mention of Peter. But I'm sure he's fine. He's a very capable boy."

Molly nodded, still blushing. Leonard continued: "The men, whoever they were, went ashore, had some kind of confrontation with the Mollusks, and then left."

"So they're off the island now?" said Louise.

"Yes," said Leonard. "And they're sailing on a course that will bring them, if the wind holds, straight to England."

"Oh, dear," said Louise.

"Yes," said Leonard. "They're coming for the starstuff."

"But," said Molly, "even if they do come for it, you said it was too well guarded to be taken."

"I'm afraid I may have been overconfident," said Leonard.

"What do you mean?" said Molly.

Leonard looked grim. "The dolphins told Ammm that one of the men on the ship was not a man."

"I don't understand," said Molly. "What *was* it, then?"

"The dolphins didn't say. Only that it was with the men, but it was not a man. And when he passed over the water, the water became cold."

At those words, Molly felt a chill herself. "What does that mean?" she said.

Leonard exchanged looks with Louise. "I'm afraid it means the Others have sent somebody . . . some*thing* . . . very formidable to retrieve the starstuff. Something with powers that are not easily countered. So I'm going to move the starstuff out of London, to a place known by only a very few of us. We will guard it there until the time comes for the Return."

"Why can't you just return it now," said Molly, "before this . . . this *something* gets here?"

"I wish I could," said Leonard. "But the Return can only happen at certain times. We have no choice but to wait for the next one."

"When will you leave?" said Louise.

"Tonight, I'm afraid," Leonard said. "Within the hour, in fact."

As his wife and daughter absorbed this unhappy news, Leonard rose, went to the large dining-room window, and beckoned. Seconds later there was a knock at the front door. Waving off the servant who appeared instantly, Leonard went to answer the door himself. He returned to the dining room with three men, all well dressed, all serious-looking, all quite large. One of the men held a leash attached to a dog, also quite large.

"Louise and Molly," said Leonard, "may I present Mister Cadigan, Mister Hodge, and Mister Jarvis. The dog's name, I'm afraid, is Hornblower."

The men removed their hats, and everyone except Hornblower exchanged how-do-you-dos.

"These men will be staying here until I return," said Leonard. "They will be outside most of the time. I've instructed Cook to feed them; they will sleep in shifts in the attic. Molly, until I return, you're to go nowhere—*nowhere*—without one of these men accompanying you, do you understand?"

Molly had questions—many questions—but she understood that now was not the time to ask them. So she simply nodded.

"Good," said Leonard. "Now, if you will excuse me, I must make some preparations."

He left the room, and the three men went back outside with Hornblower. When they were gone, Molly looked at her mother.

"We'll be fine," said Louise.

"But will Father be fine?" said Molly.

"Of course he will," said Louise, smiling bravely. But Molly saw the worry in her eyes.

In a half hour, Leonard, now dressed for travel, was ready to leave. He hugged Louise, then Molly.

"I'll be back before you know it," he said.

Louise turned away, dabbing at her face with a handkerchief. Leonard rested his hand on her shoulder for a moment, then turned to go.

To Molly's surprise, her father did not leave by the front door, as he almost always did. Instead he left by the service entrance at the rear of the house.

*As though someone is watching the house*, she thought.

Molly followed her father back through the kitchen. He paused at the door, blew her a kiss, then turned and left. Molly held the door open for a moment, watching until her father's tall form had disappeared completely into the swirling fog of the dark London night.

*Be careful*, she thought.

## CHAPTER 16

# One Look Back

As dawn approached, Peter was growing desperate.

He'd been flying behind the ship for hours now—far longer than he'd ever remained aloft before—and it was a demanding kind of flying, not the effortless swooping Peter enjoyed so much on the island. He dared not slip too far back from the ship, lest he lose sight of it and become lost. But he also dared not get too close or too high, lest he be spotted in the moonlight.

He flew behind the ship, low to the water, only a few yards above the swirling wake, keeping a sail between him and the lookout high up in the crow's nest. This positioning required intense concentration, and over the hours it took its toll.

All at once, Tinker Bell's shrill warning chimed in his ear. Peter startled, his bare toes catching in the churning wake. He pointed his arms up and strained higher, just in time to miss a wave. He'd dozed off, sinking to within inches of the wave tops.

*That was close!*

"Thanks, Tink," he whispered, having regained some altitude. She didn't answer, instead flitting off a few yards to resume pretending that she was ignoring him.

*It's a good thing she came along*, he thought.

Exhaustion wasn't Peter's only problem: he was also hungry, and very thirsty. He hadn't thought about any of this when he'd left the island, but obviously he would need food and water. The only place he was going to get them was on the ship. But exactly *how* would he get them? He licked his salt-parched lips. He knew he'd have to solve the water problem soon.

Peter looked back at the reassuring shape of Mollusk Island. Each time he'd looked, as the night wore on, the island had grown smaller; now it was but a bump on the horizon. Soon it would be gone altogether, leaving him and Tink alone with the ship and its dangerous inhabitants. This had seemed like such a good idea when he'd explained it to the others. Now he wondered if he'd made a terrible mistake. For the dozenth time, he thought about turning back. If he did, it would have to be soon. Once he lost sight of the island, the ship would be his only hope.

Peter looked ahead and noted with alarm that the sky had grown lighter, changing from black to a dark blue. Soon sunlight would flood the sea, and Peter would be exposed. He had to either turn back now or hide—and if he was going to hide, he had to find a place very soon.

Peter drew closer to the ship and drifted upward, toward the top of the sternmost of the ship's four tall masts. The mast was intersected by five stout horizontal poles; Peter knew, from his one sea voyage, that these were called yards. The ship's sails hung from these yards; depending on the wind and the ship's course, the crew would climb up and furl—hoist up—or unfurl the sails as needed.

Peter noticed that the sail on the topmost yard was only loosely furled. He moved steadily closer, now directly above the stern of the ship. He kept his eyes trained down, watching the few men on deck at this early hour—the man at the wheel, an officer standing next to him, and a few sailors standing well forward. They were all looking toward the promise of the sun on the horizon. Satisfied that no one was looking up, Peter flew high to the yard and settled gently onto its smooth, weathered wood. It felt very, very good to be sitting on something firm again, even if it was a hundred feet above the deck of a moving ship.

Lying on his stomach on the yard, Peter examined the furled sail, which hung from the yard in thick folds. Peter found that, by wriggling his body, he could squirm down into one of these folds, so it held him like a hammock. There, nestled in the rough canvas, he was well

hidden—that is, unless crewmen climbed up and unfurled the sail.

But for now, Peter was too tired to worry about that. His hunger and thirst would have to wait. For now: sleep. As his eyes fluttered shut, he heard a soft tinkling and saw Tinker Bell landing on the yard just above him.

"G'night, Tink," he mumbled, so tired he barely got the words out before sleep pulled him under.

Tink didn't answer. She dropped down into the fold with him, settling into his tousled mass of reddish hair, her favorite place to rest. Almost instantly, she too was asleep.

Which meant neither of them was looking down.

Which meant neither of them saw when, in the waning moments of darkness, the black form of Lord Ombra slithered from a companionway onto the quarterdeck. Neither saw the hooded head move from side to side, as if searching, like a dog smelling something in the air. Neither saw the hood pause as it faced the aftmost mast. Neither saw it slowly train its gaze upward, upward . . . only to stop suddenly when the first rays of dawn flooded the ship in an exhilarating light.

Recoiling from the glare, the dark form moved quickly back to the companionway. Then it slithered down into the bowels of the ship, but not before stopping to take one look back, and upward . . .

Directly at the furled sail.

## CHAPTER 17

# OMBRA'S FEELING

LORD OMBRA GLIDED ACROSS the floor planks of the captain's quarters, where thick wool blankets hung over the stern windows, preventing even a sliver of sunlight from penetrating. A lone lantern suspended from an overhead beam cast a dim yellow light. The lantern rocked and tilted back and forth with the movement of the ship, sending shadows chasing along the floor and walls.

Captain Nerezza, seated at a table beneath the lantern, studied a chart of the South Atlantic, with a hand-drawn speck representing Mollusk Island. He had not heard Ombra enter, but then he never did. He kept his eyes on the chart, hoping his uninvited visitor would go away.

But Ombra came closer, gliding among the moving shadows, though he himself cast none. Standing directly over Nerezza, he spoke, his voice a low moan.

"I wonder, Captain, if it might be possible to send one of your hands aloft to inspect the mizzen sails?"

"Inspect? Inspect for what, sir?" As he spoke the word "sir," Nerezza's wooden nose whistled, as happened when he was agitated. Ombra or no, Nerezza did not like to be told, even politely, what to do with his crew.

"A stowaway, perhaps," said Ombra. "Perhaps nothing."

"Lord Ombra," said Nerezza, trying to keep the anger from his voice. "If there were a stowaway, my men would have—"

Ombra silenced him with a raised hand. Nerezza felt a chill creep along his neck.

"Humor me, Captain," groaned Ombra. "It's just a feeling I have."

*I didn't know you had feelings,* thought Nerezza.

"Ah, but I do have them," said Ombra, as if Nerezza had spoken aloud. "And I have learned to trust them."

Nerezza stammered out a reply. "Of . . . of course," he said. "As you wish. I'll send a boy up to take a look around."

"Good," said Ombra. "I will retire to my cabin."

Ombra spent the day in a tiny room, a windowless, coffinlike space. The crew had strict orders not to look in there—not that any man would.

"Yes, Lord Ombra," said Nerezza. "If we find anything, I—" he stopped, realizing that Ombra was gone.

Nerezza rose from the table and went to open the door.

He touched the handle, then gasped and drew his hand back. The handle was cold as ice.

Regaining his composure, he opened the door and ascended through a companionway.

On deck, he looked up at the mizzenmast sails and rigging; there was nothing amiss. He sighed, then called to an officer.

"Send a boy up to check the mizzen sails," he said.

The officer, puzzled, risked a question: "If I may ask, sir, check for what?"

"Just check them!" barked Nerezza. He stormed below, embarrassed to be giving orders that made no sense to him.

A *feeling, indeed*, he thought.

## CHAPTER 18

# "No Bees at Sea"

Seaman Conrad Dillinger, agile as a monkey in a tree, climbed the rigging that ran down from the mizzenmast. Even though the ship rode the sea in constant motion—up-and-down, forward-and-back, side-to-side—Conrad easily kept his balance. He didn't mind being sent up to check the sails, because he enjoyed the view so much. The ocean spread out before him like a vast blue tablecloth, interrupted by the occasional white stitch of foam on a wave.

He glanced down to the ship's deck, now far below. A few crew members mopped the decks, their heads down. Most were below, eating breakfast. Conrad could smell the biscuits and bacon from here. He glanced up at the sails; they looked fine to him, but he'd been ordered to check them, and check them he would.

---

Peter awoke to the sound of urgent bells in his ear. He yawned and was about to ask Tink what the clamor was about when she placed her tiny hand across his lips to silence him.

*What?* Peter asked with his eyes.

Tink answered with a soft flurry of bells. *A boy is coming!*

Peter, instantly wide awake, sneaked a peek over the fold of the weathered canvas. Sure enough, a young sailor—not much older than he was—was quickly climbing the rigging toward the reefed topsail where Peter hid.

*Where to hide?* Peter wondered.

Tink pointed forward. The topmost sail on the next mast was reefed, just like the one Peter was hiding in.

*There*, said Tink's bells.

Peter looked at the deck; the few crew members he saw on deck had their heads aimed down at their work as they mopped. On the main mast was a lookout in the crow's nest, but he was facing forward. But what about the sailor climbing toward him? Wouldn't he see Peter fly across?

*I'll deal with the boy*, chimed Tink. *You be ready.*

"Be ready for *what?*" whispered Peter.

But Tink was gone.

———

Conrad had almost reached the second yardarm when he heard it.

*Bells.*

But not the ship's bells, which were as familiar to Conrad as his own heartbeat. These sounded like tiny bells. Tiny . . . *beautiful* bells, coming from the furled sail above him. He looked up, and . . .

*WHOOSH!*

. . . something shot past his left ear. A bird? It was about the size of a bird, but . . . but it was *glowing*. And it moved far too fast for a bird; far too fast for Conrad to get a good view of it. He looked down, and . . .

*WHOOSH!*

. . . it shot past his head again, this time going up, and then around behind him. Trying to follow it, he twisted his head violently and swung around on the shroud one-handed, and . . .

*WHOOSH!*

. . . it shot past him again, and then . . .

*WHOOSH!*

. . . again, and this time, in his frantic, twisting effort to get a glimpse of this *thing* that was tormenting him, Conrad did something that he never would have thought was possible for a rigging rat like himself.

He lost his grip.

And then, gravity being what it is, he fell.

Peter saw the boy fall. He'd been watching as Tink swooped around the young seaman. When he was sure the boy was distracted, Peter had launched himself across the space between the masts, toward his new hiding place. But he kept his eyes on the action below him as the boy fell. For an instant the boy appeared doomed, but then he hit a rigging line and grabbed hold, stopping himself just before he crashed onto the deck.

Peter shot toward the sail, diving into its folds just as the sound of the boy's strangled shout reached the crow's-nest lookout and the men on deck. All eyes turned to the young seaman, white-faced and wobbly, clinging to the rigging. None saw the golden blur streaking toward the sail where Peter now hid.

"Thanks, Tink," he whispered as she nestled in next to him.

Tink tinkled modestly.

"I am very, very glad you came," said Peter.

*You should be*, said the bells.

———

Safely back on deck, his legs still shaky, Conrad Dillinger looked back into the rigging, an expression of puzzlement on his face. Watching him with some amusement was a leather-faced older hand who'd been swabbing the deck onto which Conrad had very nearly fallen.

"Wakes you up, don't it?" he said. "Almost fell myself once. Wakes you right up. Good thing you caught yourself, or I'd have had quite a mess to mop down here, ha-ha."

Conrad looked at him.

"Best thing is to get right back up there," said the old swabbie.

"Did you see it?" said Conrad.

"Did I see *what?*" the swabbie inquired. He spat a brown glob over the rail.

"There was this yellow *thing*. Like a bird, only too fast for a bird. More like a . . . bee. Did you see a yellow bee?"

"You're talking like you hit your head," said the swabbie. "Ain't no bees out at sea." He smiled at the sound of that, revealing a mouth nearly devoid of teeth. "No bees at sea," he repeated, and then he turned it into a song:

*"Ain't no bees out to sea if you please.*
*If you please, when you sneeze mind the breeze . . ."*

Off the old man went, mopping and singing. His song had a catchy tune; in a few moments the other swabbies were singing along with him. Conrad found himself humming along as he looked back up at the rigging. There *had* been something flying around him up there; he was sure of that. What he wasn't sure about was whether he should report this to an officer. He was worried that he'd be ridiculed, especially if he mentioned the strange feeling he'd had just before he'd managed to catch himself—the feeling of *floating*. And what about the bells? He had definitely heard bells. Should he report that? But who would believe him?

Conrad decided he would think about it later. Right now, it was time for breakfast. Following the smell of biscuits and bacon, he headed below.

Hiding in the sail far above, Peter smelled the biscuits and bacon, too.

"I'm hungry, Tink," he said. "And thirsty."

Tinker Bell responded with a stern burst of bells.

"No, I won't go down there during the day," he said. "But tonight I have to find water and something to eat, or I'll never make it to England."

More bells, softer now.

"You're right," said Peter. "Right now I need to sleep. Wake me when it's dark, would you?"

A nod from Tink, and in a minute's time Peter was fast asleep.

# $\mathcal{A}$NYTHING $\mathcal{U}$NUSUAL

"$\mathcal{W}$HAT DID HE FIND?" said Ombra.

He and Captain Nerezza were taking lunch, seated across from each other at a heavy table in the captain's darkened quarters. Nerezza detested these meals, because of Ombra's bizarre dining habits.

Ombra ate only one thing: octopus. He ate it raw, and preferably live, out of a wooden bucket, placed on the table by a nervous cook's mate, who quickly fled the cabin. Ombra would settle at the table and lean his black-cloaked form over the bucket, making hideous sucking and slurping sounds; occasionally black ink would squirt onto the table and floor. Nerezza found it difficult to eat his own food, sitting across from this grotesque spectacle.

"What did who find?" said Nerezza.

Ombra made a sucking sound, and Nerezza saw a tentacle, still writhing, disappear into the shadow beneath the hood.

"The boy you sent up to check the mizzen sails," said Ombra. "What did he find?"

"Oh, him," said Nerezza a bit smugly. "Nothing. As I expected."

"Nothing? Nothing at all?"

"Not in the sails, no."

The hooded head lifted from the bucket, and although Nerezza could not see Ombra's eyes, he felt the chill of his gaze.

"But he saw something?"

"He *thought* he saw something," corrected Nerezza. "He lost his balance and blamed it on a bee."

"A bee."

"It's ridiculous, of course," said Nerezza. "There's no bees out here. A gull is what he saw, if he saw anything. I took him off his ration of grog. He's too young for grog if he's seeing bees."

Ombra slurped down another piece of octopus. Then his hood came up again.

"You will double the watch tonight," he said, sliding his chair back and standing.

Nerezza wanted to object. He didn't appreciate doubling the watch; it would disrupt the shifts. But all he said was: "As you wish, Lord Ombra."

"If any man sees anything unusual," groaned Ombra, "I want to be told immediately." He slid toward the door, passing uncomfortably close to Nerezza, who had to fight the urge to recoil.

"Yes, my lord," said Nerezza, though what he thought was, *What are the men supposed to see? Bees?*

Ombra stopped, and Nerezza felt his gaze. "Possibly," he said. And then he was gone.

## CHAPTER 20

# THE SIGNAL

MOLLY WAITED UNTIL THE MAID had set the tea service down and left the sitting room of their splendid London home. When the maid was out of earshot, Molly moved closer to her mother and spoke in a whisper.

"Have you heard from Father?" she said.

Louise Aster poured a cup of tea and handed it to her daughter before answering.

"No, dear, not yet."

"Is that bad, do you think?" whispered Molly. "Do you think he's all right?"

"I'm sure he's fine," said her mother, pouring herself a cup. "He said it might be some time before he could get word to us."

Molly, setting her teacup down, rose and walked to the window. The sitting room looked out on Kensington Palace Gardens, one of London's finest streets, a broad boulevard lined on both sides with massive mansions. It was a typically gloomy London day, though for once it was not raining. A carriage rumbled past, clots of mud flying off the wheels, puffs of breath steaming from the horses' nostrils, the top-hatted driver hunched down into his overcoat, trying to keep warm.

On the sidewalk in front of the Aster house, looking cold but vigilant, stood the massive, sturdy form of Mr. Hodge. Molly knew that Mr. Jarvis was watching the back of the house, with the dog, Hornblower. The third guard, Mr. Cadigan, was upstairs resting. Rain or no rain, there were always two of these men standing guard outside. Sometimes Molly took them tea and biscuits, for which they were quite grateful, especially Hornblower. Molly had tried several times to engage the men in conversation, hoping to get them to talk about who, or what, they were watching for, or guarding against. These efforts had been fruitless: the men were polite, but revealed nothing.

"Oh, Mother . . . I hate to say it, but I miss Mrs. Bumbrake at times like this. She's something of a comfort, in spite of herself."

"Don't worry, dear. As soon as her sister is feeling better, she'll be back. A fortnight at most."

"I do hate this," said Molly.

"I'd rather you not use that word, dear," said her mother. "It's entirely unacceptable." She continued, "Now, what is it you *dislike?*"

"This feeling of . . . of *waiting*," said Molly impatiently.

"Waiting for what?"

"For . . . for something bad to happen."

"I'm sure nothing bad is going to happen."

"Then why are there men guarding our house?" said Molly.

Louise hesitated before she answered, and Molly saw a flicker of emotion cross her usually placid face. But all she said was, "We're perfectly safe, dear. Those men are here because your father wanted to make sure of that."

Molly's anger rose, and with it her voice. "Mother," she said, "I'm not a child. I know what kind of people the Others are. I was on the ship with them, remember? I was captured by that awful man Slank. I've seen what they'll do to get the starst—"

Molly stopped midword as her mother gave her an uncharacteristically sharp look, followed by a barely perceptible nod toward the doorway. Molly glanced in that direction and saw the maid standing there, just outside the room. She was the newest member of the household staff, a black-haired, rail-thin woman with a narrow face.

"Yes, Jenna?" asked Louise.

"Did you need anything else, ma'am?" said the maid.

"No, Jenna, thank you," said Louise. "We're fine."

Jenna bowed and left. Louise rose from her chair and crossed to where Molly was standing. Her expression was still calm, but her cheeks had a pink tinge that Molly knew meant she was angry.

"Molly," Louise said, her voice low but firm, "if you don't wish to be treated like a child, you must not act like one. Yes, the Others are dangerous. Don't you think I know that? But your father has done—is doing—all that he can to deal with the situation, and to protect us. For our part, we must be brave and do our best to maintain appearances. Above all, we must not discuss these matters—*ever*—in front of the staff."

Molly, chastened, nodded. "I'm sorry, Mother," she said. "It's just that sometimes I—"

She was interrupted by the resonating *bong* of the big front-door chime. She and her mother exchanged a *Who-could-that-be?* look. Their question was answered a moment later when Jenna reappeared in the doorway and said, "It's Master George, ma'am. To see Miss Molly."

Molly blushed, drawing a small smile from her mother.

"Please show him in, Jenna," said Louise.

In a moment, the lanky form of George Darling gangled into the room, all arms and legs and ears, a sandy-blond fourteen-year-old who would one day be a tall and handsome man, but who was still learning to operate his suddenly growing body.

"H . . . Hullo, Mrs. Aster," he stammered to Louise.

"Hello, George," she said.

"Hullo, Molly," George said, his face, particularly his pro-truding ears, turning the shade of a ripe tomato.

"Hello, George," said Molly.

"Molly, why don't you entertain George?" said Louise. "I need to speak to Cook about dinner." With a twinkle in her eyes, she left the room.

"So," said George, not quite looking at Molly. "Hullo."

"You said that already," said Molly.

"Ah," said George. "So I did."

George was a bit older than Molly, but they'd known each other since they were very small, as their families trav-eled in the same social circles. George's home was in Ennismore Gardens, just across the park from Molly's. As children they had played together for many happy hours. Now, however, they were entering the awkward stage between childhood and adulthood, and although they still enjoyed each other's company, they were unsure how to, or whether to, express that enjoyment.

This had been particularly true in the months since Molly had returned from her eventful trip to sea. George had sensed a change in Molly; he had tried more than once to ask her about her experiences on the ship, only to have Molly quickly change the subject. So he had given up on that line of inquiry. But he continued to call on the Aster house reg-ularly.

After a moment of uncomfortable silence, he said, "So,

who's the bruiser lurking out front? He gave me quite the hard look as I walked up."

"That's not a bruiser," said Molly. "That's Mister Hodge."

"All right, then," said George. "And who is Mister Hodge?"

"He's a friend of my father's."

George studied her for a moment.

"Is your father here?" he said.

"No," said Molly. "He's . . . he's away."

"I see," said George. "And your father's . . . *friend* . . . he stands outside all day?"

"Yes," said Molly. "He does."

"I see," he said.

Another uncomfortable silence, finally broken by George.

"Look, Molly," he said. "Do you . . . I mean, are you . . . I mean . . . is there something wrong?"

"Wrong? Of course not," said Molly. "What would be wrong? There's nothing wrong."

"Because if there is," said George, "and if I could—"

"There's nothing wrong," said Molly.

More silence.

"All right," said George. "I just thought that . . . I mean . . . Never mind."

Molly appeared on the verge of saying something, but she merely nodded. This was followed by more silence and increasing discomfort on both sides.

"All right, then," said George finally. "I suppose I should be going, then."

Again Molly appeared on the verge of saying something; again she held her tongue.

"All right, then," repeated George. "Good-bye, Molly."

"Good-bye," she said, and they parted, both of them feeling quite unhappy, neither of them sure why.

Jenna showed George to the door, and Molly went upstairs to her room, which was on the third floor at the front of the house, with a window looking out on the boulevard. Molly sat in the window seat and watched George trudge away, not looking back. He passed a larger person coming up the sidewalk toward the Aster house. Molly saw that it was a bobby—a Metropolitan police officer—wearing the blue uniform and distinctive domed helmet. She noted that it was not Constable Calvin, the stout, red-faced, heavily whiskered man who had walked this beat since before Molly was born, but a taller man, hawk-nosed, clean-shaven, whose uniform seemed too small for him, the frock-coat sleeves barely reaching his wrists.

As Molly watched, the bobby drew alongside the corner of the Aster property, where he passed Mr. Hodge, who was beginning his hourly circuit of the perimeter of the Aster grounds. Mr. Hodge nodded politely. The bobby did not respond, and in fact barely glanced at Mr. Hodge. Molly saw that this reaction, or lack of reaction, puzzled Mr. Hodge; he turned and watched the bobby's back for a moment. Then he shrugged and turned right, heading around the side of the house.

And because he had gone around the side, Mr. Hodge did not see what the bobby did next, although Molly, watching from her bedroom, did see it.

The bobby stopped in front of the house and looked in all directions, as if checking to see that nobody was watching him. Then he looked toward the Aster house, peering intently; Molly figured he was looking toward the sitting room.

*What is he looking at?* wondered Molly.

What he was looking at, unseen by Molly, was a hand, held close to the sitting-room window. The hand belonged to Jenna, the maid. It was holding up three fingers.

One for each guard.

From her window, Molly thought she saw the bobby's head give just the slightest hint of a nod, but she wasn't sure. The bobby then turned and walked away in the same direction from which he had come.

*I wonder what that was about,* thought Molly.

## CHAPTER 21

# THE SCUTTLEBUTT

PETER HAD NEVER FELT hungrier, or thirstier. He'd been awakened from his restless sleep by the ache of his empty belly. His lips were dry and cracked; his throat was parched.

The only good thing about the situation, as far as Peter could tell, was that since the incident with the young sailor that morning, no crewman had climbed near his hiding place. Peter had some experience at sea; he knew that as long as the wind held and the ship maintained its present course, the sailors would have no reason to do anything to the sail where he'd taken refuge. With any luck, he could be undisturbed here for days.

But he had to find food and water. Especially water. He had to find some *soon*. Unfortunately, he dared not venture out of his hiding place until darkness fell.

The afternoon hours passed slowly and uncomfortably; Peter felt increasingly cramped, hot, and sweaty in his tight canvas confinement. Finally, *finally*, the sky began to darken. At last the sun went down, and the welcome coolness of night enveloped the ship.

Peter wriggled his way toward the top of the sail. Tinker Bell poked her tiny head over the edge and looked down.

"What do you see, Tink?" Peter whispered.

Soft bells. *Some men working. Some talking. Nobody looking this way.*

"Is there a place where I can land down there, where they won't see me?" whispered Peter.

A pause as Tink scanned the deck. Then: *Yes. At the back. I'll show you.*

Tink fluttered out of the sail and hovered. Peter, moving stiffly, poked his head up from the canvas and looked around. The moon was not yet up; the rigging was dark. Peter realized that he probably would not be spotted even if somebody on deck did happen to look up. He crawled out on the yard and looked to where Tink was pointing: a darkened area of the deck toward the stern, on the port side, alongside the raised poop deck where the helmsman stood at the wheel. Peter saw that, if he crouched, he could not be seen from the helm. But he would have to be alert for anybody coming back along the port rail.

"Okay," he whispered to Tink. "Let's go."

In an instant, Tink, who could fly faster than Peter could see, darted down to the deck. Peter swooped right behind her, enjoying the *swoosh* of the cool air on his face. He crouched on the deck next to Tink, listening for a shout that would mean somebody had seen him.

Nothing.

"All right," he said. "Now I need to find water."

Soft bells from Tink. *I know where the water is.*

"You do?" whispered Peter. "Where?"

*A barrel, in the middle of the ship. The sailors get water from it with a big spoon.*

"The scuttlebutt!" whispered Peter. He remembered the term from his time aboard the ill-fated scow *Never Land*. The crew often gathered by the scuttlebutt—a water barrel with a wooden ladle—to slake their thirst and trade gossip.

"Can I get to it?" whispered Peter. "Will I be seen?"

Tink flitted forward, keeping close to the deck, then flitted back with the bad news.

*There are two men nearby.*

"How near?"

*This near.* In less than a second, Tink flew fifteen feet aftward along the rail, then back. If the men were only that far from the scuttlebutt, they would surely see Peter.

"Oh," said Peter, despondent. His throat felt more parched than ever. Since Tink had mentioned the scuttlebutt, he'd almost tasted the water.

*Wait here*, said Tink. She flitted forward again, returning about a minute later, looking frustrated.

"What happened?" said Peter.

*The spoon,* she said. *I can't lift it. It's tied to the barrel, anyway.*

Despite his discomfort, Peter had to smile, touched by Tink's effort to carry the big ladle back to him.

"It's all right, Tink," he said. "Thanks for trying."

Tink shook her head. *I'll find something smaller,* she said.

Peter looked around, but saw nothing that could be used to carry water. Small objects were not left lying about on a ship's deck, as they inevitably were blown overboard.

"Tink," Peter whispered, "I don't think—"

But Tink was gone again . . . this time over the side of the ship. Peter wondered what she could possibly be up to, but he had no choice other than to wait, which he did for several minutes, before Tink reappeared, dripping wet, proudly holding . . . a shell.

"Where'd you get that?" whispered Peter, not believing that Tink—even Tink—could have swum down to the seafloor.

*From the side of the ship,* she said.

Peter examined the shell. Sure enough, it was a barnacle shell. But *how* . . .

"How did you get it free from the ship?" he said. Barnacles were notoriously hard to remove from a hull; they clung with astonishing strength, as any sailor would agree after spending a few unhappy hours trying to scrape them off.

*I talked to it,* said Tink.

"You *talked* to it?" Peter whispered. He was about to express skepticism, but he realized that if anybody could talk a barnacle into letting go of a ship, it was Tink.

*Wait here,* she said. Clasping the shell, she zipped forward.

A few moments later she was coming back, flying cautiously, holding the shell in front of her, frowning in concentration as she struggled to avoid spilling a drop. She reached Peter and handed him the shell. He brought it eagerly to his lips. It was only an ounce, maybe less, and it smelled of barnacle, but it was the sweetest thing Peter had ever tasted. He swished it around in his parched mouth and swallowed, then licked the shell.

"Thanks, Tink," he whispered.

*I'll get more,* she said, taking the shell.

"What about the sailors?" Peter said.

*They're looking the other way.*

"Be careful," said Peter, but she was already gone.

Tink made a dozen more trips, two dozen, slaking Peter's thirst an ounce at a time. Each time, her route to the scuttlebutt took her over a certain spot on the deck. Each time she passed over that spot, she felt an odd sensation. At first she disregarded it, but it became more pronounced with each trip, until she found herself swerving around the spot. But still she sensed it, a distinctly unpleasant feeling.

A chill.

She didn't mention it to Peter; she wasn't sure what it was, and she didn't want to appear afraid. So she avoided the spot as best she could, bringing Peter his water until finally he insisted that she stop before somebody saw her.

"That was wonderful, Tink," he whispered. "Thanks again."

*You're welcome.*

"Now let's find some food," said Peter. "I'm starving."

———✦———

Directly beneath the spot on the deck that had troubled Tink was the small, tomb-dark inner cabin where Lord Ombra spent most of his time on the ship. Ombra was there now. Each time Tink had passed overhead, he too had sensed something.

He rose, glided to the door, and opened it. The gloom in the passageway told him night had fully fallen. It would be dark on the deck.

Ombra would go hunting.

# TUBBY TED'S DISCOVERY

TUBBY TED HAD EATEN three bananas for breakfast, after first eating two coconuts, a mango, and something that looked and tasted a lot like bread, which the Mollusks made out of seeds and pounded grass. They were nice enough to drop a couple loaves by each day, to keep the boys from starving to death.

Tubby Ted was in no danger of that. He was more in danger of bursting. But he decided that what he needed was another three, or perhaps another five, bananas. The boys had eaten all the ripe ones from the trees near their hut, so Ted wandered off into the jungle a ways, until he spotted a tree with a nice-looking bunch. He was searching for a stick to knock them down with when . . .

*WHOOMP!*

Suddenly, Ted was not standing: he was sitting on the ground. And *one of his legs was missing.* The left one, to be precise. This was very upsetting for a moment, until Ted realized that he could still *feel* the leg, but it had gone into the ground somehow.

*Quicksand!* he thought. The Mollusks had warned the boys that there was quicksand on the island; that it would trap a person and slowly suck him under. The boys had asked why, if it acted slowly, was it called *quick*sand. The Mollusks had replied that, as far as they were concerned, *most* English names for things were silly. The word that they used for quicksand was a deep grunt that translated roughly to "uh-oh."

But this was not quicksand: when Tubby Ted wiggled his left foot, it moved freely, and it wasn't wet. He tried to pull it free, to stand up, but could not. So he started to dig. But as he dug, to his surprise, most of the dirt didn't come up in his hand: instead, it disappeared, falling away down into the hole with his leg.

In a few moments, Ted had the hole large enough to pull his leg free. The hole was big enough for Ted to stick his head down and take a look inside. Thus, when James came along, searching for his missing friend, he saw only the backside of Tubby Ted sticking up, like a plump ostrich in shorts.

"What are you doing?" James called out.

Tubby Ted pulled his head out, clumps of dirt sticking to his hair, his sweaty face smeared with dirt and mud. A bright orange-and-green three-inch centipede dangled from his left ear, like an earring.

"Oh, hullo, James," said Ted. "I was looking for bananas."

"Under the ground?" said James, reaching out and batting away the centipede.

"No, I was going to get them from up there"—he pointed up at the bananas—"and I fell into this hole here." He pointed down. "So then I looked into it and I found a much bigger hole. A *very* big hole. It has lava walls and a dirt floor."

"Really?" said James. He stuck his head into the hole, looked around, then pulled his head out, his eyes wide.

"That is a *very* big hole," he said.

"That's what I'm saying."

"More like a small cave than a big hole."

"Much more like it." Tubby Ted was proud of his discovery, though he had no idea why James seemed so impressed.

James stuck his head down inside again, then looked back up at Tubby Ted. "Do you know what you just found, Tubby Ted?" he said.

"I do, James. I absolutely do!"

"What?"

Tubby Ted's face fell. "I'm not exactly sure. I thought you were going to tell me."

"I will," James said, turning and trotting back toward the hut. "But we have to tell the others!"

"Tell them *what?*" said Tubby Ted.

"We have work to do!" said James, now almost out of sight.

Ted took one last longing glance up at his banana bunch. Then he started trotting after James, wondering what, exactly, he had found.

## CHAPTER 23

# A Second Visit

MOLLY DIDN'T KNOW WHY she awoke. It was late at night. Her room was dark and cold, the fire only dead ash now.

She lay in her bed, listening: the house was still.

But something had awakened her.

She rose from her bed and padded in bare, cold feet to her window. Looking out, she first saw only blackness, and then the faint glowing sphere of the gas lamp on the street, fighting its lonely, losing battle to illuminate the all-enshrouding fog. She looked left and, by straining her eyes, could just make out the large, reassuring form of Mr. Cadigan at his usual nighttime post at the end of the front walk.

Then she looked to the right, past the streetlight, and gasped as she saw two shapes emerge from the fog. They were illuminated only for a moment, but that was enough for her to see that it was the same Metropolitan police officer who had walked by earlier that evening. With him was a man

Molly didn't recognize—tall and thin, like the bobby, but apparently a civilian; he wore an overcoat and top hat, not the frock coat and domed helmet of the Metropolitan Police. Molly did not get a good look at his face, but he had the bearing of a gentleman.

*Odd*, thought Molly. *Why is that man with the bobby? And why is the bobby coming by so late?*

Straining to see through the swirling fog, she watched the two men approach Mr. Cadigan, who was also keeping an eye on them. They passed directly in front of him, but neither of them looked at him, which also struck Molly as odd. Not even so much as a nod. *Not terribly friendly*, she thought. She saw Mr. Cadigan's head turn and follow as he watched them pass; he kept looking in their direction until they vanished into the fog.

Molly watched out the window a bit longer but saw nothing except gloom and dark. Finally, shivering, she slipped back into bed and snuggled under the comforter. She thought about the bobby and the man with him. She pondered whether she had reason to be troubled by this. Was she just being a scared little goose? After all, there were thousands of bobbies in London. Why should she be surprised to see an unfamiliar one walk past her house?

But why had he made a second visit? Why had he looked at her house earlier in the day? And why was he with a gentleman so late at night?

She thought about sharing these concerns with her mother. But then she remembered her mother's words to her earlier in the day: *We must be brave.*

Molly decided she *was* being a little goose, letting her fears run away with her mind. She would force herself to be brave. She wouldn't say anything about it. No reason to make trouble where there was none.

And so, after some tossing about, Molly went back to sleep.

## CHAPTER 24

# THE STOWAWAY

SOFT BELLS CHIMED in Peter's ear, and a welcome message: *I know where there's food.*

"You do?" Peter whispered, squatting in the darkness at the stern of the ship. "Where?"

Tink pointed down toward Peter's bare feet and the dark wooden deck.

*Under there.*

Peter sighed. "I *know* there's food down there, Tink. But there are men down there, too. They'll see me."

*I can bring you food. I brought you water.*

"It'll be too heavy for you, Tink," he whispered.

Tink pouted, but didn't argue; she knew she wouldn't be able to fly with anything much bigger than a grape.

"I'm going to go forward a bit," said Peter. "Maybe we can find a safe way belowdecks."

*I'll go first.*

"All right, but be careful."

*They won't see me.*

Tink flitted forward, staying low, about knee-height. Peter crawled after her on hands and knees, grateful that the night sky was cloudy and dark. From somewhere above him and to his right he heard the murmur of two men talking, and although he could not make out the words, the exchange carried the bored tone of sailors passing time. Tink darted ahead, then zipped back to Peter.

*There's an opening up there, and stairs going down.*

"Where?" he whispered.

*Just past the water barrel.*

"What's down the stairs?"

In a blink and a half, Tink flew off and returned.

*A hallway.*

"Is there anybody in the hallway?"

*No, but there's food. I can smell it. It's coming from a door at the end of the hall.*

Food! Peter felt his mouth water. Now, if he could just get down there . . .

"What about the men?" he whispered.

Tink flitted ahead, then back.

*They're looking the other way,* she said. *Out at the water on the other side.*

"All right, then," whispered Peter. "Let's go."

Following Tink, Peter crawled silently forward to the

edge of the boxlike companionway that contained the stair-well, protecting it from rain and weather. Tink stuck her tiny head around the corner, then beckoned him on. He crawled out into the open, looking to his right. As Tink had said, Peter saw two sailors on the far side of the deck, leaning against the rail and looking out to sea. Tink darted into the shadowy darkness and down the steep stairs. Peter followed right behind.

———

At exactly the moment when Tink and Peter disappeared below, a dark form oozed up from a companionway on the starboard side of the ship. Instantly the deck air cooled. The two sailors gossiping at the rail felt it and fell silent, their bodies rigid, their eyes fixed on the waves, both of them silently praying that Ombra would glide past, would leave them alone.

But the dark form stopped directly behind them. Sweating now despite the chill, they stared at the water for thirty agonizing seconds before the silence was broken by Ombra's harsh groan.

"Have you men seen anything unusual?"

"N . . . N . . . NO, sir," said one of the men, the other being too scared to speak.

"Nothing strange on deck?" groaned Ombra.

"N . . . No, sir."

"How long have you been here?"

"The whole watch, sir."

There was another uncomfortable silence. Then Ombra glided on. The men slumped with relief, then cautiously turned their heads to look. Ombra moved along the deck in a deliberate manner, his cloaked head tracking slowly back and forth.

"What's he doing?" whispered one of the two.

"Dunno, mate," answered the other. "But it can't be no good. He looks like . . . a hunting dog."

"Aye, that he does," said the first. "Like a bloodhound on a trail."

⸺◆⸺

At the bottom of the companionway, Peter and Tink found themselves in a dark corridor. It appeared to be empty, but Peter was nervous. On deck, he could escape by simply launching himself off the ship and flying away. Down here, flying was not an option. He could easily be trapped.

"Where's the food?" he whispered.

*This way,* said Tink, darting down the corridor, a tiny glowing comet in the gloom. She stopped in front of a closed door on the left side. Ahead, the corridor continued twenty more feet, then turned sharply left.

Peter tiptoed to the door and put his ear against it, listening. Nothing. He turned the iron latch and gently pushed the door open; it creaked a bit, but not so as to draw attention amid the thousand other creaks and groans of a ship tossing and moving at sea.

Peter stepped inside: the room was pitch black. But as Tink had reported, the smell of food was strong.

"Tink," he whispered. "I need some light."

Tink flitted through the doorway and, with a frown of concentration, increased her glow from the level of a candle to that of a chandelier. As the room filled with light, Peter looked around: he saw a dozen or so wooden barrels, some iron pots, and . . .

. . . a man.

The man was not three feet away, sleeping in a hammock slung from the ceiling. He was a portly fellow; the cook, Peter assumed. His blood froze as the man stirred. But the sleeper was merely shifting position, and did not wake.

Peter looked at the barrels. They were all closed, to keep the rats out. He approached the nearest barrel and ran his fingers around the rim. The barrelhead was sealed tight. He tried another, then another, then another; all were sealed. But on the next barrel his luck changed: the barrelhead moved. It had not been secured.

Peter glanced back at the cook. Still sleeping. Working the fingers of both hands under the barrelhead, he tugged, and it came free.

Ombra, the dark and deadly bloodhound, worked his way forward along the starboard side, almost to the bow of the ship. He was not pleased. He'd found nothing. Whatever, whoever, he was after was not to be found to starboard.

He slithered across to the port side and, still moving his head back and forth, began making his way toward the stern. Suddenly, he stopped. He could feel it now: a warmth, a glowing—something foreign to him. He moved on, more quickly now.

Tink made a soft sound—not so much a word as a feeling.

*Danger.*

Peter looked away from the barrel, from which he had been pulling pieces of salt pork, which he stuffed into his shirt. He mouthed a question, making no sound.

"What?"

Tink crossed her arms, as if cold, and shivered.

*I don't know,* she said. *Something bad. Coming.*

Peter searched her face and saw an expression he'd never seen there before: fear.

Ombra's dark shape slithered sternward along the port rail. As he neared the companionway that Peter and Tink had gone down, he slowed, then stopped. The dark hood peered down into the companionway for a moment.

Then the cloak glided forward, and started to descend.

———◆———

Tink's sound was urgent now.

*Hurry!*

"All right," whispered Peter, stuffing a last piece of salt pork into his shirt. He grabbed the barrelhead and hastily put it back onto the barrel.

Too hastily. Peter didn't get it on right. The barrelhead slid across the opening and fell to the floor with a loud clatter.

The cook woke instantly.

"Hey! What . . . WHAT ARE YOU DOING?" he bellowed, struggling to get out of the hammock.

*Come!* rang Tink in Peter's ear, but he needed no persuading. In two steps he was out of the room and into the corridor. He turned right to race for the companionway.

*NO!* Tink grabbed Peter's hair in her tiny fists; she yanked with surprising force. *Not that way!*

Peter was about to ask her why, when he saw it, straight ahead—somebody, some*thing*, clad in black, coming down the companionway. He turned and ran, following Tinker Bell the other way along the corridor. They made a right-angle

143

turn to the left. Behind him he heard the bellowing of the angry cook. But now, in the instant before he turned the corner, Peter also *felt* something—a sudden, strange chill, both in the air and shivering up through him. He dared not look back; the cook was thundering down the corridor now, roaring with rage, coming after him.

"STOP, THIEF!" he bellowed.

*This way*, said the bells in Peter's ear.

They entered a corridor that cut across the width of the ship. Tink darted to the right, into a narrow passageway, and Peter quickly saw why: just ahead was a narrow companionway leading up to the deck. Tink shot up through the opening like a spark out of a chimney. Peter launched himself upward right behind her, clearing the companionway opening just as the cook, who moved with remarkable quickness for a man of his bulk, reached the bottom of the ladder.

"ON DECK THERE!" bellowed the cook. "STOP HIM! STOP THE THIEF!"

Peter found himself on the deck by the portside rail, almost to the stern. He heard the pounding of bare feet running toward him from the forward part of the ship. And now the cook's furious face appeared in the companionway.

There was nowhere for Peter to go. Nowhere on the ship, in any event. After an instant's hesitation, Peter ran to the stern and dove headfirst over the rail.

"MAN OVERBOARD!" bellowed the cook.

In a moment, three men reached the stern rail, then six, all looking down at the ship's frothy wake, ghostly white in the black night sea. There was some discussion of bringing the ship about and attempting a rescue, but this plan was vehemently vetoed by the cook.

"Good riddance," he said, to nods of agreement from the others. "We don't need a food thief on this ship."

"He's shark food, then," said one wit, drawing chuckles from the group.

But the joviality stopped instantly and the men fell silent when the air turned cool, and the dark form of Ombra oozed out of the companionway.

"Who was it?" asked the groaning voice. "Who went over the rail?"

All eyes turned to the cook, the only man who'd seen the thief.

"I . . . I can't say," he said. "I never caught a look at his face. But he was a slight one. That I'm sure of. Slight and quick. And . . ." The cook hesitated.

"And *what?*" groaned Ombra.

"Nothing, sir," said the cook, who had decided that it was wiser not to mention the strange light he'd seen darting about the thief. "Just that he was a slight one, sir. And quick."

"Get the captain," groaned Ombra. "Tell him I want a full muster of all the men on this ship. I want to know who went over the side. *Now.*"

A sailor scurried off to give the captain the unwelcome news. The rest remained at the stern, watching the wake. Nobody looked skyward; there was no reason to. So nobody saw Peter and Tink, who had, after launching themselves from the stern, flown alongside the ship at wavetop level to the bow, then arced high into the dark sky, then swooped back down to their hiding place inside the furled sail.

From there, as their racing pulses gradually slowed to normal, they watched and listened to the proceedings below: the unhappy sailors, roused from their sleep, lined up on deck to be counted, then counted again; the embarrassed anger of Captain Nerezza, forced to confront the fact that there had been a stowaway on his ship; the mysterious dark figure, silently watching it all.

"Who *is* that?" Peter whispered, pointing out the cloaked form of Ombra.

Tinker Bell shivered, and again Peter saw the unfamiliar look of fear on her face as she crossed her tiny arms.

*Bad*, she said.

Peter remembered the chill he'd felt belowdecks. Could it possibly have come from the cloaked man?

"But who *is* he?" he whispered. "How do we know he's bad?"

Tink only shivered, and shook her head. *Bad*, she repeated. *Stay away.*

Peter slid down into the canvas sail. He pulled a piece of

salt pork from his shirt and, after offering it to Tink—who shook her head with distaste—tore off a piece with his teeth and began chewing.

A hundred feet below, the sailors who'd been awakened were dismissed; they trudged back to their hammocks, muttering unhappily. In a minute, Nerezza and Ombra stood alone on deck.

"So it was a stowaway," said Nerezza.

Ombra was silent.

"Whoever it was," said Nerezza, "he's dead now."

"Is he?" groaned Ombra. "Are you sure?"

"Well, of course he is," said Nerezza. "He went over the rail. By now he . . ."

Nerezza didn't finish the sentence; Ombra was gone, having melted away into the darkness.

Nerezza stood alone, wondering who had been on his ship, and why Ombra would possibly doubt that the stowaway had drowned.

## CHAPTER 25

# GENIUS

$\mathcal{H}$OOK WAS IN A COLD RAGE.

He was never pleasant to be around, but now his mood was foul even for him. A dark fury consumed him. He'd been this way for days, ever since his utter humiliation at the hands of the cursed flying boy.

Revenge. He wanted revenge. He *would* have his revenge.

And so this day, for the first time since he had been marooned on this wretched island, he laboriously climbed to the top of the great steep peak that separated the pirate side from the side where the boys—and the Mollusks—lived. After reaching the peak, he slowly, stealthily, worked his way down the far side to a rock outcropping that gave him a good view of the Mollusk village, and the place nearby where the boys had their driftwood hut. He lay on his stomach to keep out of sight, and he watched and waited. He would wait as long as it took. He *would* have his revenge.

An hour went by. Two. And then he saw them . . .

*The boys!* Two . . . three . . . no, *four* of them. The flying boy was not among them, but Hook assumed he would be somewhere around. They were moving away from the Mollusk village, and Hook saw that they were carrying things. Two of them held stacks of large, jungle-plant leaves—*Why?* Hook wondered. One had his arms wrapped around what looked like a small stool or table. The chubby one was carrying an armful of coconuts.

Hook tracked them intently as they moved left to right along one of the many jungle paths. His view of them was interrupted by a clump of palm trees. He shifted his gaze slightly to the right, where the path became visible again.

Nothing.

Hook watched the clump of trees intently for twenty minutes. Then the boys emerged again, going back the way they had come.

But now their hands were empty.

"Ah," said Hook, with a smile that revealed his brown tooth stumps in all their jagged glory. "Got ourselves a little *hiding place*, have we?"

He stayed there, watching, and in fifteen minutes the boys appeared again, carrying more leaves and coconuts. Again they disappeared into the palm clump, again reappearing with empty hands. They made several more trips as Hook watched, thinking, plotting. The boys had made a mistake, choosing a hiding place away from the protection of the Mollusk warriors. It was not all *that* far away, but perhaps far enough to do the trick.

If he could catch them as a group . . .

Hook's eyes wandered far to the left, where his attention was captured by several low, brown shapes moving on a distant hillside. A glimmer of an idea began to glow in his sinister mind, and the more he pondered it, the brighter it grew. He continued pondering until he was satisfied he had a plan that was not only workable, but—Hook had to admit it, in all modesty—brilliant. Finally, the rage that had engulfed him for days was gone, and the joy of pure evil filled his calloused heart.

Hook rose and made his way back across the mountain to the pirate camp.

"Smee!" he shouted as he entered the clearing. "Fetch me writing tools!"

"Aye, Cap'n!" answered Smee from inside the log fort. After a minute he bustled out, in all his roundness, carrying a quill made from a parrot feather and a coconut-shell bowl filled with octopus ink. These he set on a rickety desk made of driftwood, with a stump for a chair. Hook sat at the desk and, frowning in concentration, sketched out something on a large yellow leaf that had been dried in the sun. Smee, looking over Hook's shoulder, studied the drawing, which consisted of a complex web of lines and arrows.

"What's that, Cap'n?" he asked.

"It's a *plan*," said Hook.

"Ah," said Smee. He was silent for a few moments, then said: "A plan of what?"

"Paths," said Hook. "The boys are using the same path over and over."

"I see," said Smee, although in fact he did not.

"We can't go near their hut, can we, Smee?"

"No, Cap'n."

"And why's that?"

"Them Mollusks."

"Right you are. The savages watch over the boys. But what if we was to flush 'em out and herd 'em down this path?" He pointed to his drawing.

"The Mollusks?" said Smee.

"No, you idjit," said Hook. "The boys."

"Herd the boys?" said Smee.

"Exactly!" said Hook, gesturing to his drawing. "The jungle is thick here. There's nowhere to go but down this path, is there?" He smiled. "We'll scare 'em half to death, run 'em straight away from that hut so fast they won't have time to think. They'll be running *away* from the Mollusks. A few minutes is all it'll take."

"But won't the Mollusks see us herd 'em?" said Smee.

"Ah!" said Hook, delighted with his cleverness. "But it won't be us doing the herding."

"I see," said Smee, still not seeing.

Hook sketched some more arrows onto the leaf, then sketched some crosshatch lines where one of the arrows turned right. He nodded with satisfaction.

"I am a genius," he observed.

Smee, frowning hard at the leaf, said nothing.

Hook sighed and said, "Tell Hurky to fetch the fishing net."

"The fishing net?" said Smee.

"Yes, the fishing net," said Hook. "And tell the men to collect their spears."

Smee frowned even harder. "We're going fishing with spears?"

"No, idjit," said Hook. "It's boars we're after."

"Boars?" said Smee, completely lost now. There were huge, hairy, wild pigs that roamed the island. They were vicious, aggressive, and crafty—even the Mollusks steered clear of them—but the pirates had managed to catch an injured one once. They'd cooked and eaten it, and the fresh meat had been a welcome change from the usual island fare of coconuts, fish, and the occasional boiled sea urchin.

"But, Cap'n," said Smee. "I thought we was after them boys."

"*We are*, you idjit," said Hook. "That's why we need the boars."

"But . . ." said Smee.

"It's genius, is what it is," said Hook. "We're going to let the hunted do the hunting while those of us who are usually the hunters go fishing. Genius!"

"So we're going fishing *and* hunting?" said Smee.

"NO, you idjit!" roared Hook. "Haven't you been *listening?*"

"No," said Smee. "I mean, yes."

Hook sighed the heavy sigh of a great man doomed to go unworshipped by the fools around him. "Just get the men, Smee," he said. "With spears and the net."

"Aye, Cap'n," said Smee, and he trotted off, muttering, "spears and the net; spears and the net," so as not to forget.

Hook watched him go, then returned his gaze to his drawing and his brilliant plan for getting rid of the cursed boys once and for all.

## CHAPTER 26

# St. Katherine's Dock

$S$LOWLY, LABORIOUSLY, pushed by the tide with little help from a weak, fast-fading wind, the ship inched the last half mile to its berth in London.

*At last*, Nerezza thought. He had never been so grateful to reach port. Since they'd left the strange island, he'd had little sleep. The crew, already unsettled by the presence of Lord Ombra, had been made even more skittish by strange shipboard occurrences. First, there had been the mysterious stowaway who'd gone overboard but left troublesome questions behind. Who was he? How and where had he boarded the ship? And what would compel him to jump from a ship—a ship *in the middle of the ocean*—rather than allow himself to be caught?

And then there was the mysterious light. Crewman after crewman claimed to have seen it: a small, quick light flitting about the ship, sometimes in the rigging, sometimes on the deck, often around the scuttlebutt. Nobody got near it, or even got a good look at it; whatever it was, it moved too fast.

The sailors, being as superstitious as most crews, had decided that it was the ghost of the drowned stowaway. Nerezza forbade such talk, loudly declaring that he would keelhaul any man who so much as spoke the word "ghost." But that did not quiet the anxious mutterings.

It did not help that Ombra had displayed a keen interest in these rumors, constantly demanding reports on all sightings of anything unusual, and prowling the deck at night, searching, searching . . . for what, Nerezza did not know. But he did know this: it kept him from getting much sleep.

Slank, too, was very interested in the ghost reports, and especially the mystery of the stowaway. Several times he had badgered the cook for a description of the fleeing figure, asking over and over: "Was it a boy? Could it have been a *boy* you saw?" The cook could give no satisfactory answer, protesting that he'd barely seen the figure. But Slank would not let go of it, and his relentless suspicion added to the shipboard tension.

And so Nerezza was grateful when, at last, London came into view. He stood on deck now, feeling the damp, cold air seep through his overcoat as the ship eased forward on the dark waters of the Thames—waters swarming with traffic, boats and ships of every size bearing flags from dozens of countries.

In the distance lay London's familiar landmarks—the Tower, Tower Bridge, Parliament—looking majestic even in the coal-clouded air. On the right lay the vast, busy complexity of the London docks, a forest of masts rising from hundreds of ships. Nerezza spotted the red brick of Hardwick's Warehouses.

"We'll put in to St. Katherine's," Nerezza announced to his first mate, who had been expecting this and quickly relayed the orders to the crew. "Look alive, now!" he shouted, though this was hardly necessary: the sailors were eager to get off the haunted ship and onto shore.

---

Far above, in the folds of the furled sail that had been both his hammock and hiding place for far too long, Peter eagerly awaited getting off this ship. He was hungry, having eaten nothing for two days but an old piece of meat that was mostly bone. He was also tired, having slept poorly from worrying constantly about being discovered. And he was deeply troubled by Tinker Bell's accounts of the mysterious dark form that prowled the deck below each night.

The day before, his heart had leaped as he'd heard the lookout's long-awaited call of "LAND HO!" From then on, England had been a dark line off to port; France, the same to starboard. From time to time, he'd cautiously poked his head over the top of the sail, marking the ship's progress as it drew slowly closer to its destination. He'd heard the sailors calling out the names of the landmarks: Isle of Sheppey, Canvey Island, the ominously named Gravesend, and finally the entrance to the river Thames. Now, at last, he could see the quay and docks themselves, and the huge fleet of ships in various stages of loading and unloading.

But he could see his breath, as well. For in addition to his other miseries, Peter was cold, bitterly cold. He had nothing to protect himself from the damp North Sea chill but the rags he wore and the rough canvas of the sail. He shivered constantly, longing for the warm sun and gentle tropic breezes of Mollusk Island—so far away now.

Less than a year earlier, Peter and the other boys had stood on one of these docks, about to go to sea aboard a doomed old tub carrying a mysterious trunk and a strange little girl. To Peter, that seemed like a lifetime ago. He was a very different person now from the cocky, selfish boy who'd left England. His life had changed dramatically on that voyage, and on Mollusk Island. He had fully expected to remain in his new home forever.

But now here he was, back where he'd started, his life once again intertwined with Molly's. He had to find her. But how? Peter looked out at the teeming docks, where hundreds, no, thousands of people—sailors, dockworkers, tradesmen, naval officers, customs officials, and more—scurried back and forth. Beyond them, Peter saw the impenetrable immensity of London—a confusing jumble of rundown, rickety buildings stretching into the dark distance, as far as he could see.

*How would he find Molly?*

Peter knew nothing of London—he'd never even been in the city before that fateful morning when the carriage had delivered him and the other boys from St. Norbert's Home for Wayward Boys to the docklands. He had no family in London, and—aside from Molly and her father—no friends. He had no money. He had no coat. He didn't even have shoes.

*How would he find Molly?*

Peter shivered. He had no plan at the moment. He knew only that he must find her, and quickly, before the hard men on the deck below got to her.

The dock was close now. There was much shouting and activity on the ship as its crew prepared to heave lines and tie the ship up. Peter hazarded a peek down at the deck. Directly below, standing next to the mast from which Peter's sail was suspended, was the captain, Nerezza—he of the hideous wooden nose—adjacent to Slank. Peter flinched involuntarily at the sight of Slank, who, Peter knew, would like nothing better than to slit the throat of the boy who had bested him back on Mollusk Island.

Slank and Nerezza talked quietly. Peter strained to hear, wishing he knew what they were saying.

"Tink," he whispered.

*What?* came the answer, soft bells in his ear.

"Do you think you can get close to those two men down there without being seen?"

Tink peeked down. *You mean Wood Nose and Ugly Face?*

Peter had to smile. "Yes, them."

*I'll go down the back of this pole,* she said, pointing to the mast. *They won't see me.*

"All right," whispered Peter. "See if you can find out what they're saying. But be care—"

He didn't finish, for Tink was already gone. Hoping he hadn't made a stupid mistake in sending her, Peter hid himself, settling back into the sail, worrying and waiting. And shivering.

———◆———

"Keep the crew on board?" Nerezza asked, astonished. "Is he mad? We reach London after several *months* at sea, with only a few measly hours on that wretched island, and he wants me to deny shore leave and *keep the crew on board?*"

"That's Ombra's orders," said Slank, who had just spent an uncomfortable twenty minutes below in Ombra's night-dark cabin. "He don't want word of his presence to get out until he's done with the Asters."

"All right, then," said Nerezza reluctantly. "There'll be no shore leave 'til Ombra says so."

The orders, when relayed by the first mate, brought sour faces and some angry murmurs, but the crewmen valued their skins too much to express their feelings aloud with Nerezza watching.

With the ship tied securely now, a gangplank was run out to connect the deck with the dock.

"There they are," Slank said, nudging Nerezza. "Right on time."

Two men stood off to the side of the gangplank, one tall and lean—hatchet-faced with dark, close-set eyes under bushy brows. Wearing an overcoat, woolen trousers, and the top hat of a gentleman, he looked out of place amid the squalor and bustle along the stone quay. Next to him, not quite so tall, stood a man wearing the black uniform of a Metropolitan police officer. The uniform, both Nerezza and Slank noticed, did not fit him well, being too short in both the sleeves and the pants legs.

"That's them? You're certain?" said Nerezza.

"I am," said Slank. He raised his hand, winning the attention of the two men on the dock, and gestured for them to ascend the gangplank. This they did with the deliberate steps of landsmen uncertain of their footing on a ship.

They approached the quarterdeck, stopping at the mizzenmast, alongside of which Slank made the introductions.

"Captain Nerezza," he said, "this here is Mister Gerch"—

he nodded toward the gentleman—"and this here is Mister Hampton. Or, should I say, *Constable* Hampton."

Nobody smiled at the attempted humor. Nor were any handshakes exchanged.

"Is he here?" inquired Gerch, not one to waste time on pleasantries with those he perceived to be of inferior social standing.

"Belowdecks," said Slank.

"He don't come out in the daylight," said Nerezza.

"All right," said Gerch. "Then you tell him this. Aster's gone."

"*Gone?*" said Slank, alarmed. "Gone where?"

It was Hampton who answered: "We don't know. We have somebody inside, a girl on the household staff, that says Aster left a week ago and hasn't been back since."

"What about the daughter?" said Slank.

"She's still there, with her mum," said Hampton.

This drew an ugly smile from Slank. "He left the women, did he?" he said. "Then I'd say we've got him."

"There are three guards," said Hampton. "Big ones. And a dog."

"The guards will not be a problem," said Nerezza.

Slank nodded his agreement, remembering the warrior guards back on Mollusk Island.

"So," said Gerch, "how does the . . . how does your passenger wish to proceed?"

"You're to come back at nightfall," said Slank.

Gerch said, "Then what?"

"Then our passenger comes up and tells us what we do next," said Slank. "He's not much for revealing his plans ahead of time, but if I had to guess, I'd say we're going to pay a call on Lord Aster's wife and daughter."

## CHAPTER 27

# *I*NTO THE *S*TORM

*I*N THE SAIL, PETER LISTENED, teeth chattering, as Tinker Bell delivered the bad news.

*Tonight,* she was saying. *When it's dark. They're waiting for . . .*

Here the bells stopped, and Tink shivered, which was how she indicated the dark shape that prowled the ship by night.

"Did they say where Molly's house is?" Peter whispered.

*No,* Tink answered in the curt tone she used whenever Molly's name came up. *Just that the father's not there.*

Peter frowned, considering the bleak picture Tink had painted. Molly and her mother were alone in a house, and the men on the deck below were going after them tonight. To make matters worse, these men apparently had the police, or at least some of the police, on their side. Molly's house was protected by guards, but the men below weren't worried about them. *Nor should they be*, thought Peter, remembering how the dark shape had dealt so easily with the Mollusk warriors.

Now, to make matters worse, it began to rain, a cold drizzle that found its way down through the sail folds, making Peter thoroughly miserable.

"We need to get out of here," he whispered.

Tink agreed with an immediate burst of bells: *Let's fly ashore.*

"I wish we could," said Peter. "But they'll see us. Or they'll see me, anyway."

The rain was coming harder now, the drops like cold pebbles, drumming on the canvas. Tink worked her way up to the sail opening and peeked down toward the deck.

*No one's there*, she reported. *They must have gone down to get out of the rain.*

"Really?" said Peter. "Do you think we could get out of here without being seen?"

Tink took a look at the sky. *Wait a few minutes*, she said. *It's going to rain much harder.*

Peter did not question this. Tink, being part bird, knew a great deal about the weather.

Sure enough, a few minutes later, a massive cloud bank swept in, bringing with it a blinding, drenching deluge. Peter, now too soaked to care if he got any wetter, climbed out of the sail and stood on the yardarm. He had no worries about being seen; he couldn't even see the deck through the swirling fog and rain, and he had to hang on to a rope to keep from being blown off the ship. Tink, not one to show dependence of any kind, nonetheless held on to his shirt with both hands.

"Ready?" Peter shouted.

Tink nodded, a bit uncertainly.

"All right, then," said Peter. "Let's go."

And with Tink still holding tightly to his shirt, Peter launched himself into the storm.

CHAPTER 28

# Not Safe at All

Peter, with Tinker Bell clinging to him, struggled to fly through the blinding rain, his body hurled this way and that by the swirling wind. He hoped he was heading toward the dock, but the visibility was so poor he couldn't be certain.

Angling his body downward, he descended and saw that he was over the roof of a long, low building. He followed it to an edge, then dropped as quickly as he dared to the ground. He found himself in a dim, debris-strewn alley between two warehouses. He stood for a moment, panting, hands on knees, water streaming down his body.

"Hey, there!" rasped a voice behind him. "Mind where you drip!"

Peter spun around and saw he was standing practically on top of a scrawny, bearded man sitting on the hard-packed dirt under the warehouse eave, cradling a bottle in his lap. The dirt was quickly going to mud.

"S . . . sorry, sir," said Peter.

"Sir? *Sir?* Haw-haw *harrggghhh-TOOEY.*" The man's laugh trailed off into a rough, wet cough, which turned into a spectacular spit. When he was done, he wiped his mouth on his sleeve and looked up at Peter with a broad, toothless smile. "Sorry, lad. Struck me funny is all. Nobody calls old Trumpy 'sir.' That's me name: Old Trumpy. You call me that. What does I call you?"

"Peter," answered Peter.

"A good name, Peter," said Old Trumpy. He raised the bottle to his lips and tried to take a swig, only to discover that it was empty. Disappointed, he set the bottle down again, then continued: "I had a dog once named Peter. Or maybe it was a cat. It was an animal of some kind, that much I recall. But it might not have been named Peter. Did you fall?"

"What?" asked Peter.

"One minute," said Old Trumpy, "you wasn't here. Next minute you was. But you didn't come from this way or that," he said, nodding to each end of the alley. "So I'm asking, did you fall?"

"Oh," said Peter. "Yes. From the—" He glanced up. "From up there. The roof."

Old Trumpy nodded sympathetically. "I falls a lot meself," he said. "I find it's better if I just sits and don't bother with the standing." He frowned, his eyes trying to focus on something just above Peter's head.

"What did you say your name was again?" he said.

"Peter."

"That's right," said Old Trumpy. "Peter. Well, Peter, do you mind if Old Trumpy asks you a question?"

"No."

"Is there a very small person sitting on your head?" He pointed a wrinkled hand at a spot above Peter.

Peter's own hand shot up. *Tink.* He grabbed her and, ignoring the angry peal of bells, stuffed her under his shirt.

"No, sir," he said. "I mean, no."

Old Trumpy blinked several times and looked relieved. "Good," he said. "Sometimes, when I has me rum, I sees things that ain't there. First time for a very small person, though. Usually it's snakes." He raised the bottle to his lips again, only to discover that it was still empty.

Peter said nothing. Tink, on the other hand, had a great deal to say from under his shirt, including some unkind comments about Peter's personal hygiene.

"Do you hear bells?" said Old Trumpy, glancing around.

"No!" said Peter.

"Well, I do!" said Old Trumpy, frowning. "That's another new one. Usually I just sees things."

*Let me out!* said Tink, not quietly.

"There it is again," said Old Trumpy.

"Be quiet," hissed Peter to Tink.

"What?" said Old Trumpy.

"Nothing!" said Peter.

"I thought you just said be quiet," said Old Trumpy.

"No," said Peter. "I mean, yes, I did, but not to you."

"Then who did you say it to?" said Old Trumpy.

"I, er . . . to myself," answered Peter.

"Ah," said Old Trumpy. "I does that meself sometimes. I'm talking thirteen to a dozen, and then I notice there's nobody there. The bells is new, though." He attempted another swig from the bottle. Empty still.

Peter looked toward the near end of the alley. The sky was lighter, the rain abating.

"Sir," he said. "I'm trying to find a house here in London."

"Oh, there's lots of houses here in London," said Old Trumpy. "Thousands, I should think. Shouldn't be no trouble finding one."

"But I'm looking for a certain one," said Peter. "A particular one."

"Ah," said Old Trumpy. "That could be harder."

"It belongs to a family named Aster," said Peter. "Lord Leonard Aster."

"*Lord* Aster, is it?" said Old Trumpy. "It's a *lord's* house you want?"

"Yes," said Peter.

"Haw-haw *harrggghhh-TOOEY*," said Old Trumpy, producing another impressive fountain of phlegm, from which Peter looked away.

"Sorry," said Old Trumpy. "No offense . . . What's your name again?"

"Peter."

"No offense, Peter, but you don't look like the nobility type."

"But do you know the house?" said Peter.

"What house?" said Old Trumpy.

"Lord Aster's," said Peter, trying not to show his exasperation. "Do you know where he lives?"

"Not around here, I can tell you that, haw-haw," said Old Trumpy, gesturing around the filthy alley. As he did, a rat scurried from one rubbish mound to another.

"Well, do you know where I might look for him?" said Peter.

Old Trumpy considered this question thoughtfully for a moment, then said: "Look for who?"

Peter sighed. "Never mind," he said. He started walking toward the end of the alley.

"You're off, then?" called Old Trumpy.

"Yes," said Peter, picking his way carefully over a pile of rubbish and jumping back as several rats scurried out. "I'm off."

"What's your name again?" called Old Trumpy.

Peter stopped, sighed, turned around. "Peter," he said.

"Right, Peter," said Old Trumpy. "Listen, son, you be careful out there. It ain't safe 'round these docks, especially for a young lad like you. And it ain't safe for nobody nowhere in London when dark comes." He drew a finger across his throat. "You can't trust nobody out there, lad. *Nobody*. That's why Old Trumpy stays in here."

Peter, saying nothing, turned away and resumed picking his way toward the end of the alley, leaving Old Trumpy talking to himself.

"Ain't safe for nobody," he muttered. "Not nowhere at all, not with night coming."

Then he tried another swig from the bottle, which, to his mild surprise and considerable disappointment, remained empty.

## CHAPTER 29

# A Bone to Pick

SLANK WAS WATCHING the crew of *Le Fantome* like a hawk.

He'd been at sea since the age of thirteen; he knew sailors, and he knew that London, with its many temptations, beckoned to them powerfully, despite Nerezza's orders to remain on the ship. Guards were posted at the gangway to keep the crew from walking off, but Slank knew that many of the men—if they thought nobody was watching—wouldn't hesitate to slide down a line to the dock, or even jump into the filthy Thames and swim for it. And once they'd gotten ashore and filled their bellies with grog, it was only a matter of time before they were wagging their tongues about the ship's strange voyage—and the even stranger passenger it carried.

But Lord Ombra did not want word of his presence to get out, not yet. And Slank shuddered to think of the consequences if Lord Ombra was displeased. So Slank passed the idle hours awaiting Ombra's appearance prowling the decks, keeping close watch on the increasingly restive crew.

At the moment, most of the crew had gathered forward along the rail to watch a bloody, drunken brawl taking place outside the Jolly Tar, a notorious dockside pub. With the men temporarily distracted, Slank decided to scale the rat lines that led to the crow's nest. From here, high above the deck, he had a good view of the ship and a stunning view of the city, stretching into the distance under a late-morning sky dark with coal soot.

Twenty minutes passed. Thirty. The fight ended, and the crew of *Le Fantome* went back to sitting around. Slank fixed his attention on the bow lines, then the stern, then back again. He looked port and starboard; he kept his ears attentive for the sound of whispering. A light breeze blew, bringing with it the scents of the city, some foul, some—like the smell of fresh food cooking—sweet. The furled sails slapped, a sound familiar and pleasant to any sailor. As the stiff fabric flapped, its folds opened and shut, like the bellows of an accordion.

*What was that?*

Slank stared aft, into one of the folds of a sail attached to the mizzenmast. He had the perfect angle as the breeze blew and the sail sagged open. The breeze calmed, and it slipped shut again, like a giant purse closing.

Slank frowned, trying to make sense of what he'd seen. The furled sail sagged open, and there it was again.

He quickly lowered himself from the lookout basket, scurried down the rat lines, crossed the deck, and ascended the mizzenmast faster than he'd gone aloft in years. He climbed to the folds in the second sail from the top. He pulled on the heavy sailcloth, one fold to the next, searching for what he thought he'd seen. Several men gathered on the decks below, watching, wondering what Slank was doing.

*There!* Slank reached and held the last of the folds open. He leaned over and peered down into this fold, confused by what he saw: three apple cores, eaten to the seeds; a bone, also gnawed practically to the marrow.

*A rat? But what rat would climb up here to eat? A bird?*

Slank hooked his knee around a line and lowered himself upside down into the fold of canvas, drawing mutters of interest from the sailors below. He grabbed the bone, then pulled himself back up. Steadying himself, he studied the bone, twisting it in the gray light.

Teeth marks. Not picked clean by a bird's beak, as he might have expected. Not the gnawings of a rat, either; no, these looked like human teeth marks, too small to be a man's. They were more the size of a . . .

Slank stared out toward the rooftops of London, then glanced at the decks below. Could their stowaway have left these behind? But the apple cores were not nearly rotten enough; they were far too fresh, too recently eaten. The stowaway had jumped ship weeks ago.

Slank frowned, remembering another ship and the boy who'd gone overboard at sea—only to reappear later, alive. He thought about the rumors of a ghost haunting the ship—*after* the stowaway had gone overboard.

*Could it possibly be?*

Slank stared at the bone, his grip tightening on it, as he would love to have squeezed the throat of the flying boy. If, somehow, the boy had been on the ship, and was now here in London, what did that mean for Ombra and his plan? Did Slank dare mention it? Back on the island, Ombra had cautioned him about his hatred for—his obsession with—the boy. Did he dare bring up his suspicions now, without better proof than some old bone and some apple cores? Yet Ombra himself had clearly suspected something was amiss on the ship, with his constant demands for searchers and extra guards. . . .

Slank decided that, for the time being, he would keep his suspicion to himself. He pocketed the bone and climbed back down to the deck, inventing a story to explain his unusual behavior to the watching sailors.

Yes, he'd keep quiet for now. But when he got off the ship—as he would soon enough, he'd be looking for the boy. And if he found him . . .

Slank put his hand into his pocket again and gripped the bone until it snapped.

CHAPTER 30

# SOMEHOW

PETER, WITH TINK STILL unhappily concealed under his shirt, stumbled from the alley into a cobblestone street swarming with activity. In the center of the street, barrels and crates were being hauled by horse-drawn wagons, as well as handcarts pushed and pulled by grunting, cursing men. Hurrying this way and that were sailors of many hues, in many garbs, talking and shouting in many languages. Everybody seemed to be in a hurry; everybody seemed to be in everybody else's way.

On both sides of the street, next to gutters running with stinking brown water, were shops selling clocks, sextants, canvas trousers, weatherproof coats, hammocks, rope, lanterns—all manner of goods for ships and those who sailed them. Scattered among the shops were public houses, from which came the sounds of shouting, singing, laughter, and fighting. Directly across the street from Peter, a sailor in a red flannel shirt emerged from a pub, stood for a moment, wavering back and forth, and then pitched face-forward into the gutter. Nobody took notice; the din and flow of humanity went on around him unabated.

An official-looking man strode past, wearing a blue jacket with brass buttons.

"Excuse me, sir," Peter said, stepping up to him, "can you tell me where I might find Lord—"

"Out of the way!" said the man, barely looking down as he gave Peter a shove that sent him stumbling into another man, who shoved him into yet another man, who cuffed him on the ear and pushed him away so hard that he fell into the street and had to scuttle backward like a crab to avoid being trampled by a horse pulling a wagon.

Peter leaped to his feet and pressed his wet back against a building, his heart pounding. Tink's bells sounded angrily from under his shirt.

"We *can't* fly away," he whispered. "People don't fly in London."

*But we can fly*, she said.

"But not here. I don't want them to see me," Peter whispered. A chill swept through his body, and he shivered violently. He was wet and filthy, and his feet were bare. Suddenly he became acutely aware of how cold and hungry and tired he was. Especially cold.

And night was falling.

Despair seeped into Peter's soul. He longed to be back on the island with the Lost Boys. For a moment he wanted only to sink to the ground, curl into a ball, and cry. What prevented him from doing so was the thought of Molly, and the memory of the time she had leaped from a ship in the middle of the ocean to save his life. If *he* were in trouble, she would not lie on the ground sniveling; she would find a way to help him. Now she was in trouble, somewhere in this indifferent, confusing, and cruel city. And somehow he had to find her.

Somehow.

# $\mathcal{A}$ $\mathcal{T}$INY $\mathcal{H}$EART $\mathcal{B}$EATING

TWO MILES AWAY, in her grand home on Kensington Palace Gardens, Molly paced in her room, as she had done for much of a lonely, restless afternoon. She paused every few minutes to look out the window—for what, she didn't know.

Each time she looked, the scene was the same: the street, the gloom, Mr. Cadigan standing guard. Nothing changed. Yet still Molly was drawn back to the window, time and again.

She sat on her bed, then stood again, then sat, then lay down for perhaps the dozenth time, knowing that rest would not come.

All at once she felt a burning at the base of her neck. She quickly unbuttoned the top two buttons of her blue-and-white dress and felt for the locket that hung around her neck.

It was warm.

Molly ran to her window. A hard rain poured down. She

looked down onto the broad street in front of the house, but the rain fell too heavily to allow her to see across to the mansion on the other side. Despite herself, she dared to hope that she would see her father's coach arriving, or even her father himself already at the front door.

But there was only Mr. Cadigan, at his post.

Staring out her window, she pulled the locket out from under her dress. It pulsed twice, like a tiny heart beating.

## CHAPTER 32

# A FEELING

PETER GASPED, AND his hand went to the locket around his neck.

*What is it?* said Tink, who had felt it also, the sudden warmth. *What's happening?*

"I don't know," whispered Peter, touching the locket, feeling it pulse twice. He held it for a moment, not daring to pull it out on this busy street. Then he let it go and pushed himself away from the wall. Hunching his shoulders against the cold, he started walking purposefully uphill, away from the water, toward the smoky density of London.

*Where are we going?* asked Tink, from under his shirt.

"To find Molly," said Peter.

*But you don't know where she is.*

"No," said Peter. "I don't. But I know she's here."

CHAPTER 33

# A Way Out

As the gray drizzle of evening sky turned to the murky dark of night, Peter trudged through mud-slick streets, his feet bleeding from cuts he was too cold to feel.

It would be inadequate to say that he was lost, since he'd never known where he was, or where he was going. No, he was far beyond lost. He tried to keep aimed in one direction—away from the river—but the cobblestone streets were a maze, twisting this way and that, sometimes branching off in four or five directions, sometimes stopping in a dead end, forcing Peter to retrace his weary steps. He could have been miles from where he started; he could have been only yards. He simply didn't know.

As night fell, the streets grew less busy. But they were not deserted: Peter encountered other shadowy shapes moving through the fog. Most of them, especially the women and children, scurried past, keeping their distance, their eyes avoiding Peter's. But some of the men and larger boys slowed and gave Peter hard, appraising looks, looks that made him hold his breath and tense his legs, ready to run.

Peter was working his way along a dark, narrow stretch of street when Tinker Bell, under his shirt, emitted a sharp warning sound an instant before Peter sensed something moving to his left. He jumped away from it, an action that saved him; for at that moment, a dark form lunged at him from a pitch-black alley. Peter felt a hand brush his back, the fingers grasping his shirt, trying to get a grip. Peter scrambled forward, jerking free, almost falling, catching himself with his hands on the ground as he stumbled away, hearing a grunt and a curse behind him, then the sound of heavy foot-steps right behind.

Upright again, Peter raced blindly through the fog, hear-ing the hard clomping following him. On and on he ran until, finally, the sound began to fade. Peter came to a cross street, where he turned right and kept running until he could no longer hear the footsteps at all. He finally came to a stop, breathing hard, near a gas streetlight that infused the fog with a ghostly glow.

"Thanks, Tink," he gasped.

*Why didn't you fly?* she demanded.

"I'm attracting too much attention as it is," he said. "If people see me fly, word will spread that there's a flying boy in

London, and Slank and the others could figure out that I'm here. Besides, I got away, didn't I?"

Tink, unable to come up with a counterargument, changed the subject. *I want to get out*, she said. *It smells awful in here.*

"Not yet," he said. "We can't—"

"Who're you talking to?" came a voice from behind him.

Peter whirled and emitted an involuntary yelp of surprise.

"No need for that, mate," said the voice. "It's only me."

In the pale gaslight, Peter saw that the voice belonged to a boy. He was about Peter's height, but considerably huskier. His wide face was streaked with dirt. The boy wore a threadbare coat; it was a man's coat, too big for him, but it looked wonderfully warm to Peter, who was also jealous of the boy's shoes. They were oversized, but far better than bare feet.

"So who was it?" said the boy.

"Who was what?" said Peter.

"Who was you talking to?" said the boy.

"Nobody," said Peter.

The boy stared at him for a few moments. Peter stared back, trying to look confident despite his uncontrollable shivering.

"You're cold?" said the boy.

Peter said nothing, but his chattering teeth were answer enough.

"Come with me, then," said the boy, his tone friendly now. "I know a place where you can warm up. There's food, too. Come on." He started to walk away.

Peter hesitated. The boy stopped and looked back.

"Come on," he repeated. "Do you want to stay out here and freeze to death? Or do you want to be warm?"

Peter, who wanted to be warm more than he'd ever wanted anything, started walking toward the boy. He felt the flutter of a vibration from Tink, but he put his hand gently on his shirt to silence her.

"I'll be careful," he whispered. "He's just a boy, and he seems friendly enough."

"There you go again!" called the boy.

"It's nothing," said Peter. "Talking to myself, is all."

The boy waited until Peter caught up with him, then resumed walking.

"What's your name?" he said.

"Peter. What's yours?"

"Trotter," said the boy.

"Where are we going, Trotter?" asked Peter.

"Just 'round here," said Trotter, turning onto a narrow lane lined with rickety wooden structures leaning this way and that.

"Is it your house?" said Peter.

"Sort of," said Trotter.

He ducked into a narrow, very dark alley between two

buildings. Peter hesitated. Tink vibrated again, and again he quieted her.

"Come on," said Trotter, barely visible in the deep gloom.

Peter moved cautiously forward until he reached Trotter, who continued down the alley, then turned left into an even narrower and darker alley. So complete was the blackness that Peter couldn't see Trotter, or for that matter, his own hands. From somewhere in the buildings around him he heard a baby's cry; from somewhere else, a scream. He bumped into Trotter, who had stopped.

"Sorry," said Peter.

"Here we are," said Trotter. Peter heard the creak of a door opening and felt Trotter push him through the doorway. He found himself in a room smelling strongly of smoke and sweat and filth. But it was, as Trotter had promised, warm, the source of the heat being a glowing bed of coals in an iron grate on the far side of the room.

Small shapes crouched on the dirt floor close to the fire; by its glow Peter saw that they were children, three boys and a girl, wearing clothes not much better than Peter's rags. The girl and one of the boys turned toward him. They examined him for a moment, their expressions vacant, then turned back to the fire.

Peter felt Tinker Bell stirring, but before he could move his hand to stop her, the door closed behind him, and he heard a deep voice rumble, "Who have we here?"

Peter whirled and saw a tall, heavyset man with a thick black beard flecked with pieces of food, above which protruded a sharp, beaklike nose flanked by deep-set eyes.

"His name's Peter," said Trotter.

"Well then, Peter," rumbled the man. "Here you are." His tone was pleasant enough, but it was not matched by the intense look in his eyes.

Peter took a step toward the door, but the man casually sidestepped in front of it, blocking Peter's path.

"Now then, Peter," he said softly. "No need to leave when you just got here, is there? Why don't you go over by the fire there and warm yourself?" He took a step forward. Peter took a step back.

"There's a good lad," said the man, giving Peter a shove that sent him staggering backward. "Sit down there, with them."

Peter hesitated, and instantly felt the man's hand grip his shoulder with painful force, shoving him hard to the floor.

"When I tell you to sit down," the man said, "you sit down." He turned to Trotter and said, "Fetch the supper."

Trotter went to the corner of the room and came back with a filthy cloth sack, which he handed to the man. The man reached in and pulled out a dark loaf of bread. He raised it to his mouth and tore off a large hunk with his crooked brown teeth, chewing it openmouthed, swallowing loudly.

He ate another piece, then another, taking his time, while the children on the floor watched the loaf dwindle. The man finally tore off a large piece and handed it to Trotter, who began eating it greedily.

Less than half of the loaf remained. The man held it out toward the children on the floor.

"Now then," he said. "Who wants supper?"

The children—Peter included—stared at the bread hungrily. Several reached out toward the man.

Slowly, deliberately, the man tore off a piece and tossed it to Peter.

"Company first," he said.

Peter caught the bread and took a bite. It was hard and stale, but he didn't care: it was the first food he'd had for days. He chewed slowly, meaning to make it last.

"Now you," said the man, tossing a piece to one of the boys. "And you, and you," he said, tossing pieces to another boy, and the girl.

That left one boy without bread. The boy, who was sitting next to Peter, looked at the man expectantly. The man tore off a piece of bread and held it toward the boy. The boy reached for it. The man laughed and stuffed the bread into his own mouth.

"None for you," he said, chewing. "You didn't bring me no push today, so you don't get nothing from me."

"But," said the boy, "I was . . . *OWW!*"

The man's heavy boot caught the boy on his ear, sending him sprawling on the floor.

"No back talk," said the man. "I get nothing, you get nothing." He turned to Peter. "Them's the rules here," he said. "You brings me push, I give you something to eat. You understand?"

Eyeing the man's boot, Peter said, "No, sir. What is . . . push?"

"Push," said the man, "is chink."

Peter looked at him blankly.

"It's money," said the man. "You brings me money."

"But," said Peter, "how do I get money?"

"Same way this useless lot does," said the man, gesturing at the other children. "You go griddling."

Peter's look remained puzzled.

"They're mumpers," said the man. "Lurkers. Gegors. Shivering Jemmys."

Peter shook his head.

"They're *beggars*," said the man, growing impatient. "They ask for a copper or two, looking pitiful as can be, poor things. And they brings the coppers back to me, and I gives 'em this nice warm house and a nice supper. That's the arrangement, you see? You takes care of me, and I takes care of you."

"But," said Peter, "I can't. You see I have to get to—" he left the sentence unfinished, seeing the look in the man's eye, the twitch of the man's heavy boot.

"Oh, you can, all right," said the man, very softly now. "You can, and you will. You'll go out with them in the morning, and you'll stay out there all day, and you'll come back at night with some coppers for me, or you'll feel me belt on your back. Show him, Trotter."

Trotter went to the boy sitting next to Peter—the one who'd received no bread—and yanked up the boy's shirt. Peter saw that the boy's back was covered with dark red welts, some oozing blood. Peter looked down.

"And if you're thinking of running away," said the man—correctly guessing what Peter was thinking—"you'd best think again. Trotter and me will be out there keeping an eye on you."

Peter looked up at Trotter, once so friendly, now staring down at him with a look of easy contempt. Peter remembered Old Trumpy's words: *You can't trust nobody out there.*

"If you tries to run," continued the man, "Trotter and me will find you. There's nowhere you can go on these streets where we won't find you, understand? Nowhere. And when we finds you, you'll wish you hadn't run. Ask these others, if you don't believe it."

Peter glanced at the other children; their expressions—a blend of terror and hopelessness—confirmed the man's words.

Peter considered his situation. He could escape from Trotter on the streets tomorrow, but he'd have to fly, and he very much wanted to avoid that. He also couldn't afford to waste any more time, not with the men from the ship looking for Molly.

No, the best thing would be to escape from this place now, tonight, after the man and Trotter were asleep. The door was only across the room. He'd open it quietly, and . . .

"Bedtime, then," said the man, breaking into Peter's thoughts. "You wants to get your rest, because you'll be working hard for me tomorrow. And the next day, and the next." He smiled unpleasantly. "And to make sure you don't get restless in the night . . ."

The man went to the corner, where Peter saw a filthy straw mat. The man grabbed it and dragged it in front of the door. He lay down on it and, looking directly at Peter, said: "There. Now we can all sleep nice and sound."

Then he lay down, his body completely blocking the door, and almost immediately fell asleep. Trotter went to another mattress and did the same. Without saying a word, the other children lay down where they were, curled up on the dirt floor.

In a few minutes, Peter was the only person awake. He stared at the glowing coals, listening to the man's loud, irregular snores, berating himself for being such a fool, wondering if the men had reached Molly's house, and trying desperately to think of a way out of this room.

## CHAPTER 34

# A VISITOR

IT WAS VERY LATE NOW—more morning than night—and Molly had given up on even the hope of sleep.

She'd tried reading by the light of an oil lamp, but she couldn't concentrate. Most of the time she stood looking out her window, watching Mr. Jarvis standing guard in front, under the gas streetlight.

She was watching him when a tap at her door made her jump.

Molly went to the door, expecting to be reprimanded by her mother for being awake at this late hour. When she opened the door she was quite surprised to see the new maid, still in uniform.

"Yes, Jenna?" Molly said. "What is it?"

"I was just wondering if the young lady needed any-thing," said Jenna.

"No, thank you," said Molly. She started to close the

door, but Jenna remained in the doorway, motionless, the intensity of her gaze disconcerting to Molly.

"Is there anything else?" said Molly.

"I was just thinking that, as it's quite late, perhaps the young lady should go to bed."

"Thank you, Jenna," Molly answered stiffly, "but I'm fine."

Jenna stepped forward a half step—almost menacingly, Molly thought.

"But the young lady *should* go to bed," said Jenna, her tone insistent. "To get her rest. I don't think Lady Aster would want to know the young lady was up at this hour."

Molly was shocked by this impertinence, and the implied threat. She allowed her ire to overcome her breeding as she responded with an impertinent question of her own.

"How did you know I was awake?" she said. "And why are *you* up at this hour?"

If Jenna was intimidated—if she felt any emotion at all— she did not betray it in her cool and steady gaze.

"I heard the young lady moving about, and came up to see if the young lady needed anything," she said, ignoring Molly's second question.

"As I told you," Molly said icily, "I do not."

Jenna appeared to be about to say something more, but was apparently dissuaded by Molly's expression.

"Was there anything else?" Molly said, her hand on the door.

"No, ma'am," said Jenna.

"Good night, then," said Molly, closing the door. She stood there, listening, feeling the presence of Jenna twelve inches away on the other side of the door. Finally, after a very long minute, she heard the maid's footsteps leaving.

*What cheek*, thought Molly. She sat on her bed, stewing for a bit, and as her anger subsided, troubling thoughts arose. How could Jenna have heard her moving about? She was sure she hadn't made much noise, and her room, in one of the towers at the top of the house, was a full three floors away from the maids' quarters.

*Why was Jenna awake? Why had she come up? Why was she so insistent that I go to bed?*

She sat there thinking for a few more minutes.

Then she rose and blew out the oil lamp.

Then she went back to the window and resumed watching the street.

# ℐ Walk in the Dark

The five men rode inside the cab of a black, horse-drawn taxi, Ombra and Nerezza on a bouncy bench facing Gerch, "Constable" Hampton, and Slank, the three crammed shoulder to shoulder, facing backward. The sound of the horse hooves *clippity-clop*ping on the cobblestones kept their voices from being overheard by the driver.

Nerezza pulled back the small window curtains. They had ordered the cabbie to take the long way around to the Aster house, avoiding the busier Uxbridge Road in favor of Silver Street and Church Lane. But peering out the window, Nerezza had no idea where they were; he saw only darkness. He took a deep breath; his wooden nose whistled.

Gerch and Hampton tried not to stare at Ombra, but they couldn't help themselves. Ever since the dark shape had appeared on the deck of *Le Fantome*, oozing from below more like a cloud than a man, the two had kept eyes on him, the way the fox never loses track of the hounds.

Both men jumped when the groaning voice spoke, coming from somewhere in the dark-hooded void where Ombra's face should have been: "Describe the situation at the house."

Gerch cleared his throat and straightened his posture. His voice cracked as he said, "Hampton?"

Hampton, not eager to be the object of attention of the dark thing across from him, spoke nervously in a thick Cockney accent. "One out front, name of Jarvis. 'Nother around back called Cadigan. And a third man, Hodge, inside the house."

"The location of the man inside?"

"That there varies night to night, sir," Hampton said. "But we've got a housemaid inside, keeping track for when the time comes."

"The time has come," Ombra said. "Stop the cab."

Nerezza banged his fist on the wall. Immediately the *clippity-clop* slowed, then stopped. Nerezza peered through the curtain. Nerezza saw that they were stopped now near the south end of Kensington Palace Gardens, within walking distance of the Aster mansion. He wondered how Ombra had known, with the curtains drawn, where they were, but he did not intend to ask. He opened the cab door and stepped out, followed by the others.

Nerezza paid the driver, then pressed an extra coin into

his hand and told him to await their return. The cabbie agreed somewhat reluctantly. Something about these passengers made him nervous, and his horse was acting skittish, nearly bolting when the cloaked one had approached the cab.

Church Lane was pitch black and quiet. The chilly air smelled of smoke. With Ombra gliding ahead, the group moved away from the cab, into the night. They turned left onto a broad street, holding to the side away from the string of gas streetlamps.

Halfway up the street, Ombra stopped; the others caught up.

"Mister Slank," groaned Ombra, "you will stay here and keep watch."

Slank nodded and stepped behind a tree, now invisible from the street.

Ombra resumed gliding up the street, passing several more mansions, then stopped as the light in front of the Aster house loomed in the distance. Barely discernible at the edge of its wan glow was the figure of Jarvis, standing guard.

"Mister Gerch," Ombra groaned quietly as the others reached him, "you and Captain Nerezza will remain here, out of sight. I shall signal you when Mister Jarvis is no longer a concern. Constable Hampton, you will lead the way. We'll cross the street here. Don't bother about me. You will walk past and engage Mister Jarvis in conversation. You must make sure that he stands in the light. Do you understand?"

"Yes . . . Yes, sir . . . m'lord," stammered Hampton.

"Not in the shadow, but the light," repeated Ombra. "And when I approach, you make sure his attention is elsewhere."

"Elsewhere," echoed Hampton, twitching his nose like a nervous rat. "Yes, m'lord."

"Go," groaned Ombra.

Hampton stepped into the street, crossing toward the mansion. He glanced over his shoulder to see if Ombra was following him. But he saw only Gerch and Nerezza in the distance; there was no sign of Ombra.

"Go!"

Hampton jumped at the voice, which came from . . . *where?*

Quickly he turned back and resumed walking, feeling the unseen presence behind him, looking ahead at the streetlight and the dark figure of Jarvis. Hampton did not know what was about to happen, but he did know this: he was glad he wasn't Jarvis.

## CHAPTER 36

# A FEW SECONDS

A HALF HOUR AFTER the troubling visit from Jenna, Molly
was still at her window. On the street below, Mr. Jarvis stood
under the lamppost, his thick form casting a thick shadow in
the gas streetlight.

It happened in a few seconds, and although Molly was
watching, her mind could not be certain of what her eyes
had seen.

First there was movement to the right, a form emerging
from the darkness.

The bobby. The same one Molly had seen twice before,
the one with the ill-fitting uniform.

But this time the bobby did not walk past. This time
he stopped directly in front of Mr. Jarvis and said something
to him. Mr. Jarvis said something back. The bobby took
another few steps toward Molly's left, as though walking
away, but then he stopped and said something else.

Mr. Jarvis turned toward the bobby to respond. Thus he didn't see the other man emerge from the fog to the right.

Molly didn't see the man clearly, either: even under the gaslight, he was strangely featureless, dark as the night itself. He moved swiftly, fluidly, to within two feet of Mr. Jarvis, who apparently did not hear anything, his eyes still on the bobby.

The dark man paused only for an instant before flowing back into the night, but in that instant something happened. Mr. Jarvis's shoulders slumped—that much Molly saw clearly. But there was something else, something that she sensed but couldn't quite see—something about the light, and the night. It wasn't right, Molly was certain of that, but she didn't know exactly why.

A second later it was over: the bobby turned and disappeared into the fog. Now Mr. Jarvis again stood alone in the circle of gaslight. Slowly he raised his head, and in a moment, he—and the scene outside—appeared just as it had before.

But Molly, watching from her window, felt a deep unease. Something had happened. Something was wrong.

## CHAPTER 37

# "I'll Find You"

THE ROOM WAS NEARLY dark now, the coal fire casting only a dull reddish glow. Peter stared at the dying embers, trying to think of a plan.

Tink stuck her head out of the top of Peter's shirt. She looked around, her gaze taking in the sleeping forms of the man and the children. She eased herself out and stood on Peter's shoulder, close to his right ear. In very soft tones, she said: *We're going to go now.*

Peter looked at the man sleeping in front of the door.

"How?" he whispered.

*Listen,* said Tink, and, leaning close to Peter's ear, she explained her plan. Peter frowned at first, then began to nod. When she was done, he couldn't help but smile; it amazed him sometimes, the amount of thinking that went on inside Tink's tiny head.

*Ready?* said Tink.

Peter nodded again and stood up quietly. Tinker Bell fluttered to the low ceiling and grabbed a wooden beam just above Peter's head, pressing herself flat against it. Peter took a deep breath.

Then he began to shout at the top of his lungs.

"OWWWWW!" he yelled. "MY HAIR IS ON FIRE!"

Immediately the sleeping man was awake.

"What?" he bellowed, getting to his feet. "What is it?"

"MY HAIR!" yelled Peter. "YOWWW!"

The man blinked, his eyes seeking Peter in the gloom. Now Trotter was on his feet as well. They began moving toward him. Peter waited until he was sure they were both looking at him, noted their positions, then spun around, facing away from them, and closed his eyes tightly.

"NOW!" he shouted.

Even through his eyelids, Peter saw it, the flash of brilliant white light that filled the room for a full second, like silent lightning.

He felt Tink's exhausted body drop to his shoulders, her energy, for the moment, spent.

Go, she chimed weakly. Go.

Opening his eyes in the once-again dark room, Peter spun and saw the man and Trotter both frozen statue-still, blinking, stunned, and blinded by the light. Running on tiptoes, Peter shot between them to the door. Their backs were still to him as he reached the door and found the latch. He lifted it and pushed the door. The latch rattled . . . but the door did not open.

The man, hearing the rattle, cocked his head.

*Hurry*, said Tink, clinging to Peter's neck.

"He's at the door!" shouted the man, suddenly turning. Still blind, waving his arms in front of him, he moved cautiously toward Peter, Trotter right behind him.

*Hurry.*

Peter yanked hard upward on the latch; this time he felt the door give. He pushed it open and lunged through it just as the man, roaring with rage, reached it.

Peter was in the alley now. He ran to his right. A second later, he heard footsteps behind him. His advantage was gone now: the alley was pitch black, so Peter was as blind as his pursuers. But unlike Peter, they were familiar with the alley.

Peter stumbled on something, sprawling forward on his face. He jumped up. The footsteps were upon him now.

*Fly*, said Tink, but Peter had already flung himself desperately upward. He felt his heels brush against something hairy—the man's beard—and then felt a hand grab his ankle. He kicked hard and heard a grunt, and then he was free.

"Get him," roared the man's voice. "He's climbing the wall. GET HIM."

A scuffling noise, then Trotter's voice. "He ain't here."

"I felt him!" shouted the man. "He went up right here."

"Well, he ain't here now," said Trotter.

Above them, unseen and seeing nothing himself, Peter rose tentatively in the narrow space between two buildings. Finally he cleared the roofs and began drifting away toward the pale sphere of a gaslight in the distance. From behind and below, he heard the man's enraged bellow.

"I'll find you!" he yelled. "You won't get away from me, not in London. I'll find you!"

## CHAPTER 38

# THE SHADOW THIEF

HAMPTON WAS NOT a man who was easily surprised. He'd worked for the Others before; he knew they had unusual powers, and he'd seen some strange things.

But he had never seen anything like what Ombra did to the guard under the streetlight in front of the Aster house. As he followed Ombra around to the side of the house, he still didn't know exactly *what* he'd seen. He stole a look back over his shoulder at Jarvis, standing beneath the streetlamp, not moving a muscle. Hampton returned his gaze to the dark shape gliding ahead. He wondered who, or what, was under that cloak. He was not at all certain that he wanted to know.

They rounded the corner of the house, and Ombra stopped, nearly invisible in the blackness. He turned to face Hampton, who felt a chill and turned slightly away, unable to look directly at the void under the hood.

"You understand my instructions?" Ombra groaned, barely audibly.

"Yes, m'lord," whispered Hampton. "But making him cast a shadow could be a tricky thing, dark as it is."

"I don't need much, and I don't need long," the voice groaned. "You smell like a man who smokes."

Hampton frowned, trying to make sense of this remark. Then it hit him. "Ah, I see, m'lord," he said, smiling despite his nervousness. "Perhaps Cadigan likes a bit of tobacco himself."

"Perhaps he does," groaned Ombra. "Keep his back turned to me. You'll know when it has happened."

"Right," said Hampton. He straightened his tall bobby's hat and fixed the ill-fitting uniform coat, then started toward the back of the huge, dark house, staying near the shrubbery as he walked down the cobblestone drive.

Rounding the corner of the house, he turned toward the service entrance, and permitted himself another smile: Cadigan did, indeed, smoke. Hampton smelled pipe tobacco even before he saw Cadigan's large form looming ahead.

"Who goes there?" Cadigan's voice was low and husky.

"Constable Hampton."

"What's your business?"

"Are you Cadigan, then?"

"Might be." Cadigan's tone was suspicious, unwelcoming.

"Mister Jarvis said I might have a word with you."

"Did he, then?" said Cadigan.

"That he did," said Hampton.

"Well, you've had your word, *Constable*. I'll ask you to return in the morning when I'm not on duty here."

Hampton kept walking. He needed to get past Cadigan, to turn him. But the big man moved, cutting him off. Cadigan clearly had no mind to allow a stranger—constable or no—between him and the kitchen door.

"Tomorrow, if you don't mind," Cadigan said, the politeness of his words belied by the menace in his voice.

"You mind if I smoke?" Hampton said, and before Cadigan could answer, he bent and scratched a long wooden matchstick on the side of his shoe. In the oppressive darkness the match seemed to explode, its yellow light flashing across the faces of both men. Cadigan was younger than his voice suggested. He had a broad forehead, closely cut red hair, and a thick neck. Hampton stuck a small cigar into his mouth and brought the match up with a quick and practiced motion. He sucked the cigar to life and exhaled a cloud of gray smoke that enveloped Cadigan, then was absorbed by the night.

"The thing is," he said, still holding the burning matchstick, "this here can't wait 'til morning."

Cadigan was smelling the cigar smoke, eyeing the match flame. As Hampton had hoped, Cadigan allowed his tobacco habit to overcome his reserve. He reached into his pocket and pulled out his pipe.

"D'you mind?" he asked, nodding toward the match.

"Not at all," said Hampton. Cadigan stepped close to share the flame. As he did, Hampton turned him fully around.

Cadigan sucked on the pipe. The flame grew, throwing off another burst of light. Hampton, looking over Cadigan's shoulder, saw a black shape flow swiftly across the drive, toward Cadigan's flickering shadow.

"I was told to deliver a warning," Hampton said.

"About what?" Cadigan said, again drawing on his pipe. The flame was nearing Hampton's fingers now, but he dared not let go.

Ombra's cape glided silently, swiftly toward Cadigan's shadow. Hampton watched this movement. Cadigan saw Hampton's eyes shift, and immediately spun around.

Too late.

Cadigan moaned as his shadow elongated and stretched like a water drop, moving away from him and toward the base of Ombra's cape, until only a thin neck of shadow touched Cadigan's feet. It seemed to cling to him, as if not wanting to let go; then it broke away, like a piece of taffy stretched too thin. The entire shadow raced to Ombra, forming a dark pool beneath him. Ombra lifted his right sleeve, and the shadow—writhing as though resisting capture—flowed upward to where Ombra's hand would be, though Hampton, watching all this closely, could not see a hand.

For an instant, Ombra held the shadow as a man would hold a snake. Then his left sleeve came up, a burlap sack dangling from it. The right arm seemed to wrestle with the unwilling, shifting shadow, stuffing it into the open sack until it disappeared. Then the sack vanished into the robe.

Ombra spun around, one full circle. As he did, a new shadow appeared on the ground in front of him—although there was no light behind him. The shadow slithered, serpentlike, across the ground. It attached itself to Cadigan's feet just as the match flickered to extinction.

Darkness.

Hampton heard himself breathing heavily. Cadigan stood motionless in front of him.

"Mister Cadigan," groaned Ombra, "you will resume your duties."

"Yes, m'lord," Cadigan responded tonelessly. He moved back to the doorway.

"Shall I summon the housemaid?" Hampton asked.

The hood of the cape lifted toward the sky. "No," said Ombra. "It will soon be dawn. We must return to the ship."

Ombra addressed the statue-still figure in the doorway. "Mister Cadigan."

"Yes, m'lord," answered the toneless voice.

"We will visit you and Mister Jarvis again tomorrow night. You will assist us with Mister Hodge and the women."

"As you wish, m'lord," said Cadigan.

"Yes," said Ombra. "Exactly as I wish."

Then he turned and, with Hampton hurrying behind, disappeared into the darkness.

## CHAPTER 39

# The Market

$\mathcal{P}$ETER, WITH AN EXHAUSTED Tinker Bell clutching tightly to his shirt, flew low over the dark city until, judging that he was a safe distance from the man, he alit on the peak of a steeply pitched roof. There he crouched, shivering.

"Are you all right?" he said.

*Yes,* answered Tink. *But tired.*

"That was a good plan you had back there," he said.

*Yes, it was.*

They went quiet for a while, recovering. In the east, the black of the night began to soften to a dark gray; dawn was coming as a slight glow through the coal smoke. Peter looked around and saw that he was atop a tallish building, standing alone. To one side was a railroad track; to the other an open square with rows of stalls, apparently some kind of market.

Peter was grateful that the nightmarish night was finally

ending, but he dared not let daylight catch him perched in so visible a spot. Sitting down, he slid to the edge of the roof, then dropped gently down to the square. No sooner had his bare feet touched the dirt than he began to hear sounds of the awakening day; a cough, voices, barking, cart wheels rumbling on cobblestones.

Peter tucked the protesting Tinker Bell under his shirt and walked down a row of stalls to a low stone wall separating the square from the street. It occurred to him that a market might be a good place to find food. He sat on the wall, his plan for the moment being to wait there until the sellers arrived, in hopes he might be able to beg or borrow a bite to eat, and then see if anybody could tell him the way to Lord Aster's house.

Soon enough the sellers began to arrive in ones and twos, bringing their wares in by hand and on pushcarts. But it wasn't food they were selling: it was . . . animals.

Peter and Tink had landed in a pet market, on a street called Brick Lane. The carts were stacked with cages, inside which were all sorts of small animals—dogs, cats, guinea pigs, turtles, snakes, lizards, chattering monkeys, and birds. Most of all, birds. Hundreds and hundreds of birds, big and small, native and exotic, bright and drab, sometimes dozens to a cage, twittering, trilling, tweeting, screeching.

To Peter, it was a meaningless cacophony. But not to Tink. Tink understood the birds perfectly, and what they

were saying did not please her at all. Peter felt a vibration, and then Tink's tiny, furious face poked from his collar. Quickly he covered her with his hand.

"Get back in there," he hissed.

*They want out,* she said.

"Tink, we can't—"

*They're hungry and scared. They want to fly.*

"But we—"

Peter's protest was too late. Tink had escaped through his fingers and was streaking toward a small, wiry man pushing a cart with four large cages filled with canaries, twittering and flitting around like bright yellow leaves whipped by a late-autumn wind.

"Come back!" called Peter, his voice drawing the attention of the wiry man, who turned away from his cage to look at Peter just as Tink darted past him and landed next to one of his cages. Her motion caught the man's eye, and he began to turn back toward the cart.

"No!" yelled Peter, drawing the man's narrow-set eyes back to him. He was sallow-faced and thin-lipped, with strands of oil-brown hair plastered to his forehead. Peter saw that, behind the man, Tink had found the cage door and was fiddling with the latch.

"What is it?" said the man, annoyed.

Peter tried frantically to think of something to say. Tink had the cage door open now and had stuck her head inside.

She was communicating something, somehow, to the birds, who had stopped twittering and were listening to her intently, heads cocked.

"I . . . ah . . ." Peter said to the man, "I say, it's a nice day, isn't it?"

The man looked at the sky, which was a dull, smoky gray, threatening to rain. He gave Peter a venomous look, spat on the ground, and turned back to his cart.

And saw Tink.

The man shot out his hand with the quickness and precision of one skilled in capturing small flying creatures. In an instant, Tink was caught. Peter saw Tink's head poking from the top of the man's right fist as he heard a terrified burst of bells.

*Help! Peter, help!*

But Peter was already running toward the man. "Put her down! She's mine!" he shouted. "Put her . . . *UH*."

As quickly as the man's right hand had grabbed Tink, his left fist shot out, catching Peter on his cheek. Peter's head snapped sideways, and he saw a flash of light. Then, without being aware of falling, he was lying on his back in the dirt, the right side of his face throbbing in pain.

Above him he saw the man holding Tink's struggling form close to his face, examining her. Then, after glancing down at Peter, he thrust her into the canary cage and closed the door.

Peter, woozy, his face afire with pain, struggled unsteadily to his feet.

"Let her go!" he shouted at the man. "You can't keep her! She's not yours!"

"Now she is," the man said softly. "She's all mine." He stared at her, intrigued. "But *what* is she? Ain't never seen one like her."

Peter lunged toward the cage again, but the man was too quick, and far too strong. He stepped in front of Peter and, grabbing him by the shoulders, hurled him to the ground again. The man then covered the canary cage with a piece of canvas, tying it tightly in place with a piece of rope. From within, Peter could hear the muffled sound of Tink's frantic appeals for help.

Yet again he got to his feet, standing just out of the man's reach.

"Please," he begged the man. "*Please.* Let her go."

"If you know what's good for you," said the man, taking a menacing step toward Peter, "you'll get out of here."

"No!" shouted Peter, though he took a step back. "Let her go!"

By now a half dozen other merchants had wandered over to find out what the noise was about. Peter turned to them.

"He's got my . . . my bird," he said, pointing to the wiry man. "He stole my bird!"

The man shook his head as he turned to the other sellers. He addressed them calmly, the voice of reason. "Do you believe the cheek of this one?" he said. "He tries to steal one of me canaries, and then he calls me the thief! Me, who's worked this market for ten years and more!"

The other sellers, all of whom knew the man, shook their heads at the sorry state of modern youth.

"It's not true!" said Peter desperately. "He's lying!" Seeing that nobody in the crowd believed him, he ignored his throbbing cheek and hurled himself again toward the cage. The wiry man was waiting for him. He grinned with satisfaction as he drove his fist deep into Peter's stomach.

Peter went down on all fours, unable to breathe, the pain in his belly almost unendurable. The pet sellers roared with laughter. After a few moments, Peter was able to draw in some air in small, tortured gasps. He raised his head, saw the wiry man laughing with the others, saw the canvas-covered cage, heard Tink's faint, frantic calls from within.

With agonizing effort, Peter staggered to his feet and again lunged forward, this time managing to reach the cage. He took hold of it just as the wiry man grabbed him, pulling back his fist to deliver another blow to Peter's face.

"Here now!" boomed a new, deeply authoritative voice. "What's this all about?"

The wiry man dropped his fist. He and Peter turned to

find themselves facing a police officer, a large man sporting a luxuriant walrus moustache.

"He's a thief," said the wiry man, pointing to Peter holding the cage. "Tried to steal me best canaries, he did." The wiry man appealed to the other pet sellers, who nodded in sober confirmation.

"A thief, is it?" said the bobby, grabbing Peter by his shirt collar. "Hand it over, then," he said.

"But she's *mine*!" said Peter. "I . . . OW!"

He was silenced by a sharp poke in the ribs from the bobby's stick.

"You save your talk for the magistrate," said the bobby sternly. "Not that he'll want to hear it neither."

This witticism drew a hearty laugh from the pet sellers.

"Come along, then," said the bobby. He yanked the birdcage away from Peter and handed it back to the seller.

*Peter?* In the noise of the market, only Peter heard the muffled bells. He stepped toward the cage again, only to be jerked violently away by the bobby, who began dragging him down the street, away from the market. Peter tried to jump—hoping, in desperation, to fly his way free of this predicament—but the bobby's massive hand held his arm in an iron grip.

As they reached the end of Brick Lane, Peter took a last

glance back at the pet seller, who was watching him and smiling, as he tied a second rope around his now-precious canary cage. The last thing Peter heard, as he lost sight of the market, was the distant, muffled, desperate sound of bells.

## CHAPTER 40

# THE FEAR IN HER EYES

MOLLY AWOKE TO A tapping on her door. She had finally fallen asleep just before dawn, and wanted nothing more than to snuggle deeper beneath her warm comforter. But the tapping persisted.

"Miss Aster!" called an unwelcome voice. "Miss Aster!"

Molly groaned and, throwing off the comforter, rose from her bed and padded in bare feet across the cold floor. She opened the door to find herself looking into the piercing eyes of Jenna.

"Lady Aster says she wants you down to breakfast," said Jenna.

Molly stared back for a moment, remembering Jenna's odd visit to her room just a few hours earlier. She wondered if Jenna—who looked wide awake—had slept at all.

"Tell her I'll be right down," Molly said curtly, closing the door.

She dressed quickly and went downstairs to the breakfast room, where she found her mother seated at the table, a half-finished breakfast in front of her, a reproving look on her face.

"I'm sorry, Mother," Molly said, sitting down. "I couldn't get to sleep last night. There was the strangest . . ."

She stopped in midsentence as Jenna entered the room, carrying a plate of eggs, which she set in front of Molly. Molly remained silent as Jenna bowed slightly and left the room. Louise Aster looked at her daughter expectantly.

"Yes?" she prompted. "The strangest what?"

Molly looked toward the doorway through which Jenna had just departed. Lowering her voice to a whisper, she said, "Last night—"

She was interrupted by an outburst of furious barking from the rear of the house, soon joined by loud shouts. Molly and her mother looked at each other, then jumped up and hurried out of the breakfast room and down the hall. Following the noise, they passed by the kitchen and into the staff dining room.

Inside they found a frantic scene:

Hornblower, normally a placid dog, was in a raging fury, his huge teeth bared in a fierce snarl as he barked furiously and lunged at Mr. Jarvis and Mr. Cadigan. The two men stood near the far wall, eyeing the dog, their faces pale in the bright gaslight; Molly thought their expressions were oddly

impassive, almost vacant, considering how close they were to the snapping jaws. The third guard, Mr. Hodge, was desperately trying to hold Hornblower back, gripping his collar with both hands. Hodge was a large man, but Hornblower was a large dog, and Hodge was just barely able to restrain him.

Finally, with great effort, Hodge was able to get a leash on Hornblower and drag him outside, where he tied the leash to a tree. He returned to the dining room, red-faced and panting, and sat at the table. Jarvis and Cadigan remained standing by the wall, neither having moved. Several servants, including Jenna, had come to see what the fuss was about.

Louise Aster addressed the three guards. "What on earth was that about?" she said.

Hodge shot a look at the other two men—an odd look, Molly thought—then spoke.

"I don't know, ma'am," he said. "I had Hornblower in the room with me last night—it was my night off—and when we came downstairs, as soon as he saw Mister Jarvis and Mister Cadigan, why, he just went mad. I don't understand it." Again, he looked at Jarvis and Cadigan. "He's never done anything like that before. He knows them well as he knows me."

"I see," said Mrs. Aster. "Mister Jarvis? Mister Cadigan? Have you an idea what's gotten into the dog?"

The two men shook their heads, but neither spoke. This was odd, Molly thought: both Jarvis and Cadigan were usually talkative.

"I see," said Mrs. Aster, and Molly noticed that she, too, seemed a bit puzzled by the reticence of the two men. "Well then," she went on, "I suppose it's best to keep Hornblower outside until he calms down."

Hodge nodded. Jarvis and Cadigan remained motionless.

"Well then," repeated Mrs. Aster as the silence became awkward. "Molly, let's finish our breakfast."

She left the room. Molly followed, feeling Jenna's eyes on her as she walked past the servants. Molly felt tired and confused. Everything seemed wrong: Jenna's behavior; the strange events she'd seen by the gaslight last night; Hornblower's sudden hostility to Jarvis and Cadigan; and their uncharacteristic passivity. There was something else about them as well—Molly frowned, thinking of the two of them against the wall—yes, there had definitely been something strange about the way they looked, though at the moment she couldn't quite identify it.

Molly followed her mother to the breakfast room, determined to voice her concerns.

"Mother," she said as they sat down. "There's something wrong."

"I know," said her mother quietly.

"You do?" said Molly.

"Yes," said her mother. "But we can't talk about it now." She tilted her head slightly toward the doorway; as she did, Jenna glided past.

"Mother," whispered Molly, "I'm scared."

"It's all right," her mother said, putting her hand on Molly's. "We'll be all right."

The words were reassuring, but Molly was not persuaded by them. She heard the strain in her mother's voice. And she saw the fear in her eyes.

CHAPTER 41

# $\mathcal{P}$LAY $\mathcal{I}$T $\mathcal{S}$AFE

CAPTAIN NEREZZA SIPPED warm tea from a battered mug, staring at Slank over the rising steam. They sat at the large table in the center of the captain's oversized cabin. The wan light of dawn flowed through the row of windows at the stern. A small cannon, useful as a stern chaser during combat at sea, was strapped to the wall, its brass gleaming.

Outside on the quay, weary sailors, awakened too early, rolled barrels, while others cursed and shouted as they struggled to maneuver nets filled with heavy cargo. Some sailors, having overdone the grog, slept against the wall of the Jolly Tar; one was passed out in a wheelbarrow. A typical morning on St. Katherine's dock.

"I don't like it," Slank said. "We were so close."

Nerezza said, "We have two of the three guards now. He knows what he's doing."

"We should have finished it," Slank complained. "We

should have charged in there. Who was going to stop us?"

"That's just it," said Nerezza. "We don't know, do we?"

"There were five of us! And with the two guards taken—"

"—and a third guard, we don't know where," Nerezza added calmly. "There're the other servants in the house that need taking care of. Ombra's got plans for that. And time's running short, and dawn coming. And that ain't all."

"What d'you mean?"

"You've had a small taste of what them Starcatchers can do," Nerezza said.

Slank winced at the memory of how he had been bested by the flying boy back on the island.

"I shouldn't have to tell you," continued Nerezza, "what even a boy can do if he has hold of the starstuff. Now, inside that house you have a mother and daughter, true enough. But not a normal mother and daughter, eh, Mister Slank? Not considering the father. No, them is Starcatchers. Maybe they can fly, like the boy. If they can, what good is storming in on them if they take off out the window like a pair of birds? Maybe they got powers we ain't seen yet, eh? That's what Ombra's thinking, I tell you. He don't intend to come all this way to lose them by rushing things. No, he wants to deal with that third guard, put the odds in our favor, give us the advantage when we go after Mrs. Aster and the girl, y'see? So I'd be patient if I was you, Mister Slank, unless, of course, you fancy to be the first one he sends through that door and into that house."

Slank nodded, seeing Nerezza's point. He looked out the window, pondering. Mention of the Starcatchers and the flying boy reminded him of the bone he'd found in the sail, and his suspicions. He wondered if now wasn't the time to tell Nerezza that there might be still another Starcatcher in London, maybe inside the Aster house. The thought dangled there on the tip of Slank's tongue, but he could not spit it out, for fear Nerezza would think him a fool.

Nerezza saw the worry on Slank's face. "What is it?" he said.

There it was: an invitation for Slank to reveal his suspicions.

But instead, Slank said, "I don't want to be the first one into that house. You're right about that."

"You and me both," Nerezza said.

"So we wait for tonight," Slank said.

"Right," said Nerezza. "We play it safe. And by the time the woman and the girl know we're there, it'll be too late." He took another sip of tea, heavily sugared, the way he liked it. He savored its sweetness as he swallowed.

"Too late," he said again.

## CHAPTER 42

# THE STANDOFF

THE JAIL CELL REEKED of vomit and menace. Peter sat in a corner, where he'd remained since the bobby had shoved him in there, trying his best not to be noticed by the others.

There were eleven of them: three boys younger—or at least smaller—than Peter, five boys older, and three men. Peter wasn't so worried about the men: all three were drunk and seemed mostly interested in sleeping, although one had awakened long enough to empty the contents of his stomach onto himself and onto the floor, filling the cell with an acrid stench before he fell back into a deep, snoring slumber.

No, it was the older boys who concerned Peter. They were already in the cell when he'd been brought in, and they seemed quite familiar with it, almost comfortable there. They apparently knew each other, or had at least formed into a hierarchy, as packs of males do. Their leader was not the tallest among them, but definitely the broadest: a brutish, muscular boy the others called Rafe. He amused himself by tormenting the smaller boys, punching them and threatening to stuff them headfirst into the disgustingly full wooden bucket that served as the cell's communal toilet.

Peter desperately hoped that he would not have to use that bucket; the thought repulsed him. He hoped, too, that Rafe would continue ignoring him. Peter kept his eyes cast down, not meeting anyone's gaze. His mood had descended to a level below despair: he had no idea how to get himself out of this, let alone rescue Tink or find Molly in time to warn her of the danger she was in. He had no hope at all. His stomach ached and his swollen jaw throbbed with agonizing pain.

"You," said a menacing voice.

Peter looked up, and his heart sank at the sight of Rafe's thick form looming over him.

"What?" he said.

"You got anything for me?" said Rafe. He squatted in front of Peter, his wide, grinning face only a foot away.

Peter said nothing. Why did everyone in this city want something from him?

Casually, Rafe reached his meaty hand out. Peter flinched as Rafe grabbed a handful of Peter's filthy, torn shirt.

Rafe made a disappointed face. "Can't use these pitiful rags," he said. Then he brightened as he spied the gold chain around Peter's neck. Peter inwardly berated himself for not having thought to hide it.

"Here now," Rafe said, pulling the chain out and fingering the locket. "What's this?"

Peter pushed Rafe's hand aside and jumped to his feet, moving along the wall, away from Rafe. He couldn't give up the locket. No matter what, he must not let that happen.

Rafe appeared surprised by the show of defiance, but pleased at the prospect of having some sport with his prey. He rose to his feet, smiling.

"So," he said, moving slowly toward Peter. "You want to tussle with Rafe, do you?"

Peter continued to edge along the wall, looking frantically around the cell. He saw he'd get no help from the drunks, who were sleeping, and none from the other boys, who were watching with the expressions of spectators at an execution: they were clearly grateful that somebody else was the victim.

Rafe advanced toward Peter. Peter slid sideways along the cell wall. He reached the corner; there was nowhere to go. Rafe was a yard away, smiling broadly, bringing his fists up, ready to begin the pummeling.

Peter felt his foot hit something. He looked down and saw it: the toilet bucket.

He reached down and grabbed the handle with his right hand, swinging the bucket up to waist level. The stench was almost overpowering, but Peter was driven by desperation now. He put his left hand on the bottom of the bucket and drew it back, ready to hurl its repulsive contents at Rafe.

Rafe stopped, his smug expression replaced by one of surprise, and—Peter was relieved to see—an undercurrent of fear.

"You wouldn't dare," he said.

"Yes, I would," replied Peter.

They stood facing each other in the silent cell, staring into each other's eyes for the better part of a very long minute. It was Rafe who blinked first.

"All right," he said, backing away. "You stand there in the stink." He settled down on the other side of the cell. "But soon enough you'll get tired. Soon enough you'll fall asleep. And then I'll have that thing around your neck." He hurled a hate-filled glare at Peter. "And I'll have your neck, too," he added.

Peter didn't answer. He stood in the corner, holding the bucket, enveloped in foul fumes. He would not allow his face to betray his feelings. But he knew that Rafe was right: he could not hold out forever.

## CHAPTER 43

# THUNDER DOWN THE TRAIL

$\mathcal{A}$ PIRATE NAMED CHAMBERS led the hunting party, a group of able-bodied sailors armed with swords and bamboo spears tipped with sharpened shells. They moved smartly, knowing Hook was watching from his position on the mountainside.

They trudged through the humid, thick jungle, dodging snakes as thick as an arm and spiders the size of a fist. Chambers posted a man or two at various points on the jungle paths, according to Hook's plan. By the time the hunting party had reached the herd of wild boars that Hook had seen earlier, it was down to Chambers and three others.

About a dozen of the huge, hairy, tusked beasts wallowed at the edge of a shallow watering hole, more mud than water. Chambers, using arm gestures so as not to spook the boars, positioned his men in a semicircle around one side of the watering hole. When they were set, he used the polished metal of his belt buckle to reflect a beam of sunlight toward the mountain. Then he waited.

Hook saw Chambers's ready signal, and nearly allowed a smile to bend his moustache across his face. But not yet. He observed all: the jungle treetops, the boys' hut, the paths. Squinting to his right, with some effort, he caught a glimpse of Hurky and more of his men concealed in the jungle on both sides of the trail that led past the hut. By now they would have laid the fishing net on the ground, stretching it across the path. Hook's brilliant plan was coming together.

Hook drew his sword from his belt, angled the flat of its blade into the sun, and sent a blinding flash back in the direction of Chambers. Another: two quick flashes in a row. Then he watched as Chambers went to work.

———

Chambers nodded as Hook's double signal blinked from the mountainside. He rose and waved his hand, issuing the silent command. The other three men stood, and all four of them began whooping and shouting as loud as they could. Then, pointing their spears and swords in front of them, they charged toward the wallowing boars.

This was the critical moment, because the boars might react by attacking, and if they did, they would likely tear the men to pieces. When Chambers had pointed this out to Captain Hook, Hook had boldly declared that this was a risk he was willing to take.

And so, despite the fierce faces of the shouting men, there was fear in their hearts as they saw the boars lift their heads. The hairy beasts snorted and pawed the mud, clearly considering charging. Then, to the great relief of the men, the boars turned and ran. The ground shook with their retreat; mud flew from their hooves.

———◆———

From his mountainside lookout, Hook watched delightedly as, to his left, Chambers startled the boars. The beasts took off racing down the jungle trail, heads low. At the first intersection of trails, the boars encountered a nervous pirate pointing a spear; they veered to the right, just as Hook had drawn it up. He lost them for a few seconds to the thick jungle treetops, but then the herd reappeared, running even faster, their hooves tossing up a brown cloud of dirt clods behind them.

At the next junction of jungle paths, a pair of pirates surprised the boars and turned them again. Now the animals were headed right for the thatched hut where the boys lived.

Hook chortled and finally grinned, his brown teeth showing beneath his famous foot-wide moustache as he half whispered, "I have you now, you little devils."

James felt it before he heard it.

"Run!" he shouted.

"What?" asked Prentiss, who was putting the finishing touches on a length of bamboo. The boys were currently working to improve the bamboo gutters that hung from their hut and collected rain water. When working properly, the storage system saved them repeated bucket trips to the spring-fed well dug by the Mollusks.

"Run!" repeated James. "The hideout!"

This time nobody questioned him, because now they could all feel it, and hear it: a deep rumbling sound quickly getting louder and closer. The boys dropped what they were doing and took off running away from the sound, down the jungle path and toward their hideout.

The thunder gained on them; they could not outrun it. James and Thomas, the quickest of the boys, reached the hideout first. James pulled the plant out of the way of the door. Thomas dove down the hole into the ground, face-first, with James right behind.

But as Prentiss and Tubby Ted reached the secret cave, the snorting, stampeding beasts were right on their heels, and the two boys dared not slow down. They passed the cave's secret entrance, running as fast as they could, Prentiss in the lead. They followed the jungle trail around the corner . . .

. . . and ran smack into a tangle of rope.

The rope stopped Prentiss, and Tubby Ted slammed into him from behind, the two of them falling over onto the trail. Prentiss looked back to see the oncoming boars, now only yards away, and he knew he was about to be trampled and killed.

But just then he felt the ropes tightening. Then he and Tubby Ted skidded sideways across the trail's hard-packed dirt, just as the boars reached them.

The frantic boars roared past in a blur of hairy hides and a mighty pounding of hooves. The sound faded and, in a few moments, was gone.

Prentiss, who had shut his eyes in terror, opened them, amazed to find himself ensnared in a net, along with Tubby Ted. They were saved! How lucky they were to have been caught in this net, no doubt intended for the boars!

But his mood changed quickly as he found himself face-to-face with a pockmarked pirate. The man opened his toothless mouth and laughed. His breath stung Prentiss' eyes.

———◆◆———

Hook observed all this from his mountain perch: he saw the boys take off running; he saw the boars rip past the hut—one of the animals running right through the hut, breaking a hole through the back wall of sticks, and dragging a pair of pants on his head.

Hook lost sight of the boys briefly, but then saw two of them run right into his net. They were swiftly hauled to the side of the trail as the boars ran past.

Chambers and the others, following the boars, caught up to the group with the boys. Chambers flashed his belt buckle at Hook, signaling success.

Hook flashed back with the flat of his sword: first one, then another, and finally a third. This three-flash signal warned that a patrol of Mollusks had left the compound and was quickly approaching. The pirates had to hurry.

And hurry they did.

The last thing Hook saw, before the jungle swallowed them entirely, was his sailors carrying a netted bundle over their heads at a steady trot.

And in that net were two young boys. Hook would rather have had four, but two would do for his purposes.

Oh, yes, he had plans for those two.

## CHAPTER 44

# THE COLLECTOR

THE BIRD SELLER'S NAME, as fate would have it, was Isaac
Wren. Others found his surname amusing, but Wren himself
did not. He rarely found amusement in anything: he was a
serious man, a man who never laughed, and who smiled—a
thin smile, at that—only when he got the best of an opponent in a business transaction. This was not uncommon, for
Wren was a clever dealer, a shrewd bargainer who could tell
at a glance how much a bird was worth, and what he could
get for it.

Of course, he had never seen anything like Tinker Bell.
But in the few moments he'd held her in his hand—had seen
the astonishing beauty of her tiny, delicate, terrified face,
and had heard the celestial sounds she made—he knew this
was a creature that would come along only once in a lifetime,
if that.

Wren meant to make the best of this opportunity.

Whatever this wondrous creature was, he was determined to part with it as a rich man. And he meant to sell it quickly, because he was certain that such a valuable thing must belong to somebody. The boy must have stolen it. Its rightful owner would be looking for it, Wren was certain. He intended to be rid of the creature before that owner appeared.

And so, from the moment the bobby had dragged off the annoying boy, Wren had loaded his birdcages—including the precious one wrapped in canvas—back onto his cart, and left Brick Lane. He went directly to the home of Lord Welton Pondle, a very wealthy man with whom he had dealt in the past. Pondle was one of London's most avid collectors of rare animals; he was well known among animal dealers for his willingness to pay handsome sums for hard-to-get specimens.

Pondle also—and this was why Wren went to him first—did not mind buying animals of questionable ownership. If a rare and valuable animal had been reported stolen from one collector and a remarkably similar animal happened to be offered to Lord Pondle a short while later, he would pay the asking price, no questions asked.

And so, in just over an hour after the disturbance at the pet market, Isaac Wren sat in Pondle's massive den, the canvas-covered canary cage on the floor in front of him. One wall of the den was a large stone fireplace with a coal fire burning in the grate, warding off the London chill. Two of the other walls of the room were lined with the heads, and sometimes the entire bodies, of rare, stuffed animals, many of which Pondle had killed himself. The fourth wall was almost completely covered with cases containing Pondle's very large collection of butterflies; hanging in the center was the net he had used to capture them.

After waiting for fifteen minutes, Wren heard a muttering in the hallway and quickly rose to his feet. He bowed deeply as Pondle waddled through the doorway. Pondle was a heavy man, with most of his weight concentrated toward his center, forming a vast waistline. He was tapered at both ends, with tiny feet and a small, pointed head. He had a capuchin monkey named Edgar sitting on his shoulder.

Edgar wore a collar connected by a thin silver chain to a bracelet on Pondle's left wrist. Neither Pondle nor Edgar looked happy to see Wren.

"What is it?" Pondle said, ignoring Wren's bow. "You realize you're keeping me from a meeting of the Newt and Salamander Fanciers Group?"

"I'm sorry, Your Lordship," said Wren, "but I believe when you see what I've brought you"—he pointed to the covered cage—"you'll agree that it was well worth your time. This here is something you won't see in no other collection in London. Not in all of England neither, for that matter."

"Really?" said Pondle, his annoyance grudgingly giving way to curiosity. "What is it?"

"The best thing," said Wren, "would be for Your Lordship to see for yourself." He lifted the cage and placed it on a table. Watched closely by Pondle and Edgar, he began to untie the ropes holding the canvas, first one, then the other. Then, with a dramatic flourish, Wren pulled the canvas away.

There was a flutter of yellow flashes inside the cage as the twittering birds darted this way and that.

Pondle glared at Wren.

"Canaries?" he said, his voice rising. "You caused me to miss the Newt and Salamander Fanciers Group for *canaries?*"

"No, m'lord!" said Wren, pointing to the cage. "Look there, at the bottom."

With another glare at Wren, Pondle brought his face, and Edgar's, close to the cage. It was Edgar who reacted first, emitting a screech of surprise. This was quickly followed by Pondle's sharp intake of breath as he saw the gossamer wings, the tiny, exquisite face, the impossibly expressive eyes, now wide with fear.

Pondle looked at Wren, then back at Tinker Bell, then back at Wren.

"But what . . ." he said, "what *is* it?"

"It's a fairy, sir," said Wren. He repeated it softly, for he had trouble believing it himself: "A fairy."

"Where did you get her?"

"I'm afraid I'm not at liberty to say, Your Lordship," said Wren.

Pondle gave Wren a significant look. "I see," he said, returning his gaze to Tink. A pause, then: "How much?"

Wren had been anticipating this moment, knowing that the price he could extract, and the quality of his future life, depended on how badly Pondle wanted the creature. Wren saw by Pondle's expression that he wanted it very badly indeed.

Wren took a breath, exhaled, and came out with it: "Five thousand pounds."

Pondle spun to face Wren, his face reddening. "But that's *outrageous!*" he sputtered. Edgar bared his teeth.

Wren nodded understandingly. "I agree it's a substantial sum, sir, but—"

"It's a fortune!" bellowed Pondle.

"As I say," Wren said calmly, "I certainly understand if Your Lordship don't wish to pay it. But it's not every day a man gets a chance to own such a creature as this, is it?"

Pondle stared at Tink, saying nothing.

Wren went on: "And as I say, there wouldn't be no other collector in all of England could claim to have one of these, now could there?"

Pondle kept staring at Tink.

"I brought it to Your Lordship first," continued Wren,

"because I know how much Your Lordship appreciates the truly rare item. But if the price is too high, I certainly understand." Wren picked up the canvas and made as if to cover the cage. "I'll just take it to Lord Shaftsbury, and I'm sure he—"

"Shaftsbury!" said Pondle. Edgar emitted a screech. Pondle *detested* Shaftsbury, who had once outbid Pondle on an albino ocelot, and never failed to remind him of this at social gatherings.

Pondle threw his arm out, blocking Wren's efforts to cover the cage.

"I want to hold it," he said.

Wren barely suppressed a smile. Pondle had taken the bait; the hook would soon be set.

"Certainly, m'lord," he said. He opened the cage door and carefully reached inside. The canaries darted this way and that, avoiding his hand. Tink went to the opposite side of the cage, pressing her back against the wire. Wren's hand came across the cage toward her. Just as it reached her, she darted to her left, but Wren, the experienced bird-snatcher, had seen it coming, and easily grabbed her.

Tink opened her mouth and sunk her small but sharp teeth into Wren's thumb.

"Aaah!" he said, wincing, but not letting go.

"What is it?" said Pondle, peering into the cage, Edgar peering with him.

"It's nothing," said Wren, repositioning his hand so his

246

thumb was out of range of Tink's mouth, but keeping a tight grip on her as he pulled her from the cage and pushed the door shut. "This one's a little feisty. You want to watch out for its mouth."

Eagerly, Pondle reached his sweaty hands forward, and Wren carefully pressed Tinker Bell into them. She squirmed to get free, but Pondle held her firmly, raising her in front of his face to get a good look at her; his eyes, and Edgar's, widening in amazement.

"It's beautiful," he said.

"Yes, m'lord," said Wren, sucking on his bleeding thumb, wondering if he should have asked for more money.

"I must have it," said Pondle.

"If you please, m'lord," said Wren, getting to the heart of it, "gold would be best."

Pondle looked at him. "All right," he said. "Gold you shall have." He looked back at Tink. "I have just the cage for her."

At the word "cage," Tink emitted a furious burst of bells, startling Edgar, but delighting Pondle.

"Did you hear that?" he said. "What a marvelous sound it makes!"

"Yes, m'lord," said Wren. "About the gold, if you—"

"Yes, yes, you shall have your gold," said Pondle. "As soon as I have secured this creature in the—"

He was interrupted by more bells from Tink, an

247

extended sequence of melodious tones. He was transfixed by the sound, as were both Wren and Edgar. But the monkey understood something that neither man did.

Tink was talking to the canaries.

They were not the brightest birds, unfortunately; Tink would have much preferred to be working with macaws or cockatoos, who would have grasped the situation instantly. But she had to work with the resources at hand. She had noticed that Wren, focused on capturing her and handing her to Pondle, had failed to latch the birdcage door.

*Fly out!* she called to the caged birds. *Fly out!*

The canaries, excited but confused, fluttered wildly about the cage, all speaking at once: *What? What? What? What? What?*

*Fly out!* repeated Tink.

*Fly out!* said one of the canaries, finally understanding, flitting to the cage door. The others picked up the cry: *Fly out! Fly out!*

The canary flew up against the cage door; it swung open, and the canary darted out, followed quickly by the others. By the time Wren saw what was happening and lunged toward the cage, he was too late: the canaries—seventeen in all— were now loose in the room. Wren lunged about, trying unsuccessfully to grab them, as Pondle watched the scene with alarm while Edgar leaped up and down on his shoulder, screeching loudly.

*Fly to me!* called Tink. *Fly to me! Peck the man! Peck the man!*

*Peck the man!* chorused the canaries. *Peck the man!*

Suddenly Pondle was surrounded by a swirling swarm of yellow.

"Ow!" he shouted, as the first sharp beak sunk into a roll of pink flesh on his neck. "OWWWW!"

Edgar screeched and leaped from Pondle's shoulder in an effort to escape the canaries; his weight yanked Pondle's left hand free from Tinker Bell just as he had released her with his right to swat at the attacking birds.

Tink was free.

It took her a second to get her bearings. Spying the open door, she shot toward it.

*WHAM!*

The door slammed just before she reached it. Wren, having seen Tink escape Pondle's grasp and anticipating her escape attempt, got there first. He almost grabbed Tink as well, his lunging hand missing her by an inch as she veered sharply away.

The den was chaos now: Pondle, his head still in a swarm of attacking canaries, was running blindly in circles, bellowing and waving his arms, flinging the hapless Edgar around like a rag doll.

Wren, meanwhile, had eyes only for Tink. He stalked her, occasionally leaping at her; but as quick as he was, she was quicker, managing each time to elude him. He pursued her as she flew around the den, looking desperately for an exit, but the door was shut tight and there were no windows. After several circuits, Tink landed on a stuffed moose head just out of Wren's reach. She perched on the moose's massive antlers, panting, watching Wren the way a bird watches a cat, while he stood below, also panting, watching her the way a cat watches a bird.

They remained that way for several seconds, focused on each other, ignoring the bleats of Pondle, who was now bleeding from numerous small but painful peck wounds. Then Wren had an idea. Bypassing Pondle, he crossed to the butterfly wall, grabbed the butterfly net, and yanked it free from its mounting bracket. Holding it in both hands, he moved back across the floor toward Tink, who watched him coming closer and . . .

*SWOOSH!*

. . . Tink shot away from the antlers only an instant before the net got there. Wren cursed as he yanked the handle, pulling the moose head off the wall and sending it crashing to the floor. He whirled and set off after Tink.

*SWOOSH! SWOOSH!*

Twice more he swung the net at her; the second time he very nearly got her, the wire striking her leg and sending her spinning through the air. Wren smiled grimly; she would tire, and he would have her soon.

Tink was thinking the same thing as she looked frantically around the room for a way to escape, or at least a place to rest for a moment.

And then she heard it.

*Hot!* said the voice. *Hot! Out!*

Tink, shooting across the room to escape another swing of the net, looked around for the source of the voice. Suddenly she realized who was calling to her.

Edgar.

The monkey, between jerks on the silver chain attaching his collar to Pondle's wrist, was chattering and hooting at her. She wasn't getting everything he said; he spoke a different dialect from the monkeys back on Mollusk Island. But two words—"hot" and "out"—came through clearly and repeatedly. He was also gesturing frantically toward the fireplace. There were fires on Mollusk Island, but no fireplaces; Tink did not know how a chimney worked. But she knew that if she didn't do something soon, the man with the net would get her.

Tink swooped across the room, directly at the glowing coals. She felt a SWOOSH just miss her from behind as she shot into the fireplace, gasping as the fiercely hot air hit her face. Instinctively, she turned up and away from it, into the smoky darkness of the chimney. Up and up and up she went, holding her breath to keep out the foul fumes, almost losing consciousness just as she felt the blessed coolness of the dank, foggy London air, and found herself soaring free in the night.

From the chimney behind her, she heard faint sounds: the wails of Lord Pondle, famed collector, batting helplessly at fierce, tiny, yellow birds; the sound of her savior, Edgar, hooting in delight; and—loudest of all—the curses of Isaac Wren, bird seller, who had just seen his glorious, happy, wealthy future vanish up the flue.

## CHAPTER 45

# The Cold Iron Ring

PETER ACHED ALL OVER. He ached in his jaw and belly, where the bird seller had hit him; he ached in his legs, from standing in tense readiness against the wall of the cell, braced for an attack by Rafe. And he ached in his arms and hands from holding the heavy, disgusting toilet bucket, its fumes so foul that several times he had gagged uncontrollably. Once, Peter set the bucket down, but Rafe was on his feet in an instant, ready to pounce, and Peter had to quickly pick it back up again, slopping some of its repulsive contents onto his bare feet.

He knew he could not stand this much longer. Rafe knew it, too. The stocky bully sat comfortably on the far side of the cell, watching Peter with a contemptuous smirk.

"Smells good, don't it?" he asked. "You'll be wearing that bucket on your head soon enough." This was the fourth time he'd made that joke, but the other boys hooted with laughter as though they'd never heard it before.

Their raucous reaction was silenced by the appearance at the cell door of two uniformed men. These were the jailer, a mutton-chopped man named Humdrake, and his nervous young assistant, a boy of fifteen named Kremp, all gawky limbs and Adam's apple. In one hand, Humdrake lugged a heavy, coiled chain; in the other, he held a metal key ring with a half dozen keys. He inserted one of these into the cell door, opened it, stepped inside with Kremp, then relocked the door. He faced the prisoners.

"ALL RIGHT, YOU WORTHLESS SCUM," he bellowed—while on official duty, Humdrake never spoke below a bellow—"LINE UP ACCORDING TO HEIGHT." To emphasize the command, he gave the boy nearest to him a kick. The boys began scrambling into line.

"KREMP," Humdrake bellowed to his assistant. "WAKE UP THAT SCUM OVER THERE." He pointed to the snoring drunks. As Kremp went over and began prodding them, Humdrake's eyes fell on Peter, still standing against the wall, holding the toilet bucket.

"YOU!" bellowed Humdrake. "WHAT D'YOU THINK YOU'RE DOING WITH THAT?"

"I . . . I . . ." stammered Peter. "I was—"

"DO YOU INTEND TO STEAL THAT BUCKET?"

bellowed Humdrake, who was not one to tolerate toilet-bucket thieves.

"No, sir," said Peter. "I was—"

"THEN PUT IT DOWN."

"Yes, sir," said Peter, setting down the bucket, glad to be relieved of its weight and stink.

"NOW GET INTO LINE," bellowed Humdrake, grabbing Peter by the shoulder and shoving him toward the others. Peter, avoiding a punch thrown by Rafe, got into line according to size, smallest to largest, toward the front, fourth in line. Kremp herded the drunks to the end of the line. One of them, stumbling and confused, said, "What's happening? Where are we going?"

"YOU ARE GOING TO BE TAKEN BEFORE THE MAGISTRATE," bellowed Humdrake. He had bellowed these same words many times before; it was rote bellowing. "YOU WILL HAVE A PROPER HEARING TO DETERMINE YOUR GUILT OR INNOCENCE. YOU WILL THEN BE TAKEN TO NEWGATE TO ROT."

At those words, the boy in front of Peter, who was perhaps nine years old, perhaps eight, began to cry.

"What's Newgate?" Peter whispered to him.

"A prison," sniffed the boy. "A 'orrible, 'orrible prison. Me dad died there."

Peter turned toward Humdrake, gulped, and spoke.

"Sir!" he said.

"WHAT IS IT?"

"What if . . ." said Peter, screwing up his courage, "what if we haven't done anything wrong?"

The larger boys behind Peter snorted. Humdrake turned a purplish shade of red.

"KREMP!" he bellowed. "CLOUT THAT BOY ON THE EAR!"

Kremp scuttled over and clouted Peter on the ear. Fortunately for Peter, Kremp was an inexperienced clouter, and it was not too painful.

"IF YOU DIDN'T DO NOTHING," said Humdrake, explaining the fine points of English law, "THEN YOU WOULDN'T BE HERE, NOW WOULD YOU?"

Peter saw that his only way out of this predicament would be to fly. He knew he'd be seen, but he had no choice. He'd do it quickly, he decided, the instant they were outside. Then he—

Peter's thoughts were interrupted by the clinking of chain links. He looked to the back of the line.

*Oh, no.*

Humdrake was chaining the prisoners together. He moved down the line, squatting next to the prisoners one by one, snapping shackles around their right ankles; the shackles were firmly attached to the chain. As Humdrake closed each shackle, he locked it with a small, shiny brass key on his key ring. As he approached the front of the line, Peter looked around desperately but hopelessly: the cell door was locked; there was no way out. He felt a hollowness in his stomach as Humdrake snapped the cold iron ring around his own filthy ankle.

His flying ability was useless now. He was trapped.

## CHAPTER 46

# HOPELESS

TINKER BELL WAS NOT a city girl. She'd come into being on a tropical island that she could see in its entirety from aloft, which meant that navigation was a simple matter of looking down and finding a familiar cove, rock, hill, or jungle clearing.

But now, having escaped the birdcage man and the horrid collector with the sweaty palms, Tink found herself flying over a different, and far more confusing, kind of jungle. Below her lay a vast clutter of soot-blackened rooftops, hundreds and thousands of them, stretching into the gray formless murk in every direction. Peter was somewhere down there, but Tink had no idea where.

She decided it would be best to fly toward the ship, since that was where she and Peter had started; her hope was that, in retracing their route, her path might cross with Peter's. The problem was that she didn't know which way the ship was, or where she was, as she'd been carried to the collector's house in a canvas-shrouded cage.

She flew randomly for a while, seeing no change in the rooftop terrain. Finally, growing weary, she landed on the apex of a steeply peaked roof, next to a smoking chimney. Seconds later, a pigeon alit next to her.

*Food?* said the pigeon.

*No*, said Tink. *No food. Do you know where the ships are?*

*Food?* said the pigeon. *Food?*

*No*, said Tink. *Ship?*

*Food?* said the pigeon. *Food? Food? Food? Food?*

*NO!* snapped Tink, and the startled pigeon, in an explosion of feathers, flapped off.

*Stupid bird*, thought Tink, as she wearily launched herself into the dank London air, on a hopeless quest to find one smallish boy in a city of four million people.

## CHAPTER 47

# THE DRUNKEN CENTIPEDE

WHEN HUMDRAKE WAS satisfied that all twelve prisoners were securely attached to the chain by their ankles, he opened the jail-cell door.

"COME ON, COME ON," he bellowed, yanking the first boy forward, thus setting the entire group into stumbling motion. "THE MAGISTRATE AIN'T GOT ALL DAY."

Trying to coordinate his steps with the boys ahead of and behind him, Peter shuffled forward, following Humdrake into a dim corridor, then out into the noisy disorder of the front room of the police station. It was a chaotic mass of London lowlife—pickpockets, footpads, cracksmen, dragsmen, rollers, beggars, lurkers, swindlers, mobsmen, and more—all loudly proclaiming their innocence while being duly ignored by the burly bobbies who had collared them.

The sad parade of prisoners drew little attention as, prodded by the impatient Humdrake, they shuffled, chains clinking, through the room to the big front door, then out into the muddy street. It was early afternoon, but typically dark and gray. A horse-drawn carriage clopped by; Peter and the others ducked, trying to avoid the clods of muck sent flying by the horses' hooves.

"MOVE ALONG," bellowed Humdrake. "MOVE ALONG."

And move along they did, shuffling slowly forward. With each step, Peter grew more desperate, casting his eyes left and right, trying to think how he might escape, his mind refusing to yield a plan.

They crossed several side streets before reaching an imposing gray court building, where Humdrake halted them. A steep flight of steps led up to a massive oak front door. At the top of the steps a distraught young woman, dressed in rags and holding a screaming baby, was clutching at the sleeve of a man in a guard uniform.

"They can't take him away!" the woman cried. "They can't take him! How am I supposed to live? How can I feed my baby? My baby is sick! Please—"

"Off with you!" said the guard, giving the woman a shove that sent her staggering. She collapsed and sat on the steps, sobbing, holding her bawling child.

"ALL RIGHT, THEN," bellowed Humdrake, kicking the nearest of the prisoners—the boy right behind Peter—to get the line moving. "UP THE STEPS. MOVE ALONG!"

Clumsily, hobbled by their chains, the prisoners began ascending the steps, past the sobbing woman. She raised her head, and Peter's eyes met hers for an instant; he saw her despair and felt it in his own heart. Up they trudged. They stopped at the top of the steps, and the guard began to swing open the massive door.

"GET INSIDE, THERE," bellowed Humdrake.

Peter felt the world closing in on him, his mind searching frantically for a way out.

"MOVE!"

As if guided by an unseen force, Peter's hand went to his neck, touching the familiar spherical form of the golden locket. It had been given to him by Molly's father, Leonard Aster, on the day Peter had decided he would stay on Mollusk Island rather than return with the Asters to England. Peter remembered Lord Aster's words: "You may well need starstuff someday," he'd said, fastening the locket around Peter's neck. "Keep it with you always, and use it wisely."

Peter wondered: should he use it now? Its powers were astonishing, but also unpredictable. Would they free him from these chains?

"MOVE ALONG," bellowed Humdrake.

The first boy in the chain line stepped through the doorway.

Peter made up his mind. Swiftly, he lifted the chain over

his head. Holding the locket in one hand, he flicked the tiny catch with his thumb. The locket opened, and Peter's hand disappeared inside a sphere of glowing, golden radiance. In a moment, all of Peter's physical discomforts—the cold, the hunger, the pain—were gone, replaced by a feeling of exquisite well-being. The air around him was filled with the delicate scent of wildflowers in a meadow, and haunting musical sounds—neither instrument nor voice—of unearthly beauty.

Peter had experienced this sensation before, but still, its sheer gloriousness momentarily stunned him. His feet stopped moving, thus triggering a chain reaction: the boy in front of him, his right foot having been jerked to a stop, fell forward into the boy in front of him, who fell forward into the boy in front of *him*, the three of them going down in a heap. Meanwhile, the boy behind Peter stumbled into Peter's back, and each prisoner in line behind him stumbled clumsily to a halt, some of them tumbling to the steps.

"WHAT'S THIS?" bellowed an enraged Humdrake, watching his chain of charges collapsing and staggering about like a drunken centipede. "GET MOVING! GET MOVING!"

Peter, forcing himself to ignore the glorious feeling suffusing his body, bent over and gently tapped the open locket against the shackle on his ankle. In the brilliant glow, he couldn't see what, if anything, had happened. He pulled the locket away.

His heart sank: the shackle was still locked. It was, however, no longer made of dirty rusting iron; it was now a warm gleaming yellow. It was gold.

"Lovely," said the boy in front of Peter, lying on the steps, looking back. Peter saw that he was talking as much about his mood as the golden shackle; he was feeling the effects of the starstuff. So was the boy behind Peter, who began to sing a song Peter didn't recognize, a lilting tune about a gypsy rover who came over the hill. The boy, who'd never been much of a singer, found that all at once he had a sweet voice, and he sent it soaring across the steps and into the streets, stopping passersby, who marveled at its beauty:

> *"He whistled and he sang 'til the green woods rang*
> *And he won the heart of a lady."*

The song did not, however, please the already furious Humdrake. He did not permit singing, nor displays of happiness of any kind.

"HERE, NOW!" he bellowed, charging toward the singing boy, prepared to do some serious kicking. As he approached the boy, however, his attention was diverted to the glowing sphere in Peter's hand. Humdrake had never seen a radiant golden sphere in a prisoner's possession, but he knew instinctively that this was also something he did not permit.

"WHAT'S THIS?" he bellowed, lunging for the glow. "GIVE ME THAT!"

As Humdrake grabbed for his arm, Peter yanked the locket away, causing it to emit a sparkling fountain of light, which drifted upward for a few seconds, then cascaded downward, a shimmering shower, onto Humdrake and the entire chain of prisoners, and the woman sitting on the steps nearby, holding the crying baby.

As the starstuff descended onto these people, three things happened:

The first thing was that the baby stopped crying and started smiling. The mother smiled, too, in grateful relief. She did not know it yet, but her child was no longer sick and would never be sick again.

The second thing was a radical change in Humdrake's mood. In a flash his anger was gone, replaced by a sense of powerful affection for these boys, these lads, these unfortunate urchins. Their only real crime, Humdrake now realized, was that they lacked a strong father's hand to guide them—a lack that Humdrake himself had felt keenly as a boy. No, thought Humdrake, these boys were not criminals to be punished; what they needed was direction and, yes, love. And he, Humdrake, could provide it. Take this boy in front of him right now, the scrawny one who tried to steal the toilet bucket. What inner torment the boy must have been feeling to be driven to such a desperate act! What this boy needed, Humdrake now saw, was a hug.

And so Humdrake reached out to hug Peter, only to find himself tumbling forward in a slow and weightless somersault. That was because of the third thing that was happening: Humdrake was rising into the air. So was Peter. So, in fact, were all of the prisoners. They were drifting gracefully upward from the courthouse steps, like the tail of an enormous, strange kite. Some of them were right-side up, and some were upside down, but none were even slightly alarmed. All were delighting in the experience and the view; the boy behind Peter was still singing, his high-pitched, bell-clear voice echoing down the street:

> *"And here I'll stay 'til my dying day*
> *With my whistling gypsy rover."*

The spectacle of a dozen flying people quickly drew the attention of passersby on the street below. There were shouts of surprise and alarm, then some screams; a crowd gathered and grew quickly as the uproar drew more and more spectators from surrounding streets and from the courthouse itself. Kremp, the young apprentice jailer, ran nervously back and forth on the steps; Humdrake had given him no instructions regarding what to do when prisoners floated away.

Peter and the others were now hovering one hundred

feet in the air over the increasingly chaotic street scene. Peter had shut the locket and returned it to his neck, not knowing how much of its precious contents he had left, if any. What he did know was that the starstuff now keeping the prisoners and Humdrake aloft would eventually wear off, and they would drift back to the ground. Before that happened, he needed to get his ankle free of the golden shackle. But to do that, he needed to get the key from Humdrake, who was floating about twenty-five feet away and a little above the others, smiling radiantly.

Peter tried to fly toward him, but he could not move the massive group to which he was attached.

"Sir!" he called, trying to get Humdrake's attention. "Sir! Sir!"

"YES, BOY," said Humdrake, still bellowing, although now it was an affectionate bellow. "WHAT IS IT?"

"Sir, can you please fly over to us?" said Peter.

"OF COURSE," bellowed Humdrake, and he began flapping his arms, an action that had no effect other than to make him look like an enormous mutton-chopped penguin.

"No, sir! You have to lean! Lean!" shouted Peter, but Humdrake could no longer hear him over the roar of the crowd below. Hundreds had gathered in the street, with more coming every moment. The boys around Peter were laughing, thoroughly enjoying the wonder of it all, floating above the sea of upturned faces and shouting voices.

Their euphoria was not shared by Peter, who understood, with a sinking feeling, that all he had bought with his precious starstuff was a few more minutes of freedom. The flying chain would come down, and when it did, he would again be trapped, this time for good.

## CHAPTER 48

# SOMETHING STRONG

MOLLY GASPED; her hand went to her throat.

This time it was far stronger: a pulsation from her locket, the feeling of heat, almost as if her skin were burning.

Again, she ran to the window and looked out, hoping to see her father. Again she was disappointed.

But she knew something must have happened—something strong and close by. Keeping her hand on the still-warm locket, she stared into the gloom, her thoughts racing but finding no answer.

*What could it be?*

# $\mathcal{E}$ITHER $\mathcal{W}$AY

$\mathcal{T}$INKER BELL FELT IT, TOO, but in a different way, and more powerfully. She was sitting on a roof, resting and fuming after yet another failed attempt to extract information from yet another idiot London pigeon. Then it came: it was as if an invisible wave of warm air had suddenly enveloped her, then rushed past.

Tink knew instantly what it was. She also knew, from its direction of travel, where it had come from. Forgetting her weariness, she leaped up from the rooftop and streaked low across London as fast as she had ever flown. She understood that Peter had opened the locket, or somebody else had.

Whichever it was, Peter was in serious trouble.

## CHAPTER 50

# GRASPING HANDS

THE STARSTUFF WAS wearing off. The other prisoners hadn't felt this yet: they were still giggling with glee, cavorting and spinning in midair, the chain transmitting the motion from one to the other so that they were all whirling and spinning madly in the sky. The drunks who'd been at the rear of the prisoner line were singing a song about whiskey in the jar. Some distance away, Humdrake was now floating horizontally, his face to the sky, smiling beatifically and waving his arms, doing a lazy backstroke to nowhere.

But Peter knew it was wearing off, and they were starting, ever so slowly, to descend. For the tenth time, he lunged and strained against the chain, trying to fly the mass of prisoners over to Humdrake and the shiny brass shackle key on his key ring, which dangled tantalizingly from a hook on his belt. And for the tenth time, he was unable to move the mass at all.

Unlike Peter's euphoric fellow prisoners, the crowd below had noticed that the group was beginning to come down. A contingent of police officers had gathered and, with much shouting and shoving, begun to clear out the space where it appeared the group would be landing. The bobbies did not know how these prisoners had managed to flee skyward—the word "witchcraft" was already being whispered in the crowd—but they clearly intended to take them back into custody when they returned to earth.

Slowly, slowly the prisoners descended toward the waiting bobbies, whose arms were outstretched in readiness. Peter gauged the distance: fifty feet to the bobbies' hands, now forty, now thirty, now twenty, ten . . .

Bells.

Peter spun around, looking for the source of the sound, his eye catching a blazing blur of light coming over the courthouse roof, angling downward and streaking directly toward him until, with impossible deceleration, it stopped short six inches from his face and turned into . . .

"Tink!" Peter cried.

*You smell terrible*, she said, wrinkling her nose.

"I know," he said. "Could you—"

*Who are these filthy boys?*

"We're prisoners," he said. "I need—"

*Why did you open your locket?*

Peter looked down and saw a policeman's grasping hand just five feet from his toes.

"Please, Tink, I'll explain later," he said. "Go get the keys from that man." He pointed toward Humdrake backstroking happily a few yards away, just above the outstretched arms of two bobbies. Tink, after giving Peter a what-would-you-do-without-me look, zipped over, grabbed the keys from Humdrake's belt, avoided the swiping hand of a leaping bobby, and zipped back to Peter.

Peter's cluster was almost down now; the bobbies had managed to snag the feet of the last drunk in line, and were starting to reel in the entire group. Peter grabbed the key ring from Tink and fumbled frantically through the keys, finally getting the shiny brass one. He bent over and inserted it into the hole in the shackle.

"Get that one!" shouted a deep voice just below him. "He's got a key!"

Peter felt a hand grab his left leg; he kicked it free. He turned the key, and the shackle on his right ankle opened. Another hand grabbed at him, then another. Strong hands. Peter kicked with all his strength, heard a loud "Ow!" and a curse below him, and then shot upward, away from the chain and the shackles, away from the grasping hands, away from the shouting crowd and the chaos beneath him.

He soared into the darkening sky with Tink at his side, free again, leaving the other prisoners—still obliviously euphoric—to settle slowly into the arms of the London law, captive once again, but now in possession of a story that they would be telling until they drew their last breaths on earth.

## CHAPTER 51

# THE MESSAGE FROM EGYPT

MOLLY AND HER MOTHER were talking quietly in the sitting room. It was the first moment they'd been able to find alone together since breakfast. Throughout the morning, each time one had approached the other, it seemed that Jenna had been lurking about. Finally, Louise Aster had ordered Jenna to leave the house on a trivial errand—an order that Jenna had obeyed with obvious reluctance.

Molly and her mother sat on the sofa, their heads close together, their voices low. They discussed the suspicious actions of Jenna, and the disturbing change in the behavior of Mr. Jarvis and Mr. Cadigan, as well as Hornblower's reaction. Molly, relieved to be talking about these things at last, told her mother about the unusual warmth she'd felt— twice—from her locket, and the unfamiliar policeman who'd been passing by at odd hours, and the strange man who had suddenly appeared out of the darkness when the bobby was talking to Mr. Jarvis.

"What do you mean, strange?" asked her mother.

"Well," said Molly, trying to remember what she'd seen in those fleeting seconds, "he was very dark."

"You mean, he was wearing dark clothing?"

"Yes, I suppose he was," said Molly. "But it was more than that. He . . . his whole form was the blackest of blacks, as if he were part of the night itself."

"What did he look like?"

"I couldn't see his face. He was just a black *shape*, and the way he moved, it was—" Molly hesitated.

"What?" said Louise.

"It was the strangest thing. He moved quickly, and yet so *easily*, as if there were no effort. It wasn't like a person running at all; it was like ink flowing."

"Did Mister Jarvis see him?"

"No. He was looking the other way. The bobby saw him—he had to have; he was looking right at him—but he didn't react. And the dark man was gone a moment later. It happened in an instant."

"What happened?"

"I've been thinking and thinking about that, trying to picture it," said Molly, frowning. "It was so quick, and there wasn't much light. But whatever it was, Mister Jarvis *looked* different afterward. I can't explain it very well, I'm afraid. But it was as if something that should have been there wasn't. He'd changed somehow. I'm not making sense, am I?"

Louise didn't answer, but her face filled with worry.

"What is it, Mother?" Molly asked. "Do you know who the dark man was?"

"No," said Louise. "Not really."

"But you know *something*," Molly said. "Tell me, please!"

"I can't say for certain," said Louise slowly. "I don't know if there's a connection . . . but just before your father left, he received word from Egypt, from one of our people there, an old friend of your father's named Bakari. He sent a brief message, apparently written in great haste."

"What did it say?"

"Some starstuff fell," said Louise. "A small amount. Our people detected it immediately and sent a group of six to retrieve it. They were transporting it to Cairo when something went terribly wrong. There was an ambush; somehow the Others knew exactly where they were. Bakari was the only one of the six who managed to escape."

"That's awful," said Molly, "but what does it have to do with what happened here last night?"

"Bakari said that they were betrayed."

"By whom?"

Louise put her hand on Molly's. "By one of us," she said. "By a Starcatcher."

Molly's eyes widened. "But that's impossible," she said.

Louise nodded. "So we thought as well. But Bakari's message was quite definite."

Molly frowned. "But I still don't understand what it has to do with—"

She was stopped by the tightening of Louise's grip.

"Bakari's message ended with a strange warning," said Louise. "Neither your father nor I understood it at the time."

"What was it?" said Molly.

Her mother looked out the window, then back at Molly.

"The warning," she said, "was 'Beware the shadows.'"

## CHAPTER 52

# THE LETTER

WHEN PETER FELT HE HAD flown a safe distance from the chaos on the courthouse steps, he landed on a rooftop amid a clutter of rundown homes. After looking around to make sure nobody was watching, he dropped to the ground in an alley. Tink, following him, landed on his shoulder.

*You smell terrible*, she reminded him, in case he had forgotten.

"I know," he said. "I was in a jail. It was . . . pretty awful. How did you get out of that cage?"

*The canaries helped me*, she said. *They're not too bright, but they're brave, once you tell them what to do.*

Peter smiled despite the sour smell of his clothes, the penetrating cold, and the gnawing emptiness in his belly. "Well," he said, "I'm very glad you got out. You saved me, Tink. Again. Thank you."

*You're welcome*, said Tink, literally aglow with pride,

filling the dark and filthy alley with warm, golden light.

"Now we need to find Molly," said Peter.

Instantly the alley went dark.

"What's the matter?" said Peter.

Tink made a sound that cannot be translated into acceptable English.

Peter blushed. "Tink!"

*Why do we have to find her?*

"Because," said Peter, "she's my friend, and she's in danger."

*You've had nothing but trouble since you started looking for her.*

"She'd do the same for me."

*You don't know that.*

"I do know that. When we were on the ship, she—"

Peter was interrupted by another unprintable burst of bells. Tink hated—*hated*—to be reminded that Peter and Molly had known each other before Tink existed, at least in her current form.

"Well, you can say what you want," said Peter, when she was quiet again, "but I'm going to look for her."

He walked resolutely out of the alley. After a moment of fuming, Tink followed him, as he knew she would. When she landed on his shoulder, he gently caught her in his hand and tucked her under his shirt, an action that resulted in a predictable outpouring of complaints about his aroma.

"I'm sorry," he said. "But you saw what happens when people see you. I'll get clean clothes as soon as I can."

He tried to sound confident, but he wondered how he would find clean clothes when he'd been such a miserable failure at finding Molly's house. He wandered the busy streets aimlessly for close to an hour without any workable plan presenting itself. He was walking numbly, head down, slowly being overcome by the now-familiar feeling of hopelessness, when he literally bumped into the solution to his problem.

"Here now!" said a gruff voice.

Peter, bouncing back from the collision, found himself looking up at a tall man in a bright red coat, with a sack slung over his shoulder.

A postman.

"Sorry!" said Peter.

"Mind where you're going!" barked the postman, striding off briskly.

Peter turned and followed, a few paces back, formulating a plan while half trotting to keep up with the postman's lengthy stride. Peter had never sent a letter, nor received one. But in his years at St. Norbert's Home for Wayward Boys, several of his friends had received letters, and as Peter hurried along behind the postman, he tried to remember precisely how they worked. He knew you had to write the person's name on the envelope. But would that be enough?

Peter didn't know Molly's address; all he knew was that she lived in London.

The postman, after a dozen quick, efficient stops, strode around a corner and entered the side door of a brick building. Peter went to the front and saw a sign over the door that said ROYAL MAIL. He entered and found himself in a quiet, high-ceilinged room. Along one wall was a long desk, at which several customers were writing; along the other wall were four windows, three of which were manned by clerks. Peter studied them and decided the one on the far right—a portly man with a large red nose and watery eyes behind thick-lensed spectacles—looked the least threatening. He waited until the man wasn't busy, then approached him.

"Sir," he said.

The clerk peered at him over the spectacles. "Yes, lad?"

"I need to post a letter," said Peter.

"All right," said the clerk. "Let me see it."

"I don't have it," said Peter.

The clerk removed his spectacles, massaged his forehead, then replaced the spectacles.

"You wish to post a letter," he said, "but you have no letter."

"Yes," said Peter.

The clerk glanced around the office; the other two mail clerks were both busy with customers. The clerk ducked down behind the counter, and Peter heard the sound of liquid being swallowed. The clerk reappeared; he seemed surprised to see Peter still standing there.

"Young man," he said, once he'd got his eyes refocused. "Here is the thing: we cannot post a letter if we do not *have* the letter. Or, to put it another way, we must *have* the letter in order to post it. Do you see?" By the time he said "have," the air around Peter was filled with a strong, sweetish smell.

"Yes, sir, I understand," said Peter. "What I was wondering was, could you write the letter for me?"

The clerk narrowed his eyes. "You want me to write the letter for you?"

"Yes, sir."

"And what did you want this letter to say?"

"Oh," said Peter, "it doesn't much matter."

"You want me to write a letter," the clerk said, speaking very slowly, "but you don't care what the letter says."

"Exactly!" said Peter, glad the man finally understood him.

"Just a moment," said the clerk, ducking down again. Peter heard another swallowing sound, then a sucking sound, then "Drat!" Then there was a *thunk* as the clerk, coming back up, struck his head on the counter, followed by another "Drat!" Then the clerk reappeared, rubbing his head. He looked at Peter, closed his eyes tight for several seconds, then opened them. He seemed disappointed to see Peter still standing there.

"You're still here," he said.

"Yes, sir."

The clerk stood rubbing his head, looking at Peter. Then he had an idea. Peter could see the formation of this idea on the man's face: it started as a frown, then turned into what the clerk apparently believed was a shrewd smile. The clerk glanced at his coworkers, then leaned forward through the window and beckoned to Peter.

"Come here," he said.

The "here" sent powerful fumes wafting Peter's way, but Peter held his breath and stepped forward.

"I'll make you a bargain," the clerk said. He disappeared for a few seconds. After another *thunk* and another "Drat!" he reappeared with an object concealed in his hands. After glancing around the room, he pressed the object into Peter's hands. It was a dull gray metal flask.

Leaning close, the clerk whispered: "Take this next door to the Dog and Cabbage. Give it to the barman. Tell him it's from Henry next door at the mail office. Tell him to fill it back up, and I'll be 'round after work to pay him. You understand, lad?"

Peter nodded.

"Run along, then," said the clerk.

Peter trotted next door and into the Dog and Cabbage, a dark, seedy pub with a few scattered customers staring silently at pints of bitter. A man stood behind the bar, watching Peter approach.

"You're a bit young to be in here," he said.

Peter set the flask on the bar. A hint of a smile formed on the bartender's face.

"Henry," he said.

"Yes, sir," said Peter.

"Did Henry send any money with you?" said the bartender.

"No, sir," said Peter. "He said he'd come 'round after work."

The bartender sighed, then picked up the flask, filled it from a bottle behind the bar, and handed it back to Peter.

"Thank you," said Peter, getting a nod in return.

Peter tucked the flask under his shirt with Tink, who, of course, complained. Ignoring her, Peter trotted back into the post office. He stood off a little way while Henry waited on a customer; then he went to the window and, making sure he was unobserved, handed the flask to Henry, who immediately ducked below his counter for several lengthy swigs.

When he reappeared, Peter said, "Now will you write my letter?"

"What letter?" said Henry, blinking.

"The letter you said you'd write for me, if I went to the pub and—"

"Yes, yes, all right," said Henry, looking around nervously. "No need to shout! Do have paper and pen, then?"

"No, sir."

Henry sighed. "And I suppose no envelope or stamp?"

"No, sir, but you said if I went to the pub you—"

"Yes! Yes! Shhh!" said Henry. He fumbled around his desk and produced a piece of paper. Dipping a pen in his inkwell, he looked at Peter and said, "Go ahead."

"With what, sir?"

"With the letter!" said Henry, much too loud for the post office. Every head turned his way; his two fellow clerks glared at him.

"Sorry!" he said. "Just a bit of . . . that is, I mean . . . Sorry!" To Peter, he hissed, "What am I supposed to write?"

"Just write anything," said Peter. "Write hello from Peter."

"All right," said Henry, hastily scrawling *Hello from Peter.* "Is that it?"

"And now if you could address it."

Sighing, Henry folded the letter, tucked it into an envelope, and sealed it with a blob of wax and metal stamp. He took a tuppence from his pocket and dropped it into a box on the counter. Picking up the pen again, he said, "Who is the addressee?"

"The what?"

"The addressee," said Henry. "The person to whom the letter is to be posted."

"Oh," said Peter. "Lord Aster."

Henry looked up, pen poised. "Lord Aster?" he said. "Lord *Leonard* Aster?"

"Yes, sir," said Peter. "Do you know him?"

"I know of him, to be sure," said Henry.

"And you know where he lives?" said Peter eagerly.

"Of course," said Henry.

"Then, please address the letter to him."

Henry sighed, then wrote *Lord Aster, Kensington Palace Gardens*, on the envelope.

"All right," he said, "that's—"

"And please put an X on the back," said Peter. "A big one."

Shaking his head, Henry drew a large X on the back of the envelope, then tossed it into a bin behind him. "There," he said. "Done. Good-bye." He started to duck beneath the counter.

Peter's voice stopped him: "And now the letter will go to Lord Aster's house?"

"Yes," said Henry. "Good-bye."

"When will it be delivered?"

Henry looked at the clock. "The postman for that route will leave in one hour," he said. "Last delivery today. Good-bye."

"Which postman will it be?" said Peter.

Henry blinked. "Which *postman*?" he said.

"Yes," said Peter.

"What *difference* does it make which . . ." Henry stopped, realizing that, in a contest of wills, he was overmatched. "The postman is Hawkins," he said. "The very tall one." He waited, resigned, for Peter's next question.

"Thank you," said Peter, turning to go.

Henry, startled, mumbled "Good-bye" as he watched the very strange, very determined boy leave. He spent a moment trying to fathom what on earth the boy was trying to do with his ridiculous letter. Then he shrugged, glanced around the post office, and returned to his faithful flask.

# CHAPTER 53

# $\mathcal{P}$OTATO $\mathcal{S}$OUP

$\mathcal{T}$HE ASTER HOUSEHOLD had eight servants. This was a small staff for a family as wealthy as the Asters, with a house so large. But the Asters valued privacy, and the larger the staff, the more prying the eyes, the more gossipy the tongues.

So the Asters got by with just eight. There were the three maids—Mary and Sarah, both of whom had been with the Asters for ages; and Jenna, who recently replaced another longtime family servant, a girl who had suddenly developed a mysterious ailment and had gone off to the Great Ormond Street Hospital. There were three men on the staff—Paul, the family's longtime manservant; Patrick, the coachman; and a young groom named Ben. The cook was a Spanish woman named Sierra; she had an elderly and somewhat cranky assistant, called Mrs. Conine.

On this evening, as usual, the three maids and the three men had gathered for supper in the big room at the rear of the house, next to the kitchen. When everyone was seated around the table, Paul, as was customary, said the blessing. Jenna rose and went into the kitchen, returning with a tureen of potato soup. Although usually quiet, Jenna declared loudly that the soup was delicious, and insisted that each person try some. She even returned to the kitchen and insisted that Sierra and Mrs. Conine taste it, though they both said they already had.

"Oh, please, you must try some more," said Jenna. "It's delicious!"

"It's just potato soup," said Sierra. But in the end, she and Mrs. Conine yielded to Jenna's enthusiasm and took a few spoonfuls each.

So all of them began the supper with a helping of potato soup.

All of them, that is, except Jenna.

## CHAPTER 54

# A Fine Name Indeed

Night was falling, and Peter was trotting, almost running, to keep up with Hawkins. The long-legged postman was clearly eager to be done with his rounds: he darted from house to house, dropping letters into the front-door mail slots, preoccupied with his task, which was fortunate for Peter, who was trying to remain unnoticed, blending into the homebound pedestrian throng while keeping close enough to see whether any of the envelopes was marked with an X.

He worried that he might have missed it already, which would mean that he was now following the postman *away* from Molly's house. But he had no choice other than to keep trotting along, hoping he was going in the right direction, and trying to ignore the now-constant complaints of a very unhappy Tinker Bell, still imprisoned inside his filthy shirt.

*It's almost dark*, she was saying. *Nobody will see me now.*

"Not yet," Peter puffed. "There are too many people around."

The postman was now striding along Bayswater Road, to the north of Kensington Palace Gardens. With each passing block, the houses were becoming larger and better-kept. And the mail sack was getting emptier. And the evening was growing darker.

Hawkins strode up the walk to a white corner house and pulled a letter from his sack. Peter, hovering on the sidewalk, strained to see the envelope: no X. The postman dropped the letter through a slot and came back down the walk. Peter looked away as the postman went past, then turned to follow him.

He was stopped by a grip on his arm, then an unwelcome voice: "Where are *you* going?"

Peter turned and saw Trotter, the boy who had lured him into capture by the man who wanted to make him a beggar. Peter jerked his arm free, only to feel a much more powerful, and painful, grip on his shoulder.

"I told you I'd find you," said a low voice. Peter looked up and saw the big man who'd imprisoned him, his face contorted by a triumphant sneer.

Peter looked up Bayswater Road: the red uniform of the postman was disappearing into the gloom.

"Let me *go*," Peter said, struggling. The man only tightened his grip. "LET ME GO! PLEASE, HELP!" Peter shouted, hoping to draw the attention of passersby. But with the onset of darkness, the sidewalk crowd had thinned; the few remaining pedestrians scurried past, averting their eyes from the shouting boy and the large, menacing man.

"You'll not get away this time, boy," the man said.

"Here, now! What's this!" A stranger's voice from behind Peter.

A man, apparently the occupant of the white corner house, was coming down the walkway. He was short and slight, with a large, protruding forehead, piercing eyes, and a bushy moustache. He wore an overcoat that was far too large, making him look even smaller.

"What's the matter here?" he said.

"It's none of your business what the matter is," growled the big man, tightening his grip on Peter.

The small man looked at Peter. "Is that true?" he said.

Peter started to open his mouth, but was silenced by a violent yank from the massive hand on his shoulder.

"I said it's none of your business," said the big man, stepping threateningly forward.

The small man seemed unfazed. "Isn't it?" he said. "Here, Porthos!"

In a moment, the reason for the small man's confidence appeared in the form of an enormous dog bounding down the walk. It was a Saint Bernard, but to Peter it looked more like a bear. It raced toward Peter and the big man, barking ferociously. The big man drew Peter in front of him as a shield. Trotter ducked behind them both.

"Porthos, halt!" said the small man. The huge dog skidded to a stop, growling in a deep, threatening rumble, teeth bared, its eyes trained on the big man.

"Now," said the small man mildly, speaking to Peter. "Is this man bothering you?"

Peter nodded.

"Let the boy go," said the small man.

The big man tightened his grip on Peter's shoulder.

"I said *let him go*," said the small man. He took a step forward, and the dog moved forward with him, its growl becoming more menacing.

Peter felt the big man bracing, as if he were about to attack. But apparently he thought better of it, for suddenly he removed his hand from Peter's shoulder.

"Now, get out of here," said the small man, "and don't come back."

The big man backed away, glaring. "You wouldn't be so brave if you didn't have that dog," he said.

"Ah," said the small man, smiling, "but I *do* have the dog, don't I?"

The large man spat on the ground, then turned and, with Trotter behind him, skulked off into the night.

The small man chuckled, then turned to Peter. "Are you all right?" he said.

"Yes, sir, thank you," said Peter. "And thank you for rescuing me."

"Happy to do it," said the small man, petting the now-docile Porthos. "You look cold and hungry. Would you like to come inside for a hot meal by a warm fire?"

*Yes!* said Tinker Bell, from under Peter's shirt.

"What was that sound?" said the small man.

"Nothing!" said Peter, clapping his hand over his shirt.

"Are you sure?" said the small man. "I could swear I heard bells."

"No!" said Peter. "That is, I mean . . . *I* didn't hear anything."

"Odd," said the small man, looking at Peter's shirt. "Anyway, would you like to come inside?"

"No, thank you," said Peter, tightening his grip on Tink. "I need to go. I need to find . . . Oh, no!" Peter looked up Bayswater Road; it was almost deserted now. There was no sign of Hawkins the postman.

"Oh, *no*," repeated Peter, bringing his hand to his forehead.

"What is it?" said the small man.

"I'm trying to find somebody," said Peter, his voice breaking. "The postman was going to her house, and now I don't know where he's gone."

"Who are you trying to find?" said the small man.

"Molly Aster," said Peter, looking up Bayswater Road.

"Aster?" said the small man. "Is she related to Lord Aster?"

Peter's head snapped around. "Do you know where he lives?"

"Of course," said the small man. "Everyone does in this neighborhood."

Peter's heart leaped. "Is it near here, then?"

"It is," said the small man. "Quite near. It's on Kensington Palace Gardens, not a mile from here."

"Up this street?" said Peter, pointing up Bayswater Road.

"That's one way," said the man, "but if you're in a hurry—"

"I am!" said Peter.

"Then there's a shortcut through Kensington Gardens." He pointed across Bayswater Road. "There's a path that begins just there. You follow it, and it will cross two others. You want the second path to the right, then straight on 'til you see a row of fine mansions. The one you want is the largest, grandest, white one, with two towers, one at each end."

"A white house with two towers," repeated Peter. He turned to go, then turned back.

"Thank you," he said.

"You're welcome," said the small man, still petting the huge dog. "Good luck to you." Then, looking directly at Peter's shirt, he added, "To *both* of you."

Peter put his hand on his shirt, at a loss for words. The small man smiled.

"By the way," he said. "What's your name?"

"Peter," said Peter.

"Ah, yes, Peter," said the small man. "A fine name. I'm called James . . . James Barrie. But to my friends, it's Jamie."

Peter, not knowing what to make of this, said nothing.

The man extended his hand, and Peter shook it. "We're friends now, you and I."

"Thank you, again," Peter said.

"My pleasure."

Porthos whined. The man scratched the dog's head and said, "And let's not forget Porthos! Credit where credit is due." He smiled. It was a wide smile, surprisingly big for such a small face. "Well then, Peter," said the little man. "Good-bye."

"Good-bye," said Peter as he turned and ran across the road.

"Don't forget," called Jamie, "second path to the right!" Then he turned and, with Porthos padding behind, went back to his house, muttering to himself.

"Peter," the man said. "A fine name indeed."

## CHAPTER 55

# "Take All His Air"

$H$OOK SAT INSIDE the fort walls, brooding by the fire. He watched the two boys in the bamboo cage, their lips cracked and puckered, their sad, fearful eyes trained on the cage floor. Next to them, untouched so far, sat their daily meal of starfish mush and coconut juice.

Hook was not pleased. His initial excitement over the capture of the boys had subsided into grumpiness when several days had gone by without an attempt to rescue them. It was not the caged boys Hook wanted. It was the cursed flying boy who had taken his left hand. It was Peter he dreamed of seeing strapped to a pole with a fire lit beneath him.

Hook brooded some more, his baleful gaze on the two captives. And then, as it so often did, a plan came to him.

"Smee!" he bellowed, causing the two boys to jump.

The fat little man trundled over. "Yes, Cap'n?"

"You ever been whaling, Smee?"

"No, Cap'n."

"Timing is everything."

"Yes, Cap'n."

"Timing's the difference between a hold full of blubber, or a whole lot of nothing."

"Are you a little close to the fire, perhaps, Cap'n?"

"The whale comes up for air, you see. You have to anticipate that moment. You need to have the harpoons all set and ready."

"Yes, Cap'n. But—"

Hook glared. He did not like to be interrupted in midplan. "What is it, Smee?"

"We have no harpoons."

Hook clapped his hand to his forehead.

Smee, misinterpreting this act, went on: "We have some pistols, but they mostly don't shoot. We have the swords, of course, but I ain't heard of nobody killing a whale with a sword."

Now Hook had his hand *and* his hook on his forehead.

"Maybe," said Smee, "you could poke the whale in the eye with a sword. Of course he'd still have the *other* eye, but I b'lieve, in a whale, the other eye is way over on the other side of the head, so your one-eyed whale would swim in a circle, and you could—"

"SMEE!"

"What, Cap'n?"

"You are an idjit, Smee."

"Aye, Cap'n."

"If you were to engage in a battle of wits with a sponge, Smee, my money would be on the sponge."

"Aye, Cap'n, but all I'm saying is that if we're going to catch a whale, we—"

"I'M NOT TALKING ABOUT CATCHING A WHALE, YOU IDJIT!"

Smee frowned, not wanting to contradict the captain, but quite certain that only a minute ago he had distinctly heard the captain talking about catching a whale.

"The point," said Hook, "is that the whale don't surface 'til it runs out of air."

Smee nodded tentatively.

"We haven't taken all his air," Hook said. "That's our problem. We haven't got ourselves enough bait, y'see?"

"Aye, Cap'n," said Smee, though he did not see at all.

"Round up the men," Hook ordered. "If two boys won't do the trick, let's take all his air. Let's see what the boy does when all four of his mates go missing."

"Aye, Cap'n," said Smee, waddling off, wondering how a conversation that had been entirely about whales wound up involving the boy.

## CHAPTER 56

# ℐ Very Strange Business

Just after sunset, when the sky was neither day nor night, five men boarded a black cab and rode the cobblestone streets from St. Katherine's dock to Kensington Palace Gardens. There was no talk in the cab, only a deep chill in the close air and an oppressive silence, as if the black-robed figure sucked the life from everyone and everything around him.

Finally, after a trip that had seemed interminable to Nerezza, Slank, Gerch, and Hampton, the cab slowed to a stop. Nerezza parted the window curtains and looked out. They were about twenty yards down the street from the Aster house, on the opposite side. Jarvis was standing out front. A tall postman walked past him and up the walk, deposited some letters, came back down the walk, and disappeared down the street.

"Jarvis is out front," Nerezza reported.

"Is he . . ." said Gerch, ". . . is he one of the ones who . . . who were . . ." He stopped, glancing at the still, silent form of Ombra.

"Yes," said Nerezza. "He's one of the two. The other one is Cadigan: he's at the back entrance tonight. When we give the word, Cadigan will call the third one, Hodge, outside, with the dog, so Lord Ombra can . . . can meet him. Then we'll have all three."

"And the staff?" said Gerch.

"The girl has taken care of them," said Nerezza. "Are you ready, Lord Ombra?"

The dark form, which had been utterly motionless since they had left the dock, stirred, and instantly the other four occupants of the cab felt colder, much colder. The hooded head turned toward the window, but did not touch the closed shade.

"Too soon," said the groaning voice. "Have the driver go around and return here."

"Yes, m'lord," Nerezza said, leaning out and passing the order along to the cab driver.

The black cab rumbled forward into the gloom. It passed the tall postman, who, uncharacteristically, broke his stride as he felt a sudden, sharp chill shudder through his body.

For ten minutes, the occupants of the cab rode without

speaking. Finally, the strain of the silence became unbearable to Gerch, who said, "There was the strangest report today, from the courthouse in Lambeth."

"I heard about that," said Hampton, nodding. "The flying prisoners."

Slank's head whipped around to face Hampton. "What did you say?" he said.

"I know it sounds absurd," said Hampton. "You know how the newspapers are always exaggerating everything. It's probably—"

"*What did you say about flying prisoners?*" said Slank, his face an inch from Hampton's.

"I . . . it was in the newspapers," sputtered Hampton. "Outside the courthouse, some prisoners flew into the air, then came back down again."

"A very strange business," added Hampton. "Hundreds of people claimed to have seen it. Hundreds!"

"They all came back down?" said Slank. "They were all captured?"

"I believe one of them flew away."

"A boy?" said Slank, leaning now into Hampton. "Was it a boy who flew away?"

"I don't know," said Hampton. "Why?"

"He's here," said Slank. "He's in London."

"Who's here?" said Hampton.

"You don't know that," said Nerezza.

"He's *here*, I tell you," shouted Slank, his face contorted in fury. "He's—"

"Silence!"

Ombra's voice instantly quieted Slank.

"We have work to do," said Ombra.

"I'm sorry, Lord Ombra," said Slank, hanging his head. "It's just that—"

"I know," the voice groaned. "You want the boy."

Slank nodded.

"If the boy is here," said Ombra, lifting his hooded head slightly—as if looking through the ceiling of the cab into the night sky, "and I believe you may be right about that, then you shall have him soon enough."

CHAPTER 57

# At Last

As Peter ran down the path into Kensington Gardens, Tink flew alongside his right ear, silent for a change, happy to be released from the aromatic confines of Peter's shirt.

Peter repeated the small man's directions to himself.

*Second path to the right.*

He crossed one path, then—emboldened by the darkness enveloping him—jumped and swooped upward, flying now, squinting ahead to see. . . .

And there it was: the second path.

Peter and Tink veered right, rising even higher. To their right, Peter saw a large oval pond and, looming in the distance, the massive form of Kensington Palace. Flying faster now, they crossed a broad expanse of lawn to the south of the palace. Just ahead loomed the mansions lining Kensington Palace Gardens, their windows glowing yellow in the deepening night fog.

As he drew near the end of the path, Peter slowed and settled quietly to the ground next to the wide, gently sloping street. To Tink's dismay, Peter snatched her and once again tucked her under his shirt. He hesitated, taking in his surroundings, then decided to keep to the opposite side, away from the streetlights. He trotted past one huge home after another, looking for . . .

*A white house with two towers.*

*There!* He saw it. Just ahead and across the street: a grand white mansion with a square tower at each end.

Molly's house. At last!

"Tink," he whispered excitedly. "We found it!"

*Oh, hooray,* came the bells, muffled and distinctly unenthusiastic.

Peter started forward, then hesitated. Should he just knock on the front door in his bedraggled, filthy condition? If he did, wouldn't a servant just turn him away? Perhaps it would be better to fly and try to find Molly's window and tap on it. Peter studied the house: it had a great many windows. Too many. He would try the front door first. If that didn't work, he'd think of something else.

He took another few steps, then stopped again as he saw the distinctive form of a man standing in shadow near the streetlight in front of the house. The man was no pedestrian: he stood rock-still, facing the street.

*A guard,* Peter thought.

Peter watched the man for a moment, trying to think of a plan. He decided that he would simply walk past him. If the man stopped him, Peter would say he had an important message for Molly Aster. If the man refused to let him pass, Peter would leave, then fly back into the darkness and try to find Molly's window.

Taking a deep breath, Peter began walking toward the man, but stopped and quickly retreated as he heard the clopping of hooves coming up the street toward him.

A cab rumbled out of the darkness into the glow of the streetlamp. It stopped across from the Aster house. The cab's door opened, and a man stepped out.

Peter gasped.

It was Slank.

## CHAPTER 58

# $\mathcal{V}$ISITORS

$\mathcal{M}$OLLY SAT AT HER writing table, which was illuminated by a single oil lamp sitting next to her open diary. She dipped her pen into the ink bottle and stared at the blank page, but found herself unable to form a meaningful sentence from the bits and pieces of random thoughts and vague fears swirling around her mind.

She and her mother, weary after a day of worry and suspicion, had retired early—Molly to her bedroom in the south tower, Louise to her room on the third floor. They had agreed that each would waken the other if she heard anything odd in the night—although Molly doubted that she would sleep any time soon.

She jumped as a sharp knock shattered the silence. Composing herself, she put down her pen, rose, and went to the door and opened it. She expected to see the familiar face of Sarah, who came around each evening to tend Molly's fireplace. Instead, she found herself looking into the intense, narrow-set eyes of Jenna.

"What is it?" Molly said coldly.

"I'm here to fix the young lady's fire for the night," replied Jenna, with an equal lack of warmth.

"Where is Sarah?"

"She's not feeling well."

"What's wrong with her?"

"Oh, she'll be fine; the young lady needn't worry about her," said Jenna, in a tone that, to Molly's ears, sounded oddly amused.

"I see," said Molly uncertainly. She stood aside and watched as Jenna went to the fireplace, removed some ashes, then scooped a few coal lumps from the scuttle and added them to the glowing pile in the fireplace. When she was done, Jenna turned to Molly and said, "Will there be anything else, m'lady?"

"No, thank you," said Molly.

Jenna crossed the room and paused, her hand on the doorknob. She stared at Molly with an intensity that made Molly quite uncomfortable.

"Yes?" said Molly.

"Nothing, m'lady," said Jenna.

"Then good night," said Molly.

"And a very pleasant night to *you*, m'lady," said Jenna, with a smile so unpleasant, so openly hostile, that Molly took an involuntary step back. Then Jenna swung the door shut so hard that the breeze made the lamp flame flicker in its glass chimney.

Molly stood there for a moment staring at the door, her breath coming in shallow gasps, trying to calm herself. Should she tell her mother what had happened? But what actually *had* happened? What was there to tell? That she didn't like the way Jenna had *smiled* at her?

Chastising herself for being such a ninny, Molly went back to staring at her diary. It was useless; she was too upset to write. She rose and went to her window, pushing the curtain aside and looking down at the street.

She tensed: there was a cab outside, and men were getting out. Given the darkness and the distance, their features were indistinct: *one . . . two . . . three men.* They alit from the cab not twenty feet from the stout form of Mr. Jarvis, who stood beneath the streetlight. But rather than approach the men, Jarvis remained at his post, motionless. If he saw them, he gave no indication of it.

*Odd.*

Molly knew she must tell her mother about the visitors. She was about to turn away from the window when one of the men moved closer to the streetlight. Just for an instant, Molly caught a partial glimpse of this man's face. Her heart froze; her mind raced back to a rowboat off Mollusk Island and the brutal man who had taken her captive, only to be outwitted by Peter. Was this the same man? The man she'd last seen being pushed out to sea by mermaids, his face contorted by rage and hatred?

Was this *Slank*? Could it possibly be?

Molly pressed her face to the cold windowpane, trying to get a better look. Four men had now emerged from the cab. A fifth was descending from the doorway. Like the others, he offered little more than a featureless silhouette, yet he appeared somehow darker, and he moved differently—a floating, graceful motion. Molly recognized him as the strange figure she had seen the night before.

The dark figure—he looked as if he were wearing some kind of robe—raised his right arm and gestured toward Mr. Jarvis, summoning him. To Molly's surprise, Jarvis walked over, though slowly, and stood in front of the dark figure, his head bent submissively, apparently listening. After a moment, he nodded. He unlocked and opened the gate for the others, then trudged toward the side of the house.

Whoever this dark man was, he was clearly giving orders to Mr. Jarvis, who had now left the front of the house unguarded. Molly had to warn her mother immediately. She turned from the window, strode quickly across the room, and opened the door.

And screamed.

Jenna stood in the doorway. It was as if she hadn't moved.

But she must have moved.

Because now she was holding a knife.

## CHAPTER 59

# SOMETHING ODD

JARVIS WALKED STIFFLY, like a soldier marching to a drum only he could hear, along the carriageway on the north side of the Aster mansion. A few yards behind him glided the dark form of Ombra.

The other men—Slank, Nerezza, Gerch, and Hampton—remained by the front gate with the cab. The cab driver sat still, staring straight ahead; his shadow had encountered Ombra an hour earlier.

Jarvis reached the far corner of the house and turned left, toward the back door. The only sounds were the occasional whinny of a distant horse and the cold wind rustling the tree branches.

"Cadigan," Jarvis called softly.

Cadigan's hulking form emerged from the shadows. He drew on his pipe, his expressionless face illuminated for a

315

moment by the red glow of the tobacco, then faded back into the darkness.

"Has she taken care of the staff?" Jarvis said, his voice low.

"Sleeping like babies."

"What about the lady and the girl?"

"In their chambers."

"He wants you to call Hodge outside."

"Aye."

"You're to lead him here, where we're standing," Jarvis said. "Make sure you leave the door open. And make sure your shadow ain't touching his."

"Aye."

"Do it, then."

Jarvis melted into the darkness. Cadigan opened the door and called for Hodge, who appeared half a minute later. He was a big man, even bigger than Cadigan, with shoulders that filled the doorway.

"What is it?" Hodge said.

"Something out here I want you to see," said Cadigan.

Hodge stepped out, followed by Hornblower the dog, who growled at Cadigan. Hodge started to pull the door closed behind him; as he did, Cadigan, sidestepping Hornblower, stepped forward and blocked the door, pushing it back open and sticking his head into the kitchen as if looking for someone. "Any of the staff around?" he said.

"I told you earlier: they all went to sleep early tonight," said Hodge, annoyed at having to repeat himself.

"All right, then," said Cadigan, coming back out, but leaving the door open.

Hodge was about to say something when Hornblower began barking and ran toward the corner of the house.

"Hornblower!" shouted Hodge. "Come back here!"

The dog ignored him, barking furiously as it rounded the corner.

Suddenly the barking stopped.

"Hornblower!" shouted Hodge.

A few moments later, Hornblower reappeared, walking slowly, stiffly. The dog passed Cadigan, but did not growl, or even appear to notice him. It also ignored Hodge, who frowned as the dog walked past him and into the house. Hodge then turned to Cadigan and said, with more than a little irritation in his voice, "What do you want?"

"I was wondering," said Cadigan, moving around to Hodge's right, so that Hodge had to turn to keep facing him, "if you noticed anything odd about Jarvis."

"What do you mean?" said Hodge, who in fact thought that both Jarvis *and* Cadigan had recently been acting odd. The door was now to Hodge's left; his back was toward the corner of the house, and thus he did not see the dark figure rounding the corner, coming toward him.

"What I mean," said Cadigan, "is that I'm a bit troubled by his general lack of comportment."

Hodge scowled. "What are you talking about?" he said.

"What I mean to say," said Cadigan, "and I don't in no way mean to imply this for certain, but, judging from my own reconnaissance, if you will, it seems to me that Jarvis has been displaying a certain lack of procedural rectitude, if you follow me."

"No," said Hodge. "I don't follow you. Not at all. And I don't think I should be out here, neither." He started to turn toward the door.

"Wait," said Cadigan, putting a hand on Hodge's thick right forearm.

Hodge, irritated, turned back and started to say something, but stopped when he felt the air suddenly grow colder.

Out of the corner of his left eye, Cadigan saw Hodge's shadow moving, stretching back. . . .

Instantly, Hodge slumped, the life gone from his face. Gone, too, was his shadow, replaced in a moment by another, thinner one. Now Hodge came back to life, but his expression had changed from suspicion and irritation to passiveness and docility. Cadigan saw Ombra tuck his rough cloth bag into the darkness of his cloak, then turn and glide back toward the corner of the house, where he vanished.

"This way," said the groaning voice.

"Yes, m'lord," said Hodge, pivoting and following Ombra. Cadigan followed Hodge, both men moving in the same stiff-legged manner. They rounded the house and rejoined the others near the front gate. Ombra ordered Jarvis, Cadigan, and Hodge to guard the house, then turned to Slank and Nerezza.

"You will bring the lady of the house here. Her room is on the third floor. Do not harm her. Put her in the taxi. Gerch and Hampton will see her back to the ship. You will wait here for me."

"As you wish," Nerezza said. He exhaled, the cold air causing a plume of condensation to whistle from his nose-piece.

"What about the girl?" said Slank. He very much wanted to see the girl. He vividly remembered the last time he'd seen her—she and the boy—flying away, leaving him in the rowboat, defeated. Oh, yes, he would like to see that girl again, and the look of fear on her face when she realized that she was not rid of him.

But Slank's face fell when Ombra answered: "I will deal with the girl."

Disappointed, but not about to defy Ombra, Slank turned and followed Nerezza up the walkway toward the house. A moment later, Ombra glided after them. Gerch and Hampton watched the dark form disappear silently through the doorway.

"I wonder why he wants to get the girl," said Hampton.

"I don't know," said Gerch. "But I would not want to be the girl."

# OVERHEARD WORDS

PETER, WITH TINK on his shoulder, crouched on a high tree branch directly across the street from Molly's house. His worst fears had been realized: Slank had arrived here first, along with the others from the ship, including the dark-cloaked man who aroused such fear in Tink.

Not only were they already here ahead of him, but they'd met no resistance. Although the tree branches, the fog, and the cab all conspired to obscure Peter's vision of the group across the street, he'd seen enough to understand that all of the men outside the house—including those he took to be guards—were taking orders from the dark-cloaked figure. And he had overheard enough of their conversation to catch the words "lady of the house" and "girl."

Now three of the men—including Slank and the

dark-cloaked man—were heading into the house. The other four men remained out front. Peter couldn't very well use the front door, but he had to get in somehow.

He had to warn Molly.

## CHAPTER 61

# $\mathcal{F}$OOTSTEPS

$\mathcal{M}$OLLY BACKED AWAY FROM the doorway, her eyes on the knife in Jenna's hand. It was a kitchen knife; Molly had seen Mrs. Conine chop vegetables with its long, gleaming blade, always honed razor sharp.

As Molly stepped back, Jenna moved forward, filling the doorway.

"Was the young lady going out?" she said, with mock servility.

"What are you doing?" said Molly, her eyes still on the knife.

"I'm keeping you in your room, *m'lady*," said Jenna, in a tone unlike any she had used with Molly before. Gone was any trace of subservience; in its place was only hard contempt.

"You can't do this!" said Molly, raising her voice, trying to give it a confidence she didn't feel.

Jenna wiggled the knife. "Can't I, *m'lady?*"

Before Molly could speak again, she heard a dull thumping of footsteps coming upstairs from several floors below. The footfalls were heavy: men, possibly two or three of them. Molly looked past Jenna, through her open doorway.

"Help!" she screamed as loudly as she could. "Help! She has a knife! Please, help me!"

No answer. The thumps stopped, but for only a moment; then they resumed.

"Help!" Molly called again, less hopefully. Jenna smirked, as if to say that whoever was coming up the stairs would be of no help to Molly.

The two young women stared at each other as the footsteps reached the second-floor landing, then the third. Molly waited, expecting to hear the familiar creak of footsteps on the stairway that led up to her room in the south tower. Instead, she heard a door opening on the floor below.

Then she heard her mother scream.

## CHAPTER 62

# ROUGH HANDS

LOUISE ASTER, dressed in a white linen nightgown, stared in horror. Hearing Molly's cry for help, Louise had run to her bedroom door and flung it open, only to find herself facing two hard-looking men, one with a nose that belonged on a carved wooden mask. She backed away from the doorway, her throat tightening in terror.

Slank and Nerezza stepped toward her. Louise screamed and turned to run. But Slank, moving with the speed of a striking snake, grabbed her arm with thick, calloused fingers and yanked her back toward the door. Louise cried out again, dragging her heels and throwing elbows into Slank's ribs, struggling desperately to break free. But Slank held her tightly, pulling her roughly into the hallway.

There Lady Aster felt a sudden chill engulf her body, a sensation so startling that she stopped struggling for an instant. And in that instant she caught a glimpse of a dark form moving—flowing—up the stairs to the south tower.

To Molly's room.

"RUN, MOLLY!" she shouted. "RU—"

A rough hand clamped over her mouth while another took her by the neck, cutting off her anguished voice. Nerezza and Slank both had hold of her now; she struggled, but was powerless to prevent them from dragging her down the stairs. She managed only one glance back, a glance that revealed the dark form sliding up the tower stairwell, silently, smoothly, like a monstrous leech.

## CHAPTER 63

# The Thing on the Stairs

THE SOUND OF LOUISE ASTER'S SCREAMS echoed horribly up the stairwell to Molly's room; then—even more horribly—her mother's voice was choked into silence. Molly took a frantic step toward the doorway, only to be forced back again by a threatening thrust of the blade held in Jenna's hand.

Molly spun around, looking for another way out, but there was no other way, save for the window. She ran to it and screamed at what she saw below: her mother, struggling furiously but uselessly, was being dragged down the walk by two men, toward a waiting cab.

Molly quickly unlatched the window and yanked it upward with all her strength. The window shot open. Molly reached for the chain around her neck, feeling for her locket.

Too late. Jenna had crossed the room, bringing the point of the knife to within inches of Molly's face.

"I'll take the locket, m'*lady*," she said.

"No," said Molly, backing away from the blade. She felt herself bump her writing desk; the impact caused the oil lamp to wobble, sending the shadows of the two young women dancing along the walls.

"If you won't give it to me," said Jenna, moving forward, "then I'll cut it from your neck. I might cut you while I'm at it. Sometimes I'm not too handy with a knife."

Molly saw the knife coming closer. She reached behind her, frantically feeling for anything to use as a weapon. Her right hand brushed something, and she grabbed it. Jenna flicked the knife forward expertly, catching the locket chain with the blade point, severing it. As chain and locket clattered to the floor, Molly whipped her arm forward, the ink bottle in her hand. She hurled the ink directly into Jenna's face. Jenna shrieked and brought her left hand to her eyes, but managed to hold on to the knife with her right. She took a vicious crosswise swipe at Molly, a swipe that would have slashed Molly's throat had Molly not seen it coming and ducked. Molly felt the blade edge just barely brush the top of her hair. Taking advantage of Jenna's momentary blindness, Molly lunged past her toward the door. Behind her she heard Jenna stumbling around, sightless, screaming in rage.

Molly reached the door and ran through it onto the

landing at the top of the stairs. She stopped—and shrieked again.

The dark man was slithering up the stairs toward her. Molly was looking right at him, ten feet away, but could see none of his features; where his face should have been, Molly saw only blackness. But she *felt* his presence intensely, felt the air grow cold.

Behind her, Molly heard Jenna stumbling toward the doorway, getting close now. But Molly would rather have faced a dozen knife-wielding Jennas than descend the stairway toward that faceless creeping *thing*.

Molly turned around; Jenna, her face stained a deep indigo, was coming out the door, still clutching the knife in one hand and vigorously rubbing her eyes with the other. Molly hid to the side. As Jenna stepped through the doorway, Molly stuck out her leg. Jenna tripped hard, falling forward onto the landing, the knife clattering across the floor.

Molly darted past the sprawling form of Jenna, into her room. She slammed the door shut; the last thing she saw before it closed was the dark man reaching the top of the landing. She could feel him looking at her with his formless face.

Gasping with fear, Molly fumbled with the bolt on the door, finally sliding it home. She turned and looked toward the window, her only hope of escape now. But she was four stories up; to get out that way, first she had to find the locket. She dropped to her hands and knees and, by the dim, flickering light of the oil lamp, began frantically searching the floor.

As she did, she heard a groaning sound right outside her door. And she felt the air growing colder.

## CHAPTER 64

# THE BLACK POOL

OMBRA'S SHIFTING FORM hovered alongside the blinded Jenna, who groveled at the hem of his cape, her ink-stained eyes stinging painfully. The knife, with its shining blade, lay on the floor between them.

"My lord . . ." said Jenna, "I'm sorry. Forgive me. I—"

"A knife?" came the low wheeze of Ombra's voice. "You might have hurt her."

"I beg you, my lord—"

"We *need* her, you fool."

"I only meant to—"

"You dare disobey my instructions?"

As he spoke, Ombra moved so that his cloaklike shape edged over the maid's shadow, cast by the hall's flickering wall lamp. Jenna's stinging, bloodshot eyes widened in fear.

"No!" she cried, trying to scramble away on the floor. "I'm sorry, Lord Ombra! Please!"

But it was too late. Jenna's shadow, where it touched Ombra, was turning bloodred. The coloration spread rapidly across her shadow to her feet, then through her legs into her black-and-white uniform, disappearing briefly until it appeared again on her arms, her neck, her face.

Jenna, her entire body crimson now, writhed on the floor in agony, her voice weakening.

"Please . . . no . . ."

Ombra stepped off her shadow. Instantly the redness began receding from her body, flowing back into his cape, as if sucked into a huge black sponge. Jenna's skin returned to its sallow, pale color. Her eyes wept indigo tears.

"You will remain here," Ombra said, "and await my orders. You will obey my orders *exactly*."

Jenna nodded vigorously.

Ombra turned the doorknob, pushed: the door was locked. He looked down at the bottom of the door. And then he disappeared.

Except that he had not disappeared. Where he had stood, now there was only a shadow—a black, lightless pool on the floor, next to the crack at the bottom of the door.

Silently, the shadow began to flow forward under the door, and into Molly's room.

## CHAPTER 65

# An Urgent Search

Peter perched on a narrow ledge outside the third floor of the house. He had been flying from window to window—the house had dozens—peering painstakingly into each one, looking, without success, for Molly. He'd tried opening them, but they were latched shut. He'd also considered breaking one, but the panes were too small for him to climb through.

A few minutes earlier he'd heard muffled screams; these had drawn him to the window of the room he stood outside now. He'd gotten there just in time to see a lady—not Molly—being dragged out by Slank and another man.

Now, looking down at the front walk, he saw the lady being carried roughly to the cab. She was putting up a game fight, but she was no match for the two men. Peter hesitated, wanting to help the woman, but knowing that he could not leave Molly alone in the house. He watched helplessly as the men forced the lady into the cab; two of the other men climbed in after her. The driver flicked the reins, and in a moment the cab disappeared into the foggy night.

Peter turned back to the house and resumed going window to window. His search was all the more urgent now. The dark-cloaked man had not emerged from the house. He was still inside, no doubt looking for Molly.

Peter had to find her first.

CHAPTER 66

# $\mathcal{T}$HE $\mathcal{E}$NVELOPE

$\mathcal{M}$OLLY, ON HANDS AND KNEES, swept her eyes back and forth along the floor, desperately searching by the dim lamplight for the fallen locket.

She tried not to think about what was on the other side of her door. She'd heard Jenna's voice—an awful, agonized cry, an inhuman groaning. She tried to concentrate her mind only on finding the locket, and not on whoever, *whatever*, was making that sound.

She jumped as the doorknob rattled. The door moved as pressure was applied from the other side, but the bolt held. Molly ran her hands along the floor under the writing desk, feeling for the locket. Where was it?

Suddenly the air—already chilly—grew much colder. Molly thought at first it was a gust of wind coming through the open window. But she was facing the window now, and the cold air was coming from *behind* her.

From the door.

She turned and raised a hand to her mouth. From the crack at the bottom of the door, blackness was seeping into the room. At first it was a dark line along the base of the door, but it quickly spread outward on the floor, and then began to billow upward, like a cloud made of night itself, formless at first, but gradually assuming the shape of the cloaked thing from the stairway.

For the fourth time this terrible night, Molly screamed. She backed away as the cloaked creature glided a few feet toward her. Then, from the featureless blackness that served as its face, it spoke in the hideous groan Molly had heard before, though now she could make out the words:

"Do not be afraid. I mean you no harm."

Molly struggled to control her voice. "Who are you?" she said. "Why have you taken my mother?"

"I am Lord Ombra," groaned the dark thing. "Your mother will not be harmed, provided that you do as you are told."

"What do you want me to do?" said Molly.

Ombra's shape shifted, and from somewhere—Molly could not tell where—he produced a white envelope, about six inches square. This he extended toward Molly.

"You will give this to your father," he said.

Molly looked at the envelope, but did not reach for it.

"I don't know where my father is," she said.

"If you wish your mother to be unharmed," said Ombra, "you will find him."

"But *how?*" said Molly, her voice breaking. "He didn't tell me where—"

"*You will find him,*" hissed Ombra.

The dark robes began gliding forward again, the envelope extended. Molly was about to reach for it, if only to stop this horrible thing from coming any closer. But something nagged at her. There was something odd about the way Ombra was moving. Her mind raced. *What was it?*

She looked down at the floor and back up. Then it came to her.

She was standing next to her writing desk, upon which sat the oil lamp. The lamp was to her right; her shadow was cast on the floor to her left. Ombra was not moving directly toward her; he was moving diagonally, to his right.

He was moving to her shadow. He was inches away from it.

*Beware the shadows.*

Molly reached forward, as if to take the envelope. Ombra paused in his advance and extended it to her. At that instant, Molly lunged to her right; the envelope fell to the floor. Ombra, seeing what Molly intended to do, moved swiftly after her shadow, but just before he reached it, Molly reached the lamp and blew out the flame.

The room went dark.

"That was very foolish," groaned Ombra.

Molly didn't answer. As quietly as she could, she moved in the pitch blackness toward where she remembered the door to be. She screamed when she felt the deep coldness directly in front of her and heard the hideous mocking voice only inches away.

"Do you think I'm going to let you simply walk out, little girl?" it said. "Do you think I can't see you? Do you think the darkness hampers *me?*"

Molly stumbled blindly backward into the room. She heard the door swing open.

"Jenna," Ombra groaned.

"Yes, Lord Ombra," came Jenna's eager voice.

"Come in here and relight the young lady's lamp, so she and I can become . . . *acquainted.*"

"Yes, Lord Ombra."

Molly heard Jenna moving tentatively into the room, feeling her way in the darkness to the fireplace, where the matches were kept. She heard Jenna picking up the wooden matchbox, then shuffling over to the writing desk, then lifting the glass globe. She heard the scrape of the match, saw the flame, saw Jenna's indigo-stained face, first leaning over to light the wick, then flashing Molly a smile of joyful hatred.

The lamp flared to life. Ombra turned toward Molly. Her shadow was cast behind her now. Ombra began to glide forward. Molly looked desperately around, but there was nowhere to go, nowhere but the open window. She edged toward it, but hopelessness was overwhelming her now. The window was four stories up; to jump from it was to die.

For the rest of her life, Molly would remember what happened next.

First, she caught glimpse of a pulsing glow from just under her bed: her locket. *But if it's glowing . . .*

Next, a sensation of something deeply familiar infusing her being, like a missing part of her soul had returned.

Then, finally, a voice—a voice she'd thought she might never hear again, a voice that, even in this moment of despair, swelled her heart.

"Molly!" the voice cried.

She turned and saw him crouched in the window.

"Peter!"

"Look out!" he said, seeing Ombra moving toward her, a few feet away now. Peter jumped into the room, clapped a hand over Molly's eyes, closed his own, and shouted, "Now, Tink!"

A blinding light filled the room for an instant, then was gone. Peter opened his eyes and took his hand from Molly's. Tink lay on Peter's shoulder, exhausted, nearly unconscious. Tenderly, Peter lifted her and tucked her into his shirt.

By the dim light of the oil lamp they saw Jenna at the writing table, blinking and disoriented. In the far corner of the room, on the floor by the door, was a dark, roiling, indistinct shape. Jenna stumbled toward it.

"Lord Ombra!" she cried.

The dark shape began to billow upward. Jenna, still blinking, looked around the room, her gaze finding Molly and Peter.

"Over there, Lord Ombra!" she said. "By the window."

The dark cloud, now taking Ombra's form again, began to ooze toward them.

Peter jumped to the window ledge and held out his hand.

"Come on, Molly!" he said. "Take my hand!"

"But . . . can you fly us both?" she asked.

"We have to try!" he said. "Hurry!"

Molly looked back at the advancing form of Ombra, then at Peter. She took a step toward the window, then turned. There was no time to retrieve her locket from under the bed. Quickly she bent down and scooped something off the floor: the envelope.

Holding it, she ran to the window and climbed onto the ledge, sitting next to Peter, their legs dangling out. He put his left arm around her tightly, and she put her right arm around him.

"Hold tight," he whispered, and as he strained upward with all his might, they slid off the ledge, inches before the black shape got to the window and reached, grasping, into the night, clutching only fog.

## CHAPTER 67

# THE PHANTOM LIGHT

AN INHUMAN ROAR OF RAGE, like wind from a deep, cold cave, filled the night. The sound froze Slank and Nerezza, who stood at the end of the walk, having just seen the cab, and their prisoner, off to the ship. In a moment they were joined by Jarvis, Cadigan, and Hodge, who came running from their posts around the house.

They looked toward the source of the horrible sound and saw Ombra's dark form leaning out the fourth-story window, an arm extended, pointing at something flying awkwardly, erratically, overhead toward Kensington Gardens.

Slank squinted up at it, then cursed in fury.

*The boy. The flying boy. And he had the girl.*

"Stop them!" commanded Ombra, but all five men were already pursuing the ghostly figures now passing over the streetlight. The men ran across the street, only to be confronted by the high fence surrounding the mansion opposite the Asters', its massive iron gate locked shut. Hodge, familiar with the neighborhood, led the others to the right and down an alleyway along the side of the mansion, into the park. By then the flying boy and girl were out of sight, having vanished over the roof. But Slank had not given up.

"He was falling!" he yelled. "Did you see that? He was falling!"

———

Peter was, in fact, falling.

Molly's weight was proving too much for him; he couldn't support her much longer. As they cleared the mansion roof he heard the shouts of the men coming around the side. Clinging tight to Molly, he strained desperately upward, but felt them descending, felt the dark ground below getting closer. . . .

Molly felt it, too.

"Peter . . ." she whispered helplessly.

"I know. . . ."

Dull bells sounded from beneath his shirt, where the weakened Tink clung to his collar.

*We're falling.*

"I know," he repeated.

*Do something. Drop the girl.*

"No!"

"What?" Molly said.

"Not you!" Peter said. He heard shouts from the right. He strained upward. Nothing.

More bells. *You can't fly with this cow holding you down.*

"Be quiet!"

"What?" said Molly.

"Nothing! I mean, not you!" The shouts were closer now. *Do I have to do everything myself?*

And with that, Tink, unseen by Molly, darted out of the back of Peter's collar and flew into the night.

———•••———

"This way! This way!"

Slank, now running in front, raced into the dew-soaked grass of Kensington Gardens. He stopped, the others stopping behind him. Their eyes searched the dark sky.

"They *can't* have gotten far," Slank said, frustration and rage choking his voice. "They were *sinking.* You saw that, didn't you? He could barely fly."

"There!" Hodge shouted, pointing.

The others followed his gaze, and saw it: a pale yellow light flitting through the fog about twenty-five yards away.

"That's them!" yelled Slank, breaking into a run, the others on his heels.

———•••———

Peter saw dark shapes directly ahead, closer and closer. Trees.

He and Molly were too low; they were going to hit them.

"Hang on tight," he whispered to Molly. With his last ounce of strength, he made one more desperate effort to swoop upward. For a second or two, nothing happened. Then he felt it—felt them ascending, just the slightest bit.

But not quite enough.

———✦———

Ombra stood silently in the shadow of a massive elm on the street in front of the Aster home, watching as the men returned. Their shoulders were slumped, their heads bowed; their hands empty. They had chased the mysterious phantom light halfway across Kensington Gardens, only to have it vanish. The boy and girl had escaped.

Now they trudged reluctantly toward Ombra, wondering—fearing—what the dark figure would do to them for having failed.

"My lord—" Nerezza began, only to be silenced by Ombra's upraised arm.

"Silence," said the groaning voice. "The girl took the envelope. We have her mother. Those are the important things. The girl will find her father. The message will be delivered. Slank."

"Yes, my lord."

"Find another cab."

"As you wish, my lord." Slank hurried off.

"You men," Ombra said, addressing the three guards, "will take up your positions here at the house. Jenna will tell the rest of the staff that the lady and the girl were called away in the night to join Lord Aster, and that they will be gone for several days at least. The staff will believe this; they are accustomed to the Asters' mysterious ways. I doubt the girl would be fool enough to return here, but if she does, seize her and bring her to me immediately."

The guards nodded.

"And the boy?" said Nerezza.

"Yes, the *boy*," said Ombra, and now there was anger in his voice. "The boy and his bright little friend."

The dark hood turned toward Nerezza. Nerezza thought he saw two dim red circles in the deep blackness, like glowing coals; he felt Ombra's stare, felt his face go cold as ice. Ombra's entire being seemed to swell, then subside; there was a rustling noise that sounded, to Nerezza, like the wing of a giant bat.

"You told me there was no stowaway on your ship, *Captain* Nerezza. But it seems you were wrong."

Nerezza tried to answer, but found he could not talk, could not move.

Ombra looked away, and suddenly Nerezza could move again.

"I very much look forward to meeting the boy again," Ombra said, his voice once again calm. "I have . . . *plans* for the boy."

From the south, the sound of clopping hooves came up the street. Slank had found a cab. Ombra turned away, leaving Nerezza to rub his still-cold face and to wonder what ugly fate this dark thing had in mind for the boy.

.

## CHAPTER 68

# CONVERSATION IN A TREE

PETER AND MOLLY sat next to each other high in an oak tree on the west side of Kensington Palace, shoulders just touching, listening intently for sounds of the men searching for them. They'd made a lucky landing on a wide limb and had managed, by grabbing nearby branches, not to topple off.

At first they'd sat tensely, listening to the searchers shouting nearby. But as the shouts faded into the distance, Peter and Molly began to relax. They were quiet, yet intensely aware of each other's presence. Finally Peter broke the silence with a whisper.

"Are you all right?"

"Thanks to you, yes," whispered Molly. "And you? You must be exhausted from flying us both."

"I'm fine," said Peter, though he was in fact very tired, and doubted that he could fly at all right then.

*Well, I'm not fine,* said Tink, alighting on a branch behind Molly.

"What was that?" said Molly.

"Tinker Bell!" said Peter, happy to see her back.

"Who?" said Molly.

"You met her once," said Peter. He reached past Molly and plucked Tink from the branch.

"Thanks, Tink," he said.

Tink didn't answer. She stood on Peter's palm with her arms folded; her usually golden glow had a reddish tinge, which told Peter that she was not in a good mood.

"Oh, my! Yes!" said Molly, studying her. "I remember now—the little companion bird that Father gave you back on the island."

Tink, who did not at *all* care for the phrase "little companion bird," made a discordant sound.

"Tink," said Peter, blushing. "You don't mean that."

*Yes I do.*

"You can understand her?" said Molly. She looked back and forth between Tink and Peter. "What's she saying?"

*Tell her she's a big stupid cow who nearly got us killed.*

"She says she's delighted to see you again," said Peter.

"And I'm delighted to see you," said Molly, extending the tip of her pinky toward Tink. Tink, keeping her tiny arms folded, turned haughtily around in Peter's palm so she was facing away from Molly.

"She's shy," said Peter.

"I see," said Molly doubtfully. Turning her attention back to Peter, she said, "Peter, I am so, *so* glad to see you."

Peter blushed again, grateful that the darkness hid his reddening face.

"I have so much to tell you," Molly went on. "Something dreadful is happening. These strange men have taken my mother, and my father is gone and I don't know where he is, and the maid attacked me with a knife, and then that hideous dark *thing* back there was after me, and if you hadn't shown up when you did, I—"

Molly stopped in midsentence, frowning. "But, Peter," she said, "what *are* you doing here? I mean, I'm ever so glad that you came, but I thought you were going to stay on that island."

"I was," said Peter. "Until those men came." He nodded in the direction of Molly's house. "Slank is one of them."

Molly shuddered. "I *thought* I saw him. Father told me that men had come to the island looking for the starstuff."

"How did he know that?"

"He got a message from Ammm," said Molly. Seeing Peter's puzzled look, she added, "You remember Ammm, the porpoise."

Peter nodded. He remembered now. Quite well, in fact, though it seemed like a very long time ago.

"They came to the island looking for starstuff," he told

her. "They kidnapped Fighting Prawn's daughter and forced him to tell them that your father took the chest back to England. And I heard them say they planned to use *you* to make your father give it to them. So I decided I had to come to . . . to warn you."

"But however did you get here?" Molly said.

"On their ship," said Peter.

"With *them*? But . . . how?"

"I hid in a folded sail."

"In a sail? All the way to England? Oh, Peter," said Molly, putting her hand on his arm—an act that made his entire body tingle—"that was *very* brave."

*He'd have starved to death without me*, noted Tink.

"What did she say?" said Molly.

"She agrees with you," said Peter.

"I'm sorry you had to go through that," said Molly. "But thank goodness you did! Had you not come . . . well . . . that . . . that *thing* in my room was about to get me. He called himself Lord . . . Lord . . ." Molly frowned, trying to remember. "*Ombra*, that's it. Lord Ombra."

"He, or whatever it is, was on the ship, too," said Peter. "And the island. There's something very strange about that one."

Tink shivered.

"I know!" said Molly. "What *is* he?"

"I don't know," said Peter. "But he comes out only at

night. He seems to be afraid of light. You saw what happened to him when Tink made herself bright in your room."

*And nearly killed myself*, noted Tink, still facing away from Molly.

Molly looked questioningly at Peter.

"She says it's difficult for her, making such a bright light," said Peter.

"Oh," said Molly. "Well, thank you, Tinker Bell. Thank you both. If you hadn't arrived when you did, I believe that Lord Ombra, whatever he is, was about to—this is going to sound odd, but—I believe he was trying to do something . . . to my . . . shadow."

Peter nodded slowly. "I think you may be right. On the island, I saw him do something, but I couldn't quite figure it out."

He described what he'd seen from the tree overlooking the Mollusk village, when the dark creature had seemed to suck Fighting Prawn's shadow into him. Molly, in turn, told Peter about the warning—*Beware the shadows*—that her parents had received from their friend in Egypt.

"So this Ombra, then," said Peter, "is he one of the Others?"

"He must be," said Molly. "He said that they wouldn't . . . they wouldn't . . . ."

Her words turned into sobs. Peter put his arm around her.

Tink made a sound that could be loosely translated as "Hmph."

"He said," Molly continued, her voice quavering, "that he wouldn't harm my mother if I gave this to my father." She reached into the pocket of her dress and pulled out the square white envelope.

Peter looked at it. "Should we open it?" he said.

"I don't know," said Molly. "He definitely said I was to give it to my father. But I don't know where my father is. When he found out that those men were coming, he said he had to move the starstuff."

"Was it here?" said Peter. "In your house?"

"No," said Molly. "It was being kept in a secret place here in London, but Father felt it wasn't safe there. He said he needed to move it to a safer place, because the Others were sending something . . . what was the word he used . . . something *formidable* to retrieve it."

"Ombra," said Peter.

"Yes," agreed Molly. "That must be what it was."

"Did your father say where he was taking the starstuff?" said Peter.

"Just that it was a place away from London. He said that only a few Starcatchers know where it is. They're going to keep it there until it's time for the Return."

"What's the Return?"

"Do you remember when we were on the *Never Land,* and I first told you about starstuff?" said Molly.

"Yes," said Peter. "I made you fly to prove it was real."

Tink, very displeased that they were discussing something that happened before she came into being, turned a deeper shade of red.

"That's right," said Molly, smiling at the memory. "Well, I also told you that the Starcatchers, when they find fallen starstuff, send it away somehow, so the Others can't get hold of it."

"Yes," said Peter. "I remember now."

"That's called the Return," said Molly.

"Where do they send it?" said Peter.

"I don't know," said Molly. "Only the senior Starcatchers know about the Return. It's quite dangerous, I believe."

"But is it done, then?" said Peter. "The starstuff that Ombra and the Others are after—have the Starcatchers returned it?"

"I don't know," said Molly. "Father said the Return could happen only at certain times, so they'd have to wait for the next one. I don't know when that is. Or where it is. But now I *have* to find him, Peter."

"All right," said Peter. "Then we'll find him."

"But *how?*"

"I don't know," Peter said. "But we will. I found you, didn't I?"

Molly looked at Peter's face for a moment by Tink's soft, jealousy-hued glow. Tears slid down both of her cheeks. She squeezed his hand. He felt himself float perhaps a quarter inch off the limb.

"Yes," she said. "You did find me. You're a wonderful friend."

Peter swallowed.

"All right, then," he said. "Where do we start?"

"Well," said Molly, wiping her tears, "it looks to me as though you start with a change of clothing. And a pair of shoes."

Peter looked down with embarrassment at his filthy, stinking, tattered clothes, his bare feet black with mud.

"I'm sorry," he mumbled. "I . . . this was all I—"

"Oh, Peter," said Molly, squeezing his hand again, "don't apologize! But you must be awfully cold."

Peter, suddenly realizing how cold he was, shivered.

"We need to get you somewhere warm," said Molly, who was coatless and quite chilly herself.

"I don't think we can go back there," said Peter, pointing toward her house.

"No, definitely not," said Molly, remembering Jenna, and the guards who had turned into captors. She thought for a moment.

"I know," she said. "We can go to George's house."

"Who's George?" said Peter.

"He's a friend of mi . . . of my family," said Molly. "He's very nice, in a stuffy sort of way. He lives not far from here, about a ten-minute walk across the park. He'll help us, I'm sure."

"Good," said Peter, though he felt just the slightest bit troubled by the thought of George.

"All right, then," said Molly. "Let's get down out of this tree. Can you help me, Peter?"

"Of course," said Peter, putting his arm around her.

*Let her drop*, said Tink.

"What did she say?" said Molly.

"She said to be careful," said Peter, shooting a hot look at Tink to tell her to keep her bells to herself.

## CHAPTER 69

# A CRY ON THE WIND

JAMES AWOKE WITH A START.

*What was that sound?*

Dawn was just breaking on Mollusk Island, the sun shooting pink rays into a brightening sky. Thomas lay next to James, sleeping soundly.

"Wake up," said James, shaking him.

"*What*," said Thomas, turning away, irritated.

"Listen!" said James.

Thomas, hearing the urgency in James's voice, sat up, fully awake now.

"Is it the boars?" he said, his face filling with fear.

"No," said James. "Listen."

They remained silent for fifteen seconds, twenty . . .

Then it came again, a faint cry carried on the wind.

"That sounds like . . . Tubby Ted!" said Thomas.

"Let's go," said James.

In the desperate scramble to escape the wild boars, Tubby Ted and Prentiss had never made it to the boys' underground hideout. After waiting hours for their friends to appear, James and Thomas had set out to search for them. They'd gone over the familiar island paths, but with no luck. Then they searched farther from their hideout, venturing deeper into the jungle, higher up the mountainside. Still nothing.

Finally they were forced to consider the awful possibility that the missing boys were not lost but had been caught by the boars—or the pirates. If the pirates had them, James knew he had to ask the Mollusks for help. He had planned to do so this morning.

But then he'd awakened to Tubby Ted's cry for help.

Now James was sprinting through the jungle toward the sound, leaping over logs, holes, vines, rocks. Thomas, shorter-legged but quick, followed as closely as he could.

The next cry they heard was clearer, and closer.

"HELP!"

No question: Tubby Ted.

"SOMEONE HELP ME!!"

James opened his mouth to answer, but caught himself. It wasn't like Tubby Ted to be up this early. What if this was a trap set by the pirates? If so, he and Prentiss were walking—no, *running*—right into it. James raised his hand and stopped Thomas, the two of them huffing to catch their breath.

"Why are we stopping?"

"Because," James answered, "that's Tubby Ted's voice, and that, over there, is the sunrise. Have you ever known Tubby Ted to be awake at sunrise?"

Thomas shook his head.

"It could be a trap."

"Good point."

Tubby Ted cried out yet again. They were quite close now.

"What do we do?" Thomas whispered.

James thought about turning back, going to the Mollusks for help. But what if, when they returned, Tubby Ted was gone?

Another cry. James made up his mind.

"Watch where you walk," he said, taking a tentative step off the trail, into the thick jungle. "There could be a pit or a snare."

With their eyes on the ground, the two boys moved cautiously ahead, pushing through the dense vegetation toward the sound of the cries, which now seemed to be coming from only a few feet away; though in the tangled mass of vines and leaves the boys could see only inches ahead.

James and Thomas pushed toward the sound and stumbled into a clearing. Lifting their heads, they found themselves face-to-face with Tubby Ted.

Except that Ted's face was upside down.

He was hanging from a rope tied to his ankles. His face

was ablaze with bright red insect bites. Tears streamed from his eyes, but because he was inverted, they flowed down his forehead.

"Ted!" said James. "Are you—"

"I'm sorry," said Tubby Ted. "I wouldn't have done it. But they've got Prentiss."

"Done what?" James asked.

"Who has Prentiss?" said Thomas.

At that moment, a heavy rope net fell around them both, its weight knocking them to the jungle floor. It stank of old fish and sea muck. As they struggled to escape it, four men emerged from the jungle and quickly closed up the net.

James understood his mistake too late: he'd been so intent on where he was stepping that he'd paid no attention to the trap waiting in the treetops. Two pirates hoisted the net, turning it and the boys upside down. With the world inverted, James watched as the rope tied to Tubby Ted's ankles went slack. Tubby Ted cried out, and from James's perspective, fell upward and hit a ceiling of dirt as a *whoof* of air escaped from his lungs. Then Ted was replaced in James's view by the bearded face of a pirate, pressed close, his breath reeking even more than the net.

"You two fishies will make a *fine* catch for old Captain Hook," he said.

The other three pirates roared with laughter.

"I'm sorry," said Tubby Ted.

Two pirates strode triumphantly into the fort, carrying between them the net holding James and Thomas, still upside down and very uncomfortable after the long, jouncing trek over the mountain. Behind them, prodded by the other two pirates in the hunting party, trudged the exhausted Tubby Ted.

Hook stood in the center of the compound, waiting, a snarl of happiness on his face.

"So my plan worked," he said.

"Like a charm," said one of the net-carriers. "We hung the fat one up like you said. Cried like a baby, he did. Brought these two running right into the trap."

"I am a genius," observed Hook. There was no response. Hook glared at Smee.

"Aye, Cap'n," said Smee. "A genius."

The pirates untied the net and upended it, dumping James and Thomas into the dirt. Hook moved so that he stood directly over James, the tips of his scuffed boots just touching the boy.

"Welcome back," Hook said softly.

James looked into Hook's piercing stare, then turned his head away.

"Thought you'd escaped me, did you?" said Hook. "Well, let's see if your flying friend can rescue you *now*, boy. This time you won't be out in the open, or near the spring. You'll be in a *cage*, boy, with your three little friends. How d'you like that?" Hook spat a brown glob that splatted into the dirt an inch from James's head, then said, "Put the little bilge rats into the cage."

Rough hands shoved James, Thomas, and Tubby Ted across the compound to a box of lashed bamboo, about six feet square and four feet high. James saw hands clutching two of the bamboo poles from the inside: Prentiss. The pirates untied an elaborate series of knots, opened the top of the cage, and heaved the boys inside—two pirates being required for Tubby Ted. The boys crouched silently as the pirates carefully retied the top. Then, when the pirates had left, James spoke.

"Prentiss, are you all right?"

Prentiss' face, like Ted's, was covered with insect bites, some of them now oozing scabs.

"Yes," said Prentiss, though his lip was quivering. "I'm all right, except the bugs—"

"The bugs at night are big enough to wear shoes," said Tubby Ted. "The bites sting at first but itch something awful a few hours later."

"But the bats are the worst," Prentiss said. "Fruit bats the size of cats, with faces like little monkeys. They come out around dusk and dive and dart through the night sky like . . . like, I don't know what."

"Like bats," Tubby Ted said.

"Yes," agreed Prentiss.

"But that's not the worst," Tubby Ted said. "It's the slugs I can't stand. Long, slimy, yellow slugs that come out when you're asleep. They must like the salt on your skin or something, because I had—" Tubby Ted made a face.

"Sixty-seven," Prentiss said. "Ted had sixty-seven of 'em on him yesterday morning. Could barely see his face for all the slugs."

"And the food they give us is *awful*," said Tubby Ted.

"We've got to get out of here," James said in a whisper.

"How?" said Prentiss. "They have this cage"—he pushed at a bamboo pole—"tied tight with knots that we can't reach."

"And there's guards all day and night," said Ted.

"And," said Prentiss, "they told us that if we try to escape, they'll kill us."

"Right," said James, peering between poles at the pirates. "But if we don't escape, Hook will use us as bait to catch Peter." He looked at the other boys. "And once he has Peter, he'll kill us all anyway."

## CHAPTER 70

# RELUCTANT ALLIES

MOLLY AND PETER, with Tink sitting on Peter's head, made their way out of Kensington Gardens, into Hyde Park. The fog had turned the night nearly pitch black; Peter had no idea where they were or in which direction they were headed. But Molly, who'd spent much of her childhood roaming these grounds, forged ahead confidently, with Peter stumbling behind. This troubled Peter just a bit—having gone so quickly from heroic rescuer to passive follower.

What troubled him more was Molly's height. When last he'd seen her, back on Mollusk Island, they were the same height; if Peter stood up straight—as he tended to do when he was around Molly—he could even make himself a bit taller.

But when they'd climbed down from the tree and, for a moment, stood next to each other, Peter noticed that Molly was now taller—not by much, but taller nonetheless.

He thought Molly noticed it, too, though she said nothing.

Now, as he trotted along behind her in the darkness, a part of Peter's mind strayed from their current predicament to the troublesome fact that she was growing older and he was not. How much had she changed? What would this mean for their friendship? Would they—

"*Oof*," he said, running into Molly's back, nearly knocking her over and getting a mocking chime from Tink. "Sorry! I . . . I didn't see you stop. What is it?"

"That's Kensington Road," Molly whispered. Ahead, Peter saw the dim sphere of a streetlight, with paler echoes on either side. "George's house is just down there, past Prince's Gate in Ennismore Gardens."

They walked forward and crossed Kensington Road, deserted at this late hour. In a moment they were on a grand street lined on both sides with massive mansions standing shoulder to shoulder.

"George's house is just down here to the left," said Molly, setting off briskly. In a minute she stopped in front of a particularly fine home, with marble steps leading up to a front door flanked by massive pillars.

Molly stopped at the base of the stairs, looking up at the door, frowning.

"Are you going to knock?" said Peter.

Molly shook her head. "No," she said. "George's parents are very . . . proper. If they see y—"

She looked at Peter in his filthy rags, with Tinker Bell on his head. "If they see *us* at this time of night, they may become quite alarmed. They might even call the police, and we don't want that. One of those men back there was a constable, or at least disguised as one. We don't know who the real police are. And even if we did, how could I explain the situation to them? If I start talking about the Others, and starstuff, and the shadow creature—"

Peter nodded. Having recently escaped from the police, he had his own reasons for not wanting to be seen by them. "So what are we going to do?" he said.

"George's room is in the back," she said. "We'll go 'round through the alley, then see if we can find a way to wake him."

They walked past the mansion and turned left into a lightless alley. Gingerly, they felt their way to the end and around to the back of the Darling house. All the windows on this side were dark; what little light there was came from a streetlight on the next street over.

"George's room is on the third floor, on this corner," said Molly, pointing. "That window there."

Peter wondered how she knew that.

Molly was studying a large elm that stood next to the house. "If we could get up to that branch there," she said, "we could tap on the window."

"I can fly up there," Peter said.

Molly looked doubtful. "But George doesn't know you,"

she said. "He'd probably think you were a burglar and sound the alarm. Can you help me up? If I could just get to that lower branch there—" She pointed to a limb about ten feet away. "I think I could climb the rest of the way."

"All right," said Peter. "Hold on to my neck."

Molly stepped close and draped her arms around him. There was an awkward moment as they embraced—awkward, yet strangely pleasant for both—then Peter said, "On three, jump as hard as you can. One . . . two . . . *three*."

They sprang upward together, floating just high enough that Molly could grab the limb and clamber onto it. From there, with Peter's help, she was able to climb to the limb at the third-floor level. Then, with Peter crouching behind, she crept out onto the limb to the window.

She took a breath, then made a fist and rapped on the glass three times.

Nothing.

Three more raps, harder this time.

Still nothing.

Molly had drawn back her fist to try again, when she gasped; a pale, puzzled face had appeared in the window. Molly's fist became a waving hand.

"George!" she whispered. "It's me! Let me in!"

The look of puzzlement on George's face turned to recognition. The window slid open.

"Molly?" George said quite loudly. "What are you doing—"

"*Shhh!*" said Molly. "Don't wake your parents! May I come in?"

"But how did you—"

"I'll explain," said Molly. "But *may I please come in out of this tree?*"

"Oh, yes, of course. Sorry!" George pushed a large telescope away from the window, then helped Molly into his room. He was wearing a long nightshirt and a tasseled nightcap, which made his ears seem to protrude even more than usual.

"You must be freezing," he said, noticing that Molly wore no coat. He began to close the window.

"No!" whispered Molly.

George looked back at her.

"There's someone else in the tree," she said. "A friend."

"*What?*" said George, sticking his head out the window. Seeing Peter, he raised up and smacked his head hard on the window frame.

"OW!"

*Another idiot*, observed Tinker Bell.

"Quiet," said Peter, stuffing her into his shirt.

Rubbing his head, George said, "Who on earth are *you?*"

"I'm Peter," said Peter.

"He's a friend of mine," said Molly. "He's cold. Please let him in."

"But . . . but . . ." said George, his aching brain in danger of being overwhelmed.

"*Please*, George," said Molly.

"Well, I mean . . . I suppose if—" said George.

"Oh, *thank* you," said Molly, brushing past George and helping Peter through the window. For a moment Peter and George studied each other; neither seemed impressed with what he saw. Peter saw a gawky, stiff, and—unfortunately— tall boy with dark eyes, pink cheeks, and large ears. George saw a compact, wiry boy with an impish face and a tousled nest of reddish hair, barefoot and clad in filthy, torn rags. Under George's scrutiny, Peter suddenly became acutely aware that he had not bathed in a very long time.

"Well then!" said Molly. "George, this is Peter. Peter, George."

The two boys continued to regard each other doubtfully.

"I suppose I should explain," Molly said.

"Yes," said George, turning to her. "Please do."

"All right, then," she said. "It's a bit complicated"—she gave Peter a look. "But I'll try." She took a deep breath, exhaled, then said, "Some men came to my house tonight and took my mother."

"*What?*" said George. "Took her *where?*"

"I don't know," said Molly. "They forced her into a cab and took her away."

"But . . . who are these men?"

"They're evil men, George. They've taken my mother because they want something from my father. They're using her as leverage to get it."

"So they're kidnappers!" said George. "But, Molly, that's *awful*! Did you tell the police?"

"No," said Molly.

"Why on earth not?"

Molly looked at Peter again, then said, "I can't, George. I think the police may be involved. And there are"—she glanced at Peter—"other reasons."

"Well then, let me tell Father," said George. "He knows some very important people. He can . . ."

"*No*," said Molly, with an urgency that made George flinch. "You mustn't tell *anybody*. You could put my mother in even worse danger. Please promise me, George. *You mustn't tell anybody*."

"All right," said George reluctantly. "But if you don't want help, why are you here?" He glanced at Peter as he said this.

"We have nowhere else to go," said Molly. "We were getting cold."

"But what about your own house?"

"We can't go there," said Molly. "The men who . . . who took my mother are still there."

"They're in your house *now*?" George threw his hands up, then let them fall at his sides. "Well, if you're not going to ask the police for help, what *are* you going to do?"

"I don't know yet," said Molly. "I need to think about it. But for now, I was hoping that you could let us stay here, and perhaps lend us some warm clothes."

George eyed Peter's filthy figure with a look of open distaste. Peter looked back defiantly.

"Please," said Molly.

George sighed. "I suppose I could find some old things," he said, "from when I was smaller."

Peter bristled, standing up straight.

"I don't need charity," he said.

*Yes you do,* chimed Tink.

"Be quiet," said Peter.

"What did you say?" said George.

"Nothing," said Peter.

"Yes, you did," said George. "I heard you say something."

The two boys glared at each other until Molly stepped between them.

"Please," she said. "Please don't argue, not now. I've got to find my father. I've got to help my . . . my . . ." Molly buried her face in her hands, sobbing.

George and Peter both looked down, ashamed.

"I'm sorry," said George.

"Me too," said Peter.

*She even cries like a cow,* said Tinker Bell.

"Be quiet," said Peter. George heard him, but let it go.

"I'm sorry," said Molly, wiping her eyes on her sleeve.

Both boys shifted position, as if about to comfort her, but neither moved. For a moment there was no sound except for Molly sniffling.

"All right, then," George said finally. "I'll go get some clothes for . . . for—"

"Peter," said Peter.

"Right, Peter," said George. "And, Molly—"

"Yes?"

"Whatever help you need," said George, "I'm . . . I mean—"

"Thank you, George," said Molly. She put her hand on his arm, an act that caused both George and Peter to redden, but for quite different reasons. The boys exchanged a look, and two things were clear to both of them:

One was that they were, for now, allies.

The other was that they were most definitely not friends.

## CHAPTER 71

# THE SECRET PLACE

GEORGE HAD FINALLY fallen asleep. He was snoring on the floor, having insisted that Molly, being a girl, should take his bed. Molly had refused, insisting that Peter, being the most tired, should take the bed. Peter, of course, had refused.

So the bed was empty, and all three young people lay on the floor. George was the only one who'd managed to fall asleep, despite the fact that he was using a cricket bat as a pillow. Molly and Peter lay next to each other, both exhausted but too agitated by the night's events to find the comfort of slumber. Tink—who had been hidden, unhappily, under the bed while George was awake—now sprawled on Peter's chest.

Peter had cleaned himself up, somewhat, in George's washbasin and was wearing a pair of George's old knickers and a white cotton shirt, both finer than any clothing Peter had ever owned himself. George had also given him stockings and a pair of shoes that were a bit too large, but far better than nothing.

For the better part of an hour, the only sound in the room was George's rhythmic drone of a snore. Then Molly whispered, "I'm going to open it."

"Open what?" whispered Peter.

"The letter that . . . Ombra *thing* gave me," whispered Molly.

"I thought he said to give it to your—"

"Father, yes. But I don't know where Father is, and there might be something in the letter that will help. Tinker Bell? Do you think you could give me a bit of light?"

*I'm too tired.*

"What did she say?" whispered Molly.

"She said she'd be delighted," said Peter, prodding Tink to her feet.

By Tink's soft golden glow, Molly broke the wax seal on the envelope and pulled out a single sheet of paper bearing words written in compact, precise penmanship. Together, she and Peter read the message:

*Lord Aster,*

*You are in possession of certain property unlawfully taken from the ship Never Land. I am in possession of your wife. I propose to make an exchange.*

*You are to send a representative to the center of Tower*

*Bridge at midnight. He will receive instructions for the exchange from my representative, who will be holding a red lantern. My representative will be on the bridge each night at midnight for seven nights. If you do not respond within that time, or if you make any effort to dispose of the property, you will not see your wife again. Likewise, if you, or anyone, should attempt to rescue your wife, she will come to the gravest harm.*

*I trust that, as a man of reason, you will agree that your wife's well-being is more important than your continued possession of property that rightfully belongs to others.*

*Most sincerely,*

*Lord Ombra*

Molly put the letter down and looked at Peter, despair filling her face.

"He's going to kill her," she whispered.

"No, no," said Peter, draping his arm somewhat awkwardly over Molly's shoulders. "We'll find your father."

"But how?" said Molly. "This"—she held up the letter—"doesn't tell us anything. I don't know where to start."

"You must know somebody who knows where he went," said Peter. "Aren't there other Starcatchers in London?"

"Yes, but Father has always shielded me from most of his Starcatcher activities. He said I wasn't old enough yet to—" She stopped and sat up straight. "That's it!"

"What?" said Peter.

"The Tower," said Molly.

"What tower?"

"The Tower of London."

"What about it?"

"Before Father moved the starstuff," Molly said, "he said it was somewhere here in London—somewhere well guarded. I think he meant the Tower."

"Why?"

"Sometimes," said Molly, "when Father has business in the City, he takes me along. Three times this year, when he was done with his meetings, we stopped at the Tower. It was always at night, after visiting hours. A certain guard, a man with a thick white beard, would let Father pass, but Father always made me wait with the guard. If I asked why, Father would make some joke about not wanting me to get my head chopped off. He'd be inside for fifteen minutes—half an hour, at most—then he'd come out and we'd go home."

Peter thought for a moment, then said, "So you don't *know* the starstuff was even in there."

"No, I don't," agreed Molly. "But it makes sense. It's a well-guarded place, and Father visited it, and he obviously was keeping the reason secret, even from me."

"But even if the starstuff *was* there," said Peter, "it's not there now, is it?"

"No," said Molly. "But if I go in there, I might find somebody who knows where Father has gone."

"All right," said Peter. "Let's go."

Molly smiled, grateful that Peter had included himself. She looked at the window; the black of night was giving way to the gray of dawn.

"We'll have to wait until tonight," she said. "The Tower is full of visitors during the day. And we need to go when we're certain to find the guard who let my father in."

"All right," said Peter. "But what do we do today?"

"I suppose we'll have to stay here with George," said Molly.

"Oh," said Peter.

They both looked at George, still snoring on his cricket bat.

"He's really not such a bad sort," said Molly. "Once you get to know him."

Peter said nothing.

*You're jealous!* said Tinker Bell.

"I am not," said Peter.

"What did she say?" said Molly.

"Nothing," said Peter. Then, turning away from Molly, he lay back down on the hard wooden floor and tried, with little hope of success, to fall asleep.

CHAPTER 72

# ᴛHE WARDER AND THE WATCHER

PETER AND MOLLY spent a long, restless day hiding in George's room. After eating the scones that George had managed to spirit away from the breakfast table, they spent most of the time dozing and staring out the window at the gray London sky. They tried reading some of George's books, but most of them were about astronomy, and quite technical; neither Peter nor Molly found them particularly interesting. Tink spent the day under the bed, out of George's sight; and though she was not happy about it, she was at least quiet.

The one moment of tension occurred when the housemaid came to tidy up George's bedroom. George managed to turn her away with a story about not wanting her to disturb the baby bat that he had found and was nursing back to health. The housemaid found this quite believable, as the

Darling house did, in fact, have a colony of bats in the attic, and the maid was terrified of them. She scurried away, muttering about the insanity of wanting to make a bat any healthier than it already was.

Other than that, the day was a slow, dull procession of uneventful hours. George tried several times to get Molly to tell him more about her predicament, only to be rebuffed, to his irritation and Peter's not-very-well-concealed enjoyment. George was also quite miffed that, when night finally fell, Molly borrowed two coats from him, and money for a taxi—then refused to let him accompany her and Peter, or even to tell him where they were going.

"But why *not*?" he said.

"I can't explain," said Molly. "Not now. But you can't go."

"Then why is *he* going?" said George, pointing at Peter, who stared back with just enough of a smile to infuriate George.

"Because he . . . I'm sorry, but I can't explain that either," said Molly. Seeing George's angry look, she added, "Please, George, trust me. I'm ever so grateful for your help—we both are—but right now, I can't tell you anything more."

"Fine, then," said George, plopping himself on his bed with a look that said it was not a bit fine. "What are *you* doing?" he said to Peter, who was on his hands and knees, reaching under the bed.

"Nothing," said Peter, surreptitiously snagging Tink and tucking her into his shirt.

"We'll be back later," said Molly. She pushed George's telescope aside and opened the window.

George sat silently, staring at the floor.

"Good-bye, then," said Molly, as she climbed out onto the tree limb, followed by Peter, who shut the window behind them.

"Is he looking out the window?" asked Molly.

"No," said Peter. "He's still moping on the bed."

"Then please fly me down," said Molly.

She wrapped her arms around his neck and they slid off the branch, descending quickly but safely to the ground. With Molly leading the way, they went back to Kensington Road, where they found a cab waiting by a low, green cabmen's shelter. As they approached, Peter tucked Tinker Bell under his coat.

"To the Tower of London, please," Molly told the driver.

"Tower's closed now," he answered.

"I know," said Molly.

The driver shrugged, and Molly and Peter climbed into the cab.

They rode in silence, listening to the clopping of hooves. The streets were largely empty, and the cabbie made good time into the City, then down toward the river and along Thames Street.

The cab stopped. "Here we are," said Molly, peering out the window. She and Peter got out of the cab. The massive stone outer wall of the Tower loomed ahead. The street was deserted and dark, except for a single gas lamp doing battle with the swirling river fog.

The driver looked around. "Are you sure you want to be left here?" he said.

"Yes," said Molly, paying him.

Shaking his head, the driver flicked the reins. In a moment the cab was swallowed by the night.

"This way," said Molly. She led Peter to the southwest corner of the Tower compound. There, a stone causeway spanned the broad grassy ditch that had once been the moat. At the end of the causeway was an arch, flanked by two rectangular towers. Molly, with Peter following, crossed the causeway and entered the arch. It was lit—barely—by a lone hanging lantern. Their footsteps echoed from the cold stone walls as they passed through, unchallenged.

"Where's the guard?" Peter whispered.

"At the next gate," Molly answered.

Once through the arch, they found themselves on a second causeway. Ahead, Peter could make out another archway, this one flanked by cylindrical towers. It, too, was lit by a single lantern, and by its flickering light, Peter saw a man wearing the dark overcoat and distinctive flat-topped hat of the Yeoman Warders, or "Beefeaters," who had guarded the

Tower for centuries. He was a large man with a thick white beard. His right hand was curled around a stout wooden staff with a pointed metal tip.

As Molly and Peter approached, the guard took the staff in both hands and, in a gruff voice, called, "Who goes there?"

"It's me, sir," said Molly, stepping closer. "Molly Aster. Leonard Aster's daughter. I've been here before."

The Warder studied her by the lantern light and nodded. "Yes, you have," he said, his voice softening just a bit.

"I need to go inside," she said.

The Warder frowned. "*You* want to go inside?" he said. "Where's your father?"

"He's away," said Molly. "He sent me here on an important errand."

"And who's this?" The Warder nodded toward Peter.

"He's . . . a friend," said Molly. "He needs to go inside, too."

The Warder shook his head.

"I'll let you in," he said. "I know your father, and I know you. But I can't let him in."

"Please," said Molly.

"I'm sorry, miss. Orders is orders."

"I know that," said Molly. "But this is urgent. Something terrible has happened."

"What is it?" said the Warder.

"I . . . I can't tell you," said Molly, remembering Ombra's letter and the threat to harm her mother.

"Then I can't let him in," said the Warder.

Molly thought for a moment. "All right," she said. "I'll go in alone."

"But, Molly—" Peter protested.

"It's all right," interrupted Molly, giving Peter a look that was clearly intended to send a message, though he could not tell what the message was.

"I'll go inside," she said, "and you can wait *outside*, back through there." She gestured toward the first archway they had come through. She stared at Peter, as if waiting for him to grasp what she was getting at. But he still didn't see it.

Molly rolled her eyes. "Just don't *fly away*, all right?"

Peter felt like such an idiot, he nearly smacked himself in the head.

"Ah," he said, nodding. "I see."

"Good," said Molly, turning back to the Warder. "I'm just trying to remember," she said. "My father said I should go to the . . . the—"

"The White Tower?" said the Warder. "That's where he usually goes."

"Yes, of course," said Molly. "The White Tower. "That's the . . . the—"

"The tall one in the middle," said the Warder.

"Exactly," said Molly, walking past the Warder, through

the archway. She turned and, with a significant look, called back to Peter: "I'll see you *soon*, then."

"Right," said Peter, turning and trotting back toward the first archway, getting an earful of mocking bells from Tink.

*I thought she was going to have to draw you a picture.*

"Be quiet," he said.

He trotted back through the first archway. He stopped and looked around, his eyes sweeping the causeway and the street beyond. Seeing nobody, he turned and launched himself upward and toward the looming wall of the Tower compound. In moments he vanished, shrouded by fog and darkness.

A moment later, a man in dark clothing emerged from the moat ditch. He'd been keeping low, hidden from view, yet with a good look at the causeway. The man stared for a moment in the direction toward which Peter's flying form had just disappeared. Then, keeping to the shadows, he crept away from the old moat and began running toward the river.

## CHAPTER 73

# The Messenger

Nerezza sat at the writing table in his dim cabin aboard *Le Fantome*, his brain still echoing with the scream that, a minute earlier, had risen through his ship.

It was a woman's scream, piercing and short, as if something had suddenly cut it off. It came from below, from the locked hold where Louise Aster was being kept prisoner. A few minutes earlier, Lord Ombra, accompanied by a terrified sailor carrying a lantern, had gone down there. Then came the scream. Now the ship was silent, as every man aboard waited—like Nerezza—for the next awful sound from below.

But there was nothing more. After several silent minutes, the door to Nerezza's stateroom creaked, causing him to jerk involuntarily. He felt the now-familiar chill as the dark form of Ombra slithered into the room.

"Yes, my lord?" said Nerezza, trying to keep his voice

from betraying his annoyance at the fact that Ombra did not knock.

Ombra glided wordlessly forward, until he was directly in front of where Nerezza sat. There was a movement of his dark form, a subtle shifting of shape, and from somewhere, Ombra produced a burlap sack. He held it up for a moment, then dropped it on the table. Nerezza recoiled: the sack was moving—bulges forming and subsiding, traveling from end to end, as if some living thing, or things, were trying to escape.

Ombra emitted a low wheezing rattle that, Nerezza realized, was probably as close as Ombra came to laughing.

"They will not harm you," groaned Ombra. "They just want to go . . . *home*. The addition of Lady Aster has made it a little crowded in there. She does not enjoy being confined."

As if to demonstrate Ombra's point, the sack seemed to lunge toward Nerezza. He jerked away, nearly falling backward off his chair.

Ombra groaned, "As for the other Lady Aster—or, I should say, what is *left* of Lady Aster, in the hold—she is quite docile now, and will make no attempt to escape. But she is to remain under watch and be kept well fed. She must appear in good condition when the time comes to reunite her with her husband."

"Yes, Lord Ombra. I'll give the orders." Nerezza hoped

this might be the end of it, and that Ombra would leave his cabin and take the sack with him.

But instead, Ombra cocked his hood oddly and said, "Wait! What's that?" The hood swiveled silently on the broad, dark shoulders. "I believe we have a visitor."

Nerezza had heard nothing, but in a moment a crewman appeared in the doorway and knocked.

"What is it?" said Nerezza.

"Begging your pardon, Cap'n. A messenger. For the . . . For *him*," said the crewman, indicating Ombra. "Says it's urgent."

"Very well. Send him in," said Nerezza.

The crewman hurried up the companionway stairs. There was shouting and the sound of more footsteps.

Ombra explained: "Gerch and Hampton stationed men at various locations in the city that Lord Aster has been known to frequent. These men were ordered to watch for the boy and the girl, who are no doubt looking for Lord Aster themselves. I believe our visitor to be one of these men."

A moment later, a small, pale, nervous man entered the cabin, panting hard. Ignoring Nerezza, he approached Ombra, his expression fearful.

"My lord," the man said. "I saw . . . I—" he stuttered to a stop, staring at the faceless void beneath Ombra's hood.

"What is it?" groaned Ombra, his wheezing voice serving only to make the man more agitated.

"I . . ." The man stopped again, frozen.

Ombra glided forward until the edge of his cloak touched, then covered, the shadow cast by the messenger in the cabin's flickering lantern light. The man's face went slack; a moment later his fearful expression returned as Ombra pulled away.

"He's seen them," said Ombra. "The boy and the girl."

"Where?" said Nerezza.

"At the Tower," said Ombra, moving swiftly to the doorway.

"Are you . . . Is he sure it was them?" said Nerezza.

"Yes," said Ombra, now oozing up the companionway. "The boy flew over the wall."

"Shall I call for a carriage?" said Nerezza, following the dark form up the ladder.

"No," said Ombra. "The Tower is close by. Bring ten men. And Mister Slank."

On deck, Ombra stood impatiently by the gangplank while Nerezza shouted commands. Within two minutes he had assembled a party of ten tough, trusted men. Slank was the last to arrive on deck; the moment he did, Ombra turned and glided down the gangway, followed by the others. At the bottom Ombra turned left, going west along the quay; the men had to trot to keep up with his swiftly flowing form.

"What is it?" Slank huffed, catching up to Nerezza.

"They're at the Tower," said Nerezza.

"Both of them?" said Slank. "The boy, too?"

"The boy, too."

"Good," said Slank, patting his belt to make sure he had his knife.

## CHAPTER 74

# The Ravens' Cries

Peter and Tink, having soared high over the guard at the gate, descended cautiously into the Tower complex. They found themselves on a cobblestone street, lit—barely—by smoky torches stuck at intervals into the high stone walls on either side.

"Molly?" Peter called softly, as his feet touched the ground.

"Here," said a voice behind him, so close that he jumped in surprise, drawing a mocking chime from Tinker Bell.

"This way," said Molly, setting off up the shadowy street, Peter and Tink following. In a few yards they came to an opening on the right, with stone steps leading down to an archway and an iron gate. Beyond the gate they could make out the stone wharf alongside the black waters of the Thames.

"That's Traitor's Gate," said Molly. "It was used to bring

prisoners into the Tower. And this"—she pointed to a stone structure rising into the night sky on their left—"is the Bloody Tower."

"Why's it called that?" said Peter.

"Two boys were murdered there one night," said Molly. "One smothered, one stabbed."

"Why?" said Peter.

"They were in line for the throne," said Molly. "Not always a safe place to be. Some say their ghosts still roam these grounds. Come on."

She set off again. Peter, after another glance at the Bloody Tower, followed. They had gone only a few steps when . . .

*CAW! CAW! CAW!*

Molly shrieked and jumped back into Peter. The two of them clung together, frozen by the harsh, inhuman sound coming from the darkness just ahead and to the left.

*CAW! CAW! CAW!*

Tink emitted a peal of laughter.

*It's a bird, you ninnies.*

"What did she say?" whispered Molly, still clinging to Peter's arm.

"She says it's a bird," said Peter.

"Oh," said Molly, sounding embarrassed as she quickly let go of Peter. "The ravens."

"Ravens?" said Peter.

"They live here," said Molly. "It's a tradition. The legend is that, if the ravens ever leave the Tower, disaster would befall England."

Now Peter saw them amid the shadows—a half dozen large, black, sleek birds.

*They want to know if we have meat,* said Tink.

"Meat?" said Peter.

*They eat meat,* said Tink.

"They eat *meat?*" said Peter.

"I've heard that," said Molly. "The Warders feed them."

*CAW! CAW!*

*And biscuits soaked in blood,* said Tink.

"Tell them we don't have any," said Peter.

"Any what?" said Molly.

"Biscuits soaked in blood," said Peter.

"Well, of course we don't," said Molly.

Tink landed amid the ravens, who gathered around her glowing form. There was a brief conversation conducted in bells and caws. Tink returned to Peter and, pointing to a break in the wall to their left, said: *The White Tower is up that way.*

"The ravens say the White Tower is up that way," Peter told Molly.

"I know that," said Molly, setting off through the opening in the wall.

*Of course,* mocked Tink. *She knows everything.*

They walked up a sloping green, and in a few minutes were standing at the base of the massive central White Tower, its ninety-foot walls disappearing from view as they rose into the night fog. The exterior was dark, save for a torch to the right illuminating the base of a steep stone staircase. Molly and Peter went to it and, after a glance up at the forbidding structure looming over them, began climbing the steps.

The scuffing of their feet prevented them from hearing the sound, faint in the distance behind them, of the ravens cawing again, more agitated than before. Tink heard it, but—not wanting to leave Peter—chose to ignore the ravens' cries.

The cause of those cries was now gliding along the wharf outside the Tower, looking for a way to get in.

## CHAPTER 75

# TRAITOR'S GATE

GUIDED BY THE pale light of two lanterns, the men trotted
to keep up with the dark shape of Ombra as he moved
swiftly along the river. To their left stood the Tower Bridge,
only one of its two great towers visible, the other hidden in
the distance by the dense fog swirling over the Thames. To
the right rose the massive stone wall surrounding the Tower
of London.

Ombra stopped before an opening in the wall, leading to
a gate blocked by another wood-framed gate with iron bars.
Beyond the gate, stone steps rose to a street inside the Tower.

"Traitor's Gate," Slank said to Nerezza. "It's how high-
class prisoners was brought in. Princess Elizabeth herself was
brought through here when Bloody Mary put her in the
Tower."

The dark hood turned his way, and Slank instantly
regretted having spoken.

"Spare us the history lesson," groaned Ombra. "Captain Nerezza, take the men to the Tower entrance, but keep out of sight of the guard. Mister Slank, you are to engage the guard in conversation. When you see me approach, raise a lantern."

Slank and Nerezza nodded, then led the men away along the fortress wall, toward the Tower entrance. When Slank glanced back at Traitor's Gate, Ombra had disappeared.

Beneath the gate's bottom timber, warped from weather and weight, a shapeless pool of dark oozed forward like a wind-blown puddle. Once clear of the gate, it swirled upward, gaining height and a capelike form, the arms extending outward, then the hood upward, covering whatever dark entity existed within.

The *caw caw* of the ravens stopped. The birds themselves, normally restless, held perfectly still.

Ombra slithered soundlessly, swiftly up the Traitor's Gate steps, turning left when he reached the street. Keeping close to the wall, he followed the street to the tower that Molly had passed through—and Peter had flown over—a few minutes earlier.

Standing under the tower archway, his back to Ombra, was a guard. Ombra hung back against the wall, waiting, invisible in the darkness.

In a few minutes the guard shifted as he heard boot steps

approaching along the causeway. Then Slank came into view, lantern in hand.

"Tower's closed," the guard said.

"I know, I know," said Slank, slurring his words as if drunk. "I apologize for troubling you, sir, but I seem to be lost." He kept coming toward the guard.

"Wherever you're going," said the guard, putting both hands on his staff, "it's not here."

"No, no, no, of course not," said Slank, coming still closer. "I was hoping you could give me directions."

At that moment the guard felt a sudden intense chill behind him. Before he could turn to investigate, Slank raised the lantern. The guard's shadow appeared on the cobblestones behind him. It was motionless for a moment, then it began bending and stretching as it was sucked to the dark form of Ombra, who plucked it into the air and stuffed it into the burlap sack. Now the guard stood motionless, shadowless, his face drained of all expression.

"Summon the others," Ombra said to Slank.

Slank turned and waved his lantern. In a moment Nerezza appeared on the causeway, followed by the rest of the men. When they arrived, Ombra said, "The boy and the girl have gone to the White Tower. This way."

He turned, flowing through the archway. The men followed, each giving a wide berth to the tower guard, who stood unmoving, still holding his staff, staring ahead at nothing.

## CHAPTER 76

# McGuinn

$\mathcal{M}$OLLY AND PETER reached the top of the stone staircase and found themselves in front of a heavy oak door. Molly tried the iron handle; the door was locked. She knocked, waited, then knocked again; no answer. She pounded the door with her fist, hard, for a full fifteen seconds. Still nothing.

She was about to pound again, when they heard footsteps inside. A few seconds later a two-inch-square panel in the door slid open.

"Who is it?" It was a man's voice, high-pitched, suspicious.

"It's Molly Aster," said Molly. "Leonard Aster's daughter."

A lantern appeared in the panel opening.

"Let me see your face," said the voice.

Molly moved close to the opening so her face was illuminated by the lantern light.

"Well, well," said the voice, suddenly warm. "It *is* you. Hello, Molly."

"Is that . . . Mister McGuinn?" said Molly.

"It is indeed," said the voice. "Hold on a moment."

The panel closed.

There was a sound of heavy metal bolts sliding, and the door swung open, revealing a portly man, barely taller than Molly but as big as a barrel around his middle. He wore a gray nightshirt, his white hair tufting in all directions, his feet stuck into unbuckled shoes; clearly he'd been sleeping.

The man waddled forward and gave Molly a hug, stiffening when he caught sight of Peter over her shoulder.

"Who's this?" he said, stepping away from Molly and raising the lantern to Peter's face. His eyes widened when he caught sight of Tink sitting in Peter's hair. "And what's *that*?"

"That's Peter," said Molly, "and that's Tinker Bell."

McGuinn frowned. "Hold on," he said. "You're the boy from the island!"

"Yes," said Peter.

"Well then," said McGuinn. "Come in, come in."

He ushered them inside, closing and bolting the door behind them. They found themselves in a vast, echoing room. In the shifting lantern light, Peter could just make out distant walls and pillars rising to a high ceiling.

"I didn't expect to see you here," said Molly. To Peter, she said, "Mister McGuinn is an old friend—our families have known each other for, well, centuries. But the McGuinns live in York."

"Oh," said McGuinn, "I'm here quite often. There's always a senior Starcatcher on duty. But what are *you* doing here, Molly?"

"I'm trying to find my father," said Molly.

"He's not here," said McGuinn.

"I know that," said Molly. "But this is the only place I could think of to look."

"But your father is—"

"I know," said Molly. "He's taking the starstuff to the Return. But something urgent has come up. Men came to my house yesterday and took my mother."

"No!" said McGuinn, putting his hand on Molly's arm.

"Yes," she said. "They want to exchange her for the starstuff."

"The Others," McGuinn said grimly.

Molly nodded.

"But your father left guards," said McGuinn.

"He did," said Molly. "And they're helping the Others."

"That can't be!" said McGuinn. "Those men are—"

Molly cut him off. "The Others changed them somehow," she said. "One of the ones who came, he . . . he calls himself Lord Ombra, I don't think he's even a man. He seems to be able to take control of people. I know this sounds impossible, but somehow he seems to . . . to take their shadows."

"Oh, my," said McGuinn, running a hand through his unkempt mass of hair. "It's true, then. We'd received a message about that from Egypt."

"Yes," said Molly. "Mother told me."

"When we heard about the shadow business," said McGuinn, "and that the Others had come to that island . . ." He looked at Peter again, frowning. "But how did *you* get here from the island?"

"I hid on their ship," said Peter.

McGuinn nodded. "Molly's father said you were a brave lad."

Peter blushed.

"So," continued McGuinn, "when we got word of this shadow business, and the ship heading to London, we decided to move the starstuff away from here in preparation for the Return. Your father insisted on doing it himself, Molly."

"I know," she said. "I figured out that it must have been kept here. I know Father came to the Tower at night; sometimes he brought me. But he never let me go inside with him."

"No, he couldn't," said McGuinn. "Only senior Starcatchers are permitted in the Keep."

"What's the Keep?" said Peter.

McGuinn hesitated, then said, "Well, I suppose since you already know there's something here, I can tell you this much: the Keep is a Starcatcher sanctuary, here in the Tower. It's been here for centuries."

"Here?" said Peter. "But aren't there lots of visitors here?"

"Oh, yes," said McGuinn, smiling. "But they don't know the Keep exists. In fact, most of the Tower workers have no idea it's here. It can't be entered—it can't even be seen—except by those who know how."

"Well," said Molly, "we don't need to see it. We need to find my father, or get a message to him, and quickly. Ombra's letter says we have seven—no, six—nights to make the exchange."

McGuinn's expression became somber, his voice softer.

"I'm afraid that's a bit of a problem, Molly."

Molly frowned and said, "What do you mean?"

"Your father left strict instructions. Nobody is to be told where he has taken the starstuff. Not even you."

"But this is an emergency," pleaded Molly. "Surely if he knew that my mother—"

"No," interrupted McGuinn. "He still wouldn't want me to tell. He knew very well what the risks were when he gave the instructions. You must understand the stakes: we're safe-guarding the largest quantity of starstuff to fall in centuries—in human memory, really. That's why the Others have gone to such extremes to get it back. We *cannot* allow it to fall into their hands. To do so would be to give up everything the Starcatchers have spent generations achieving. It would be a terrible tragedy for humankind. *Nothing* is more important than getting the starstuff safely to the Return, Molly—not even our families. As Starcatchers, we must accept the risks involved. Your father understands that. You must try to understand it, too."

Molly hung her head. A tear dropped from her eye and splashed on the stone floor. McGuinn reached out and put a hand on her shoulder.

Molly shook it off.

"No," she said, looking up at McGuinn, her eyes red but defiant. "I *don't* understand. And I don't believe that Father would want to let my mother die at the hands of that . . . that *creature*."

"Molly, please," said McGuinn. "You must—"

He was interrupted by a sudden burst of sound from Tinker Bell.

"What is it?" said Molly.

"Men are here," said Peter. "A lot of men."

"I don't hear anyone," said McGuinn.

"If Tink says men are here," said Peter, "they are."

CHAPTER 77

# Wolves on the Steps

As Ombra rounded the corner of the Bloody Tower, the ravens again fell silent. The dark form drifted up the gently rising cobblestone pathway to the White Tower. Nerezza, Slank, and the men followed, their shadows shifting by the light of the swaying lanterns.

Ombra stopped at the base of the stone steps leading up to the tower. When the men had gathered round, he spoke in a low groan, his words barely audible.

"We enter here," he said. "Captain, you will post two men at the door to prevent any escape."

Nerezza said, "Begging your pardon, my lord. But if we want to prevent escape, shouldn't we *surround* the Tower?"

"I am . . . *informed* by the guard," said Ombra, "that this is the only door to the White Tower."

"But, my lord," said Nerezza, remembering Ombra's

wrath when the children escaped the Aster house, "what if they fly?"

"The windows are barred," replied Ombra. "There will be no escape that way."

Nerezza nodded.

"When we enter," continued Ombra, addressing the men, "you will spread out and search the tower. You will find Aster's daughter, and you will bring her to me unharmed."

"And the boy?" said Slank.

Ombra paused for a moment, then said, "I shall need him only for a moment, Mister Slank. Then you may have him."

Slank smiled. Ombra turned toward the waiting men, the faceless hood scanning their faces. Each man felt the cold stare as it swept across.

"The girl is most important to me. She must be brought to me unharmed. *Unharmed*. Is that understood?"

The men nodded.

"Good," said Ombra. "There will be ten gold sovereigns to the man who finds her."

The men nodded, eager now to get inside.

Ombra raised his right arm and pointed to the door. "Go," he said.

With a roar, the men charged up the steps, as hungry for gold coins as wolves for meat.

CHAPTER 78

# A Deadly Fall

Peter, Molly, and McGuinn heard it clearly now: men shouting, and the sound of boots—many boots—tromping heavily up the stone steps outside.

"Could it be Warders?" said Molly.

"No," McGuinn answered, his eyes on the door. "They're in their barracks. Nobody is supposed to be here at this hour."

The footsteps reached the top of the stairs outside. The door handle rattled. A voice outside shouted, "It's locked!"

"Break it down!" shouted another voice, which Peter recognized instantly.

"Slank," he said.

"Oh, no," said Molly. "How did *he* find us?"

"Who is it?" said McGuinn.

"He's with the Others," said Molly.

"Oh, my," said McGuinn. He jumped as a heavy body

heaved into the door behind him, the crash echoing through the vast stone room. There was another crash, then another, accompanied by shouting and cursing. The old oak creaked and groaned—but remained closed.

"It's holding," said McGuinn grimly. "That door was built for battle."

"Are there any other entrances?" said Molly.

"No," said McGuinn. "The White Tower was designed to be defended. This is the only way in."

"Or out," noted Peter.

There was another resounding crash as bodies heaved against the door—more cursing, more shouting.

And then a sudden silence.

McGuinn, Peter, and Molly stood still as statues, listening, barely breathing.

Then, from just outside the door came a faint wheezing sound. Tink made a noise Peter had come to know well.

"Ombra," he said.

"The door!" said Molly, recalling the encounter with Ombra in her room. "He's going to come under the door!"

As she spoke the cold air grew colder, and a pool of blackness began to seep through the crack at the bottom of the massive door. Tink flew to Peter's ear, chiming urgently.

"The lantern!" Peter said. "Put the lantern near him!"

McGuinn hesitated, puzzled.

"He doesn't like light!" said Peter. "Put the light on him!"

McGuinn brought the lantern down to the middle of the black pool coming under the doorway. Instantly it shrank back, though two dark tentacles on either side kept advancing. McGuinn swung the lantern right, then left, driving the tentacles back. But as soon as he moved from one part of the pool to another, the part he'd abandoned began advancing again. Molly and Peter watched helplessly as McGuinn moved the lantern back and forth, back and forth, his motions increasingly frantic. But it was quickly apparent that his lantern was not enough to stop the thing coming under the door.

"Wait!" said Molly. "Can't Tinker Bell stop it again?"

Tink started to respond, but Peter cut her off: "She can stop it once, but then she'll be too tired to do it again. It will come right back. We need something else." He turned to McGuinn. "Are there more lanterns?"

"Yes," McGuinn answered. "Downstairs." He nodded to the right, not taking his eyes off the relentless seeping blackness. Peter ran along the wall and found an archway opening onto a staircase.

"Hurry!" shouted McGuinn. Peter glanced back and saw he was losing his battle with the dark shape on the floor, its tentacles protruding farther and farther into the room.

With Tink lighting the way and Molly right behind, Peter entered the cramped staircase, which descended in a tight spiral, round and round, leading them to a landing with an archway opening to another vast room. A lantern hung in the center of the archway. Peter floated up and unhooked it, then floated down. He glanced into the room and gasped as, in the gloomy distance, he saw a dozen or so shapes . . . the shapes of men.

"Who's that?" he said to Molly.

"It's suits of armor," Molly said.

"Hurry!" McGuinn's voice, tinged with panic, echoed down to them. "I can't keep it out!"

Holding the lantern, Peter ran back up the stairs, with Molly right behind. As they reached the main room they saw the reason for McGuinn's distress: Ombra was inside now, billowing upward to his full height. McGuinn, still holding his lantern, was backing away from the dark shape, which was now flowing toward him.

"Don't let him touch your shadow!" shouted Molly.

McGuinn looked down. The lantern was in his right hand, casting his shadow to the left. Ombra was gliding that way.

"Hold the lantern in front of you!" shouted Peter.

McGuinn quickly swung the lantern forward. Ombra flinched, stopping just for a moment. The lantern was now between Ombra and McGuinn—and McGuinn's shadow. McGuinn was still backing toward Peter and Molly, now standing only a few feet away in the archway leading to the landing.

"Look out!" shouted Peter, as Ombra, moving with astonishing quickness, darted to McGuinn's left. McGuinn swung the lantern that way, but as soon as he did Ombra was swooping right, like a giant bat. McGuinn stepped back quickly toward Peter and Molly, the three of them now moving onto the landing. With nowhere else to go, they started backing down the steep spiral staircase, McGuinn and Peter keeping the two lanterns in front of them, and their eyes on the relentless dark thing coming toward them.

Then it happened. In the jostling on the staircase—three bodies, two lanterns—McGuinn's shadow wound up on the outside wall for an instant. In that instant, Ombra pounced.

"No!" shouted Molly, seeing the dark shape darting to the shadow. McGuinn saw it, too. He lurched backward and, awkward in his unbuckled shoes, missed a step. As Ombra touched his shadow, McGuinn screamed and jerked away, flailing the air and letting go of the lantern. It smashed on the stairs, spewing oil, which burst into flame, filling the staircase with light. Ombra recoiled from the flames, detaching from McGuinn's shadow and oozing back up the stairs; at the same time McGuinn, unconscious, went over backward and, before Peter and Molly could grab him, fell down the steep staircase, his head hitting the stone with a sickening sound.

Molly screamed and ran down to McGuinn; Peter, still holding the lantern, followed.

McGuinn's eyes were open, but his head was at a terrible angle.

"No," Molly said. "No." She touched McGuinn's lifeless, out-flung hand, then began to sob.

Peter put his hand on her shoulder, unable to think of anything to say.

Tink had no such problem.

*We need to get out of here*, she said.

From upstairs came the sound of shouting, the thunder of feet. Ombra had opened the door; the men were inside. Peter looked back at the staircase. The lantern fire was still blocking it, but the flames were lower now.

"Come on, Molly," Peter said softly but urgently, pulling Molly to her feet. "We have to go."

"Where can we go?" said Molly, her eyes still on the fallen McGuinn.

The shouting of the men was louder now.

"I don't know," said Peter. "But we can't stay here."

CHAPTER 79

# THE SILENT STRUGGLE

"SILENCE," SAID OMBRA, in a voice that, while not loud, was heard by every man in the cavernous room. Instantly the shouting stopped. Slank, Nerezza, and the men gathered around the dark hooded figure who had just let them into the White Tower.

"Two men will remain by this door," Ombra said. "The boy and the girl are downstairs. They have blocked the stairs with a fire. Captain Nerezza, take four men and extinguish the fire, then search the lower floor. Mister Slank, there is another staircase at the far end of this room. You will take the rest of the men and go down that way."

The men were divided and—eager to win the gold sovereigns—ran off in search of Peter and Molly. They left Ombra standing alone in the center of the vast dark room. He was motionless, but not idle: inside his dark form an intense, silent struggle was taking place between Ombra and the last flickering flame of the life that had once been Senior Starcatcher McGuinn.

Ombra, forced by the lantern fire to let go of McGuinn's shadow, had been unable to absorb it completely. The part that Ombra now possessed, unable to survive in fragmented form, was dying. It was also, in its death throes, resisting Ombra's efforts to extract the information he most wanted: the location of the starstuff, and the site of the Return.

McGuinn—or what was left of McGuinn—fought hard against the cold blackness enveloping him, absorbing him. But he was weak, and Ombra was strong. McGuinn had given as little as he could, but as the last spark of his being died, Ombra was satisfied that he had obtained just enough.

Now he wanted the children.

## CHAPTER 80

# THE METAL MAN

Peter could see them now—the shadowy shapes of men on the spiral staircase, using their boots to stamp out the remaining flames of the dying lantern fire. They would be coming down very soon.

"Molly," he said. "We have to leave *now*."

Molly took one last look at the body of McGuinn, then gestured across the room and said, "There's another staircase over there."

"Come on, then," said Peter.

They started across the room, and were passing the display of medieval suits of armor when Tink sounded a soft warning.

"What is it?" said Molly.

"She says men are coming down the other way," said Peter.

They looked ahead and saw an archway. There was light

moving inside. Somebody was coming down the far staircase.

"Are there any other stairs?" whispered Peter.

"I don't think so," said Molly.

"Then we're trapped down here."

Molly looked around at the suits of armor. There were several dozen, their shiny steel plates reflecting the light from the lantern in Peter's hand.

"We'll have to hide," she said. "Put out the light."

Peter blew out the lantern. The center of the room was now nearly pitch dark. At both ends they could see men descending stairs. The searchers were moving slowly, hampered by darkness and the fact that each group had only one lantern. But eventually they would converge on the center of the room.

"In here," said Molly, tugging Peter into the display of armor. They positioned themselves in the middle of a cluster of suits, peering out between them. The searchers at each end of the room had spread out and were moving, slowly and methodically, ever closer to where Peter and Molly stood.

"What are we going to do?" whispered Molly.

Peter had been thinking about that, and the only plan he could come up with was to try to fly out. He knew he couldn't carry Molly far; his hope was that he had enough starstuff left in his locket to enable her to become airborne. The ceiling was high; Peter's plan was to try to swoop over the men and get to the staircase. He knew that if—*if*—they managed to get upstairs, they would likely encounter more men . . . and Ombra. But for now he had to worry about the men closing in on them.

"We'll have to fly over them," he whispered, pulling the locket out from under his shirt. Molly nodded, immediately grasping the plan.

Peter put his thumb on the catch and was about to flick the locket open. Suddenly, the locket became warm—almost hot.

Then it started to glow.

"Molly," he whispered, "the—"

"Peter," she interrupted. "Look."

Peter turned—and saw it. The suit of armor directly behind him was also glowing—not the color of steel, but the same color as the locket—a soft, radiant gold.

Then it began to move. As Peter and Molly watched in openmouthed amazement, the suit of armor slowly, silently, raised its right hand.

"What's happening?" whispered Peter.

"I don't know," whispered Molly.

*Touch it,* said Tink softly.

"What?" whispered Peter.

*Touch the metal man's hand with your locket.*

"What's she saying?" whispered Molly.

"She says I should touch the hand with the locket," whispered Peter.

Molly looked around; from both sides of the room, the searchers were getting closer.

"Then do what she says," she whispered.

Peter raised the locket and touched it to the golden knight's hand. For a moment, nothing happened. Then the floor began to move. Peter and Molly grabbed each other as they realized that they were sinking on a square slab of stone, about four feet on each side. Silently they descended into a dark chamber beneath the floor of the big room. Above them was the square hole through which they had descended. They could hear the searchers very close now.

"They'll see us down here," whispered Peter.

*Get off the stone*, said Tink.

Quickly, Peter stepped off the floor slab, pulling Molly with him. Immediately the knight and the slab rose back into place, pushed silently upward by a thick marble column rising from the floor of the chamber.

For a moment Molly and Peter were in total darkness. Then, suddenly, the chamber was bathed in a soft yellow light, which seemed to be coming from everywhere and nowhere. They found themselves in what looked like a large study, furnished with a long table, a dozen comfortable chairs, a writing desk, one large wall entirely covered with shelves crammed with thousands of books, and another wall covered with an enormous floor-to-ceiling map.

"Well," said Molly, "I guess we've found the Keep."

## CHAPTER 81

# THE SECRET

THE TWO SEARCH PARTIES—Slank's and Nerezza's—met at the armor display in the center of the room. They surrounded the suits of armor, then searched through them thoroughly. They found no sign of the boy and girl.

"I don't understand it," said Slank, standing among the motionless steel knights, frustration raising the pitch of his voice. "I could have sworn I saw a light right here."

"You probably saw our lantern," said Nerezza.

"No," said Slank. "It was—"

He stopped in midsentence, feeling—as did the other men—the familiar, unwelcome coolness in the air.

Nerezza and Slank turned to face Ombra. For a moment there was silence; neither man wanted to deliver the bad news. Finally Nerezza spoke.

"They're not here, my lord," he said.

Another silence; the air seemed to grow even colder. Nerezza and Slank both felt the faceless stare.

"They are here," groaned Ombra. "I saw them."

"Yes, my lord," said Nerezza, "but we—"

"*SILENCE.*"

The hideous voice echoed through the vast stone room. Not a man was breathing.

"You will search this room again," said Ombra, softly now. "And if you do not find the children, you will search the floor above this, and then the upper floor. The boy and the girl are here somewhere, and you will find them."

"Yes, my lord," said Nerezza. To the men he said, "You heard him. Find them!"

The men began scouring the room again. Ombra remained where he was, facing the suits of armor. In his dissection of the fragment of soul he had managed to extract from McGuinn, Ombra had concentrated on learning, in what little time he had, the location of the starstuff, and the Return. But he'd sensed that McGuinn was holding back something else as well—another deep secret, something about the White Tower.

Ombra stared at the armor, sifting through the dreamlike swirl of images he'd seen in the last instants of his struggle with McGuinn. There was something there, something tantalizingly close. . . .

*What was it?*

CHAPTER 82

# The Keep

Down in the Keep, bathed in golden light, Peter and Molly stood still, listening to the muffled sounds coming from the room above—shouts, boots scraping on stone. After a minute the sounds began to move away. For now, it appeared, they were safe.

"Now what?" said Peter.

"Well," said Molly, "since we're here, we might as well have a look around. Perhaps we can figure out where Father went."

Peter walked over to the bookshelf. He removed a book at random; it was leather-bound and dust-covered, clearly very old. He opened it to a random page and squinted at the writing.

"It's not in English," he said.

Molly came over and had a look. She wrinkled her nose.

"Latin," she said.

"Can you read it?"

"A bit," she said. "But very slowly. And"—she gestured at the thousands of dusty volumes—"where would I start?"

They walked over to the huge wall map. It displayed the earth—Europe and Africa in the middle, the Americas off to the left, Asia to the right. Looking closer, they saw that it was covered with hundreds of finely drawn red lines. Most of the lines converged in London; from there they radiated out all over the planet, each ending in a tiny gold star with a date next to it. Some of the dates were centuries old.

"Starstuff," said Peter.

Molly nodded. "This is where they keep track of it. I had no idea there was so much."

Peter moved close to the map, his eyes roaming back and forth until he found what he was looking for.

"Look," he said, pointing to a tiny dot in the ocean, far from land, connected to London by not one but two red lines—one meandering, one arrow-straight.

Molly smiled. "Mollusk Island," she said. She traced the meandering line with her finger. "This is us on the *Never Land*. What a voyage *that* was!" She moved her finger to the straight line. "And this is me going home, with Father and the starstuff." She followed the line back to London, then said, "It only shows the shipments reaching London. It doesn't show where they go for the Return from here."

"And you're sure the Return isn't here?"

"Yes," said Molly. "It's somewhere else." Her eyes roamed around the room, then fell on the writing desk. On it was a stack of papers. Molly went over, picked them up, and began sifting through them. But her expression quickly changed from eagerness to disappointment when she saw that they were financial documents—invoices, purchase orders, bills of lading, customs forms. She sighed.

"I suppose even Starcatchers have bills to pay," she muttered. She was about to set the papers back down when she noticed something.

"Wait a minute," she said.

"What?" said Peter.

"Look at this." Molly was holding an invoice from a wine merchant listing various bottles of wine and their prices.

Peter looked. "What about it?"

"Here," said Molly, pointing to the margin. There, in bright blue ink that contrasted with the black used to write the rest of the invoice, was the letter S, drawn in a fanciful cursive, followed by the numbers 1030 and 246.

Peter looked again, and again asked, "What about it?"

"That's Father's writing," said Molly.

"Are you sure?"

"Absolutely. He's got a specially made pen that he loves, and this is the color of ink he uses. And that's how he writes the letter S, with that odd curlicue."

"What does it mean?" said Peter.

Molly frowned. "I've no idea. But this invoice is dated only last week. Father must have written this very shortly before he left." She studied it a moment longer, then tucked it into the pocket of her dress. "Let's see if we can find anything else that might be helpful," she said.

Molly and Peter spent the next half hour looking around the Keep, but found nothing else that seemed remotely helpful. Finally, Molly, after having gone through the stack of financial documents for the fifth time without finding anything new, hung her head in discouragement.

"This has been a waste of time," she said. "No, it's much worse than that. Mister McGuinn is dead, and we've found *nothing*."

"You didn't kill him," said Peter. "Ombra did."

"But I led him here," said Molly. "I thought I could be a hero, saving Mother. I'm a fool."

"No you're not," said Peter.

*Yes she is*, said Tink, though Peter could tell her heart wasn't really in it.

"What did she say?" said Molly.

"She said, um, she said it's been quiet upstairs for a while," said Peter.

Molly listened for a few seconds, and nodded; there were no more boot steps on the floor above, no shouting.

"I suppose we should try to get out of here," she said. "We're never going to find Father if we stay here."

"How do you suppose we get out?" said Peter.

*The way you came in*, said Tink. *The metal man.*

Molly looked at Peter. He pointed to the marble column beneath the slab of floor that had carried them down to the Keep. They went over and studied its smooth, cream-colored surface, but found nothing that suggested a way out. Then Molly spotted something gleaming on the wall nearby.

"Over there," she said.

Peter followed her eyes and saw it: a small golden star set into the stone. He went to it and again removed the locket from his shirt. As he did, both locket and star began to glow.

"Stand away from the column," he said. As Molly complied, he touched the locket to the star. The column began to slide silently into the floor, the golden knight descending on its square slab of stone. When it reached the floor of the Keep, it raised its hand. Molly and Peter stepped onto the slab, and Peter touched his locket to the knight's palm.

Silently, they rose into the lower room of the White Tower, hoping that nobody was waiting for them in the darkness.

## CHAPTER 83

# OMBRA'S PLAN

NEREZZA WAS FRUSTRATED. Slank was furious.

*Where were the boy and the girl?*

The men had thoroughly searched the bottom floor of the White Tower; then the middle floor, where they had come in. Now they had finished scouring the upper floor. They had checked the windows: all were blocked by close-set iron bars. They had two men guarding the tower's only door. There was no other way for the boy and the girl to escape. And yet they were nowhere to be found.

Reluctantly, Nerezza and Slank approached Ombra, who stood alone in the center of the upper floor. The rest of the men hung back, watching, grateful that they did not have to deliver the bad news.

"My lord," said Nerezza. "We can't find them."

"They are here," said Ombra.

"But, my lord, we—"

"They are here."

"Yes, my lord."

"You will have the men search the tower again."

"Yes, my lord."

Nerezza and Slank turned to go back to the men and give the order. Slank was halted by Ombra's groan.

"Mister Slank," he said.

Slank turned back.

"You will get a lantern and come with me."

"Yes, my lord." Slank took a lantern from one of the men and returned to Ombra, who glided to the front staircase and began descending the spiral steps. He knew better than to ask Ombra what they were doing.

In fact, Ombra was not sure himself. Something was drawing him to the lower floor again, some fragment of a thought that he had extracted from McGuinn, undefined but tantalizing. Ombra had gone to the lower floor several times, drifting through the armor, trying to make sense of the murky jumble of vague images he had captured. Each time he had given up in frustration.

But something was drawing him back. He was certain the children were still in the tower. He didn't know where they were hiding. But now, as he slithered down the staircase, he had a plan for drawing them out.

## CHAPTER 84

# A VOICE IN THE DARK

PETER AND MOLLY peered through the suits of armor, their eyes straining to see across the vast darkness of the lower room.

"I think they're gone," Peter whispered.

"From this floor, yes," whispered Molly. "But they're still in the tower." Her words were confirmed by the distant echoing sounds of searchers calling to each other.

"Do you think we could make it to the front door?" said Peter.

"I doubt it," said Molly. "They'll have it guarded."

"Is there another way out?"

Molly frowned, remembering her visits to the tower. "I don't know," she said. "If there is, it would be upstairs." She thought about the front staircase and shuddered, thinking of the fallen form of McGuinn lying there in the darkness. Unable to bear the thought of stepping over his body, she pointed toward the rear staircase. "Let's go this way," she said.

Cautiously, they crept out from among the suits of armor and crossed the floor to the archway leading to the rear stairs. Inside the spiral staircase it was blacker than black.

"Should I have Tink light the way?" whispered Peter.

"We'd better not," said Molly. "They might see."

Slowly, feeling their way with their feet, they began to make their way up the stairs. They had gone four or five steps when Molly stopped, putting her hand on Peter's arm.

"Did you hear that?" she whispered.

"What?" whispered Peter.

"Shh. Listen."

They listened, and after a moment's silence they both heard it.

A woman's voice echoing plaintively across the room they had just left.

"Molly!" said the voice.

Molly's grip tightened on Peter's arm, so hard that he winced in pain.

"*Mother,*" she whispered. "Peter, that's my mother!"

"Molly," called the voice, closer now. "Please, help me!"

Molly started down the stairs. Peter grabbed her.

"Wait," he whispered.

She jerked her arm free. "That's my *mother*, Peter."

"Molly!" the voice called again, closer still.

Molly was about to call out when Peter clamped his hand over her lips. They struggled silently on the dark staircase, Peter whispering harshly in Molly's ear.

"*Think*, Molly," he said. "It could be a trick."

He felt her hesitate, then stop struggling. She nodded her head. He removed his hand from her mouth.

"I'm sorry," he whispered.

"No," she answered. "You're right."

"Molly!" called the voice. "Please come out! I need you, Molly!"

Together, Molly and Peter crept to the bottom of the staircase. Molly peered through the archway and gasped. Coming toward her, along the lower room's long side wall, was a woman's shadow cast by the wavering light of a lantern. Its source was invisible, blocked by the armor display. Molly saw the shadow raise its hands in a pleading gesture, and again heard her mother's voice:

"Molly! Please!"

"It's her," Molly whispered. "Peter, it's *her*."

Tink made a soft warning sound.

"No," said Peter. "Look."

Lady Aster's shadow had moved closer along the wall, and now they could see where, at its base, it tapered into a long, dark teardrop shape that stretched across the floor.

The teardrop shadow connected to Ombra.

He glided toward them, his black hood swiveling left and

right, hunting; its movement independent of those of the shadow.

"Molly!" The shadow's plaintive voice pierced Molly's heart. "Please!"

Molly stared at the oncoming shapes, frozen. Peter grabbed her by the arm, pulled her back into the archway.

"It's not her, Molly," he whispered. "It's not."

Molly allowed herself, reluctantly, to be pulled back, her eyes refusing to leave the shadow.

"Come *on*," whispered Peter, pulling her to the stairs.

Finally Molly turned and followed. She put her hands to her ears to stop the pitiful sound coming from below.

"Molly . . . *please*."

With Peter leading, they quickly ascended the steps to the middle floor, the one where McGuinn had let them in to the White Tower. Across the cavernous dark room they saw the flickering of a lantern and the shadows of men searching; clearly they would not be able to get to the door through which they had entered. There was no sign of a door on the side of the room where they now stood.

Tink made the warning sound again.

Peter and Molly looked back and saw the reason: lantern light now shone from below on the stairway behind them. Then the beseeching voice came again. . . .

"*Molly!*"

Ombra, having crossed the lower room, was now

ascending on their side. The searchers on the middle floor were coming closer. Peter and Molly saw they had no choice now but to take the stairs to the upper floor. Without speaking, they tiptoed quickly up the staircase. The upper room was very dark; they could just make out the shapes of several columns toward the middle. Peter and Molly listened for a moment, hearing nothing. Peter broke the silence.

"Now what?" he whispered.

"Let's see if there's a window," answered Molly.

Cautiously they moved along the back wall. They came to an opening in the wall; the darkness there was just slightly less black. Peter reached into the opening, feeling with his hands.

"It's a window," he whispered. "But it has bars on it."

Molly was about to answer, when a deep voice thundered at them.

"WHO'S THAT!" it shouted.

Peter and Molly froze, neither one breathing. The voice was coming from the shadows near a column no more than twenty-five feet away.

"I SAID, WHO'S THAT?" the voice repeated.

Silence.

"BLACKIE!" the voice boomed. "BRING THE LANTERN! THERE'S SOMEBODY UP HERE!"

Instantly there was shouting from below, the pounding of heavy-booted feet on stone, light coming up the stairs.

Peter and Molly, having nowhere else to go, ran along the rear wall, away from the stairs, toward the corner of the room. In the darkness, Peter nearly slammed face-first into the side wall. With Molly behind him, he felt along the wall and came to an opening.

"In here!" he whispered.

They ducked into the opening and found themselves in a pitch-black space, so narrow they could touch the walls on either side. Behind them the shouting was louder. Ahead of them was . . .

*A hole,* Tink said.

"What?" whispered Peter.

*There's a hole,* she said.

"Where?" said Peter.

"What?" said Molly.

*Right in front of you,* said Tink. She flitted forward and, for just a second, glowed softly, illuminating a low wooden platform set into the rough tower stone. In the center of the platform was a hole, a bit more than a foot in diameter.

Molly recognized it instantly, it being one of the more popular attractions on the tower tour.

"The garderobe," she whispered.

"What's that mean?" whispered Peter.

"It's a toilet," whispered Molly, blushing.

"Where's it go?"

"Outside."

"You mean, just . . . outside?"

"Yes."

"Come on, then," whispered Peter. "Tink, give us a little light."

By Tink's soft glow, Peter climbed onto the platform, sat, and stuck his feet into the hole. He slid forward into it, then raised his hands over his head as he went through. It was a tight fit, but he made it. He disappeared for a moment, then his head popped back up through the hole.

"Come on!" he urged Molly. "It's a bit of a drop, but I'll hold you."

Molly looked doubtful.

*She thinks she's too good to go down a toilet,* observed Tink.

The searchers' shouts were quite loud now. One came from just outside the narrow opening leading to the garderobe.

"Come *on,*" repeated Peter.

Gingerly, Molly stepped up onto the wooden platform. Peter ducked out of the way, and she put her legs through, being careful to tuck her dress. She began to slide forward, and raised her arms. She slid halfway through . . .

And got stuck. Her hips were just a bit too large for the opening. She began kicking her feet, trying to wiggle through, but she didn't budge.

"I'm stuck," she whispered.

Peter, hovering in the darkness on the underside of the

hole, couldn't hear her, but he saw what was happening. He wrapped his arms around her legs and tugged downward. Still, she did not move.

A voice boomed from right outside the garderobe.

"BRING THE LIGHT OVER HERE." Boots clomped closer. Molly saw the light coming now. She wiggled and kicked furiously, one of her shoes catching Peter in the ribs, sending him tumbling away into the night.

A man entered the garderobe, lantern in hand. He saw Molly and let out a yell of triumph.

"IN HERE!" he shouted. "SHE'S IN HERE!" Other men piled into the space behind him, the walls too close set to let them pass the man with the lantern.

"GRAB HER!" shouted a voice.

The man with the lantern reached forward to grab Molly by the arm, then immediately jerked backward, roaring in pain as he felt Tinker Bell, moving almost too swiftly to see, punch a tiny but hard fist into his right eye. The man staggered backward, knocking down the man behind him, who knocked down the man behind him. As they fell, yelling, the lantern went out, and at the same moment Molly felt Peter's arms around her legs once again. She raised her arms again, and, as Peter yanked from below, she wiggled with all her strength; this time she felt herself sliding, one agonizing inch, then another. The fallen men were clambering to their feet. Molly felt a hand grope for her, grabbing at her face.

She opened her mouth and bit down on it with all her strength. The hand was yanked away as the owner screamed in pain, and Molly, with a last, desperate wiggle, fell through the hole.

"Hang on!" shouted Peter, fighting desperately to slow her descent. Molly clung to his neck, feeling him strain against her weight, not sure how far they had to . . .

*THUMP.*

They hit the ground quite hard, but fortunately feet-first. They fell and rolled, tangled up in each other's arms. From above them—quite far above, Molly could now see—a light appeared in the garderobe hole, and there was a great deal of angry and confused shouting.

A sudden silence, and then, drifting down through the night, a horrid groaning voice, indistinct but clearly enraged.

Quickly, Molly and Peter disentangled themselves, rose to their feet and, with Tink flitting behind them, began to run.

CHAPTER 85

# $\mathcal{D}$ARK $\mathcal{K}$ITES

TWO CARRIAGES, each drawn by four horses, waited on the quay near a gaslight at the bottom of *Le Fantome*'s gangplank. The horses were unusually restless, their hooves shifting on the stones, their breath steaming.

The cause of their restlessness glided silently up to the rear carriage, keeping to the shadow side, unseen by the driver until he heard a strange, wheezing voice next to him.

"Driver."

"Eh, Guv'nor?" The driver turned and leaned down, then gasped as he found himself looking into an empty hood. Before he could speak again, Ombra slid onto the driver's shadow, cast by the gaslight onto the quay. The driver's head sagged. He now cast no shadow at all.

Ombra's voice rasped into the chilly air: "Sit up."

"Yes, my lord." The driver lifted his head and stiffened his back.

Ombra glided swiftly up to the front carriage. The driver glanced back and saw a dark shape approaching: a shadow moving within a shadow.

"You move smooth as water," said the driver jovially. "Don't even look like you're walking!"

"I'm not."

A moment later Ombra's sack was a little fatter, and the second driver was as still and obedient as the first.

Ombra turned and signaled Slank, who stood waiting on the deck of Le Fantome, holding the arm of a smaller figure draped in a plaid blanket. Slank strong-armed the figure down the gangplank, and as he did, the blanket slipped, revealing the ashen face and matted, oily hair of Lady Louise Aster. She descended the gangplank woodenly, like a child learning her first steps. When they reached the quay, Slank pushed her into the first carriage, then climbed in after her.

Next off the ship was Gerch, who took a seat alongside to the driver of the first carriage; and Hampton, who sat alongside the second driver. Two of Nerezza's men followed, taking positions on the footholds at the back of each carriage. Both men were armed with dagger and pistol.

Nerezza came down the plank next, carrying a sea bag. He was followed by four of the men who had accompanied Ombra to the Tower. They tied bags and a trunk to the roof of the second carriage, then climbed inside.

Ombra spoke quietly to the driver of the first carriage, so

quietly that even Gerch, sitting right next to the driver, did not hear the destination. Then Ombra slithered into the carriage, closing the door and taking his seat across from Slank and Lady Aster. Slank shivered as the air inside the carriage suddenly felt much colder. Lady Aster sat immobile, her face vacant of expression.

"Soon enough, my *lady*," Ombra groaned, "you'll be seeing your husband again."

Lady Aster stared straight ahead through bloodshot eyes.

"Perhaps you'll see your little girl as well," said Ombra. "At the Tower, your old family friend Mister McGuinn was kind enough to . . . *share* with me . . . where the Return is to take place. I suspect he may have told young Molly as well. If so, we shall have quite the family reunion, shall we not?"

Slank was watching Louise Aster's face; it revealed nothing.

"Oh, yes, my *lady*," hissed Ombra. "I have plans for your happy little family."

Slank thought he saw a flicker in Louise Aster's eyes, the tiniest hint of emotion cross her haggard face. Then it was gone.

"Signal the driver," groaned Ombra.

Slank raised his fist and banged sharply twice on the roof of the carriage.

The horses heaved. The carriages rattled and shook as they began to move, their wheels rumbling on the stone.

They rolled forward into the last of the lingering London night.

The rumble of the wheels was suddenly joined by another, harsher sound.

*Caw! Caw!*

The sound came from a half dozen ravens circling high above Ombra's carriage, following it obediently, like dark kites on invisible strings.

## CHAPTER 86

# An Offer of Help

By the time Molly and Peter made it back to George's house, the eastern sky was showing the first dull-gray streaks of dawn. Molly and Peter were cold and exhausted. After fleeing from the White Tower, they had hid in a dark alley for the better part of an anxious hour until they were sure they were safe from their pursuers. Then, lacking the money for a cab, they had walked all the way back to George's house, taking a roundabout route so as not to expose themselves on the busier streets.

Now, at long last, they were in the tree outside George's bedroom window. As Molly tapped on the glass, Peter tucked the complaining Tinker Bell back into his shirt.

In a moment George's sleepy face appeared. He opened the window; Molly and Peter climbed into the room.

"Thank you," said Molly.

George, wearing his nightcap and nightshirt, merely

nodded, watching Molly, obviously waiting for her to say more. When she didn't, he spoke, his voice low but angry.

"Listen," he said. "This won't do."

"What won't?" said Molly.

"This business of you and," George said, gesturing at Peter, "your *friend* here staying in my room and traipsing in and out my window at all hours. I can't keep hiding you here, Molly. You come here in the middle of the night and tell me your mother's been kidnapped and there are men in your house, and yet you don't let me tell Father, you don't let me help you, and you won't tell me what's happening, and—"

George paused, his face reddening, then went on: "Molly, I want to help you. But I can't help if you won't let me."

Molly sighed. "You're right, George," she said. "You've been very gracious, and I've been horribly rude. But this is something very, very dangerous. I don't want to involve you or your family."

"Molly," said George. "You and I—that is, my family and yours—are already involved. We have been for years. If I were in trouble, you'd help me, wouldn't you?"

Slowly, Molly nodded.

"Well," said George, "that's how I feel. About you." His face was now the color of a beet. "About helping you, I mean."

The room fell silent. Peter, though standing just two feet

from Molly, felt as if he were a thousand miles away. He hated the way she was looking at George.

"You're right," she said finally.

"Molly," Peter cautioned. She waved him off.

"No, Peter, George is right," she said. "We've nowhere else to turn at this point."

Now it was Peter's turn to sulk, but Molly ignored him.

"I need to find Father," she said. "He's the only person who can deal with the Oth . . . with the kidnappers. But he's gone from London on a . . . a confidential business trip, and I don't know where he is. Tonight Peter and I went to a place where we thought we might get some information about where he's gone, but we found nothing. No, wait, that's not quite true. We found this."

Molly reached into her pocket and pulled out the wine merchant invoice she'd found in the Starcatchers' Keep. She handed it to George, who looked at it and frowned.

"I don't understand," he said.

"Neither do I," said Molly. "But I know that's my father's handwriting, in the blue ink. And I know he must have written it just before he left London."

"S," George read, "ten thirty, two forty-six."

"I thought perhaps it was an address," said Molly. "But I can't make anything of it."

"You say he wrote this just before he left London?" said George.

"Yes," said Molly.

"Hang on," said George, striding from the room. He was back in ten minutes, this time holding a sheaf of papers.

"What're those?" said Molly.

"Train timetables," said George.

Molly's face lit up.

"George!" she said in a voice that stabbed Peter's heart. "That's brilliant!"

George blushed as he dumped the timetables onto the bed.

"Give a hand, then," he said, his attempt to sound gruff undermined by his obvious pleasure.

"Come on, Peter!" said Molly.

"What are we doing?" said Peter, feeling like an idiot.

"We're looking for a train that leaves at ten thirty and arrives at two forty-six," said George, with more than a hint of condescension in his voice.

"And that somehow involves the letter S," added Molly, grabbing a timetable and settling on the floor to study it.

Without speaking, Peter picked up a timetable and joined the other two in their search. It was tedious going, wading through long lists of train numbers, cities, and times. It reminded Peter of school—something he'd had nothing to do with for quite a while. Several times, feeling the effects of another sleepless night, Peter felt his eyes closing. He had in fact dozed off entirely when he was awakened by George's unwelcome voice.

"Hang on," said George.

"What?" said Molly.

"Look at this," he said, thrusting a timetable toward Molly. She looked at the number marked by his finger.

"So it departs at ten thirty from Waterloo Station—" she said. Her eyes scanned across a column of figures. "And it arrives at two forty-six at . . . *Salisbury*. That's it! Father took the train to Salisbury!"

"What's in Salisbury?" said Peter.

"I don't know," said Molly. "But I have to go there."

"What?" said George. "Now?"

"Yes," said Molly. "I've got time to make the train. Can you lend me the money for a ticket?"

"Well . . . yes, of course," said George.

"And Peter as well?" said Molly. "I'll repay you, I promise."

"*He's* going with you?" said George.

"Yes," said Molly.

"If he is," said George, "then I am."

"No," said Molly.

"Why not?" said George.

"Because . . ." said Molly, "because your parents wouldn't allow it."

"My parents left yesterday for Paris," said George. "I'll tell the housekeeper I've gone to spend a few days with a friend. I've done that many times."

"It's too dangerous," said Molly.

"You're going," retorted George. "*He's* going."

"But he . . ." Molly searched for words, then gave up. "George, it's just too complicated."

"Yes," said George. "And that's why you need all the help you can get. You wouldn't even know to go to Salisbury if not for me."

Molly had no answer for that.

"If you want me to buy the tickets," said George, "you have to let me go with you."

Molly hung her head, thinking.

"All right," she said.

"Molly!" said Peter.

She looked at him. "He's right," she said. "I have to take whatever help I can."

"But what about the . . . your family's business?"

"Right now," said Molly, her tone grim, "all I care about is getting my mother back. If George can help, then I want him to come with us."

"All right," said Peter, though it was clear he did not think it was. Molly and he exchanged a long look, but neither spoke.

"I'll get dressed," said George, breaking the silence. "We'll take a cab to Waterloo Station."

## CHAPTER 87

# The Golden Weather Vane

An hour into the train ride from London to Salisbury, Peter announced that he wanted some fresh air and left his seat to stand in the open space between the clattering, jostling train carriages. Here, after making sure nobody was watching, he opened his coat and allowed Tinker Bell out. She perched on his shoulder, looking at the engine smoke billowing overhead, and wrinkled her nose.

*Why do we have to stay on this loud, smelly thing?* she asked. *Why can't we just fly?*

"You know Molly and George can't fly," he said.

*So? YOU can fly.*

"But I'm with them," he said.

*But you're not one of them.*

"What do you mean?"

*They live in this awful cold place. They're stuck on the ground. You live on our island, and you can fly. You're not like them.* Tink put her tiny face close to Peter's. *You're like me.*

Peter looked at her, then stared out at the fields rushing past. He wondered: was Tink right? Had he become more fantastic creature than person? Was there any place in England for someone like him? Could he ever be Molly's friend, the way George was her friend? If he never grew old, could he be the friend of *any* normal person?

Standing on the rumbling platform, Peter felt keenly aware of how out of place he was here, how far from home. And for the first time, he understood where his home really was.

"You're right, Tink," he said softly. "I am like you."

At that same moment, back in the train carriage, George turned to Molly and asked, "How did you come to know Peter?"

"I met him on a ship," Molly answered.

"Really? And how did you become friends?"

Molly thought back to the eventful voyage aboard the *Never Land*—her discovery that the ship carried a trunk filled with starstuff; her desperate decision to enlist Peter as an ally in her effort to get the precious trunk away from the Others; the attack on the ship by the infamous Black Stache; the storm at sea that marooned them on the mysterious Mollusk Island; the struggle there, pitting children and mermaids against murderous pirates, and the even-deadlier Slank, with hostile natives and a giant flying crocodile thrown in for good measure; and, above all, the courage and resourcefulness Peter had shown, risking his life to save Molly's, and the starstuff.

These images and more ran through Molly's mind. But all she said to George was: "I needed help. And Peter helped me."

George nodded. "That's very admirable," he said. "But I'm still puzzled by your continued . . . *association* with him."

"Why?"

"Well, he's not exactly your sort of person, is he?"

"What do you mean?" said Molly.

"I mean," said George. "The way he talks. His level of education. His . . . his *breeding*. Is he really a suitable companion for someone of your background? I mean, your family, your father—"

"My father," interrupted Molly, "considers Peter to be one of the finest young men he has ever met." She glared at George.

"I see," he said.

"No," said Molly, turning away. "You don't."

George, realizing he had badly misjudged the situation, spent several minutes trying to think of something diplomatic to say, but could come up with nothing before Peter returned. The three of them rode the rest of the way in silence.

Arriving, at last, in Salisbury, they descended from the carriage and stood on the platform as the train chugged away. The day was chilly, but for once the sky was clear; sunlight bathed the gentle hills of County Wiltshire. Molly, Peter, and George walked through the station, emerging onto a muddy, well-traveled road. Several coaches-for-hire stood waiting, their horses tied to posts, their drivers presumably just across the road, refreshing themselves at the Railway Tavern. In the distance the sky was pierced by the tall, sharp spike of the Salisbury cathedral.

"Now what?" said Peter.

"I imagine we could ask somebody if he has seen Molly's father," said George.

"Ask who?" said Peter.

"Well, *someone* must know," said George, irritated. "Have you got a better idea?"

"Not yet," said Peter, looking George straight in the eye. "But I will."

The two boys glared at each other. Molly was paying no attention to them. She was staring at the cathedral tower.

"I've been here," she said.

George and Peter looked at her.

"Father and Mother brought me here," she said. "It was years ago—I was small. But I remember that cathedral."

"What else do you remember?" said Peter.

Molly frowned, thinking back. "It was summer. We

450

stayed at a large house. It was on a winding road, next to a river. There was a wooden bridge nearby. Father took me there and we would try to catch fish." She paused, then her face lit up. "And I remember something else—Mister McGuinn was there!"

"Are you sure?" said Peter.

"Who's Mister McGuinn?" said George.

"He's . . . that is, he was an . . . an associate of my father's," said Molly. "And I'm sure he was there. And I remember something else: I think the house may have had a weather vane, a *golden* weather vane." She looked at Peter. "With a star on the top."

"That's *it*," said Peter softly.

"That's what?" said George.

"That's where Father must be," said Molly. "That's why he came to Salisbury. We need to find that house."

"Do you have any recollection of how you got there?" said Peter.

"No," said Molly. "But I'm sure we took the train to Salisbury. I remember that cathedral. We started out from here."

"Then so will we," said George. Without another word, he strode across the road and into the Railway Tavern.

"What's he doing?" said Peter.

"I don't know," said Molly.

In a minute George emerged from the tavern

accompanied by a coach driver, a slight man with the face of a ferret.

"This is Mister Peavey," said George, when they reached Molly and Peter. "He says he's very familiar with this area."

"Lived here all me life," said Peavey. "I knows every inch of Wiltshire." He grinned, revealing six teeth, widely spaced. "Every inch."

"Then perhaps you can help us," said Molly. "We're looking for a house, quite a large house, on a winding road, next to a river."

"Lots of those around here, missy," said Peavey. "Lots of those."

"It's near a bridge," said Molly.

"Could be any number of houses," said Peavey. "Any number."

"And it has a . . . a *golden* weather vane," said Molly. "Shaped like a star."

Peavey hesitated before he answered. "Well, now," he said. "That narrows it down a mite, don't it?"

"So you know the house?" said Molly eagerly.

"Maybe I do," said Peavey. He stroked his chin. "Of course, maybe I don't."

"Look here," Peter said angrily. "If you know where—"

"Allow me," interrupted George, putting his hand on Peter's arm, to Peter's great annoyance. "I believe what

Mister Peavey is saying is that his memory might need some assistance."

"A smart young lad, this one," Peavey said.

George pressed something into Peavey's hand. Peter heard the clink of coins.

Peavey grinned. "Now that you mentions it," he said, "I believe I might know the very house you're looking for. Take you there in an hour, I can."

"Excellent," said George, winking at Molly, who grinned back at him in a way that made Peter's stomach clench. George opened the door to the coach and gallantly helped Molly climb inside.

"Thank you, George," she said. "That was clever of you."

"Not at all," said George, climbing in after her. "It's just a question of knowing how to get things done." He said this without glancing back at Peter, but he figured Peter's expression would be quite unhappy.

He was quite correct.

Close to an hour later, with sunset nearing, the coach came to a stop in front of an enormous country house. Its driveway was guarded by a massive iron gate, on which was a sign that read: SE MONA.

George hopped to the ground and helped Molly out of the coach. Peter followed.

"Well?" George asked.

Molly studied the house, then shook her head. "No," she

453

said. "I don't think this is it." Her eyes swept upward. "Wait a minute!" She turned angrily to Peavey and said, "That's the *moon*, not a star!"

Peter and George looked up. Sure enough: the weather vane was crescent shaped.

"Same thing," said Peavey. "One a them planets."

"It's *not* the same," said Molly.

"Well, missy," said Peavey, "that there's the best I can do."

Peter was looking at the sign. "Maybe the . . . the Semonas can help us find the house."

"The who?" said George, with a condescending smile.

Peavey cackled. "Se Mona ain't the name of the people who lives here," he said. "That there is the name of the house. It's Old English, it is. Quite a few of the big houses round here has got Old English names."

"*Se Mona*," said George. "Means 'the moon.'"

"You speak Old English?" said Molly.

"Well, not *fluently*," said George, trying without success to sound modest. "But I've studied it enough to get by. The house you stayed at with your father—do you recall if it had a name?"

Molly frowned. "It might've," she said. "But I don't remember what it was."

"What's the Old English word for *star*?" said Peter.

"I believe it's *steorra*," said George.

Peter looked at Peavey. "Is there a house named *Steorra?*"

"Never heard of one," said Peavey.

"What about 'light'?" said Molly.

George asked Peavey: "Are any of the houses named *Leoht?*"

"Not so as I know."

"What about 'return'?" said Peter, with a glance at Molly.

George shut his eyes, deep in thought. When he opened them, he said to the driver, "Is there a house by the name of . . . *Gecierran?*"

At the sound of the name, Peavey flinched.

"You know the name?" said George.

"Yes, I know it," said Peavey. "But I don't know that I'd want to go there, if I was you."

"Why not?" said George.

Peavey hesitated, then said, "There's talk that strange things happen there. For years and years. People stay away from there."

"What kinds of strange things?" said George. "Ghosts?" He smirked at Peter and Molly. "Witchcraft?"

"Yes," Peavey said, in a quiet voice that erased George's smirk.

Molly and Peter exchanged a look.

"We want to go there," said Molly.

Peavey nodded slowly. "All right, then," he said. "But it'll cost extra."

"We'll pay," said George.

"Get in, then," said Peavey. "It's a half hour away."

But it was sooner than that when the roofline of the grand house came into view. On the highest peak, clearly visible in the last rays of the setting sun, was a weather vane.

And atop it, gleaming gold, was a five-pointed star.

## CHAPTER 88

# A GOOD FRIEND OF HIS

THE POUNDING ON the carriage roof startled Slank awake. He opened his eyes to see Nerezza parting the curtain. Ombra leaned past Nerezza to see out the carriage window, Nerezza pressing himself back into the seat to avoid contact with the dark form. Lady Aster stared unflinchingly ahead.

Ombra studied the scene out the window. The sun had set; a full moon was just rising in the clear evening sky, still low on the horizon but bright enough to illuminate the countryside. The carriage, after a full day of travel, had reached its destination—a dirt track on a small rise overlooking a patchwork of fields that ran for miles. Fifty yards away, at the end of the track, sat a stone cottage, chimney smoking, and a few tumbledown outbuildings of weathered wood.

"No neighbors," Nerezza said. "And a good view. As you requested, my lord."

Ombra made a noise that sounded like agreement. "Mister Slank," he groaned. "Take Gerch and look around."

"Yes, my lord."

Slank climbed out; he and Gerch headed off toward the cottage. A few minutes later they returned.

"The outbuildings are empty," Slank reported. "There's two people in the cottage—an old woman knitting, and an old man splitting kindling in the kitchen."

Ombra slid out of the carriage. "Stay with her," he said, indicating Lady Aster. He glided swiftly down the dirt track to the cottage. He paused at the door, where he seemed to melt and spread, losing height and shape until he was nothing but a pool of darkness, which quickly disappeared under the doorsill.

The pool reappeared inside the cottage, where an old woman sat knitting by the dim light of a candle and a dying fire. A low doorway behind her led to the kitchen, from which chopping sounds could be heard.

Feeling a sudden chill, the old woman raised her head, looking first at the window, then the door, but not seeing the dark shape oozing across the floor. She returned to her knitting, but only for a moment, as she saw some motion from the corner of her eye.

"John, is that—" she said, but those were her only words before Ombra, now back to full height and form, covered her shadow.

The knitting stopped. The woman slumped forward, a ball of yarn tumbling from her lap to the floor.

The chopping sound from the other room stopped. "Bea?" said a man's voice. "Did you say something? Bea?"

Silence. Then the sound of shuffling steps. The old man appeared in the low doorway, his right hand holding an ax. He looked at his wife's slumped form, then saw the dark shape standing next to her.

"Who the devil are you?" he said.

"Not the devil," groaned Ombra, gliding forward. "But a good friend of his."

The man raised the ax, gripping it with both hands.

"Stay back," he said.

Ombra kept coming.

"I warn you," said the man.

Ombra kept coming.

The man swung the ax, a swift overhand stroke cleaving the dark shape cleanly top to bottom, the ax head burying itself in the floor. The cloaked form split into two detached halves, which, as the man watched in horror, quickly flowed together into their original form and resumed coming at him. The man was too stunned to move as Ombra reached his shadow and sucked it away.

"You will take your wife to the barn," Ombra groaned. "You will remain there until I say otherwise."

"Yes, my lord."

The man helped the woman from her chair. Ombra opened the door, and they walked out. The woman was still holding a strand of yarn; the other end was attached to the yarn ball, which tumbled behind the couple, dancing in the dry leaves as they walked to the barn.

Ombra faced the men waiting by the carriages and gestured for them to approach. As they did, Ombra looked out over the fields, swiveling his hooded head until he saw what he was looking for. It was more than a mile away, but clearly visible by the light of the rising moon.

The site of the Return.

As Ombra stood looking at it, a half dozen black shapes glided out of the night and fluttered to rest on the roof of the cottage.

*Caw! Caw!*

Ombra turned to the ravens, then slowly raised his arm, pointing toward the Return site. Immediately the ravens took wing again. Ombra watched their swift passage across the fields. He did not know when the Return would be—in his struggle with the soul of McGuinn, he had not managed to get that information—but this was *where* it would be. Sooner or later, the Starcatchers would have to bring their precious starstuff to this place.

And when they did, Ombra, and the ravens, would be waiting.

CHAPTER 89

# No Choice

"*H*ERE WE ARE," called Peavey as he pulled the reins, bringing the carriage to a stop. "Gecierran."

Peter, Molly, and George climbed down from the coach. Night was newly fallen; a fat moon was rising in the cold, clear sky. They stood on a lonely stretch of the road that followed the meandering path of the Avon river, a few miles from the village of Upper Woodford. On one side of the road was a stand of trees; along the other ran a high stone wall broken by an iron gate. Through the gate, by the moonlight, they could see a driveway lined with evergreens leading to a massive mansion sitting between road and river, dark and unwelcoming.

"I'm off, then," said Peavey, as George handed him the fare.

"Maybe you should wait," said George. "In case there's nobody here, or it's the wrong house."

"Sorry," said Peavey, flicking the reins. "I said I'd take you here. Didn't say I'd stay."

"But—" said George.

"Sorry!" called Peavey as the carriage rumbled away, quickly disappearing around a curve, leaving the trio standing in the dark road.

"Well," said George, after a moment's silence. "As he said: 'Here we are.'"

"Yes, we are," said Peter, looking at the dark woods across the road.

Molly was studying the house. "This is it," she said. "I'm sure."

George tried the gate. "It's locked," he said.

"Perhaps there's a bell," said Molly.

The three of them looked around for a minute, but found neither a bell nor any other means to signal the house that visitors were at the gate.

"I could climb over," said George. He jumped up and grabbed the top of the stone wall with his fingertips, but was unable to hold on. "Here, Peter," he said, "give me a hand."

Peter smirked.

"What's so funny?" said George.

"Look over there," said Peter, pointing across the road.

George turned and looked. "I don't see anything," he said, and turned back.

Peter was gone.

"What?" said George. "Where—"

"Over here," said Peter, now standing inside the gate.

"But, but . . ." sputtered George. "How did—"

"Peter," Molly scolded.

"What?" answered Peter innocently. He tried to lift the massive iron latch, but it was locked. "I suppose I'll have to—"

He was cut off midsentence by a sharp warning sound from Tink.

*Behind you!*

But before Peter could turn around, he was encircled by two huge, hairy arms, one around his chest, and the other around his neck. He was lifted high off the ground, unable to make a sound, the breath squeezed from his lungs by the frightening strength of the arms. Molly screamed, then rushed to the gate and grabbed the bars, a look of horror on her face.

"Peter!" she cried. "Don't move!"

Peter, his lungs burning, fought the urge to thrash and twist. He felt Tink struggle from inside his coat, held shut by the massive, gripping arms.

A voice spoke from behind Peter, from the shadows of the trees lining the driveway. It was definitely a man's voice, but it spoke in grunts and low, guttural sounds.

As soon as the voice stopped, the hairy arms released Peter. He fell to his knees, gulping cold air. He turned and saw his assailant's massive, hairy body, topped by an equally massive head, with a long, dark snout tipped with a wet, black nose.

A bear. And quite a large bear at that.

Peter blinked and, still on his knees, edged away from it.

"Now then," said the voice from the shadows. "Who are you, and why are you trespassing on this property?"

Peter tried to answer, but his mind was too busy thinking about the bear. It was Molly who spoke.

"My name is Molly Aster," she said. "I'm looking for my father, Leonard Aster. It's urgent that I find him."

A short pause, and then the voice said, "Who are the others?"

"This is George Darling," said Molly, pointing to George. "And that's Peter, from the island. My father knows them both."

Another pause. Then a man stepped out of the shadows. He was a large man—nearly as tall as the bear, wide as a bull. He wore a broad-brimmed hat. Most of his face was covered with a thick, wild tangle of beard. He held a shotgun in the crook of his right arm.

"You stay where you are," he said. "All three of you. You are not to move."

The man spoke again, but this time in those same low, guttural tones, clearly addressing the bear. To Peter's surprise, the bear appeared to be listening, then responded with similar-sounding noises. The man then raised his head and made a series of strange barking sounds. Finally he switched back to English, addressing Peter, Molly, and George.

"Karl here," he said, gesturing toward the bear, "will be watching the young man inside the gate. The two of you," he said pointing to Molly and George, "are also being watched." The man turned and walked toward the house, boots crunching on gravel. "Remember: you're not to move."

Outside the gate, George slowly swiveled his head, surveying the area. He gasped as his eyes reached the woods across the road.

"Molly," he whispered.

"What?"

"Over there," he said, nodding.

Molly looked, and also gasped. Not thirty feet away, staring at them with eyes that glowed a luminous yellow in the moonlight, were three enormous wolves.

"Are they . . . *guarding* us?" whispered George.

"I believe so," said Molly.

"But how can they . . . I mean, wolves, Molly. And a *bear*. How can—"

"Be quiet, George," said Molly.

The silence stretched over several long, tense minutes, with Peter kneeling, still as a stone, three feet from the giant bear, while George and Molly stared at the wolves, and the wolves stared back.

Finally came the crunch of gravel again, and the large

man reappeared on the driveway, still carrying the shotgun. He walked past Peter, took a key ring from his belt, and opened the gate.

"Come in," he said to Molly and George. As they passed through the gate, George looked back over his shoulder. The wolves were gone.

"You can get up," the man said to Peter as he locked the gate.

Peter stood, keeping his distance from the bear.

The man grunted something to the bear. The bear grunted back and lumbered off into the shadows.

George gaped at the departing figure. "Molly," he whispered, "that man was *talking to the bear*."

"Be quiet, George," said Molly.

"This way," said the big man, starting down the driveway, followed by Molly, then Peter, then George, who was still glancing back toward the receding form of Karl the bear.

Peter moved next to George and said, "You should meet her porpoises sometime."

The mansion was even larger than it appeared from the road, a sprawling structure built of stone in a checkerboard pattern, alternating light gray and dark gray squares. Its windows—eight panes each, four on top and four below—were dark; the only light visible was a lantern burning over the front door.

The large man stopped a few yards from the house and gestured toward the door.

"Go on," he said.

Molly, Peter, and George walked past the man. Molly opened the door and, followed by the boys, stepped inside. They found themselves in a large room, rustically furnished, with massive oak ceiling beams and a huge fireplace blazing brightly. Molly's eyes went instantly to the tall figure in the center of the room.

"Father!" she said, and she ran to his arms.

For several long moments they hugged tightly, Molly's face buried in her father's shoulder. Finally they separated. Tears slid down Molly's face as she looked up into her father's eyes, where she saw tenderness losing ground to anger.

"Molly," he said, "you should not have come here."

"I know, Father, but—"

"Do you understand how—" He caught himself and shot a glance at Peter and George, both listening intently. "But I'm being rude." Aster walked over to the boys, his face softening just a bit as he shook hands with Peter.

"Peter," he said. "This is a bit of a surprise. How are you?"

"Fine, sir."

"And what on earth are you doing in England?"

"It's a long story, sir."

"I've no doubt that it is. You can tell me later. George, how are you?"

"Fine, sir. A bit surprised by the bear. That man outside appeared to be talking to it. And there were *wolves*."

Aster sent a baleful look in Molly's direction.

"Yes, well, animals can be trained to do amazing things, now can't they?" he said.

"But—"

"Yes, yes, amazing things," said Aster. "You and Peter must be very hungry."

"Well," said George, "I—"

"Good, good," said Aster. "Down that hallway to the right is the pantry. Plenty of food. Please help yourselves."

"But—"

"I insist," said Aster, pushing Peter and George toward the hallway. "Molly and I have some matters to discuss."

When they were gone, Aster turned to Molly. He kept his voice calm, but his tone was deeply displeased.

"I know you're an intelligent person," he said, his eyes boring into hers. "So I cannot for the life of me imagine what possessed you to come here—"

"Father, I—"

"Let me *finish*. To come here, jeopardizing the Return, and to bring those boys, including *George Darling*, for heaven's sake, who has *no business* getting involved in this. Do you realize the danger you've put yourself, and them, in?"

"Father, they've got Mother."

Aster's eyes widened. "*What?* Who?"

"The Others. They came to the house and took her."

"Took her where?"

"I don't know."

"But what about the guards?"

"They're working with the Others."

"*What?*"

"The Others are controlling them," said Molly.

"But . . . *how?*"

"There's a shadow man," said Molly. "I don't know how he does it, but somehow he takes people's shadows, and then he controls them."

"Shadows," said Leonard, frowning. "We received an odd report from—"

"Egypt," said Molly. "Mother told me. 'Beware the shadows.' That's what happened to the guards. This hideous creature came to our house. He calls himself Lord Ombra. He took Mother, and he tried to take my shadow. If not for Peter, he'd have gotten it."

"Lord Ombra," said Aster.

"He gave me this," said Molly, pulling Ombra's note from her pocket. "He told me to give it to you."

She handed the note to her father. He read it, then read it again.

"Oh, dear," he said softly.

"That's why I had to find you," she said.

"But how on earth *did* you find me?"

For the next ten minutes, Molly told her father what had happened since he left London—the strange comings and goings outside the Aster mansion; the odd behavior of the maid Jenna; the arrival of Slank, Ombra, and the others, and the kidnapping of Louise Aster; Molly's and Peter's flight from the house, and their decision to take refuge in George's room; their visit to the Tower; McGuinn's death; their discovery of the Keep; the eerie, horrifying appearance of Louise Aster's shadow speaking in Louise Aster's voice but attached to Ombra; their desperate escape from the White Tower through the garderobe; the decoding of the numbers scribbled on the invoice they'd found; the train trip to Salisbury; the cathedral spire that jogged Molly's memory; and the coach driver's recognition of the name *Gecierran*.

Aster reacted only twice: he buried his face in his hands for a moment at the news of the death of his old friend McGuinn, and he managed a wan smile at the garderobe escape. Other than that, he listened intently to Molly's account. When she was done, he began asking her questions, most of them about the strange being named Ombra. He made her go over each memory several times, pressing for more and more detail.

Finally, he said: "So, from what you know, this Ombra came into contact with—took the shadows of—Cadigan, Hodge, and Jarvis."

"Yes."

"And possibly the household staff."

"Yes. Certainly Jenna, but perhaps all of them."

"And . . . your mother."

"I fear so, yes."

"All right," Aster said softly, more to himself than to Molly. "All right."

"What do you mean?" said Molly. "What's all right?"

"I mean that none of those people knows where the Return is," said Aster. "Not even your mother knows that. She and I agreed that I would not tell her, in case something like this ever happened. She doesn't know, so she can't tell anyone. This Lord Ombra doesn't know where we've taken the starstuff. The Return is safe."

Molly stared at her father.

"The Return is safe," she said.

"Yes."

"But what about *Mother?*" said Molly. "What about *that?*" She pointed to Ombra's letter, still in her father's hand. "He says Mother will come to the gravest harm if you don't give him the starstuff. The *gravest harm*, Father. He's going to *kill* her."

Aster looked down, ran his hand through his hair, and looked up. Molly saw anguish in his eyes.

"Molly," he said softly. "You must understand what's at stake here."

"I *do* understand," she said. "What's at stake is Mother's life."

Aster flinched, then went on: "I will do everything in my

power to save Louise. But the one thing I cannot do—the thing your mother would not *want* me to do—is allow the starstuff to fall into the hands of the Others."

"But—"

"Molly, *listen*. This is an enormous amount of starstuff, the most we've ever recovered. If the Others get hold of it, a thousand years of work and sacrifice by the Starcatchers before us will be for nothing. *Nothing*, Molly. The world will become a terrible place. All of humanity will suffer. The plague, Molly. The Dark Ages. This would be worse than those. We must not allow it. We *cannot*."

"But if you return it," said Molly, "Mother will die."

"If the Others get it," said Aster, his voice grim, "I fear she will die anyway. Do you think they would let *any* Starcatchers live?"

"I don't know what they would do," said Molly. "But I do know that if you return it, Ombra will kill Mother. Isn't that right?"

"But—"

"*Isn't that right, Father?* Answer me."

Aster hung his head. "Yes."

"Then you can't do it," she said. "You *can't*."

Aster looked at his daughter, and now both of their faces glistened with tears.

"Molly," he whispered, "I'm afraid I have no choice."

## CHAPTER 90

# GEORGE'S THOUGHT

GEORGE AND PETER sat next to each other at a rough plank table, chewing hard. Neither boy had said a word since they'd entered the pantry and discovered a loaf of fresh-baked brown bread and a hefty block of Wiltshire cheese. They were now consuming these as fast as they could, each wanting to be sure the other boy didn't get more. Both were good competitive eaters, Peter having trained at St. Norbert's Home for Wayward Boys, and George at boarding school.

They were eating ravenously in silence when Molly burst through the pantry door. It hit the wall with a loud *thwack*. Molly's eyes were red and swollen, and her face glistened with tears. George and Peter stood, both eyeing what remained of the torn loaf.

"Molly, what's wrong?" said Peter, his mouth spewing bread crumbs.

"We're leaving," said Molly.

"*Leaving?*" said George, ejecting a chunk of cheese. "Now?"

"Yes, *now*," said Molly. "We must return to London immediately."

"But why?" said Peter. "We just got here."

"To rescue Mother," said Molly.

"But I thought your father—" began Peter.

"My *father*," said Molly, interrupting, "doesn't care about Mother."

Peter swallowed a chunk of bread with some difficulty and was about to speak when Leonard Aster appeared in the doorway behind Molly, his expression stern.

"Molly," Aster said, "that's quite enough."

Molly ignored him.

"I'm leaving," she said to Peter and George. "You can go with me or stay here, as you choose."

"Molly," said Aster. "You are *not* leaving."

"Yes, I am," she said.

"No," said Aster. "You are my daughter, and you shall do as I say. I will not have you wandering the countryside at night. *Especially* not this night."

Molly stared at her father, then nodded slowly. "So it's to be tonight," she said. "The Return is tonight."

"Molly," said Aster, glancing at George. "You mustn't—"

"I don't *care!*" shouted Molly. "I don't *care* if George finds out about the Return. I don't *care* about you and your starstuff and—"

"*Molly!*" Aster grabbed his daughter by the arms, pressed his face to hers. "You *must not* talk about these things."

Molly jerked herself free.

"I don't *care!*" she shouted. "All I care about is Mother."

"And you think I *don't?*" he asked.

"If you cared," said Molly, "you'd save her."

"And you must believe me," he said. "I shall do everything in my power to do just that."

"Except," she said, "the one thing that *would* save her."

"Please, Molly," Aster said. "Please try to understand."

He reached out and touched her shoulder gently. She pushed his hand away. Aster stared at his daughter for a few moments, weariness and sorrow furrowing his face. Then he turned his attention to Peter and George, neither of whom had moved a muscle.

"I'm sorry you had to see this," he said. "This is a . . . a very difficult time for us."

Neither boy spoke.

"First thing tomorrow," said Aster, "I will arrange to send you all back to London. But for tonight you must remain here. I'm going out for several hours with Mister Magill—the man who, ah, greeted you at the gate. The three of you will be safe and comfortable here. You must not, under any circumstances, try to leave." Aster looked pointedly at Molly.

"The house will be watched. If you *do* try to leave, you will be prevented from doing so in a manner that I regret to say could be quite unpleasant. Do you understand me?"

Peter and George, remembering the bear and the wolves, nodded. Molly did not react.

"All right, then," said Aster. He looked at Molly again, as if about to say something more, shook his head, then left.

The next half hour passed in unhappy silence. Molly sat at the pantry table, staring straight ahead, resisting Peter's and George's awkward attempts to console her. George was clearly eager to ask questions about the confrontation between Molly and her father, but sensing that this was not a good time, he managed to restrain himself.

The silence was broken by the sound of horses outside, and the crunch of wheels on gravel. Molly, Peter, and George exchanged glances, then ran to the large main room and looked out the window. By the light of the moon, now high in the cloudless sky, they saw three horses, two of them hitched to a wagon. They also saw Leonard Aster put a large cloth sack into the wagon. From out of the shadows appeared the large bearded man, Magill, holding a rolled-up piece of canvas. Behind him shuffled Karl the bear. The bear was carrying a trunk made of smooth, dark wood, with hinges and latches that gleamed gold in the moonlight.

"There it is," said Peter.

"There *what* is?" said George.

476

"Be quiet," said Molly.

Karl laid the trunk gently in the wagon bed and slid it forward, then climbed in after it, moving with surprising speed and grace despite his massive bulk. The bear lay down next to the trunk. Magill covered both bear and trunk with the piece of canvas, then climbed onto the wagon seat and picked up the reins. He and Aster exchanged a few words, then Aster mounted the horse. Magill raised his head and made some of the odd barking sounds he'd made earlier; then he cocked his ear, listening. He nodded at Aster, and both men flicked their reins, starting up the driveway.

At the end of the drive, Aster dismounted and opened the gate. When the wagon had passed through to the road, Aster led his horse through, closed the gate, locked it, and remounted. In a moment the little procession was gone from view.

"All right," said George. "I have a few questions, if you don't mind."

"Be qu—" began Molly.

"*No,*" said George. "I will *not* be quiet. I am sick and tired of not knowing what's happening. Without me, you'd never have gotten as far as Salisbury, let alone found this house. I've spent a good deal of time *and* money on your little quest, Molly, not to mention risking being eaten by wolves. I think I'm entitled to some sort of explanation."

Molly sighed. "All right," she said.

"Molly—" Peter warned.

"No," said Molly. "George is right. He's been a loyal friend, and without him we'd never have gotten this far. He's put his life at risk for me. I owe him the truth." She looked out the window. "And I don't much care about Father's precious secrets now anyway," she added bitterly.

Peter shook his head, but said nothing.

"My family," Molly said to George, "belongs to a group that for centuries has been protecting a very precious, but very dangerous, substance."

"This 'starstuff,'" said George.

"Yes," said Molly. "That's what's in the trunk you just saw."

"What is it?" said George.

"It's something that falls from the sky," said Molly. "It has amazing powers. Magical powers."

"*Magical* powers?"

"Yes."

George looked skeptical. "Molly," he said, "I'm a student of astronomy. I know quite a bit about what falls from the sky. It's rocks, Molly. Just rocks. I've never heard of any . . . starstuff."

Peter smirked.

"What's so funny?" said George.

"Nothing," said Peter.

"The reason you haven't heard of starstuff," said Molly,

"is that Father's group works very hard to keep it secret. They collect it when it falls, so that people, especially evil people, can't get hold of it."

George's expression remained skeptical. "And what do they do with it?"

"They return it."

"Return it to where?" said George, smiling. "To the heavens?"

"Yes."

"But that's impossible!" sputtered George.

"Apparently, it's not," said Molly. "They've been doing it for centuries."

"But how?"

"I don't know," said Molly. "I've never seen it done. Very few have."

"So you don't *know* that this Return thing actually happens," said George, in a tone that Peter found quite irritating. Molly, for her part, remained calm.

"It happens," she said. "That's where Father has gone now."

"I see," said George doubtfully. "And these . . . evil people you're keeping the starstuff from," he said. "Are they the ones who kidnapped your mother?"

"Yes," she said. "Their leader is this hideous creature, Lord Ombra. He has terrible powers. He can take a person's—" Molly paused, and decided that if George was skeptical about starstuff, he'd be even more so about Ombra's peculiar and fearsome abilities. "He's very powerful," she went on. "And ruthless."

"And where is this . . . Ombra now?" said George.

"In London," said Molly. "He took Mother to exchange her for the starstuff. But Father refuses to make the exchange. And Ombra said that if he doesn't get the starstuff, he will . . . will—" Molly fought to control her voice. "He will kill my mother." Molly put her face in her hands, sobbing.

"Perhaps he's just bluffing," George said softly.

Molly shook her head. "No," she said. "He'll do it. He's a horrible, horrible creature. Peter and I saw him kill a man, an old friend of my family." In that instant a picture came into Molly's mind—a vivid image of McGuinn's desperate effort to fend off the relentlessly advancing Ombra, and his fatal fall on the steep stairs of the White Tower. "He won't hesitate to—"

Molly stopped.

"Oh, dear," she said.

"What is it?" said George.

Molly ignored him. "Peter," she said, her tone urgent. "Do you remember when Ombra chased us down the stairs at the tower, and Mister McGuinn fell?"

"Yes," said Peter. "I won't soon forget *that*."

"Did Ombra touch his shadow?"

"McGuinn's?"

"Yes," said Molly. "*Think*, Peter. Did he touch it?"

Peter thought back to the terrifying confusion on the dark, narrow staircase—McGuinn swinging the lantern, trying desperately to fend off Ombra, then Ombra's sudden darting attack, and McGuinn's scream just as he lost his balance. . . .

Peter frowned, trying to trap that instant in his mind. Then he nodded. "Yes," he said. "It was just for a moment, before he fell. But yes, I think Ombra touched his shadow."

"I think so, too," said Molly.

"I don't understand," said George. "What difference does it make if he touched his shadow?"

"McGuinn knew the site of the Return," said Molly. "He wouldn't tell us, but he knew. And if he knew, and Ombra got his shadow—"

"—then Ombra knows where the Return is," said Peter.

George said, "But how does touching a person's shadow—"

"Not now, George," said Molly, waving away his question. "Peter, I feel such a fool. Father asked me several times whose shadows Ombra took, and somehow I never thought of McGuinn."

"It was just for an instant," said Peter. "We don't *know* that Ombra found out."

"But he *could* have," said Molly.

"Yes," said Peter. "I suppose he could have."

"And if he did," said Molly, "he'll be at the Return now. He'll be waiting for Father."

She and Peter stared at each other.

"I have to warn Father," she said. She ran to the door and grabbed the latch.

A sharp warning chime sounded from under Peter's shirt.

*She'd better not open that.*

"Molly!" shouted Peter, running toward her. "Don't—"

Too late: Molly had the door open. She screamed and slammed it shut.

Peter got only a moment's glimpse of the huge gray shape on the doorstep.

"Wolf," Molly gasped.

*I told her.*

"What's that ringing sound?" said George.

Ignoring him, Molly went to the window.

"There must be half a dozen out there," she said.

Peter and George, joining her, saw the dark shapes, the glowing eyes.

"I don't think they want us to leave," said George.

Molly's shoulders slumped. "No," she said.

"Molly," said Peter. "I can leave."

"How?" snorted George. "Do you intend to *fly* over the wolves?"

"Yes," said Peter.

George turned to Molly: "Has he gone mad?"

She ignored him, speaking to Peter. "It's no use," she said. "We don't know where the Return is. Father's been gone a half hour or more, on horseback. He could be anywhere. How will you find him in the dark? How will you even know which direction to go?"

"I can try," said Peter. "I've got a full moon to help me."

Molly shook her head. "You don't know this countryside, Peter. Without knowing where the Return is, you'll just get lost flying 'round out there."

"But what choice do we have?" said Peter.

"I don't know," said Molly, staring hopelessly out the window.

"Hang on," said George.

"What?" said Molly.

"It *is* a full moon," said George.

"Yes," said Molly, irritated. "Peter just said that."

"Well, I just had a thought," said George. "I'd been hoping to observe it through my telescope, though it's been rather cloudy the past few days, but tonight—"

"George," interrupted Molly. "What *are* you talking about?"

"An eclipse," said George. "A total lunar eclipse. Tonight." He pulled a watch from his pocket and consulted it. "In about an hour, in fact. The moon will pass through

Earth's shadow and disappear for . . . let me see . . . I believe it's fifty-three minutes."

Peter and Molly stared at him.

"Go on," said Molly.

"Well," said George, "I was just thinking that the eclipse might have something to do with the Return."

Molly nodded. "I know it has to be at a certain time," she said. "Father was very definite about that. And he knew the time months ago."

"Lunar eclipses can be predicted years in advance," said George. "It's quite a coincidence, don't you think? The Return and the eclipse, both tonight?"

"Yes," said Molly. "Quite a coincidence."

"So if you're right," said Peter—a bit grudgingly, in part because he didn't exactly know what an eclipse was—"the Return will take place in about an hour?"

"Yes," said George.

Molly sighed. "But even if that's so," she said, "we know only *when* it will happen. We still don't know *where*."

George smiled a self-satisfied smile.

"What?" said Molly.

"If I'm right," said George, "I know exactly where they've gone."

## CHAPTER 91

# ☊HE ☊ESTINATION

☊HERE WAS NOBODY OUTSIDE the tiny village of Amesbury on this chilly night. The sound of horse hooves clopping brought faces to a few windows. Peeking out from behind curtains drawn against the cold, the villagers saw a man on horseback followed by wagon and driver—nocturnal travelers, not an especially unusual sight on this well-traveled road.

The villagers could not see the silent loping gray shapes keeping pace with the horse and wagon, off to either side of the road, their paths taking them through the fields, out of sight.

The little procession passed through the village and disappeared up the road. The curious villagers went back to their firesides.

Two miles west of Amesbury, the road rose to a ridge. Reaching it, Leonard Aster reined his horse to a stop.

Behind him, Magill halted the wagon, raised his head, and barked. On either side, the wolves stopped, waiting, watching.

Aster and Magill surveyed the scene. Before them lay the Salisbury Plain, rising gently to the horizon, the full moon illuminating it for miles. Just ahead the road forked. The left fork bore southwest, eventually making its way to the city of Exeter. The right fork bore gently northwest, toward the heart of the rolling grasslands of the Salisbury Plain.

On the left side of that road, a half mile away, clear as day in the bright moonlight, stood their destination. Slowly, carefully, the two men swept the landscape with their eyes: it appeared to be deserted. Aster checked his pocket watch, then nodded to Magill. They flicked their reins and, flanked by the wolves, started forward toward the Return.

## CHAPTER 92

# Not Much Time

"Stonehenge," said George.

Peter frowned; Molly gasped.

"Of *course*," she said. "It's right near Salisbury, isn't it?"

"It's quite close," said George. "I've been there a half dozen times, at least. I doubt it's five miles from this house."

"Stonehenge?" said Peter. "The rock pile?"

"It's not a *pile*," said George. "It's a man-made circular arrangement of huge stones. Some say it was built thousands of years ago—before the Romans."

"But what do giant stones have to do with the Return?" said Peter.

"Nobody knows for certain why it was built," said George. "But it has something to do with the heavens. The main axis of the circle lines up almost perfectly with the midsummer sunrise and the midwinter sunset. Some say Stonehenge also was used to predict lunar eclipses."

487

"Like the one tonight," said Molly.

"Exactly," said George. "So if this Return of yours has to happen during the eclipse, Stonehenge would seem to be the place for it."

"All right," said Molly. "We must go there now."

"Um," said George, looking out the window. "Have you forgotten the wolves?"

"No," said Molly. She turned to Peter, pointing to the chain around his neck, and said, "How much have you got?"

"I don't know," said Peter. "I used some in London."

"Well, let's hope you have enough," said Molly. "Enough for two, actually."

"Two?" said Peter. "*He's* going?"

"Yes," said Molly. "We need him to show us where Stonehenge is. George, can you find Stonehenge? From here?"

"I suppose I could," George said. "But how—"

"We need to find an upstairs window," said Molly, walking toward the staircase at the end of the big room.

"But," said George, "what about the—"

"You'll see," said Molly, over her shoulder. "Come on."

Upstairs they found a window that, with a bit of effort, the three of them were able to open. As chilly air flooded the room, they leaned out over the broad sill and looked down. On the ground, fifteen feet below them, they saw three pairs of glowing yellow eyes looking back.

"There had *better* be enough," Peter said. "This wouldn't be a good time to fall."

"No," said Molly, eyeing the wolves.

"I don't understand," said George. "What are you talking about?"

"We're going to fly to Stonehenge," said Molly.

"So you're *both* mad," said George.

"You're going to fly with us," said Molly.

"Oh, of *course* I am," said George. "I'm going to just flap my wings and *fly* over those wolves!"

Molly and Peter looked at him.

"What?" he said.

Peter said, "There's no need to flap."

"Peter," said Molly, "may I have your locket?"

Peter removed it and put it in Molly's hand. She held up the small golden sphere, showing it to George, who eyed it with open skepticism.

"George," she said. "I'm going to put some starstuff on myself, then on you. It's going to feel strange, but in a pleasant way."

"What about Peter?" said George, smirking. "Doesn't he get any of this magical starstuff?"

"He doesn't need it," said Molly. "He can already fly."

George laughed out loud. "Ah!" he said. "How lovely for young Peter!"

"George," said Molly. "This isn't a joke." She put her thumb on the locket clasp.

"Isn't it?" said George. "Because it certainly—"

George stopped in midsentence, mouth gaping, as Molly opened the locket. Instantly her hand was enveloped in a warm golden glow. She tilted the locket slightly, and the glow flowed down her arm, gently surrounding her, being absorbed into her, as she emitted a soft, barely audible *Ahhhh.*

"Give me your hand, George," she said.

Cautiously, he held out his right hand. Molly tilted the locket over it, and the glow swirled and cascaded along George's arm.

"Oh, my," he said. "This is . . . it's . . . *Ahhhhhhh.*"

"Yes," said Molly. She closed the locket and handed it back to Peter.

*Can I come out now?* chimed Tink.

"I hear bells!" said George. "They're quite lovely."

"Tink wants out," Peter said to Molly.

Looking at George, Molly said, "Why not? I don't suppose it makes any difference now."

Peter opened his shirt, and Tink emerged, blinking. She hovered for a second, then landed in the tousled red mass of Peter's hair, where she sat, stretching.

George stared at her.

"Molly," he said. "There's a pixie sitting in Peter's hair."

"Yes," said Molly.

Tink chimed.

"She prefers to be called a birdgirl," said Peter.

"I see," said George, still staring at her.

"Listen, George," said Molly. ". . . George? George?"

Reluctantly, George looked away from Tink. "Yes?"

"We're going out the window now," she said. "We're going to fly."

"Capital!" said George.

"The trick is to lean forward," said Molly. "You lean forward, then you swoop, then you soar."

"Lean, swoop, and soar," said George. "Got it."

"Here we go, then," said Molly. "Peter, perhaps you should go first."

Peter, with Tink still in his hair, climbed onto the windowsill, then slid off, hovering in midair.

"Look at that!" said George, smiling hugely. "Brilliant!"

Below Peter, the wolves growled.

"What was that?" said George.

"The wolves," said Peter.

"Ah," said George, his smile dimming. "I'd forgotten about the wolves."

"Don't worry about them," said Molly, guiding George up onto the sill. "Just remember: lean, swoop, soar."

"Lean, swoop, soar," said George. He sat on the sill, legs dangling out.

The wolves were growling louder now.

"Are you quite sure," he said, "that they . . . WOOOOOOO!"

Aided by a hard shove from Molly, George slipped off the windowsill. For a moment, he hung motionless in the air, his eyes and mouth wide open in wonderment. Ever so slowly, he began to drift downward. The wolves moved into position directly beneath him.

"Lean," said Peter.

The wolves rose on their hind legs, jaws snapping. George was now staring at them, as if hypnotized.

"George!" shouted Molly, climbing onto the sill. "Lean!"

George remained motionless as he drifted down, his dangling feet now only a few feet above the wolves' jaws.

*He's not very bright, is he?* observed Tink.

Peter darted to George and grabbed his arm; Molly slid off the sill and grabbed his other arm. Together they swooped him away, then up, the snapping jaws just missing his shoes. As howls of frustration echoed behind them, the trio, with Tink flitting ahead, soared into the moonlit sky, chill night air rushing past their faces.

"George," said Molly. "Are you all right?"

George, having torn his eyes away from the rapidly receding wolves, was now looking up, gazing with wonder at the clear night sky, at the moon and the stars he had studied for so many hours, squinting into the eyepiece of the telescope in his room in London. Now, as he rose above the

492

trees, with the open sky spreading to the horizon all around him, he felt as though he were part of the heavens, as though if he reached his hand out he could touch the moon itself.

"Yes," he said. "I'm . . . it's *wonderful*, Molly. Wonderful."

"Good," said Molly. "Now which way is Stonehenge?"

"Stonehenge?" said George.

*Not very bright at all*, said Tink.

"Yes," said Molly, struggling to be patient. "We're going to Stonehenge, remember?"

"Ah," said George. "Right. Stonehenge. Let's see. The river's over there." He looked around the sky. "And there's Ursa Major, so Polaris would be . . . Ah, there it is. So we want to go . . . that way. How does one turn?"

"One leans," said Molly. "Like this." She leaned and swooped left, followed by Peter and Tink.

George gave it a try and, after wobbling a bit, executed a passable left turn. "Brilliant!" he said.

"Now what?" said Molly.

"Up ahead there," said George, pointing, "will be a village."

"I think I see the lights," said Peter, squinting toward the horizon.

"That will be Amesbury," said George. "From there we can follow the road. It's only about two miles from the village to Stonehenge."

"Let's go, then," said Molly, leaning forward. "We need to get there before the starstuff wears off."

"It wears off?" said George.

"Oh, yes," Molly called back. Even as she spoke, she was aware of a slight weakening of the starstuff's power. "*Lean*, George!" she shouted.

Then, more to herself than anyone else, she added, "We haven't much time."

## CHAPTER 93

# A Raven's Eye

THE RAVENS STOOPED atop the ancient weather-scoured gray stones, their gleaming, beady eyes darting in every direction. Every few seconds the largest of the birds fixed his sight on two distant pinpricks of yellow—the windows of the cottage where Ombra waited.

For hours the ravens, restless yet infinitely patient, had watched the empty grassland. Then one of them saw it—a faraway movement no human eye would have detected.

*Caw!* came the alert. Then again, *Caw! Caw!*

The others saw it now: tiny shapes, a rider and a wagon approaching on the road from the village.

The large raven flapped his wings, roiling the still air with a shudder of feathers, and lifted into the sky. It grew smaller, an occasional *caw* marking its progress toward the dim lights of the distant cottage.

Nerezza, dozing in a chair, sat up with a start, awakened by scratching at the cottage window. Carrying a dripping candle, he walked stiffly toward the sound, his back sore from the long carriage ride.

He pulled back the curtain and jumped: there stood a large raven, head sideways, big black eye pressed toward the glass. Nerezza, furious at himself for being scared by a bird, raised his fist to bang the glass.

Then he felt the chill just behind him.

"Let him in," groaned Ombra.

Without turning around, Nerezza fumbled with the latch and got the window open. His candle's flame danced as the bird hobbled inside and ruffled its feathers. It faced Ombra, suddenly still as death.

"The candle," said Ombra.

Nerezza breathed heavily, his nose whistling, as he brought the candle close to the bird's left side, so its shadow was cast on the windowsill. The raven made no effort to avoid the flame. Ombra raised his right arm and touched the shadow.

"Two men," Ombra groaned. "One on horseback, one driving a wagon. On the village road."

Ombra withdrew his hand. The raven, with a loud *Caw!* flapped off.

"Just two of them?" said Nerezza. He immediately regretted

speaking, as Ombra turned to face him, his empty hood gaping.

"If that is Aster," Ombra said, "as I believe it is, it makes no difference whether he has one man with him or a hundred. He is in possession of immense power, Captain; far more than we have. We have the element of surprise, and we have his wife. But we must not underestimate the power he has. Is that clear, Captain?"

"Yes, my lord."

"Summon the men, and have Slank bring Mrs. Aster. We leave immediately."

"Yes, my lord."

In a minute's time they gathered in front of the cottage: Ombra, Nerezza, and Slank holding the limp arm of the vacant-eyed Louise Aster. They were joined seconds later by a half dozen men, two of whom carried rifles. They set out across the grassland, Ombra gliding effortlessly ahead. The men had to trot to keep up with him; Slank was practically carrying the passive Louise Aster.

They approached Stonehenge from the southwest, directly opposite the entrance from the village road. Ombra chose a path that took them past several ancient burial mounds, keeping them out of sight of the road.

Twice the large raven fluttered to a landing on Ombra's shoulder, then took off again. The second time, Ombra turned and gathered the others around. Speaking in a barely audible moan, he said: "They will arrive soon on the far side

of the stones. Just ahead is a ditch. You will conceal yourselves in it and await my orders." He pointed to the two men
with rifles. "You will position yourselves on either side of me.
Mister Slank, you will keep Mrs. Aster close at hand."

The men, ghostly silhouettes in the moonlight, moved
forward into the shallow ditch that surrounded Stonehenge.
The large raven fluttered forward and joined the other sentries atop the ancient stones.

For a moment, the night fell silent.

And then, from the distance, came the gentle *clippity-
clop* of approaching horses.

## CHAPTER 94

# The Return

Aster and Magill approached the great stones from the northeast, climbing the gently rising hillside where Stonehenge was erected thousands of years earlier by people unknown, for reasons unknown.

As the two men drew near the tightly grouped arrangement, they began to see its various elements clearly in the bright moonlight.

Most dominant from the outside were the sarsen stones, standing in a circle one hundred feet across, each stone thirteen feet high and seven feet wide. Some were still supporting horizontal stones, called lintels, though most of those had long since fallen. Within the sarsen stone circle were the remains of another circle of smaller stones, known as bluestones, about six feet high, many of them now toppled or missing. Inside the bluestone circle stood the mighty trilithons, each made of two huge vertical stones, only a few inches apart, supporting a lintel. At one time there were five of these structures, the tallest standing twenty-four feet high. Three were still intact.

The entire grouping was surrounded by an ancient ditch, forming a circle more than three hundred feet across. On the northeast side of this ditch was an opening, which led out to the road. Standing next to the road, far from the main grouping, stood a lone sarsen, sixteen feet tall. This was known as the Heel Stone. It was here that Leonard Aster halted his horse, signaling for Magill to stop the wagon behind him. The men studied the main stone grouping. They saw nothing unusual, other than some dark birds perched atop the central trilithons. Aster's eye lingered on the birds for a moment, as he realized they were ravens.

*Like the ravens at the Tower,* he thought. *Odd.*

Seeing no other humans, Aster signaled to Magill, who uttered a series of soft barking sounds. Instantly the wolves emerged from the field. Five took up sentry positions along the road; the sixth began a slow surveillance around the perimeter of Stonehenge.

Aster and Magill rode forward toward the main stone grouping. At the break in the ditch they came to the Slaughter Stone, a massive sarsen slab lying on its side, its uneven surface marked by hollows that, some said, once collected the blood of those who were sacrificed on it. Here Aster dismounted, tying his horse to a shrub. Magill climbed down from the wagon and removed the canvas covering. With a growl, Karl, the enormous bear, rose and clambered down from the wagon bed. He picked up the dark trunk and set it gently on the ground.

Aster opened the cloth sack. He removed a golden helmet, which shone like fire in the moonlight, and set it on the wagon bed. Next came a pair of golden boots, followed by a pair of golden gloves and a golden suit, both fashioned of a thin material that flexed like cloth.

Aster glanced up at the moon and frowned. The left side of the moon's surface was distinctly darker than the right. It was not the sharply defined darkness that appeared on the sun in a solar eclipse, but the gradual shading of the lunar eclipse.

"It's starting," Aster said. He quickly shrugged off his coat and removed his boots, then began putting on the golden suit.

Magill watched unhappily.

"Wish you'd let me do this," he said.

"I appreciate that, Magill," said Aster. "But it's too dangerous."

"I could take Karl out there with me," said Magill. "Never seen the danger Karl couldn't handle."

Aster smiled and shook his head. "I'm afraid even Karl is no match for what's in there," he said, pointing to the trunk. "Somebody has to open the trunk when the eclipse reaches totality, and the moon is dark. Whoever that is has to be wearing this suit. Anybody else . . . any *thing* else . . . would die instantly."

"But some has withstood it," said Magill. "I've heard that."

"That's true," said Aster. "Every once in a great while somebody comes along who can tolerate starstuff in large quantities." He thought of Peter and his unwitting exposure back on the island—an exposure that gave him the power of flight, and agelessness, and . . . nobody knew what else. "But that's a very rare quality," he continued. "I doubt that more than a few people on Earth could survive being exposed to what's in that trunk. Could you give me a hand with these gloves? They're rather snug."

In a moment, with Magill's help, Aster was clad from neck to toe in the gleaming gold suit. He looked at the moon again; the shadow had deepened and broadened, and the moon now had a pronounced reddish hue.

"All right," he said to Magill. "I'll take the trunk in now. When the Return begins, the light may attract somebody from the village. You must not, under any circumstances, allow anyone to enter the stone circle. Nor must you or any of the animals enter. No matter what you see, or what you hear, once the Return has begun, *you must stay away*."

"What if there's trouble?" said Magill. "What if you need help?"

Aster laid a gold-gloved hand on Magill's shoulder. "I'll

be fine," he said softly. "And if I'm not, there's nothing you, or anybody, can do."

Aster put on the gold helmet. It covered his head and neck entirely; it had two holes in front, each covered with a fine gold mesh, which protected his eyes but enabled him to see quite well. With the helmet snugly in place, Aster bent and grabbed the trunk—which was much lighter than its bulk suggested—and hoisted it easily to his shoulder.

"Wish me luck," he said, his voice a bit muffled by the helmet.

"Good luck," said Magill.

With that, Aster turned and began carrying the trunk toward the heart of Stonehenge.

---

The wolf slowly circled the outer edge of the ditch, ears erect, eyes searching, nose sifting the thousands of scents drifting in the night air. As the wolf reached the southwest side of the ditch it stopped. Just ahead, in the moonlight, a dark thing rose from the ditch. The wolf sniffed. The thing had the silhouette of a man, but it did not smell like a man. It did not smell alive.

The thing oozed out of the ditch and toward the wolf. The wolf growled and bared its teeth. It was not so much afraid as puzzled; it could not understand why the thing was not warned off by the growl, the bared teeth.

The thing came straight at the wolf. The wolf lunged, jaws wide. It snapped at the thing. The jaws caught nothing, except a sensation of cold, as though they had tried to bite a winter fog. The wolf stumbled awkwardly, confused, having anticipated resistance, but finding none. It regained its footing and turned to snap its jaws again.

Too late.

———◆———

Molly knew the feeling well.

"It's wearing off, Peter," she called.

They had passed over Amesbury and were flying along the road to Stonehenge, now clearly visible ahead. They were still about two hundred feet in the air, but Molly could feel the ground pulling on her, gently but relentlessly. The same was happening to George, but he was happily oblivious, swooping this way and that with a smile the width of his face, occasionally declaring to nobody in particular, "Brilliant!"

"Can you reach Stonehenge?" said Peter.

"I don't know," said Molly, looking ahead. "It's going to be close."

"It would be a good thing if you could," said Peter, pointing at the road.

Molly looked down and saw three . . . now four wolves loping directly beneath them, looking up.

*They look hungry,* said Tink.

"What did she say?" Molly asked.

"She said we're almost there," said Peter.

———◆———

Ombra stuffed the scout wolf's shadow into the burlap sack. The shadowless wolf sat looking up at him, motionless.

Ombra spoke to it, not in a human tongue, but in guttural sounds.

*You saw nothing,* he said. *Go.*

The wolf trotted off, continuing its circuit of the stones, taking no notice as it passed the group of humans crouching in the ancient ditch. A few moments later the wolf was out of sight. Nerezza and Slank had their eyes on Ombra, who stood with his hood pointing upward as if listening for something.

There was a flutter of wings, a black shape flickering in the dark. A raven landed on Ombra's shoulder. It leaned its head toward the hood, holding it there for a few seconds, then fluttered into the air and was gone.

Ombra moved close—uncomfortably close—to Nerezza and Slank. He spoke in a low, barely audible groan: "A man in a gold suit—I assume it is Aster—is carrying a trunk toward the center of the circle."

"Do we take him?" whispered Nerezza.

"We move in," said Ombra. "But carefully. If he sees

us, or hears us, he has the power to destroy us in an instant."

Nerezza and Slank exchanged glances: was there a hint—just a hint—of *fear* in Ombra's voice?

"Single file," groaned Ombra. "Riflemen behind me. Be ready to fire on my command. Mister Slank, bring Mrs. Aster. Captain Nerezza, you and your men will follow Mister Slank. *Silently.*"

The men stood. Slank pulled the limp form of Louise Aster to her feet. Ombra turned and glided across the open area toward the central grouping of stones, moving slightly to his right in order to take a path that kept him hidden from view by one of the massive outer sarsen stones. Reaching this stone, he signaled for the others to halt behind him. Ombra flattened himself against the stone and slid slowly around it, looking less like a living thing than a random moon-cast shadow.

Just ahead, providing excellent cover, was a smaller standing stone, a remnant of the inner bluestone circle. Ombra oozed back and beckoned the two riflemen forward, positioning one on each side of the bluestone. From here they had a clear view of the central trilithons.

With the riflemen in place, Ombra oozed forward into the bluestone's shadow, where he became essentially invisible. There he waited.

He would not have to wait long.

Leonard Aster moved slowly, stopping every few feet to survey the area. He had seen nothing, and expected to see nothing. Had there been intruders, he was confident that Magill's wolves would have detected them. Still, he was cautious.

He had passed through the outer sarsen circle, then the inner bluestone circle. He was now approaching the central trilithon stones, some towering high above him, others lying on the ground, where they had fallen unknown centuries ago.

Aster's objective was the Altar Stone, a huge slab of sandstone lying on its side, broken in two, now embedded in the ground and almost entirely covered by fallen pieces of what had once been the tallest trilithon. Reaching this jumble of broken stone, Aster stopped and gently set the trunk down so that its wood touched an exposed corner of the altar stone. A raven fluttered past, so close that Aster ducked involuntarily. He looked up at the moon. It was now almost fully engulfed in shadow.

*Just a few minutes,* thought Aster. *If that.*

He knelt and prepared to unlatch the trunk. At long last, the Return was at hand.

Molly was not going to make it. Strain as she might, she was losing altitude rapidly; now she was fifteen feet above the wolves—now five of them—trotting directly below her feet, growling ominously. George, finally aware of the peril, was even lower, flapping his arms in a frantic, fruitless effort to gain altitude. Stonehenge was one hundred yards up the road.

"Peter," Molly said. "We can't—"

"I know," Peter said, swooping close. "Take my hand. You too, George."

With Molly holding one of his hands and George the other, Peter strained upward with all his might. He was able to hold them level for another twenty yards, but then their weight began to overcome his ability to fly. Down they dropped, toward the waiting jaws.

"I'm going to have to put you down," said Peter, sounding far calmer than he felt. "When I do, you start running toward Stonehenge."

"But," said George, looking down, "what about the—"

"Don't worry about the wolves," said Peter. "I'll take care of them."

*You will?* said Tink. *How?*

"What did she say?" said Molly.

"She said not to worry," said Peter. "Hang on."

With a grunt and a sudden violent swoop forward, Peter carried the now-heavy forms of Molly and George ten yards farther on, and set them down just ahead of the approaching wolves.

"RUN!" he shouted, turning to face the oncoming pack.

The first wolf reached him a second later, snarling, lunging. Peter shot upward, leaving it snapping at the air, then dropped straight down, his feet landing hard on the wolf's back. The wolf howled in pain and fury and turned, but Peter had again launched himself upward; the slashing teeth missed his leg by an inch. The other wolves, responding to the plight of their fellow pack member, converged on the spot, leaping and snapping at Peter, who danced in the air just above their heads, shouting to keep their attention.

Meanwhile, unnoticed by the wolves, Molly and George were running up the road toward the Heel Stone, illuminated now by the gentle light of a million stars, as the moon now was a mere ghostly circle.

"What do we do when we get there?" huffed George.

"We look for Father," said Molly, looking up at the moon. "If we're not too—"

She stopped and gasped.

"What?" said George. Then his eyes followed her gaze, and he said, "Oh, my."

Looming in the road fifteen feet ahead, standing eight feet tall if he stood an inch, was Karl the bear. He dropped to all fours and began moving toward them, growling.

"You, there!" said George, in a voice that would have sounded more impressive if it had not broken in the middle of "there" and shot up two full octaves. "Stop, I say! Stop!"

Karl did not stop. He came steadily forward, growling louder now.

A warning chime sounded in Molly's ear. Molly had heard Tink make that sound before. And, in a flash, she remembered what it meant.

"George!" she said. "Close your eyes!"

"What?" he said, staring at Karl. "Why on earth should . . . OW!"

He yelped as Molly slapped her hand over his eyes, at the same time closing hers tightly. Karl's eyes, on the other hand, were very close and very wide open when Tink flashed a brilliant burst.

With a roar, Karl, temporarily blinded and befuddled, reared up and swiped his huge paws through the air, hitting nothing.

Molly opened her eyes and pulled her hand from George's face.

"Come on!" she said. Then, remembering something, she stopped, turned, and knelt to pick up the fallen form of Tink lying on the road, glowing faintly. Gently, Molly put Tink into her coat pocket and began running up the road toward the Heel Stone, with George close behind. Behind them, Karl continued to bellow and swipe at the empty air.

<hr />

Aster had seen the bright flash of light in the distance; he had heard the deep roar, unquestionably Karl. He didn't know what was happening, and he didn't have time to find out. Whatever it was, Magill and the animals would have to deal with it. The eclipse was total now. The moon was visible only as a shadowy circle in the sky.

Aster knelt next to the trunk. He unfastened the two golden latches. He took a deep breath, then exhaled.

It was time.

———◆———

A raven glided out from the looming starlit shapes of the trilithons. It fluttered to a landing at the base of the bluestone, in the pool of darkness that was Ombra. Moments later it took flight again, disappearing into the darkening sky.

Ombra rose and spoke to the two riflemen, his voice low but urgent.

"Aster is behind that stone," he said, pointing to one of the standing trilithons. "Follow me. *Quickly*."

He glided forward, bent low, and came up to the trilithon, the riflemen crouching just behind him. The trilithon's two massive vertical stones were separated by only a few inches, forming between them a vertical crack several feet deep. Ombra moved forward, oozing into this space, disappearing entirely between the uprights. Through the opening on the other side he saw the gold-clad man—Aster, he was certain—kneeling next to a wooden trunk. Aster's goldgloved hands reached out and unfastened the two latches.

He was about to open the trunk.

Ombra shot back out of the space.

"Now," he whispered urgently, waving the riflemen forward. "Shoot him *now*."

The riflemen moved around the stone quickly. Too quickly. One of them caught his foot on the corner of a stone embedded in the ground. He fell forward, his rifle clattering on the hard-packed dirt. Aster's head turned toward the sound; he saw one rifleman sprawled on the ground, the other raising his weapon, taking aim.

Without an instant's hesitation, Aster flung the trunk lid open.

The ravens screamed and scattered into the sky.

And out came the sun.

Or so it seemed: the center of Stonehenge erupted in a brilliant ball of light. The gold-clad figure of Aster appeared to be on fire as he stumbled away from the glare. The rifleman on the ground screamed and crawled away, dragging his weapon. The other rifleman, a more disciplined warrior, turned his eyes from the light for a moment, then slowly forced himself to look again, training his rifle sight on Aster.

"*No!*"

The voice was Ombra's, but it sounded weak.

"Do not shoot him!"

Ombra was on the ground a dozen yards behind the riflemen. He had been forced back by the light burst, like smoke blown by the wind. His shape was distorted, flattened.

"Do not shoot!" he repeated, slithering away from the light. The rifleman lowered his rifle, turned, and stumbled after the retreating form.

Nerezza ran forward, meeting Ombra at the bluestone circle.

"What happened?" he said. Shielding his eyes, he looked toward the brilliant sphere of light and the figure of Aster now moving toward cover behind a huge fallen stone. "Why didn't they shoot him?"

"I called them off," said Ombra. "We cannot kill Aster while the trunk is open. It must be closed. And only Aster can get near enough to close it." Ombra looked at the sky. Nerezza followed his gaze and saw something he'd never seen before: in the middle of the ghostly reddish circle that was the moon, a pinpoint of greenish light had appeared. As Nerezza watched, the pinpoint became a tendril of light, reaching outward from the moon, farther and farther, like a tentacle feeling its way downward toward Earth.

"We have little time," said Ombra. "We must force Aster to close the trunk."

"But if we can't shoot him," said Nerezza, "and we can't get near him . . . what can we do?"

Ombra's dark hood swiveled slowly away from the moon, toward Nerezza.

"Get Slank," Ombra said. "Tell him to bring me Lady Aster."

Gasping for breath, Molly, with George just behind, reached the Heel Stone. A moment earlier the sky over Stonehenge had erupted with a brilliant flash of light; the center now bathed in a brightness that was difficult to look at directly.

"What is that?" said George. "Is that the Return?"

"I'm sure it's the starstuff," said Molly. "But it's still there, on the ground. The Return hasn't taken place yet. Father must be inside there. I need to—"

"Would you look at that," interrupted George, pointing up.

Molly looked up and saw the strange tendril of green light coming out of the moon, stretching toward Earth, its lower end moving back and forth, causing the rest of it to form gentle, undulating curves. To Molly, it looked like a giant snake seeking prey.

George stared in wonder as the light came closer to Earth. "That thing is thousands of miles long," he said. "*Tens* of thousands. It must be traveling at a *fantastic* speed!"

Tearing her eyes away from the light snake, Molly looked back toward the glowing center of Stonehenge.

"I need to get in there," she said. "To warn Father."

"Why?" said George. "Obviously the Return is about to start. And once the starstuff's gone—"

"But it's *not* gone yet," interrupted Molly. "And if

Ombra's anywhere nearby, he'll see that thing"—she pointed at the green light, drawing ever closer to Stonehenge—"and he'll try to stop the Return. I need to get in there and warn Father."

"You're not going anywhere," said a deep voice.

Molly and George turned as the tall, wide figure of Magill stepped out from behind the Heel Stone.

"You're supposed to be back at the house," he said. "You've got no business here."

"Please," said Molly. "Listen. I need to warn my father. There's a—"

"You can't go in there," said Magill. "Your father left orders. *Nobody* goes in there. Too dangerous."

"*Please*," Molly said desperately, starting toward the light. "He doesn't know that—"

"*No,*" said Magill, moving to block Molly's path. "You can't . . . *OOW!*"

George had played a bit of rugby at Harrow, and his tackling technique wasn't half bad. He'd taken a three-step running start, then launched himself, his goal being to hit Magill from the side, waist high, driving him away from Molly. Unfortunately, Magill was considerably taller than George's usual targets; George had connected, noggin-first, with Magill's right knee.

The collision proved extremely painful for both parties. Magill yelped as he skipped sideways on his left foot, both hands holding his knee. George thudded to the ground, moaning, clutching at his throbbing skull.

Molly, her obstacle removed, took off running toward the light.

———◆———

Leonard Aster crouched behind a fallen trilithon stone, a few feet from the open starstuff trunk. Warily he poked his head out; squinting in the brilliant light, he looked toward the place where, only moments ago, he'd seen two men with rifles. When he'd stumbled blindly away, looking for cover, he had expected at any moment to be shot, or at least hear shots fired. But there had been nothing. And now the men were gone.

Aster concluded that they'd been driven off by the fierce light radiating from the starstuff. The air around him hummed with energy; even with the gold mesh protecting him, he could barely see through the glare.

Cautiously, he stood and looked up, his eyes scanning the sky. *There it was.* Relief flooded through him as he saw the green tentacle of light writhing toward the glowing center of Stonehenge. It was only a few hundred feet above the top of the trilithons now—close enough that Aster could see it was actually a column of light several feet in diameter. Its end was now aiming directly at the open trunk, and descending.

*Only a few seconds now . . .*

The column was coming lower, perhaps one hundred feet now. The hum in the air was louder. Aster's eyes again swept the area and stopped suddenly. Aster took a step backward, as if he'd been struck.

*It couldn't be.*

But it was. Walking toward him from the bluestone circle, arms outstretched, was his wife.

"Louise!" he shouted, waving his arms. "Stay away!"

She kept coming. Her face, starkly illuminated by the brilliant light, was pale and drawn, her eyes wide open, staring unblinking into the glare. She was already perilously close. If she got much closer, Aster knew, she would die.

He looked up: the green light column was directly above the starstuff. The hum was almost deafening. He looked at Louise: she was still coming. To stop her, he would have to leave the trunk—something he was trained never to do. But he could not stand there and watch her die.

Aster began to run toward Louise. After three steps he stopped, frozen by something he heard behind him—a familiar voice, barely audible over the hum. He turned.

*No.*

Molly was coming toward the light.

"GO BACK, MOLLY!" he shouted. But she didn't hear him. She wasn't even looking at him.

She had seen her mother.

Now Molly was running forward, tears streaming down

her face, oblivious to the danger. In that instant Aster understood that both his wife and his daughter were about to perish in a cataclysm that he had unleashed. He might— *might*—be able to save one of them; he could not save both.

In that instant Leonard Aster made a decision that went against a lifetime of Starcatchers training, and centuries of Starcatchers tradition. In that instant, in the hum and the glare, he became a husband and a father.

Leonard Aster closed the trunk lid.

The world went black.

The brilliant light was gone. The hum was gone.

Aster could see nothing. He blinked hard, trying to force his eyes to adjust to the sudden darkness.

"Molly!" he shouted.

"Here, Father!" she called, stumbling forward, also sightless. "I saw Mother!"

"Molly, you must not come closer!" he said. "You must get away from here."

"But—"

"I'll get your mother," shouted Aster. His eyes adjusting now, he saw Louise. She was quite close. If he could get to her quickly, move her behind one of the stones, he might have time to run back to the trunk, open it, and complete the Return. He looked up: the green light column was just above the tops of the trilithons, swaying back and forth as if seeking the trunk.

Aster turned toward his wife. His golden suit, illuminated by the green light column now directly overhead, gleamed like a beacon.

———•••———

"There!" said Ombra.

The riflemen took aim at the shining figure as it ran toward Louise Aster.

"Now!" said Ombra.

The two guns fired almost as one.

The shining figure went down.

———•••———

Molly heard the shots and screamed as she saw her father crumple to the ground.

"Father!" she shouted, stumbling toward the gold-suited figure, now lying facedown on the hard-packed dirt, unmoving. She reached her father and knelt next to him. Gently, she turned him over, and gasped. The front of his golden suit was bathed in blood. It looked black in the eerie green light as it poured from a wound in his chest.

"Oh, no, no, *no*," she said.

She looked up, desperate. Directly in front of her stood her mother.

"Mother," Molly said. "Help me! Father's hurt!"

Louise Aster said nothing, looking at her daughter with

an expression devoid of any emotion, her wan face painted a pale hideous green by the overhead light.

"Mother," Molly repeated softly. *"Please."*

But she saw no concern, no hint of recognition in the empty eyes looking back at her.

And then, in the strange green light, Molly saw the dark shape of Ombra gliding across the open ground, followed by a half dozen men. They were heading directly for the trunk, which lay on the Altar Stone, twenty-five feet from where Molly knelt by her wounded father. Molly glanced up; the green column of light lingered overhead, snaking back and forth, though it seemed farther away than before. She knew the eclipse would be over soon, ending any chance of effecting the Return.

Despair filled Molly's soul. Her father was dying; her mother had become somebody, or some *thing*, that she no longer knew. And now the Others, in the form of the horrid Ombra, were about to gain possession of the starstuff that both her parents had sacrificed so much to safeguard.

*Not if I can help it*, Molly thought, struggling to her feet.

"Get the girl!" groaned Ombra.

Molly was running now. A few steps and she was almost to the trunk. She reached toward the lid, but suddenly strong hands grabbed her dress, and strong arms yanked her back. A raspy voice spoke close to her ear.

"Hold up there, missy," said Slank.

Molly struggled and kicked, but she was no match for Slank's muscles. He gripped her tighter, pinning her to him.

"No use, missy," he whispered.

Molly looked toward the trunk: Ombra and the other men were now standing next to it, the men eyeing it warily, aware of the power it contained. Molly looked up; the green snake of light was higher still, clearly receding. It was over. She had failed. The Starcatchers had failed. Slowly, Molly lowered her eyes.

*Hang on. . . .*

Molly caught just a glimpse of a shape swooping low over the tops of the sarsens from the northwest. It was hidden by the tall trilithons now, but Molly knew what it had to be, moving that fast . . .

"PETER!" she shouted at the top of her lungs.

Every head, including Ombra's, swiveled to look. And so everyone had an excellent view as Peter swerved expertly around a massive trilithon support, missing it by a quarter inch at best. Everyone saw it, but nobody had time to react, least of all Peter's target.

"Hello, Slank!" shouted Peter, delivering a high-velocity kick to Slank's head as he shot past.

Roaring in pain and rage, Slank staggered backward, involuntarily freeing Molly. He reached for his belt and yanked out a pistol, pointing it skyward, aiming it at the hated boy. Peter turned and began coming back. He was moving fast, but Slank was a good shot. As Peter, who had not yet spotted the pistol, drew close, Slank's finger tightened on the trigger. He inhaled. With Peter dead in his sights, he fired.

And as he did, a tiny figure struck his gun hand. Tinker Bell had little mass, and she was still a bit groggy, not having fully recovered from her earlier encounter with Karl the bear. But she was able to hit Slank's hand with just enough speed to mar his aim.

The bullet whistled past Peter's head.

"Thanks, Tink!" Peter shouted, swerving into the sky. Slank roared a curse and hurled the pistol after Peter's fleeting form. One of the riflemen fired at Peter, but also missed. Peter darted down and again swooped through the trilithon area. Some of the men ran after him.

"Ignore the boy!" groaned Ombra. "The trunk! Get the trunk!"

As Ombra sought to organize the men, Peter circled and flew past Molly.

"Get your father and mother!" he called. "Get them away from here!"

"Father's been shot!" shouted Molly.

"Attend to your mother, then," said a voice behind her. Molly turned. It was George.

"I'll get your father," he said. He went to Aster's prone

body and, with a grunt, managed to heave the unconscious, bleeding man onto his shoulder. Molly ran to her mother, took her arm, and began to pull her away from the center of Stonehenge. George followed, staggering under Leonard Aster's weight. Molly looked back: Peter was still swooping back and forth over the trilithons.

*What is he doing?* Molly wondered. As she pulled her mother away, her eyes went back to the trunk.

Ombra, ignoring the flying boy, was directing one of the men to close the latches. The man did so gingerly, not pleased to be touching the trunk. When he was done, Ombra gestured to him and another man.

"Pick it up," he said. "It cannot harm you now."

As the men warily reached down to pick up the trunk, Peter swept overhead.

"NOW!" he shouted.

One of the men yelled and pointed. The others' eyes followed. From behind one of the massive upright trilithon stones emerged the enormous furry mass of Karl.

"Shoot him!" groaned Ombra.

The two riflemen fumbled for their weapons, but Karl, moving with astonishing speed and agility, was upon the men before they had a chance to aim. With a swipe of his enormous paw, he sent the closest of the rifles skidding across the dirt like a twig. Both riflemen turned and ran, one still clutching his weapon but not daring to stop and try to use it.

The other men started to follow, but found their path blocked by the forbidding form of Ombra.

"Get the trunk!" growled Ombra. "I will deal with the animal."

The men, their eyes on the bear, did not move. Ombra glided forward. Karl kept coming. The green column of light was now above Karl and slightly to his right, casting a shadow to the bear's left. Ombra swerved toward it.

"Look out!" shouted Peter. But his warning meant nothing to the bear, which, preparing to fight the oncoming dark shape, reared up on its hind legs, an act that only lengthened and exposed its shadow.

Ombra flowed swiftly toward it.

A chiming sound filled the air—a sound both Karl and Ombra had heard before. Both knew what it meant; neither had time to do anything about it.

Tink flashed her brightest flash. She was exhausted, and this effort was far weaker than the one she'd managed earlier that evening, the one that had foiled Karl out on the road. This flash, intended to protect him, was half as bright, if that. But it was enough for now.

Ombra, emitting a screech that made Peter's skin crawl, flattened into an elongated black teardrop shape and was driven back out of the trilithon area. The other men stumbled after him. Karl roared in blind confusion, lunging this way and that.

"Mister Magill!" shouted Peter urgently. "Get him out of here now!"

Magill, who'd been waiting for Peter's call, sprinted out of the darkness and ran to Karl. The big man growled as he approached; Karl immediately dropped to all fours. Magill took a handful of the huge bear's neck fur and began leading him away from the trilithons. He looked back at Peter, who had landed next to the trunk.

"Be careful, lad," he said.

"I will," said Peter. "Please find Molly. She went that way. Her father needs help."

"All right," said Magill. "Good luck." He turned to go.

"Wait!" said Peter.

Magill looked back.

"Give this to Molly," said Peter. He removed the locket from his neck. Peter didn't know whether there was any starstuff left, or—even if there were—whether it would be enough to heal Leonard Aster, assuming he was still alive. He threw the locket to Magill, who caught it one-handed, nodded, and was gone.

Peter knelt by the trunk. He looked up: the green snake was still there, still searching back and forth. But it was clearly higher now; it was receding. Peter glanced at the moon; the ghostly reddish circle was just a shade lighter. The totality was ending.

Peter reached for the first of the two trunk latches.

"Shoot him!"

The groaning command came from behind him, but from a distance. He opened the first latch.

He winced at the crack of a rifle shot; blinked as a bullet *twanged* off a trilithon stone next to him, rock fragments stinging his face.

"You missed!" came the groaning voice. "Fire again!"

He reached for the second latch.

*UNNNH.*

Peter did not hear the shot that hit him; only his own grunt as the bullet tore through his left shoulder, hurling him forward onto the trunk. He slid facedown onto the dirt, wondering why he didn't feel anything.

He struggled to get back up. His left arm didn't work. He rolled sideways and the world became a red blur as the pain suddenly shot from his shoulder, surging through his body. He struggled to clear his vision, and got to his knees. The trunk was still in front of him, one side smeared with a dark liquid that Peter realized was his blood. He reached his hand for the second latch.

Then he felt the cold.

Half turning, he saw the dark form, saw Ombra's cape moving onto the shadow cast next to his kneeling body. His hand touched the latch as the cape touched his shadow.

It lasted for only a few seconds, the struggle between the boy and the dark thing for Peter's soul. Neither combatant had ever been in a fight so intense; each was surprised by the other's strength and resourcefulness; each learned something from the other. Paradoxically, it was Peter's grievous wound that saved him: the pain surged from him into Ombra, and the shock was enough to weaken Ombra's attack for an instant.

In that instant, Peter, who had never lost sight of his goal, opened the second latch and flung open the trunk.

In the next instant, as the world filled with light, Peter felt Ombra's hostile presence leaving his body. Then he heard Ombra's scream, which seemed to come from everywhere—as, in fact, it did, Ombra having disintegrated into thousands—millions—of tiny shadows, of specks of dark dust, of near-nothingness, blown far across the landscape in every direction, disappearing into the distance, leaving nothing where he had been but an old burlap sack lying on the ground, open and empty.

The last thing Peter felt was the wonderful warmth flowing into the hole in his shoulder, taking his pain away. The last thing he saw was the green column of light plunging down toward the light pouring from the open trunk, like a giant cobra striking. Peter saw that, and then he saw nothing.

---

Slank, Nerezza, and the other men saw the blinding flash, heard the horrid scream.

Nerezza and Slank looked at each other.

"What now?" said Nerezza.

"We go back," said Slank, refusing to accept that the boy had beaten him again. "We still have a rifle. We can—" He stopped, seeing the fear in Nerezza's eyes, and those of the men, who were backing away.

"What is it?" said Slank. He turned.

Wolves. Huge wolves. Five of them. Moving toward the men, spreading out.

Hunting.

Slank turned back: Nerezza and the other men were running away across the grassland.

With a curse of rage, Slank took off after them.

———

Molly also saw the brilliant flash and heard the unearthly scream.

*Dear God,* she thought. *Please don't let that be Peter. . . .*

In her arms, Molly cradled the head of Leonard Aster, who, she knew, was dying, or dead. She had removed his helmet; his face was white, his eyes open but sightless. Whether he breathed at all, Molly could not tell.

Nearby stood her mother, or the walking corpse her mother had become. George stood next to Louise Aster.

"Molly," he said, pointing. "Look."

The light column was changing color. At the base it had

turned from green to a startling blue, which even now was turning gold. The color transformation was moving progressively up the column, into the sky, at astonishing speed; in the next few seconds, it had traveled from Earth to the moon. A second later, in the blink of an eye, the column was gone altogether.

The strange light had been seen by millions of people, in England and beyond; there would be newspaper accounts in which astronomers would explain that the unusual celestial display was actually a rare, but not unheard of, form of aurora borealis, or northern lights. This explanation would be almost universally accepted, except among the residents of the village of Amesbury. But they had learned, as their ancestors had learned over the centuries, to keep their views to themselves.

George was staring at the moon.

"It's done, then," he said. "The Return. It's done."

"Yes," said Molly, looking down at the lifeless face of her father. "It's done."

As she spoke, something dropped onto the dirt next to her. It gleamed in the light of the moon, now emerging from shadow.

"Peter told me to give you that," said Magill, who was trailed by the now-docile Karl.

Molly snatched the locket off the ground.

*Please let there be some left.*

532

She held the locket over her father's chest, opened it, tilted it.

*Yes!*

The golden light poured from the locket, bathing her father's chest, flowing toward the wound, flowing into it. She looked at his face; nothing. She shook the locket; no more light flowed from it. Had it not been enough?

"Molly—"

Leonard Aster's voice was weak; to Molly, it had never sounded so wonderful.

"Father!" she said. "Oh, Father—" she was sobbing now, her tears falling on her father's face. "I'm sorry," she said, dabbing them with her sleeve. "I'm so sorry—"

"No," he said, "I'm the one who's sorry, Molly. You only wanted to help. But the starstuff, is it—"

"Gone," she said.

He frowned. "The Others? Did they—"

"No," she whispered. "The Return. It happened, Father."

Leonard closed his eyes. "Thank God," he said.

⸻

So focused were Molly and her father on their reunion that neither noticed the shadow. It was one of a number of shadows that had emerged, cautiously at first, from the burlap sack that Ombra had left behind. One went trotting off in search of a certain wolf; several others set off across the grassland in the general direction of London. A particular shadow raced along the ground among the Stonehenge stones, darting this way and that, until it found what it was looking for.

Louise Aster blinked. "Where am I?" she said.

"Mother!" said Molly, getting to her feet.

"Molly?" said Louise. "Leonard, is that you?"

"Louise!" said Aster, also standing, with some effort.

The three of them embraced; words, for the moment, being impossible.

Then Molly jerked away. "Oh, no," she said.

"What?" said Leonard.

"Peter!" she said, pointing toward the trilithons. "He was in there!"

"We must go find him," said Leonard, his face grim. "He'll need help, if he's not . . . If he hasn't . . . Molly, you stay here. Magill, come with me."

"I don't think we should go in there," said Magill gravely.

Molly looked stricken. "Why not?" she said.

Magill's face broke into a broad smile.

"Because he's right there," he said.

They all turned at once. Walking toward them— unsteadily but purposefully—was Peter. In his hands, gently, he held the sleeping form of Tink. His hair was a wild tangle; the front of his shirt was torn and dark with blood.

Molly, tears streaming down her face, ran to him, put her arms around him, hugged him hard.

"Peter," she said. "I was so worried!" She looked at his bloody shirt. "But you're hurt! Are you all right?"

Peter looked at her somberly for a moment. Then he smiled a smile so broad that his teeth shone in the moonlight.

"Never felt better in my life," he said.

## CHAPTER 95

# A Swift, Sure Shadow

THEY SPENT THE REST of the night at Gecierran, having traveled back to the mansion in a moonlit caravan of humans, horses, bear, and wolves.

They ate ravenously, then fell, exhausted, into bed, all of them sleeping late except Leonard Aster, who rose at dawn and rode to Salisbury to make travel arrangements and to send and receive a series of encoded telegrams.

He returned shortly after noon with a coach to collect the others. They traveled to the Salisbury train station, where they boarded a train with a coach reserved just for them. Once the train was moving, Leonard, with his wife by his side, addressed Molly, George, and Peter.

"First," he said, "I want to thank the three of you for what you did. Without you, there would have been no Return. The starstuff would now be in the hands of the Others. And Louise would be . . . Well, I'd rather not think about that." Leonard looked at his wife, who squeezed his hand, her face pale but peaceful.

"So," said Aster, "I'm deeply grateful to all of you. And, Molly, I owe you an apology. I obviously underestimated your resourcefulness, your abilities, and your courage—as, apparently, did the Others. I don't expect you to make a habit of disobeying me, young lady. But this time, I'm glad you did."

Molly and her father exchanged warm smiles. Then Leonard turned his attention to George.

"In a way, George, I'm sorry you got caught up in this business," he said. "We Starcatchers have worked extremely hard to keep our mission—our very existence—secret. And I'm certain your parents would not be pleased to know that, because of your connection with the Asters, you wound up being chased by wolves and a bear on Salisbury Plain."

George smiled.

"But Molly tells me she'd never have found the Return without you," continued Leonard. "And had you not been with her, I'd likely still be lying on the ground by the Altar Stone. You're a young man of great courage, George. From the bottom of my heart, I thank you."

Aster extended his hand; George, blushing, shook it.

"I'm in no position to ask favors of you, George," said Leonard. "But I'm afraid I must do so now. You know what the Starcatchers are; you know what kind of enemy we face, and the stakes for which we are fighting. I must ask you to tell nobody what you've learned—*nobody*, not even your parents. Ever."

George nodded solemnly. "I won't, sir," he said. "I promise."

"Thank you, George," said Leonard. "And now for you," he said, turning to Peter. "It seems I'm making a habit of this, Peter. This is the second time I must thank you for saving my daughter's life; and to that debt of gratitude I must add thanks for saving my own life, and that of my wife. Not to mention all you have done for the Starcatchers."

Peter blushed a deep red. Tink, sitting in his hair, said: *To hear him talk, I had nothing to do with it.*

"What did she say?" asked Molly.

"She said thank you," said Peter.

"Actually," said Leonard, his eyes twinkling. "She said, 'To hear him talk, I had nothing to do with it.'"

"You understand Tink?" said Peter, amazed.

"I do," said Leonard, "and I want to tell her that the Starcatchers will be forever grateful to her for her courage and her selflessness."

Tink, for once, was chimeless.

"Peter," Leonard went on, "I made an offer to you once before, and you refused. But I want to make it again: please stay with us in London. You can live with us, as a member of our family. You can attend any school you wish. Your needs will be provided for. Your—"

Leonard stopped; Peter was shaking his head.

"I'm sorry, sir," he said. "But I must get back to Never Land as soon as possible."

"Never Land?" said Aster.

"The island," said Peter. "Mollusk Island. We call it Never Land, because . . . well, because it sort of is. Anyway, I must get back there, sir. There's pirates, and my mates need me."

"I understand," said Leonard. "But we need you too."

Peter looked at him questioningly.

"This morning," said Leonard. "I exchanged telegrams with a number of other members of our organization. I told them about our experience with this Ombra at the Return. As you know, Ombra—or something very much like him— was also a problem for us recently in Egypt. This morning I learned that, over the past few months, there have been a half dozen attacks on Starcatchers by these creatures . . . these shadow thieves."

"So there's more than one," said Molly.

"I'm afraid so," said Leonard. "Evidently the Others have a new ally—or a new master; we're not sure which. But the Starcatchers, after centuries of having the upper hand, now find ourselves facing a formidable new opponent—an opponent that would have defeated me at Stonehenge, had you three not been there. Peter, you are a very special young man. You have unique abilities. Twice now you've played a critical role in helping us defeat the Others. I've no doubt that we're going to need your help again."

"And you shall have it, sir," said Peter. "I'll come back if you need me, I promise. But for now, I must return to Never Land."

Aster nodded. "To be honest," he said, "I expected you to say that." He looked at Molly; she was looking down. As Leonard watched, a tear landed on the coach floor below her.

"All right, then," said Leonard. "As soon as we reach London, I'll arrange for a ship to take you back."

"Thank you, sir," said Peter. "But I think it's best if I fly."

"Fly?" said Aster. "All the way to the island?"

Peter nodded. "It's much faster," he said. "And with Tink to guide me, I'm sure I can find it. She talks to birds."

"But, Peter," said Molly, looking up, dabbing her eyes. "You can't fly all that way. It's too far. What happens when you need to rest?"

"I've been thinking about that," said Peter. "I was wondering if perhaps Ammm could help me along the way. Perhaps he knows a whale or two? A whale makes a fine resting place."

Leonard nodded, smiling. "I think that could be arranged," he said. "I believe Ammm knows a number of whales."

"Who's Ammm?" said George.

"A porpoise," said Molly. "He's a friend of my family."

"Ah," said George, no longer easily surprised by Molly's family.

The rest of the trip to London passed quietly. Molly, Peter, and George—all still a bit weary from the events of the previous days—dozed; Leonard and Louise sat close together, speaking quietly. A coach met them at the Waterloo train station and took them to the Aster mansion. There they had a happy reunion with the household staff, except for the new housemaid, Jenna, who had disappeared several days earlier and had not returned. Leonard Aster immediately sent a messenger off with encoded instructions, which would quickly find their way to the coast and thence to Ammm.

George, after one last round of thank-yous from the Asters, went home. As he left, he and Peter shook hands solemnly. They were no longer enemies; each had come to a grudging respect for the other. But for reasons they could never state aloud—and in fact could only barely acknowledge in their thoughts—they knew they would never truly be friends.

With George gone, Molly and Peter went to the sitting room, where they sat quietly, talking little, awaiting nightfall. It came soon enough. When the sky was fully dark, Peter and the three Asters climbed the stairs to Molly's room.

Peter went to the window and raised it. Cold air flowed in, but nobody seemed to notice.

"You're to fly to the Isle of Wight," said Leonard. "There's a lighthouse there next to the Needles—some huge jagged rocks sticking out of the sea. Ammm will be waiting for you there."

"You're certain you can find your way?" said Louise.

"Yes, ma'am," said Peter, pointing to Tink, who stood on the windowsill, eager to be off. "Tink will get me there."

Leonard put his hand out. "Good luck, Peter," he said.

Peter shook his hand. "Thank you, sir," he said.

"Be careful, Peter," said Louise, giving him a hug and a quick peck on his cheek.

"Yes, ma'am," he said, blushing.

Louise stood back. Molly and Peter looked at each other awkwardly.

"Leonard," said Louise. "Perhaps we should—" She nodded toward the door.

"Yes, of course," he said. The Asters left the room.

Peter and Molly stood silently for another moment, then Molly said, "Thank you, Peter. For leaving the island. For finding me. For everything. Thank you."

"You're welcome," he said. "I, uh, it was, I mean, I wanted to see you, Molly. Not just to help you. But to . . . see you." He was blushing furiously now.

"Did you mean what you said to Father?" she said. "About coming back, if we need you again?"

"Yes," said Peter.

"Then I hope we do, soon. Need you, I mean. Not because I want something bad to happen, but because—" Now it was Molly's turn to blush.

"Me too," said Peter.

And then, having virtually lost the ability to speak to each other, they hugged. It was awkward for a moment, as Peter had to rise on tiptoes. But then it was not awkward at all; it was at once the happiest moment either of them could remember, and the saddest.

And then it was over. Gently, Peter pulled himself away and walked to the window.

"Good-bye, Molly," he said, his voice barely a whisper.

"Good-bye, Peter," she said.

Peter turned and put one foot up on the windowsill. Tinker Bell flitted out the window, hovering, waiting for Peter.

"Tinker Bell!" called Molly. "Take good care of him!"

*Don't worry, Molly,* chimed Tink.

"What did she say?" asked Molly.

"She said don't worry," said Peter. He gave Molly a little wave, turned, slid his body onto the sill, and slipped out into the night.

Molly ran to the window and looked out; she saw them

rising high against the moonlit sky—a bright, darting speck of light followed by a swift, sure shadow.

Molly watched them until they were gone, then watched some more, feeling the cold night air wash over her face, chilling her tears.

CHAPTER 96

# OVER THEIR HEADS

TEN DAYS SQUATTING in the bamboo cage. Maybe eleven days. James had lost count.

The pirates let them out once a day, one at a time, under guard, to relieve themselves. They also ate once a day, usually some awful concoction such as starfish mush cooked in coconut milk, with the occasional bony fish. The rest of the time they squatted in filth and boredom, virtually ignored by their captors.

Thomas and Prentiss passed the time playing tic-tac-toe, writing the X's and O's in the dirt on their forearms. They had played hundreds of games, perhaps thousands. Every one ended in a draw.

Tubby Ted passed the time discussing food: how much he missed it; what dishes he would have if he could have whatever he wanted; what order he would eat these dishes in. He could go on about this for hours. He *did* go on for hours.

James mostly stared at the sky, waiting for Peter to appear, *willing* Peter to appear. James also watched the pirate camp, looking, so far without success, for an escape plan. That's what he was doing on this particular sunny afternoon, when Prentiss, preparing to draw an O on Thomas's arm, asked a question he had asked, in one form or another, several times a day.

"What if he doesn't come back?"

"He'll come back," said James. "He said he'd come back."

"But what if he can't *get* back?" said Prentiss.

"Or never made it to England in the first place?" said Thomas.

"He made it," said James. "And he'll be back."

"If I made it to England," said Tubby Ted, "I'd eat a whole pie. A mincemeat pie. That would be first. Then I'd—"

"Shut up, Ted," said the other three boys in unison.

"Well, if he doesn't come back—" began Prentiss.

"He will," said James.

"But if he doesn't," said Prentiss, "what will they do with us?"

James had no answer to that. He, too, worried about what would happen to them if Hook decided that Peter was not returning, and the boys were no longer needed as bait. The more James thought about it, the more he knew that he had to think of an escape plan. But it seemed hopeless: the cage was built of stout bamboo poles, lashed together with thick rope, tied on the top—where the boys could not reach—with complex, seamanlike knots.

If James had a knife, or any kind of sharp edge, he could cut the rope, through the cracks between the bamboo poles. But he had no knife. A few days earlier, he'd hidden a fish bone from their daily meal; that night, he'd spent hours sawing away at the rope with the bone. It had no effect at all.

Thomas marked an X on his arm; Prentiss added an O.

"Draw," said Thomas. They began another game, this time on Prentiss' arm.

A screeching from the jungle drew the attention of all four boys.

"It's the monkeys," said James, pointing to a tree at the edge of the clearing, where a dozen or more lithe dark shapes darted from branch to branch. The boys had become quite familiar with the monkeys, which came into the pirate camp each night, scavenging for scraps of dropped food after the pirates fell asleep.

"They're eating something," said Tubby Ted.

James squinted at the monkeys. They were eating, and fighting over, small purplish fruits.

"Figs," he said. "Those are fig trees over there. The pirates get figs from there, too. They dry them out and eat them. Not that they let *us* have any."

"Figs," said Ted. "I *love* figs."

"Well, tell that to the monkeys," said Thomas. "Maybe they'll give you one."

"I could eat a hundred," said Ted. "I could eat *anything* right now. I feel like that old sailor, the one who brought us that horrible food back on the *Never Land* . . . What was his name?"

"Hungry Bob," said Prentiss.

"That's right," said Ted. "Remember he used to bring us that horrible slop with bugs in it, and he *ate* it? He told us he even ate rope once, remember?"

"Yes!" said Prentiss, smiling for the first time in more than a week.

"Well, right now," said Ted, "I could eat—"

"Wait a minute," said James, putting his hand on Ted's arm. *"Wait a minute."*

"What?" said Ted.

"That's it," said James.

"What is?" said Ted.

"It's brilliant," said James. "Ted, you're a genius!"

"I am?" said Ted. "But what did—"

"Shut up," said James. He peered out through the cage bars, looking for the short, round form of . . .

There he was.

"Mister Smee! Sir!" called James. "Excuse me, sir, may I please have a word?"

Smee waddled over.

"What is it, boy?" he asked. "I can't let you out, if that's what you want. Cap'n's orders." Smee felt sorry for the boys, and had even once tried to suggest to Hook that he consider freeing them. Hook had responded by throwing a coconut at Smee, which Smee took as a sign of disagreement.

"No, sir, it's not that," said James. "It's . . . our mouths. We have sores, and our teeth hurt. Hurt something fearful. And it's the same for all of us."

"No, it's not," said Ted. "I don't h—OOOF." Ted was silenced by James's elbow hitting his shrunken but still ample stomach.

"James is right, sir," said Prentiss, catching on. "Our mouths hurt something awful. Don't they, Thomas?" Thomas quickly nodded in agreement.

Smee said, "Teeth hurt? Sores in the mouth? *All* of you? Oh, my." The little man looked around the pirate compound. As usual, it was a hive of inactivity: most of the pirates were sleeping, including the two who were supposed to be guarding the gate in the tall wooden wall surrounding the fort. In the distance, two men were throwing knives at a tree, trying—so far without success—to hit a hairy spider the size of a dinner plate. Smee turned back to the boys, a conspiratorial look on his spherical face.

"All right," he whispered. "I'll get something for your mouths. But you can't tell nobody. 'Specially the cap'n."

"We won't, sir," said James. "We promise."

Smee, glancing around nervously, waddled off toward the driftwood hut that served as the kitchen for the pirate fort.

"What was *that* about?" said Ted. "My mouth's not sore."

"Yes, it is," said James. "If you want figs."

"Figs?" said Ted. "What do figs have to do with it?"

James sighed. "There's a thing called scurvy that pirates get," he said. "Their mouths get sore. The way they fix it is by eating fruit. Figs, for instance."

"Ohhh," said Tubby Ted, nodding. "Now that you mention it, my mouth definitely hurts."

"That's better," Prentiss said.

At that moment, Smee came back out of the hut carrying a small bundle wrapped in a leaf. He was trying to look inconspicuous, which made him look very conspicuous, but fortunately none of the other pirates appeared to be paying attention. He brought the bundle to the cage and pushed it through the bars into James's hands.

"Remember," he whispered. "Don't tell nobody."

"We won't, sir," said James, as Smee waddled hastily away. "Thank you, sir."

With Smee gone, James unwrapped the leaf. Inside were figs, a half dozen, their aroma mouthwateringly sweet.

Tubby Ted eagerly reached for one. James swatted his hand.

"What?" said Ted.

"These aren't for us," said James.

"But we need them!" said Ted. "For our scurvy!"

"We don't *have* scurvy, you twit," said Prentiss.

"Then why do we have the figs?" said Ted, practically in tears.

"They're for the monkeys," said James.

"The monkeys have scurvy?" said Ted.

"No," said James. "But they have sharp teeth."

———•———

Well after dark, after the last of the pirates had lumbered, burping and scratching, off to his hammock, James nudged Prentiss awake. They divided the figs, which were soft and juicy. Quietly, carefully, the boys reached up through the cracks of the bamboo cage, finding the rope that held the top on tight. They each chose a small section of rope and began mashing the sticky figs into it, making sure the rope was soaked through with juice.

Then they waited.

Less than ten minutes later, they heard the first gentle thump of a monkey landing on top of the cage. It was quickly followed by another, then another, until there were at least a dozen up there, gnawing furiously on the sweet rope. At times a monkey, apparently not getting its share, would screech, causing James and Prentiss to exchange alarmed looks. But the pirates, accustomed now to jungle noises, slept on.

After a half hour, the activity on the cage roof lessened, then stopped. One by one, the monkeys scampered off, looking for other treats. James and Prentiss pressed their hands against the top of the cage and, at a nod from James, pushed up.

The top lifted easily. The cage was open.

"Now what?" whispered Prentiss. "Do we run for it?"

James shook his head. "No," he whispered. He pointed to the fort's gate, in front of which lay two pirates. "We can't open the gate without waking those two."

"Then what?"

"We put the ropes back on the top here, so the cage looks tied. Then we wait for daylight. They open the gate first thing in the morning and leave it open all day. Soon as we see our chance, we run for it. It'll have to be early, before they come to open the cage and see it's untied. So we have to be ready."

Prentiss nodded. They positioned the rope pieces on the cage top, then gently lowered it back into position. Then they lay down, waiting for dawn. Neither got an instant's sleep.

⟶⟶⟵⟵

The sun broke across the island, waking the jungle birds, stirring a breeze in the palm fronds. Thomas and Tubby Ted sat

552

up sleepily, finding James and Prentiss awake, on their knees, peering out of the cage.

"What is it?" said Thomas.

"Shhh," said James. "They're opening the gate."

Thomas looked: the two guards, yawning, were pulling open the two massive gates, which swung inward.

"So?" said Thomas. "They do that every day."

"The top is untied," said James, pointing to the chewed-through ropes hanging down.

"It worked!" said Thomas. "The monkeys!"

"Shhh," cautioned James.

"Are there any figs left?" said Tubby Ted.

"No," said James, peering through the bars again. "All right, the gates are open now. We need to do this soon, before they come to let us out. The overnight guards are about to go get some breakfast. Their replacements usually don't get to the gate for a few minutes. That's when we run."

They waited, watching. As James had predicted, the two guards left the gate and ambled toward the food hut. Meanwhile, nobody appeared to be stirring in the large hut where most of the men slept.

"Now," whispered James, sliding the top of the cage off. "Quietly." He climbed out the top, followed by Prentiss and Thomas. Tubby Ted slung his leg over, then stopped.

"Come *on*, Ted," said James, looking around. Men's voices came from the sleeping hut.

"I'm stuck," said Ted. "My leg is stuck." Sure enough, his leg had gone between two of the cage poles and was now wedged through to the knee.

"Here," said James, reaching out. "Grab my arms. Prentiss, Thomas, lend a hand."

The three of them grabbed Ted's arms and heaved.

"OW!" Ted cried. "It's still stuck!"

"Quiet," said James. "They'll hear you."

But it was too late: a hairy face stuck out of the sleeping hut; a bloodshot eye spotted the boys.

"They're escaping!" shouted the pirate. "The boys is loose!"

"Pull!" shouted James, and with a desperate heave, they yanked Tubby Ted out of the cage. The four of them tumbled to the dirt as pirates began to spill out of the hut.

"Run!" shouted James, and the boys sprinted toward the unguarded gate.

"GET THEM!" roared Hook, stumbling from his private hut, still in his nightshirt, sword in hand. "GET THEM!"

James, keeping behind the other three boys, glanced back over his shoulder. The pirates, led by Hook, were close behind; too close. With a sinking heart, James realized that even if he and his mates got through the gate, they would quickly be recaptured outside.

Then he looked forward, and yelled in surprise.

*The gates were closing.*

One gate, in fact, had just bumped shut. As Prentiss and Thomas darted through the opening, the other half of the gate moved, also closing. James couldn't see who was doing it, but clearly, somebody was pulling the gate shut from the outside. Tubby Ted barely squeezed through the closing gap. Would there be room for James?

"Hurry up, James!" shouted a voice . . . a voice James knew well.

With a furious last burst of speed, James lunged through the opening just as the second gate slammed shut.

As James stumbled forward and fell to the ground, he heard the sound of bodies thudding into the other side of the gates. Without looking back, James rose and sprinted after his friends, toward the safety of the green, welcoming jungle. The last thing he heard as the thick foliage closed around him was a scream of unearthly fury.

———•◦•———

It took Hook almost a full minute to reduce his rage to the point where he could form recognizable words.

"BACK UP, YOU IDJITS!" he roared, kicking his men furiously, randomly. "BACK UP SO WE CAN OPEN THE GATES!"

The men scrambled to escape Hook's boots, clearing the way so the gates could be swung open. Hook's mind churned: *Who had shut the gates? Was it the cursed natives?* Whoever it was, Hook would have his revenge, and he'd have it right now. He'd rip their hearts from their chests barehanded. He'd . . .

"Hook!"

The sound of that voice froze Hook, froze the men— froze them all, still as a painting.

It froze them for two reasons: the first was that it was a voice they all knew well.

The second was that it came from *over their heads.*

Slowly, ever so slowly, Hook raised his eyes and looked up into the sky.

And that was when it hit him, right in the face.

A mango.

# ABOUT THE AUTHORS AND ILLUSTRATOR

$\mathcal{D}$AVE $\mathcal{B}$ARRY is a Pulitzer Prize–winning author of more than two dozen books, including *Dave Barry's Money Secrets*, *Dave Barry's Complete Guide to Guys*, *Dave Barry Slept Here*, *Big Trouble*, and *Dave Barry Hits Below the Beltway*.

$\mathcal{R}$IDLEY $\mathcal{P}$EARSON is the best-selling author of twenty-two novels, including the young adult novel *The Kingdom Keepers* and the adult thrillers *Cut and Run*, *The Pied Piper*, *The Diary of Ellen Rimbauer*, *Beyond Recognition*, *Probable Cause*, and *Undercurrents*.

$\mathcal{G}$REG $\mathcal{C}$ALL has worked for clients in music, entertainment, and publishing. His work has garnered many honors, including the ADDY award.

Visit www.davebarry.com
Visit www.ridleypearson.com